"ENTERTAINING."
—*Roanoke Times & World News*

"The world's leading 'feelgood' thriller writer is back with another tale of malevolent horsing around. Dick Francis . . . is again on the winning track with DRIVING FORCE."
—*The Sun* (Calgary, Alberta)

"Is there any aspect of horse racing that Dick Francis hasn't turned into a thriller? Yes: the horse-van business. . . . And it's the basis for the freshest, most energetic Francis book in years."
—*Kirkus Reviews*

"A fine example of Francis's many virtues. . . . The man is unique, and in that regard, irreplaceable: here's hoping he lives to be 102, giving us 30 more years of his (as he calls them) 'little adventure stories' "
—*Mostly Murder*

DRIVING FORCE

Dick Francis

FAWCETT CREST • NEW YORK

My Thanks To

LAMBOURN RACEHORSE TRANSPORT

and
John Hughes
Robert Schulman
Professor Ellie J. C. Goldstein
Professor Jeremy H. Thompson

and

Merrick and Felix
as always

A Fawcett Crest Book
Published by Ballantine Books
Copyright © 1992 by Dick Francis

Library of Congress Catalog Number: 92-22793

ISBN 0-449-22139-3

This edition published by arrangment with G.P. Putnam's Sons.

Manufactured in the United States of America

First International Ballantine Books Edition: November 1993
First Mass Market Edition: February 1994

1

I had told the drivers never on any account to pick up a hitchhiker but of course one day they did, and by the time they reached my house he was dead.

The bell by the back door rang as I was heating up leftover beef stew for a fairly boring supper, consequence of living alone, and with barely a sigh and no premonition I switched off the hot plate, put the saucepan to one side and went to see who had come. Friends tended to enter at once while yelling my name, as the door was seldom locked. Employees mostly knocked first and entered next, still with little ceremony. Only strangers rang the bell and waited.

This time it was different. This time when I opened the door the light from inside the house fell yellowly on the stretched scared eyes of two of the men who worked for me, who stood uncomfortably on the doormat shifting from foot to foot, agonizedly and obviously expectant of wrath to come.

My own response to these clear signals of disaster was the familiar adrenaline rush of alarm that no amount of dealing with earlier crises could prevent. The old pump quickened. My voice came out high.

"What's the matter?" I said. "What happened?"

I glanced over their shoulders. The bulk of one of the two largest in my fleet of horse vans stood reassuringly in the shadows out on the tarmacked parking area, the house lights raising gleams along its silvery flank. At least they hadn't run it into a ditch: at least they'd brought it home. All else had to be secondary.

"Look, Freddie," Dave Yates said, a defensive whine developing, "it's not our fault."

"What isn't?"

"This four-eyes we picked up . . ."

"You *what*?"

The younger one said, "I told you we shouldn't, Dave."

In him the anxiety whine was already full-blown, since wriggling out of blame was his familiar habit. He, Brett Gardner, already on my list for the chop, had been hired for his muscles and his mechanical know-how, the whining nature at first unsuspected. His three months' trial period was almost up, and I wouldn't be making him permanent.

He was a competent watchful driver. I'd trusted him from the start with my biggest and most expensive rigs, but I'd had requests from several good customers not to send him to transport their horses to the races, as he tended to sow his own dissatisfactions like a virus. Stable lads traveling with him went home incubating grouses, to their employers' irritation.

"It wasn't as if we had any horses on board," Dave Yates was saying, trying to placate. "Just Brett and me."

I'd told all the drivers over and over that picking up hitchhikers while there were horses on board invalidated the insurance. I told them I'd sack any of them instantly if they did that. I'd also told them never, ever, to give any lifts at all to anyone, even if the van was empty of horses, and even if they knew the lift-begger personally. No, Freddie, of course not, they'd said seriously; and now I wondered just how often they'd disobeyed me.

"What about the four-eyes?" I said, my annoyance obvious. "What's actually the matter?"

Dave said desperately, "He's dead."

"You ... *stupid* ..." Words failed me, drowned in anger. I could have hit him, and no doubt he saw it, backing away instinctively, fright rising. All sorts of scenarios presented themselves in rapid succession, none of them promising anything but trouble and lawsuits. "What did he do?" I demanded. "Try to jump off while you were moving? Or did you run him over ..." And dear Christ, I thought, let it not be that.

Dave's surprised shake of the head put at least those fears to rest.

"He's in the van," he said. "Lying on the seat. We tried to wake him when we got to Newbury, to tell him it was time to get off. And we couldn't. I mean ... he's dead."

"Are you sure?"

They both reluctantly nodded.

I switched on the outside lights to flood the tarmac with visibility and went over with them for a look-see. They skittered one on each side of me, crabbing sideways, making unhappy deprecating flapping movements with their hands, trying to shed their guilt, to justify themselves, to get me to understand it was unfortunate but not, definitely not, as Dave had said, their fault.

Dave, of about my own height (five nine) and age (mid-thirties) was primarily a horseman and secondarily a driver, usually traveling with animals that for some reason weren't being sent with enough attendants of their own. I'd seen him and Brett off that morning to pick up nine two-year-olds locally for a one-way trip to Newmarket, their owner being in the process of transferring his entire string from one perfectly good trainer to another in a typical bad-tempered huff. It wasn't that man's first expensive across-country flounce, and no doubt not his last. I'd shipped his three-year-old colts for him the previous day and was booked for fillies on the morrow. More money than sense, I thought.

I knew the nine two-year-olds had arrived safely in their new home, as Brett had made the customary calls to my office both when he reached his destination and at the start of his return journey. All the vans were equipped with mobile phones: the regular reporting calls were a useful routine, even if the older drivers thought one fussy. Fussy Freddie they might well call me behind my back, but with a fleet of fourteen vans zigzagging round England most days carrying multimillion fortunes on the hoof, I couldn't afford ignorance or negligent mistakes.

The front cabs of big horse vans were always pretty roomy, having to accommodate several attendants besides one or sometimes two drivers. The cabs of my nine-horse vans could hold eight people at a pinch, not in pullman comfort but at least sitting down. Behind the driver and the two front passenger seats a long padded rear seat usually gave support to four or five narrow bottoms: on this occasion, its entire length was occupied by one man lying on his back, feet towards me, silent and no longer worried about time.

I climbed into the cab and stood looking down at him.

I'd expected, I'd realized, some sort of tramp. Someone with a stubble, smelly jacket, grubby jeans, down on his luck. Not a prosperous-looking middle-aged fat man in suit, tie and gold onyx signet ring, with leather-soled polished shoes pointing mutely to heaven. Not a man who looked as if he could have bought other more suitable transport.

He was certainly dead. I didn't attempt to feel for a pulse, nor close the sagging mouth or the half-open lids behind the thick-lensed glasses. A rolled-up horse rug had provided him with a pillow. One arm had fallen by his side, the hand with the ring resting laxly on the floor, near but not touching a black briefcase. I jumped down from the cab, shut its door and looked at the worried faces of my men, who would no longer meet my eyes.

"How much did he pay you?" I asked bluntly.

"Freddie!" Dave wriggled in embarrassment, trying to deny it, happy-go-lucky always, likable, but of variable good sense.

"I'd never ..." Brett began, fake indignation always ready.

I gave him a disillusioned stare and interrupted. "Where did you pick him up, why did he want a ride, and how much did he offer?"

"Dave fixed it," Brett said accusingly.

"But you had your cut." I took it for granted; not a question.

"Brett asked him for more," Dave said with fury. "Demanded it."

"Yes, well, calm down." I began to walk back towards the house. "You'd better sort out what you're going to tell the police. Did he give you a name, for instance?"

"No," Dave said.

"Or a reason for wanting a lift?"

"His car had broken down," Dave explained. "He was at the South Mimms service station, pacing about and sweating round by the diesel pumps, trying to get the driver of an oil tanker to take him to Bristol."

"So?"

"So, well, he had a fistful of readies but the tanker was going to Southampton."

"What were you doing by the diesel pumps anyway?" I asked.

They'd had no need to take on more fuel, not just going to Newmarket and back.

"We'd stopped there," Dave said vaguely.

"Dave had a stomachache," Brett enlarged. "The squits. We had to stop to get him something for it."

"Imodium." Dave confirmed, nodding. "I was just walking past the pumps on my way back, see?"

Bleakly I led the way into the house, going through the back door into the hall and then wheeling left into the big all-purpose room where I customarily spent much of my time. I drew back the curtains, revealing the horse van out on the tarmac, and stood looking at it while I phoned the police.

The local constable who answered knew me well, as we'd both spent much of our lives in the racing center of Pixhill, a big village verging on small town sprawling

6

across a fold of downland in Hampshire, south of Newbury.

"Sandy?" I said briefly, when he answered. "This is Freddie Croft. I've a slight problem . . . One of my vans picked up a hitchhiker who seems to have died on the journey. Do you mind coming over? He's outside my house, not along at the farm."

"Dead, do you mean?" he asked cautiously, after a pause.

"I mean dead. As in not breathing."

He cleared his throat. "You're not having me on?"

"Sorry, no."

"Well, all right. Ten minutes."

Pixhill's token police force consisted of Sandy alone, a Wild West outpost on the frontiers of law and order. Pixhill's police station consisted of an office-room in Sandy's house, where his chief activity was writing up records of his daily patrols. Out of hours, like now, he would be watching television in scruffy clothes, drinking beer and casually cuddling his children's mother, a plump lady perennially in bedroom slippers.

In the ten promised minutes before he sped importantly onto my tarmac in his official car with every available light flashing, I learned not much more about our unwelcome deceased guest.

"How was I to know he'd die on us?" Dave said aggrievedly as I put down the receiver. "Do someone a favor . . . Yeah, well I know you told us not to. But he was going on something chronic about how he had to get to Bristol for his daughter's wedding or something . . ."

I looked at him in disbelief.

"Yeah, well," Dave said defensively, "how was I to know?"

7

"It was all Dave's idea," Brett assured me.

"Did you talk to him?" I asked them.

"Not that much," Dave said. "He chose that seat behind us, anyway. Didn't seem to want to talk."

"I told Dave it was all wrong," Brett complained.

"Shut up," Dave said angrily. "You could have refused to drive him. I didn't notice you saying you wouldn't."

"And neither of you noticed him dying, either?" I suggested with irony.

The idea discomfited them, but no, it appeared, they hadn't.

"Thought he was asleep," Dave said, and Brett nodded. "So then," Dave went on, "when we couldn't wake him . . . I mean, you saw how he looks . . . well, we'd just pulled off the motorway at the Newbury junction . . . we were going to drop him at the Chieveley service station there so he could get another lift on to Bristol . . . well . . . there he was, dead, and we couldn't roll him out onto the ground, could we?"

They couldn't, I agreed. So they'd brought him to my doorstep, like cats bringing home a dead bird.

"Dave wanted to dump him somewhere," Brett whined virtuously. "Dave wanted to. It was me said we couldn't."

Dave glared at him. "We *discussed* it," he said, "that's all we did."

"You'd have been in real trouble if you'd dumped him," I said, "and not just from me."

Sandy, still buttoning himself hastily into his dark blue uniform, arrived at that moment to take charge in the slightly pompous manner he'd developed over the years. One look at the corpse set him summoning help over his radio, resulting presently in a doctor and a host of unanswerable questions.

The dead man did, it seemed, at least have a name, discovered via a walletful of addresses and credit cards. Sandy brought the wallet down from the cab and showed it to me, where I waited on the ground outside.

"K. K. Ogden. Kevin Keith Ogden," he said, picking his way through the contents with stubby fingers. "Lives in Nottingham. Mean anything to you?"

"No." I shook my head. "Never heard of him."

He hadn't expected anything else.

"What did he die of?" I asked.

"A stroke maybe. Doc won't say before the postmortem. No sign of foul play if that's what you mean."

The archaic words "foul play" had always seemed faintly ridiculous to me, but in this case I was grateful to hear them.

"I can use the van tomorrow, then?" I asked.

"Don't see why not." He thought it over judiciously. "You might want to clean it, like."

"Yup," I said. "Always do."

He looked at me sideways. "I thought you had a rule never to give lifts."

"Dave and Brett are in big trouble."

With a glimmer of sympathy for the two men, he looked across to where they waited by the house door and said, "You didn't get your iron fist reputation for nothing, Freddie."

"What about the velvet glove bit?"

"Uh huh. That too."

Sandy at forty had thickened round the waist and softened to puffiness of cheek and jaw, but the resulting air of rustic unintelligence was misleading. His superiors at one time had posted him away from Pixhill, in accordance with their belief that a policeman became too cozy and forgiving if left too long in one small neighborhood, and had sent cruising cars in from outside to do his rounds. In Sandy's absence, however, the petty crime rate of Pixhill had soared while the detection rate plummeted, and after a while P.C. Sandy Smith had been quietly reinstated, to the overall dismay of the mildly wicked.

Smart young Dr. Bruce Farway, a recent Pixhill arrival who had already alienated half his patients by patronizing them insufferably, climbed down with agility from the cab and told me brusquely not to disturb the body before he could arrange for its removal.

"I can't imagine why I should want to," I said mildly.

He eyed me with disfavor. We'd disliked each other on sight a few months ago and he'd not forgiven me for disagreeing with his diagnosis on one of my drivers and paying for a private second opinion that had proved him wrong. No humility and precious little humanity could be diagnosed in Bruce Farway, though he could be nice to sick children, I'd heard.

Leaving him issuing brisk instructions over his car phone, Sandy and I went across to the house where he took brief statements from Dave and Brett. There was bound to be an inquest, he informed them, but it shouldn't take up much of their time.

Too much, I thought crossly, and they both unerringly read my expression. I told them I'd see them in the morning. They weren't comforted, it seemed.

Not much later Sandy freed them to walk away down to the pub where they would spread their news item through the local lightning grapevine. Sandy shut his notebook, gave me an insouciant grin and drove back to his house to phone the hitchhiker's hometown police force. Only Bruce Farway remained, impatiently waiting out by his car for the arrival of Kevin Keith Ogden's onward transport. I went out to him, for an update.

"They wanted to leave him here until tomorrow," he exclaimed, affronted. "I insisted they come tonight."

Grateful for that, I asked if he'd like to wait in the house and, with a hesitant shrug, he accepted. In the big sitting room, I offered him alcohol, Coke or coffee. Nothing, he said.

He looked with a downturned mouth at the row of framed racing photographs along one wall, mostly pictures of myself in my jockey days sitting on the backs of high-leaping horses. In a village dedicated to thoroughbred racing, where the four-footed aristocrats brought more jobs and more prosperity to the area than all other industries put together, Bruce Farway had been overheard to say that lives lived in racing were wasted. Only selfless service given to others, as for example by doctors and nurses, was praiseworthy. Jockeys' injuries, he considered, were self-inflicted. No one understood why such a man had come to Pixhill.

I thought I might as well ask him, so I did. He gave me a surprised glance and went over to the window to cast his gaze briefly at the cooling immobile horse van.

"I believe in general practice," he said. "I believe in a continuing service to a rural community. I believe in treating the family, not the illness."

All marvelous, I thought, if he hadn't looked at me superciliously down his nose in a conscious glow of superiority while he spoke.

"What did our body die of?" I asked.

He compressed his already thin lips. "Obesity and smoking, I daresay."

In another century, I thought, he would have condemned witches to the stake. For the good of their souls, of course.

11

Thin, fervent, bigoted, he fidgeted impatiently by the window and finally asked a question of his own.

"Why were you a jockey?"

The answer was too complicated. I said merely, "I was born to it. My father trained steeplechasers."

"Does that make it inevitable?"

"No," I said. "My brother captains cruise ships and my sister's a physicist."

He removed his attention wholly from the horse van with his mouth opening in astonishment. "Are you serious?"

"Certainly. Why not?"

He couldn't think why not and was saved from fishing for a reply by the telephone's ringing. I answered and found Sandy on the line, slightly out of breath and fluttering notebook pages.

"The Nottingham police," he said, "will want to know where South Mimms is, exactly."

"They've surely got a map!"

"Mm. Well, tell *me*, like, then I can make a better report."

"You've surely got a map as well."

"Oh, come on, Freddie."

I relented, smiling. "The South Mimms service station is north of London on M25. And I'll tell you something, Sandy, our friend Kevin Keith was not taking a direct route from Nottingham to Bristol. In fact, from Nottingham to Bristol you'd never go near South Mimms in a million years, so just tell the Nottingham police to go easy on the relatives because whatever our corpse was doing in South Mimms he wasn't going straight from home to any daughter's wedding."

He digested the information. "Ta," he said, "I'll tell them."

I put down the receiver and Bruce Farway asked, "What daughter's wedding?"

I explained how Dave had been persuaded to give the lift, even against express orders.

Frowning, Farway said, "You don't believe in the daughter, then?"

"Not all that much."

"I don't suppose it matters why he was in ... where did you say ... South Mimms?"

"Not to him, anymore," I agreed, "but it'll waste my drivers' time. The inquest, and so on."

"He couldn't help dying!" the doctor protested.

"He's a damn nuisance."

With plain disapproval Farway went back to watching the horse van. A boringly long time elapsed during which I drank scotch and water ("Not for me," Farway said), thought hungrily of my recongealing stew and answered two more phone calls.

The news had traveled at warp speed. The first voice demanding facts was that of the owner whose two-year-olds had gone to Newmarket, the second that of the trainer who was having to see them leave his stable.

Jericho Rich, the owner, never wasted time on polite opening chat, saying without ceremony, "What's this about a dead man in your van?" His voice, like his personality, was loud, aggressive and impatient. His name, on official documents, was Jerry Colin Rich. Jericho suited him better, if only for the noise.

While I told him what had happened, I pictured him as I'd very often seen him in parade rings at the races, a stocky gray-haired bully given to poking holes in the air with a jabbing finger.

"You listen to me, fella," he said now, shouting down the

13

line. "You pick up no hitchhikers while you work for me, understand? That's what you've always said and that's how I like it. When you take my horses you don't take anyone else's. That's the way we've always done business and I don't want any changes."

I reflected that once his whole string had gone to Newmarket I wouldn't be doing much more business for him anyway, but alienating the cantankerous old beggar would all the same be unwise. Give him a year or two and I might be ferrying him back.

"What's more," he was saying, "when you take my fillies across tomorrow, take them in a different van. Horses can smell death, you know, and I don't want those fillies upset."

I assured him they would go in a different van, even though, as I didn't bother to tell him, the cab would be reeking of disinfectant, not death, come pickup time in the morning.

"And don't send the same driver."

It wasn't worth arguing about. "All right," I said.

He began to run out of steam, which is to say, to repeat himself. I offered him always a soft cushion of agreement as being the fastest way to blunt the sword of his anger, especially when his grievances reached the third or fourth recycle. We went through the same conversation twice more. I promised yet again to send a different van and a different driver and finally, though muttering away and still not satisfied, he clicked himself off.

He'd owned five or six hurdlers in the past, which I'd ridden for him regularly. I'd had a lot of practice in absorbing the Jericho tantrums with my own temper intact.

Thanks to the Rich decibels, Farway appeared to have

heard the whole repetitious exchange because he gave me his unexpected opinion.

"It wasn't your fault your drivers picked the man up."

"Maybe." I paused. "The captain goes down with the ship, my brother says."

He stared. "Do you mean you think it *was* your fault?"

I thought chiefly that it wasn't a good time to discuss ultimate responsibility in the abstract. I wished more simply that Kevin Keith had given up the ghost in someone else's cab. A pity, I thought, that the oil tanker had been going to Southampton.

Michael Watermead, in striking contrast to Jericho Rich, spoke in soft hesitant super-educated tones over the telephone and started by asking if the nine two-year-olds that had left his care that morning had arrived safely in Newmarket.

I was certain he already knew, but I assured him that they had.

Resentment at having had to part with them would have been natural, but Michael seemed to have his feelings well in control. Tall, fair and fiftyish, his habitual air of dither fronted an effective, above middle-rank operation of sixty good stables in three attractive quadrangles, usually healthily full. His horses liked him, always a good character reference. They nuzzled his neck if he were near enough: they came to look out of their stalls at the sound of his step in the yard. I'd never ridden for him, as he trained only Flat horses, but since I'd acquired the transport business and had grown to know him, we'd become, on a business level at least, good friends.

The third son of a baron, he trained for a distantly royal personage thirty-somethingth from the throne, a snob-value combination that had brought him Rich's custom in the first place. The deterioration in the first flush of gratification on both sides—there were no longer many owner-strings as big as Rich's nor as talented in depth—had been complete, both men throwing me asides along the way from euphoria to disillusion.

"The man's impossible!" Michael had exclaimed over some particular transport demand from Jericho. "Totally unreasonable."

"My horse lost the race on the journey to Scotland," Rich complained. "Why does he send them so far? It costs too much and they arrive tired." He overlooked entirely Michael's successful forays to France with the same animals.

I remained strictly neutral and nonpartisan through all owner-trainer differences out of a strong sense of self-preservation, starting right back in my early racing days over fences when an incautious criticism had got back to its target and very nearly cost me my job. I'd become adept at sympathetic noises with the minimum of actual comment, even to friends.

Getting my own way softly had eased my whole path through life and in business had served me well. I was better at placating than confronting, at persuading than commanding; and I wasn't defeated much.

Michael said slowly, "Is it true your van brought back . . . a *dead* man?"

" 'Fraid so."

"Who?"

I explained yet again about Kevin Keith Ogden, and I told him that Jericho Rich had already demanded a different van and driver for his fillies on the morrow.

"That man," Michael said bitterly. "Despite the hole it makes in my yard, I'll be glad to see the last of him. Vile-tempered oaf."

16

"Will you fill up the hole?"

"Oh sure, in time. I've got ten boarded out that I can bring in now, for a start. Losing Jericho's a blight, but not a disaster."

"Great."

"Lunch on Sunday? Maudie will call you."

"Fine."

" 'Bye."

A man could drown in Maudie Watermead's blue eyes. Her Sunday lunches were legendary.

Farway, still by the window, was growing impatient, repeatedly consulting his watch as if the constant checking would make time go faster.

"Scotch?" I offered again.

"I don't drink."

Dislike or addiction? I wondered. Probably plain disapproval, on the whole.

I looked round my spacious familiar room, wondering how he would see it. Gray carpet with a scattering of rugs. Cream walls, racing photographs, my mother's china parrot collection in an alcove. Edwardian mahogany desk, green leather swiveling chair. Sofas with ancient fading chintz, tray of drinks on a side table, padded cream curtains, table lamps everywhere, bookshelves and a potted plant, all leaves, no flowers. A lived-in room, not excessively tidy, not a decorator's triumph.

Home.

An unenthusiastic black van at long last crawled onto the tarmac and parked between the horse van and my door. It had long black windowless sides and black windowless rear doors, and I realized it was, in fact, a hearse. Sandy in his official car returned in its wake.

Farway, exclaiming, hurried out to meet him and the

three men who emerged phlegmatically from the hearse to set about their task. I followed in Farway's wake and watched the unloading of a narrow stretcher which seemed to be covered on the upper surface with a lot of dark canvas and several sinewy straps.

The man who seemed to be in charge of things said he was from the coroner's officer and produced paperwork for Farway to deal with.

The other two climbed with the stretcher up into the cab, followed by Sandy, who soon descended again bringing with him a grip and a briefcase. Both bags were of leather, battered but originally good.

"Belongings of the deceased?" Sandy asked.

Farway thought so.

"They are not my men's," I agreed.

Sandy put the bags on the tarmac and then went aloft again to return with a plastic bag containing booty collected from the body—a watch, a cigarette lighter, a packet of cigarettes, a pen, a comb, a nail file, a handkerchief, glasses and the onyx and gold ring. He itemized them aloud to the coroner's officer who wrote at his dictation, then attached a label saying, "Property of K. K. Ogden," and stowed them in his car.

While Sandy and the coroner's officer climbed back into the cab, I squatted down beside the bags and unzipped the top of the grip.

"I don't think you should do that," Farway protested.

The grip, half-full, held overnight necessities; shaving kit, pajamas, clean shirt, nothing very new, nothing out of the ordinary. I closed the zip and snapped open the briefcase, which wasn't locked.

"Hey," Farway said.

"If a man dies on my property," I said reasonably, "I'd like to get to know him."

"But you've no right . . ."

I looked anyway through the meager contents, which seemed to me wholly uninformative. A calculator. Writing pad, nothing written on it. A bunch of postcards in an elastic band, all the same, a view of a country hotel, advertisement handouts. A bottle of aspirins, a packet of indigestion tablets, two small airline-size bottles of vodka, both full.

"Look here," Farway said uncomfortably.

I shut the briefcase and stood up. "All yours," I said.

The undertakers took their time, and when they finally brought Kevin Keith out it was through the front passenger door, not via the grooms' door further back through which we had all so far climbed to reach the rear seat. It appeared that, death having done its stiffening work, the only way out for the body was to load it forward onto the stretcher laid along the front seats: so it came out that way, feet forward, wrapped amorphically in canvas, retaining straps in place.

As bodies went, it appeared that this one was heavy and awkward in shape, the bent right arm being impossible to straighten. Certainly respect for the dead as such was markedly absent, the problem seeming to present itself rather as of the order of extricating an obstinate grand piano from a small angular attic. I supposed body-collectors got used to it. One of the men, besides remarks like "Heave now" and "That arm's jamming on the door," was assessing the chances of his football team on the following Saturday. They lifted the stretcher unceremoniously through the open back doors of the black hearse as if engaged in trash disposal and I saw them transfer the canvas-wrapped Ogden off the stretcher into an opened metal coffin.

19

Farway too, more used to corpses than I, was taking the removal of this one prosaically. He told me he wouldn't be doing the postmortem himself but it looked to him like straightforward cardiac arrest. Plain unlucky. The inquest should be a brief formality. He would be certifying death. I might not be called.

He said good night neutrally, folded himself into his car and followed the hearse as it rolled away off my tarmac. Sandy, taking with him the grip and the briefcase, drove off peacefully in the rear.

All suddenly seemed very quiet. I looked up at the stars, eternal in the face of mortality. I wondered if Kevin Keith Ogden had known he was dying, lying along a leatherette bench seat behind a thundering engine.

I thought quite likely not. There had been times when I'd been knocked out in racing falls, when the last thing I'd seen had been a whirling blurring vision of grass and sky. After the impact I wouldn't have known if I'd died; and I'd thought sometimes, gratefully waking up, that an unaware death would be a blessing.

I climbed yet again into the cab. The rolled-up horse rug still bore the imprint of Ogden's head and there was an un- appealing stain halfway along the seat, threatening action on the morrow. Damn the man, I thought.

Brett had left the key in the ignition, another taboo in my book. I stepped over into the front compartment and re- moved the key ring, checking that at least the brakes were on and all but the cabin lights were off. Finally, switching off those interior lights also I jumped down from the pas- senger door, locking it behind me.

The front passenger door and the driver's door both locked with the same key that started the engine, a large complicated key supplied by the manufacturers. I locked the driver's door—Brett hadn't—and with the second more ordinary key on the ring locked the grooms' door. A third key locked the small compartment under the dashboard that contained the mobile telephone power switch and various documents, which I'd checked and found secure.

I walked again right round the van, making a last inspection. Everything seemed as it should be. The two ramps for horses were up and bolted. The five doors for humans, two for the front seats, three for the attendants, were similarly immovable. The flap over the intake to the diesel tanks, fastened by the fourth and last key on the key ring, was proof against siphoning thieves.

Feeling all the same uneasy I went back to the house and locked the back door behind me, which I didn't do always. I stretched out a hand to switch off the outside lights and then changed my mind and left them on.

The fleet usually spent the night inside a large brick-walled converted farmyard, the wide strong entrance gates padlocked. The nine-van standing alone on my tarmac seemed unaccustomedly vulnerable, even though rigs of that size were seldom stolen. There were too many identity numbers engraved on too many parts, quite apart from the name CROFT RACEWAYS painted in about six places, the whole thing hardly inconspicuous for anyone trying to avoid notice.

I reheated the old stew, sloshed some red wine into it for excitement and ate the result while leaving the sitting room curtains open so that I could see the horse van all the time.

Absolutely nothing happened. My unease slowly abated, and I put down its existence simply to the fact of Ogden's demise.

I made and received a few more telephone calls, checking particularly with my senior driver that all the other vans were back at the farm. The rest of the day's journeys, it seemed, had for once gone uneventfully to plan: no mixups over time, no engine troubles, no equipment or attendants left behind. All the drivers had filled in their log sheets and popped them as requested into the letter box of the office. The padlocks were on the gates. No keys were anywhere accessible. Despite the dead passenger, the overall message I received was that the boss could relax and go to bed.

The boss, in the end, did just that, though from my bedroom, which was over the sitting room, I still had a clear view of the horse van out under the lights. I left the curtains wide open and although I never slept with them fully closed I nevertheless woke several times because of the continuing unusual brightness outside. At about three in the morning I became suddenly fully alert, disturbed by more than plain light. Disturbed by a moving flash across the ceiling, indistinct, like sheet lightning, seen through my eyelids.

The weather had been mild recently, though it was still early March, but it seemed to me that the temperature had dropped ten degrees in the past few hours. In bare feet and sleeping shorts I stood up and went to the window, shivering.

At first sight nothing seemed changed. Shrugging, I half turned to return to the warm bed and then stopped stock-still in serious alarm.

The grooms' door, through which we'd all climbed, was slightly open, not securely locked, as I'd left it.

Open.

I stared hard, but there was no mistake. There was a black line of shadow where the door no longer fitted flat and snugly into position. The flash of light I'd seen must have been a reflection from its window as the door had been opened.

Without considering clothes I sprinted headlong downstairs and along to the back door, unlocking it, throwing my feet into gumboots and snatching an old raincoat from a peg. Trying to fit my arms into its sleeves I ran across the tarmac and pulled the door wide.

There was a figure inside there, in black, as surprised to see me as I to see him. At first he had his back towards me, then when he whirled round with a fierce exclamation, more an explosion of escaping breath than an actual word, I saw that his head was covered with a black hood, his eyes alive through holes, the cliché disguise of robbers and terrorists.

"What the hell are you doing?" I yelled at him, trying myself crazily to climb up after him. Stupid thing to do in gumboots: the stepholes weren't designed for their clumsy width.

Black-mask snatched up the rolled horse rug, gave it a fast shake to open its folds and threw it over me while I was still halfway up. I slid off the toeholds, stepped back unbalanced into a void and landed in a heap on the tarmac. The black figure, dimly seen, jumped over onto the driver's seat, unlatched the door on that side, leaped athletically to the ground and ran for the shadows, lithe and scudding.

Perhaps in sneakers I could have made it a contest. In gumboots and an unbelted raincoat still only half on, it was hopeless. I stood up disgustedly, disentangling myself from the horse rug, fastening the raincoat belatedly and listening in vain for any sound of departing footsteps.

None of it made sense, nor did standing around shivering in inappropriate clothes in the middle of the night. There was nothing worth stealing in the van save perhaps the radio or phone, but the black figure hadn't seemed to be attacking either. He hadn't in fact seemed to be doing anything in particular, when I looked back to my first sight of him, but simply standing in the cab with his back to me. There had been dust and streaks of dirt on his clothes. As far as I could remember he hadn't been carrying anything. No tools, not even a flashlight. If he'd opened the grooms' door with either a key or a lockpick, he must have put it in a pocket.

The keyhole of the grooms' door was in the handle itself. There was no key in the lock, nor, when I looked, any obvious scratches or signs of force or tampering.

Cold and cross I threw the horse rug back into the cab, shut the grooms' door and the driver's side door and went back to the house to fetch the keys again to relock them.

Out of respect for my carpets I slid my feet out of the gumboots and padded through the hall and across the sitting room to the desk, not bothering to switch on any lights in there owing to being able to see perfectly well because of the glow outside. I retrieved the keys from the desk drawer, retraced my steps, resumed the gumboots and clomped back towards the wheels.

Coming close, I saw without belief that there was a black moving shadow again inside the cab. Monstrous, I thought, and what in God's name could he want? He was standing behind the driver's seat, feeling forward into the storage shelf that spread across the whole width of the cab high and above the front seats, projecting out over the windshield. The spacious shelf, common to all of my fleet, was used by the drivers and attendants to stow their personal belongings, often changes of clothing and occasionally a sleeping bag and pillow. There was a full-length mattress installed for the use of several of the drivers who slept there habitually

on overnight stops, preferring it to cheap lodgings. Brett
had told me he expected better. Your own choice, I assured
him.

The busy figure in the cab saw me coming and was out
and away again before I could reach him. I ran in his wake
sluggishly, as if through treacle, my bare feet half-sliding
out of the boots at every stride. He headed down the drive
and seemed to melt into the shadows of the trees by the
exit to the road.

Uselessly, I followed him to the road itself, but he was
nowhere to be seen. It was a country road, unfenced, with
open gateways to other houses. Trees and bushes by the
hundred, hiding places unlimited. It would have taken half
an army to find him.

Puzzled and dispirited I retraced my way back to the
van. The driver's door stood wide open, as he'd left it. I
climbed up clumsily and stood behind the seat, as he had,
looking into the storage shelf, switching on the cabin light
for a better view.

The shelf was empty except for the mattress and a plastic
carrier-bag which proved on inspection to contain remains
of Brett-type sustenance: screwed-up wrappers from chocolate bars, an empty sandwich-shaped casing bearing a label
announcing "Beef and Tomato," with the price underneath,
and two empty Coke cans.

I put the bag back where it had been. It was each driver's
business to keep his own van clean and I didn't feel like
picking up after Brett. Whatever he and Dave had been
doing that day, giving lifts to moribund businessmen
seemed just the start of it. Those two would have a lot of
explaining to do in the morning.

I carefully locked the doors again, and again walked
back to the house, but once inside felt far from reassured.

The agile visitor had got into the van the first time without breaking a window or other observable force and presumably could get in again the same way.

Without knowing in the least what he wanted, I still didn't like the idea of his returning a third time. It also occurred to me disturbingly that perhaps he intended to *leave* something, or destroy something, or disable the van altogether. In alarm and doubt I shed the gumboots and raincoat and ran upstairs for substitutes in the shape of two sweaters, jeans, socks, and shoes I could run in. I pulled my own old sleeping bag from a cupboard and with a last check through the window to see if a third visitation was in progress—no sign of it—I went downstairs for a padded jacket and gloves.

With all these aids to warmth, I crossed yet again to the van and settled myself in the front passenger seats, moderately comfortable in body if not in mind.

Time slid by.

I dozed.

No one came.

2

Predictably, I woke stiff and cold as soon as nature's lighting system began creeping into the electric stuff, and I trailed yawning across to the kitchen for warmth and coffee. The newspapers and the mail arrived. I sorted through the bills, read the headlines and turned to the racing pages, ate some cornflakes and answered the first phone calls of the day.

My routine working hours started at six or seven and normally ended at midnight, Sundays included, but it was a way of life, not a hardship. It was the same for trainers, all of whom seemed to believe that if they were up and caring for their horses by or before dawn, everyone who worked for them should be available likewise.

Plans tended to change overnight. The first call on that

27

day, a Friday, was from the trainer of a horse that had got cast in its stable and injured himself by threshing about on the floor, trying to get himself back onto his feet.

"The bugger's twisted his off-hind. My head lad found him, hopping lame." The big healthy voice reverberated into my ear. "He can't run at Southwell, sod it. Strike him off your list, will you?"

I said I would. "Thanks for letting me know."

"I know you run tight schedules," he boomed. "The four for Sandown are OK. Don't send that Brett for them, he's a whiner, he upsets my lads."

I assured him he wouldn't get Brett.

"Right, Freddie. See you at the sports."

Without wasting time, I buzzed my head driver and asked if the vans for Southwell had already left.

"Warming up," he assured me.

"Cross off Larry Dell. Their horse got cast."

"Got you."

I put down the kitchen receiver and went through to the sitting room where most of the desk top was taken up by the week's comprehensive chart indicating which van was going where with whose horses. I wrote it always in pencil because of the constant changes.

On an adjacent table, easily reached by swiveling the green leather chair, stood a computer, monitor and keyboard. Theoretically, it was easier to call each van to the screen to enter or rearrange its journeys, and actually I did keep the details of the journeys recorded there permanently once they'd been completed, but for an advance overview I still clung to my pencil and eraser.

Along at the farm, in the main office, my two bright secretaries, Isobel and Rose, kept the computer competently accurate and up to the minute, and despaired of my old-fashioned methods. The terminal in my sitting room was a sort of substation upon which appeared all the changes they'd made on the main computer, and that was what I chiefly used it for: checking what had been organized in my absence.

In return, I typed in any changes which came in before or after their office hours and, one way or another, we had not so far left any expectant runner waiting in vain for the coach to take it to the ball.

I checked down the list on what looked like a typical Friday for the first week of March. Two vans going north to Southwell, where the all-weather track held both Flat and jumping races all winter. Four vans collecting runners for the afternoon's program of steeplechasing at Sandown, south of London. One nine-horse van taking broodmares to Ireland. One six-van taking broodmares to Newmarket, one taking broodmares to Gloucestershire, another taking mares to a stud down in Surrey: the thoroughbred breeding season in full flood.

One van was out of action, scheduled for maintenance. One was going to France. One would be taking Jericho Rich's fillies to Newmarket. Brett and his nine-horser, standing outside my window in the strengthening dawn, were due to spend the day shuttling a whole string for a trainer moving to Pixhill from out on Salisbury Plain: not long journeys but multiple and, from my point of view, good profit.

The following week would see the Cheltenham Festival, peak of the steeplechasing year, with the Flat season proper getting into gear the week after, its crowded program bringing me six months of good business. March was sigh-of-relief time, the fogs and freezes of winter relaxing their paralyzing menace: there was no income to be made from a row of vans standing silent in the snow, but the drivers had to be paid all the same.

My head driver phoned back. Harve by name, short for Harvey.

"Pat's got flu," he said. "She's in bed."

"Shit."

"It's a bugger, the flu this year. Knocks you out. It's not her fault."

"No," I said. "How's Gerry?"

"Still bad. We could put those broodmares off till Monday."

"No, they're near to foaling. I promised they'd go to Surrey today. I'll sort something out."

Pat and Gerry were reliable drivers: if they said they were too ill to work, then they were. Reshuffle required.

"Dave can do the Gloucestershire broodmares, instead of Pat," I said. Dave was a slow driver, and I didn't send him out behind the wheel unless I had to. "Those mares have no deadline."

"Yeah. OK."

"I want him here first though. When he turns up at the farm, send him along here. Brett too."

"Will do," he said. "Is it about the dead man?"

"It is."

"Silly sods."

"And tell Jogger I need him p.d.q. Tell him to bring his slider."

"He won't be in for half an hour."

"That will do."

"Anything else?"

"Sure to be, in five minutes."

He laughed and went away, leaving me thinking, as I often did, that I was lucky to have him. When I'd been a

jockey Harve had been my weighing-room valet, bringing
my cleaned saddles and fresh breeches to the races every
day. Valets were a bit like theatrical dressers, although one
valet would "do" ten or so jockeys regularly. It was a
close personal service: one could keep few physical secrets
from one's valet.

When I'd hung up my boots and bought the transport
business he'd appeared to my surprise on my doorstep.

"I'm here to see if you'll give me a job," he said for
openers, coming straight to the point.

"But I don't need a valet anymore."

"Not that. I don't want to keep on with that. My old
dad's died and the weighing room's not the same as when
he was there, and I want a change. I'm sick of the wash-
tub. How about it if I drive for you? I drive hundreds of
miles every week anyway; have for years."

"But," I said slowly, "you'd need a Heavy Goods Vehicle license."

"I'll get one."

"The vans aren't like cars. You'd have to take a course."

"If I get the license, will you give me a job?"

I'd said I would because we'd always got on easily together, and in that casual way I'd acquired the best lieuten-
ant one could imagine.

He was sandy-haired, strong-armed, about my own age,
an inch or two taller. Dryly disillusioned, he was quick to
denigrate but in a way that made one smile. Brett, he had
remarked to me once, shifted the blame before you even
realized there was a fault. "He carries a bagful of alibis
around with him, ready to pull one out."

I went upstairs, showered, shaved, tweaked the duvet
straight on my bed and returned in short time to my desk
and the uninterrupted view of the horse van.

31

Jogger, the company mechanic, swept up the drive in his truck and squeaked to a halt nose to nose with the horse van. Spry, bowlegged, bald and cockney, he eeled out of the truck and stood looking at the horse van while scratching his head. Then he came over to the house in the peculiar gait that had earned him his nickname, a rolling motion like that of speed walkers, almost running but with one foot on the ground all the time, elbows tucked in.

I went to the door to meet him and we walked back to the van together, he impatiently slowing his scuttling progress to match mine.

"What's the boil, then?" he said.

He spoke his own sort of cockney rhyming slang, and indeed I often thought he made most of it up himself, but I was used to it by that time. For boil, read boil and bubble, trouble.

"Just check it all over, will you?" I answered. "Take a good look at the engine. Then slide under, make sure we're not leaking or carrying additions."

"Gor," he said.

I watched him check the engine, his eyes swift, fingers delicate, head nodding with certainties.

"All hunky-dory," he said.

"Good. Go over the rest."

He went along to his truck and brought out the flexible stick, with mirror attached, that could be angled to reveal invisibilities round corners, and also the low platform on casters, on which he lay on his back to slide under the vans for quick underguts inspections.

"When you're done, I'll be in the house," I said.

"Am I looking for anything particular?"

"Just for anything you don't understand."

He peered at me speculatively. "This van went to Italy earlier, dinnit?"

I agreed that it had. "Went last Friday, returned by Tuesday evening." There had been no problems or holdups, though; as far as I knew, of course.

"That Brett never cleans it proper. Got no Jekyll."

Jekyll and Hyde, I thought: pride.

"Brett had Wednesday off," I said. "Harve drove a load of colts to Newmarket that day in this van. Brett took it to Newmarket and back yesterday. A couple of odd things have happened, so . . . carry on with the check."

"You talking about that stiff?"

"Partly."

"He didn't have no chance to duff the van up, though, did he?"

"I don't know any more than you," I said. "And get a move on, Jogger, I've got to get this thing cleaned and out on the road within an hour."

He lay down philosophically and shoved himself trustingly out of sight, except for his feet, under ten or so tons of steel. Just the prospect of it gave me a sort of claustrophobia, which Jogger knew about but loftily forgave. My failing increased his self-esteem: it did no harm.

I went back to the house and Harve phoned.

"Dave's on his way along to you now," he said with agitation. "But he says Brett's packing his bags."

"He's doing *what*?"

"Dave says Brett's not a complete thicko, he knows his trial three months is nearly up and that you won't keep him on. He's ducking out first. That way he can go around saying he gave you the chuck, not the other way round. He'll be whining all over the place about how hard he

33

worked here, Dave says, and how you never appreciated him."

"He can get on with it," I said. "The thing is, what about today?"

"The Marigold shuttle," Harve said. "Brett was doing that."

"Exactly. Who else have we got?" I knew the answer as soon as I asked. We had me.

"Well . . ." He hesitated.

"Yes, all right. I'll do it if there's no one else."

"It's not just the shuttle," he went on unhappily. "Vic's wife says he's got a temperature of a hundred and three and no way is he driving to Sandown."

One of those days.

"They're both here at the farm," Harve went on, "Vic and his missus. He says he wants to go, she says she'll divorce him. You can see he's got a fever, though."

"Send him home, he'll just spread the flu around more."

"OK. But . . ."

"Give me a minute. Inspiration will strike."

He laughed. "Hurry it up," he said, disconnecting.

I sucked my teeth. If racehorse trainers hadn't been as fussy as they normally were, I could have traveled the two Surrey-bound broodmares in one of the vans taking 'chasers to Sandown. The van could have dropped off the two racers, taken the mares to their destination and returned to Sandown to bring the 'chasers home. I might have risked it if I hadn't been sure the trainer in question would get to hear of it from his grooms: and the trainer in question would never ever let his own horses travel with any horses from any other stables. Sending his runners in company with broodmares would lose me his custom instantly and evermore.

I went out to the nine-horse van. Jogger was nowhere to be seen but when I yelled his name a pair of boots slid out into view, followed by grease-clogged trousers, filthy army sweater and a dirt-streaked face.

"You're right, we've picked up a stranger," he reported, and added, grinning with yellow teeth, "Did you know? You must have known."

"No, I didn't." Nor was I pleased. Very put out, in fact.

"Have a decko," he encouraged me, removing himself from the slider and slyly offering me his place.

"I'll take your word for it," I said, staying upright. "What have you found?"

"I'd say it's stuck on with a magnet." He gave me his opinion judiciously. "It's a sort of tin box. Like a big cash box, lid downwards."

"Shiny?" I asked.

"Course not. Want it out?"

"Yes, but wait . . . um . . . we've got three drivers now with flu. Would you do a run yourself, just to help out?"

He rubbed his greasy hands down his trousers and looked dubious. Driving meant cleaning and there was no doubt he felt happier dirty. I seldom asked him to drive more than his regular test runs on all the vans, when he listened to their resonances as to a language and heard trouble before it happened.

"Broodmares, not to the races," I explained.

"Well, then . . . when?"

"Lunchtime."

"Bonus?"

"Sure, if you do your regular maintenance work as well."

He shrugged, lay down again on the slider and disappeared. I went back to my desk, phoned Harve and told him, "Jogger."

"He's driving?" He sounded incredulous. "He agreed?"

"The broodmares to Surrey," I confirmed. "It's Phil whose van is in for maintenance, isn't it? Wake him up, twist his arm, sob stuff if you like, tell him his day off's postponed, we need him to take Vic's van to Sandown."

"OK."

"That should cover it," I said.

"Fingers crossed."

"Come down here yourself, would you, when you have a minute?"

After the briefest of pauses he said, "Right."

He would be wondering what I wanted but not to the level of worry. At least, I hoped not.

Dave at that point bicycled in across the tarmac and leaned his rusty conveyance against my woodpile. Dave did have a car, even rustier than the bike, but it spent most of the time out of action. One day, he'd been saying for months, he would equip it with retreads and get it back on the road. No one believed him. He spent his money on greyhounds.

He knocked on the outside door on his way in and appeared in the sitting-room doorway with the martyred air of having stepped out of a tumbril.

"You wanted me, Freddie?" He was nervous but trying for bravado; not a success.

"I want you and Brett to clean that van. It's due out again before nine."

"But, Brett . . ." He stopped.

"Go on."

"Harve told you, didn't he? Brett says he'll be waiting

at the office door for his P45 the second Isobel gets there, then he's off."

"He's due some wages and holiday money," I said, unruffled. "You get back on your bike and go and tell him he can have it now, here, in cash, but cleaning that van is yesterday's job, and if he doesn't finish it, his unemployment dates from yesterday morning. No pay for yesterday, understand?"

"You can't do that," Dave said uncertainly.

"Want to bet? By rights, he should give me a week's notice. And ask him if he thinks he might ever need a reference."

Dave gave me a hollow look.

"Hurry and fetch him," I said. "And come back yourself."

When he'd gone I switched on the computer and brought Brett and his affairs to the screen. Every journey he'd done for me was listed there, with dates, times, horses' names, expenses and notes. The day before's journey of nine two-year-olds to Newmarket had been entered only as "proposed": no dead bodies yet cluttered the entry.

His terms of employment were there, along with days worked and holiday entitlement earned: no problem at all to put together his present due. I printed a copy of the income information, ready to give to him.

Through the window I watched Jogger heel-and-toe his way towards the house, a grayish-brown shape like a big shoe box in his hands. He came into the sitting room and plonked the object down on my chart, not caring about mundane considerations like dirt. He looked surprised when I asked him to lift the box up again so that I could spread a newspaper under it.

"I had a hell of a job getting it off," he said. "Like a limpet mine, it was."

"Where's the magnet?" I asked.

"Still stuck to the chassis, behind the second fuel tank. Super-glue job, most like. This box came off in the end, though I had to use a tire iron. No one meant it to move, I'm telling you."

"How long would you say it's been there?"

The box was thick with grime except for a clean circular saucer-sized patch on its underside where it had been in contact with the magnet.

Jogger shrugged unhappily. "It's not in a place I need to inspect all that often."

"A week? A month? More?"

"Dunno," he said.

I picked the box up in the newspaper and shook it. It was comparatively light, with no rattle.

"Empty," Jogger said, nodding.

About fifteen inches by ten by six deep, it was a strong old-fashioned gray metal cash box with rounded corners, a recessed carrying handle and a sturdy lock. No key, naturally. A dent on one edge from the tire iron. The carrying handle, stuck into its recess, wouldn't lift up.

"Can you open it?" I asked. "Without breaking it."

Jogger gave me a sideways look. "I could pick the lock if I fetch my tools and you squint the other way."

"Go on, then."

He decided to take the box out to his truck for the job and presently with a yellow grin returned with it open.

Nothing inside, not even dust. I put my nose down to it. It smelt surprisingly clean inside considering the grime on the outside. It smelt even fresh, like talcum powder or soap.

"How difficult was it to search underneath?" I asked.

"Easy, on a slider. Very easy over an inspection pit, if you knew where to look. I nearly missed it, though. It's the same color as everything else under there. See, that's it, you wouldn't expect to see it, unless you knew it was there. You'd have to park that bit over the pit, too, which you wouldn't normally do."

"How long since you had Brett's van over the inspection pit?"

He raised his eyebrows. "Did an oil change, checked the air brakes, say five weeks ago. Total overhaul must've been before Christmas. Don't remember the day."

"The computer will have it," I said.

Jogger looked across at the dark screen without favor. He liked to be able to invent memories, not have them checked.

"Thanks, anyway," I said warmly. "I wouldn't have found this cash box myself in a million years."

The yellow teeth made a brief appearance. "You want to get under there," he said.

But no, I didn't.

Dave came back on his bicycle followed by Brett, slowly, in his car, neither of them showing much appetite for the morning. They came into the sitting room, greeted Jogger unenthusiastically and looked without reaction at the dirty gray cash box lying open on the newspaper.

"Has either of you seen that before?" I asked neutrally.

Uninterestedly, they said they hadn't.

"It's not my fault the horse van wasn't cleaned," Brett said defensively. "Sandy Smith wouldn't let me near it last night."

"Clean it now, will you, while I assemble your pay packet?"

"It was Dave's idea to give that man a lift."

"Yes, so you said."

"I wouldn't have done it on my own."

"That's bloody unfair," Dave protested furiously.

"Both of you shut up," I said. "Clean the van."

Seething, they both went out and through the window I watched the rigidity of their anger as they marched towards the task. Undoubtedly the picking up of the hitchhiker had been Dave's doing, but I found I could forgive his irresponsibility more easily than Brett's self-righteousness. They had both for sure pocketed Kevin Keith Ogden's money, although nothing would get them to say how much.

Jogger said, pointing at the cash box, "What do you want me to do with that?"

"Oh . . . just leave it here. And thanks."

"Where's Brett off to in that rig today?" he asked, following my gaze through the window.

"Nowhere. He's leaving the firm. I'll be driving it myself."

"Straight up? Then I'll do you a favor."

I switched my attention to his grubby, lined, fifty-three-year-old face, the wily exterior of an old soldier who knew every skiving trick of the trade but lived by his own code of strict honesty in some respects, notably for anything that moved on wheels.

"You've got a strong active uncovered magnet under that rig," he informed me. "If you're not careful, it'll pick up iron bars and such and you could catch them on something or back onto them and maybe pierce a fuel tank or worse."

I moved my head in appreciation. "What's best to do?"

"I'll stick something over it, if you like."

"Thanks, Jogger."

He heard the real gratitude in my voice and nodded

briefly. "What've we been carrying, eh?" he asked. "Carpets?"

I was mystified. *"Carpets?"*

"And rugs. Drugs."

"Oh." I understood belatedly. "I hope not." I pondered briefly. "Keep it to yourself for now, Jogger, will you? Until I get it sorted out."

He said he would, a promise easily given that might last into the third pint that evening up in the pub, but no further.

At close quarters he smelled of oil and dust, those constant companions, and also of stale smoke and a general earthiness. I found it less objectionable than the overpoweringly sweet after-shave and clashing medicinal mouthwash of one of the other drivers, whose odor pervaded his whole horse van, even overriding the scent of horses.

As far as possible, each driver drove one particular horse van all the time, making it his own. I'd found they all preferred it like that, and they also looked after the vehicles better that way, kept them cleaner, understood their idiosyncrasies and generally treated them with pride as their personal property. Each driver kept the keys of his own van in his possession and could personalize his own cab if he cared to. Several of them who liked to sleep on board had rigged curtains for the windows. Pat, now sick with flu, carried fresh flowers and an ingenious folding changing room in hers. I could almost infallibly have told which van I was in simply by the cab.

Brett's cab was consistent with how little of himself he'd committed to the job; devoid of anything personal. I would be glad to see the back of him even though it compounded the driver shortage.

Saying he'd fetch something for the magnet and that he'd better get on with things if he was going to Surrey with the broodmares, Jogger joggled his way back to his truck, loaded the slider and drove off. Dave hosed down the outside of the horse van and cleaned the windows with a squeegee. Brett swept internal debris carelessly out through the grooms' doors onto the tarmac.

The inside plan of the thirty-five-foot-long horse van made provision for three sets of three stalls, with spaces between the sets. The horses' heads protruded forwards into these spaces, where often sat an attendant traveling near them.

The width of the van allowed for three stalls only if the horses traveling were of average build. Heavily muscled horses, like older steeplechasers, needed more room and could travel only two side-by-side. The same for broodmares. When we took mares with foals, the three stalls across converted to one single large one. So nine two-year-olds or three mares with foals could be accommodated.

These versatile arrangements are easily achieved by many cleverly designed swinging partitions, all of them of wood, covered with soft padding, to avoid injuries and bruising. We loaded the horses and bolted the stalls as needed around them.

The floors of the stalls were of thick black rubber to stop the horses sliding about, and sometimes we sprinkled the surface with shavings to catch the droppings, especially on long journeys. At each destination, the attendants or the driver would sweep the stalls clean of the muck: the nine-horse van had therefore arrived home reasonably clean already, having come back empty from Newmarket.

A narrow cupboard at the rear of each van contained brooms, a shovel, hose, squeegees and mop. We also took a bucket or two, feed sometimes for the horses, and several plastic jerrycans of drinking water. The locker under the attendants' bench seat—where Ogden had died—housed spare tack in the form of head-collars, ropes, straps, a horse blanket or two and a first-aid kit. Behind the driver's seat lay an efficient fire extinguisher; and that was about all we carried except for the attendants' own belongings up on the shelf with the mattress. The grooms mostly took with them clean tidy clothes to change into for leading their charges round the parade ring, changing back into working things for the return home.

Day after day, all over the country, fleets of horse vans like mine ferried all the runners to the races, most days about a hundred runners to each meeting, on bad days, down to, perhaps, thirty. Most of the runners that were trained in Pixhill traveled, luckily, in my vans, and as at least twenty-five trainers were in business in the district, I was making money, if not a fortune.

For all steeplechase jockeys in their early thirties the urgent question arose, *what next*?" One life lay behind, unfilled time lay ahead. I'd been driving horse vans by the age of eighteen for my father, who had owned his own transport; driving some of his horses to the races, looking after them, riding them in amateur races, driving home. By twenty, turning professional, I'd been retained by a top stable, and for twelve years after that I'd finished each season around second to sixth in the jockeys' list, riding upwards of 400 jump races a year. Few jump jockeys lasted longer than that near the top owing to the physical battering of falls, and at thirty-two time and injuries had caught up with me, as they'd been bound to do in the end.

From jockey to full-time horse transporter had been a jolting change of outlook in some ways, but familiar territory in others. Three years into the new life, it seemed as if it had been inevitable all along.

I made up Brett's pay packet with cash from my safe as promised and typed the information into the computer, so that along in the office Rose could incorporate it into the P45, the leaving-employment form that showed pay earned and taxes deducted for the fiscal year. One way and another she hadn't had much practice at P45s, as the turnover in drivers had proved small.

Brett's envelope in hand, I went out to the horse van where he and Dave were now standing on the tarmac glaring at each other. Having removed the hose from the outside faucet beyond the woodpile, Dave stood with its green flabby plastic loops over his arm, apparently childishly arguing that it was Brett's job to put it away in its cupboard.

Give me strength, I thought, and asked Dave nicely to put it away himself. With bad grace he climbed with it into the van and Brett watched him spitefully.

"That's not the only time Dave's picked up a hitchhiker," he said.

I listened but didn't reply.

Brett said, "It's him you ought to sack, not me."

"I didn't sack you."

"As good as."

His sharp young face lacked any sort of humor and I felt sorry for him that he should go through life making himself disliked. There seemed to be no way of changing him; he would go whining to the grave.

"You'll have to leave a forwarding address with Isobel," I said conversationally. "You might be called on for the inquest on yesterday's passenger."

"It's Dave they'll want."

"All the same, leave an address."

He grunted, accepted his pay packet without thanks and

drove off, Dave coming to earth again by my side and looking after him balefully.

"What did he say?" he asked.

"That you'd picked up other hitchhikers."

Dave looked furious. "He *would*."

"Don't do it, Dave."

He listened to the weight I put into the words and, unsuccessfully trying to joke, said, "Is that some sort of threat?"

"A warning."

"It don't seem fair to leave people standing by the roadside."

"It may not seem fair to you," I said, "but just grit your teeth and do it."

"Well . . . OK." He gave me a halfhearted grin and promised not to give any lifts on his way back from leaving the broodmares in Gloucestershire that afternoon.

"I'm serious, Dave."

He sighed. "Yeah. I know it."

He retrieved his rusty bike from the woodpile and squeaked away down the drive, wobbling aside for Jogger, who was returning in his truck.

Jogger had brought with him a book-sized piece of wood with a cluster of nails driven into it. The nailheads would stick to the magnet, he said, but not so firmly that he wouldn't be able to get the whole thing off at the next overhaul. The wood would prevent the magnet from picking up anything else.

I took his word for it, and watched him roll expertly under the chassis without using the slider, taking only seconds to put the insulating wood in place. He was up on his feet giving me a sideways yellow smile in an instant.

"That didn't take long," I said thoughtfully.

45

"If you know where to look, it's a piece of cake."

Harve arrived at that moment, crossing with Jogger's departure. We walked together to the house and I showed him the grime-laden cash box, explaining where Jogger had found it. He looked as puzzled as I felt.

"But what's it *for*?" he said.

"Jogger thinks we've been entertaining drugs unawares."

"What?"

"Smuggling cocaine, perhaps?"

"No." Harve was adamant. "No one could do that without us knowing."

Ruefully I said, "Maybe one of us does know."

Harve didn't agree. Our drivers were saints, he implied.

I told him about the night visitor, who'd come in black disguise and entered the horse van.

"He had a key to the grooms' door," I said. "He must have done. There's no damage to the locks."

"Yes," Harve said, thinking, "but you know those groom-door keys don't open just one van. I mean, I know for a certainty that my own van has the same key as Brett's, here. Quite a lot of them are duplicated."

I nodded. The ignition keys were individually special and couldn't be copied, but the grooms' door locks came from a different, smaller range, and several of the vans had keys that fitted others.

"What was he doing *inside* the cab?" Harve asked, "if this thing . . . this hiding place . . . was underneath?"

"I don't know. He had dirt on his clothes. Maybe he'd already looked underneath and found the hiding place empty."

"What are you going to do about it?" Harve said. "Tell Sandy Smith?"

"Maybe. Sometime. I don't want to run us into trouble if I don't have to."

Harve was happy with that. "We don't want the Customs to hear of it," he said, nodding. "They'd hold us up for hours, every crossing. They'd treat it as specific information received, I wouldn't wonder."

His pleasant face was only lightly anxious, and the unwelcome discovery, I supposed, didn't merit the instant pushing of panic buttons.

"OK," I said, "let's get on. I'll come along to the farm for fuel and start the shuttle."

I locked the house while Harvey left, then followed along to the farmyard, less than a mile away, nearer to the heart of Pixhill.

Harve, his wife and four towheaded children lived next door to the farmyard in what had been the old farmhouse. The old farm barn was now Jogger's domain, a workshop with inspection pit and every aid to mechanical perfection that he could cajole me into buying.

What had once been a cowshed was now a small canteen and a suite of three offices with windows looking into the farmyard, from where one could watch the horse vans come and go, each to and from its own allocated parking space. A small stable block with room for three horses was sited in the space between the end of the stretch of offices and the high wall of the barn. We sometimes housed our passengers there temporarily if they were due to leave or arrive in the middle of the night.

Several of the day's sorties had already begun. The other nine-van had already left to collect the broodmares bound for Ireland. The two Southwell vans' spaces were empty also. Jogger was driving Phil's van over to the barn for its overhaul.

I drew to a halt by the diesel pump and topped up the tanks.

Normally we refueled on return in the evenings to avoid water problems from air condensing overnight in quarter-full tanks, a tip I'd learned from a pilot friend. We also hosed down the vans at that point and cleaned the insides with disinfectant so they were fresh and ready to go in the mornings.

Brett, I noticed, had removed the remains of his picnic, but his solution to the stain on the bench seat had been not to clean it off but to fold the horse rug and lay it along the seat to cover it. Typical, I thought.

In the offices Isobel and Rose were consulting their machines, turning up the heaters and drinking coffee from the canteen next door. Rose said she had already given Brett his P45 and taken his mother's address and was glad to be rid of him.

Rose, plumply middle-aged, kept the financial records, seeing to the pay packets, sending out bills, preparing checks for my signature, keeping track of the pennies. Isobel, gentle, young, clearheaded, answered the telephone, took the bookings and chatted usefully with many trainers' secretaries, harvesting advance notice of their stables' requirements.

Rose and Isobel had an office each, in which they worked from eight-thirty to four. The third office, less busy-looking, less personal, was technically my own but was used just as much by Harve. The documentation of the vans was kept in there, and also duplicates of the ignition keys, in a locked drawer.

In spite of the flu, in spite of Brett, in spite of Kevin Keith Ogden, that Friday's work seemed to be going smoothly.

The driver due to transfer Jericho Rich's six fillies to Newmarket had already arrived in the farmyard, as for some unspecified reason Michael Watermead had wanted them to leave his stable earlier in the morning than the load of two-year-olds the day before.

I explained to Nigel, the driver, that Michael wouldn't be sending any of his own grooms to care for the fillies ("Jericho can whistle for favors, bloody man") but that a car with a couple of grooms would be coming over from the destination trainer in Newmarket.

"They did the same yesterday with Brett and the day before with Harve, so you shouldn't have any trouble," I said.

Nigel nodded.

"And don't pick up any corpses on the way home."

He laughed. He was twenty-four, insatiably heterosexual, found life a joke and could call on inexhaustible stamina, his chief virtue in my eyes. Any time we needed long night-driving I sent him, if I could.

Trainers often had a favorite among the drivers, a particular man they knew and trusted. In Michael Watermead's case there was a driver called Lewis, at that moment warming his hands round a mug of tea and listening to Dave's self-justifying account of the last ride of K. K. Ogden.

"Didn't he said anything?" Lewis asked interestedly. "Just snuffed it?"

"Makes you think, doesn't it?"

Lewis agreed about that, nodding his close-cropped head. In his twenties, like the majority of the drivers, he was willing, resourceful and strong, with a tattoo of a dragon on one forearm and a reputed past as a biker. The rave-up history had raised my doubts to begin with, but he'd proved thoroughly reliable at the wheel of his glossy super-six van, and Michael, who had exacting standards, had taken to him firmly.

In consequence, Lewis drove prestigious horses to big meetings. The Watermead stable at that moment housed "Classic" contenders, with representative runners in both the Guineas and Oaks; and all of the drivers had already put their money on the Watermead star three-year-old colt, Irkab Alhawa, which, if all went well, Lewis would be driving to Epsom, in June, for the Derby.

He was, that morning, setting off to France to collect two two-year-olds that an owner had bought to be trained in Michael's yard. As he was going alone, without a relief driver—agreed with Michael—he would have to take rest stops on the way and wouldn't be back until Monday evening. He would sleep as usual in his cab, which he preferred.

I checked with him that he had the right documents and food and water for the two-year-olds, and watched him set off cheerfully on the errand.

Harve having gone through the rest of the day's program again with me, I set off myself towards chilly gale-swept Salisbury Plain to get to grips with the yo-yo shuttle which could take until evening and give me a headache. The headache would result from the voice and personality of the trainer on the move, a forceful lady in her fifties with the intonation and occasionally the vocabulary of a barrack room parrot. I wanted nevertheless to please her, aiming for all her future business.

She strode across to the van when I pulled up in her yard and produced the first squawk of the day.

"The boss himself!" she proclaimed ironically, seeing my face. "Why the honor?"

"Flu," I said succinctly. "Morning, Marigold."

She peered beyond me to the empty passenger seats. "Didn't you bring a handler? Your secretary said there would be two of you."

"He's had to drive today. Sorry."

She clicked her tongue in irritation. "Half my grooms have got the bug. It's a pest."

I jumped down from the cab and lowered the two ramps while she watched and grumbled, a wiry figure in a padded jacket and woolly hat, her nose blue with cold. She was moving to Pixhill, she'd told the racing press, because it was warmer for the horses.

She'd made lists laying out the order in which her string was to travel. Her depleted force of grooms led the horses up the ramps into the van and I bolted the partitions round them until the first nine were installed.

Marigold—Mrs. English, as the grooms called her—encouraged the loading with various raucous epithets and an overall air of impatience. I certainly could have done with Dave's knack of imparting confidence to horses while leading them up ramps: Marigold's method tended to frighten them upwards so that I bolted several of them quivering and wild-eyed into their stalls.

She had decided to drive herself in her car to Pixhill to be ready in the new yard when I and the horses arrived. Four of her grooms traveled with me in the cab, all of them apparently enthusiastic over the move, the nightlife of Pixhill being seen as hotly wicked when compared with the winds of Stonehenge.

Her new yard was an old yard in Pixhill, now modernized and enlarged. Its first nine inhabitants clattered down the ramps and were directed loudly to their new homes by Marigold with a list. I shoveled the droppings onto muck sacks supplied by her grooms and put the van shipshape for the second foray.

Pleased, Marigold told me that as I was doing the work myself she wouldn't need to travel backwards and forwards all day to supervise and would entrust the next loading to me entirely. She gave me the list. I thanked her. She looked on me kindly. I thought with satisfaction that I would glue her to me as a permanent customer by nightfall.

With such profitable thoughts I set off back to Salisbury Plain and had my complacence shattered by Jogger on the phone.

"Hi ho Silver," he said cheerfully, "we've got another couple of lone rangers."

"Jogger . . . you've lost me."

"Limpets," he said helpfully. "Barnacles. Stuck to the ships' bottoms."

"Where are you, exactly?" I asked.

"In your office."

"Is there someone else with you?"

"Nothing wrong with your uptake, is there? Do you want to talk to Constable Smith? He's here now."

"Wait," I said, "do you mean what I think you mean? For lone rangers, do I understand . . . strangers?"

"You got it."

"Like the cash box?"

"Like, but not twins." Jogger paused, letting me hear a rumble from Sandy Smith's familiar voice. "Constable Smith," Jogger said, "wants to know when you'll be back. He says there was a warrant out for that stiff."

3

I spoke to Sandy.

"What warrant? What for?"

"Fraud. Dud checks. Skipping hotels without paying. Petty stuff, mostly, it seems. The Nottingham police wanted him."

"Too bad," I said.

"Had you ever seen him before, Freddie?"

"Not that I know of."

"He'd welshed on a bookie or two."

People who failed to pay bookmakers weren't necessarily my best buddies, as I pointed out.

"No," Sandy agreed, "but he must have had something to do with racing if he asked for a lift in a horse van."

"Dave said he was propositioning a tanker driver first. Maybe he had something to do with oil."

"Oh, very funny."

"Let me know the result of the postmortem, will you?"

"Well, all right, but I don't expect I'll get it today."

"Anytime," I said. "Come in for a drink."

He liked to do that, because sometimes I would keep him up to date with any local villainy I didn't like the look of. On the other hand, the villainy going on on the undersides of my vans needed more understanding before, or if ever, I told Sandy about it.

I spoke to Jogger again briefly, asking him to phone me without fail when he returned from Surrey.

"Won't hammer or bucket."

With a sigh I heard him disconnect and reached Marigold's old yard again before it clicked. Hammer and nail or bucket and pail.

Fail.

Most of the way I thought instead of the limpets and wondered what to do about them. I thought I might usefully set up an opportunity for advice without committing myself, so I pulled the van into a roadside parking space, fished out my diary for the number and got through to the Security section of the Jockey Club in Portman Square in London, asking for the head man.

Everyone professionally engaged in racing knew Patrick Venables by name and most of them by sight. Transgressors wished they didn't. Such sins as I'd been guilty of having luckily escaped his notice, I could go to him for help when I needed it and probably be believed.

Fortunately I found him in his office. I asked him if he would by any chance be going to Sandown races the next day.

"Yes, but I'm also going this afternoon," he said. "If it's urgent, come today."

I explained about the flu and the driver shortage. "But I can drive one of my vans to Sandown tomorrow," I said.

"Right. Outside the weighing room."

"Thanks very much."

I resumed the journey, loaded the appointed horses, drove them and the two grooms to join Marigold. She told me loudly I should have brought more than two grooms with nine horses and I explained that her head lad had said two only, he'd had another one go home sick and he wasn't feeling too well himself.

"Blast the man," she screeched.

"You can't argue with a virus," I said pacifically.

"I've got to get all the horses over here today," she yelled.

"Yes, well, we will."

I cleaned out the van, smiled reassuringly, shut up the ramps and made the third leg of the shuttle. Twenty-seven deliveries, I thought, seeing the third load rattle down the ramps into their new home, and supposedly two more trips to make, though the head lad had ominously told me Mrs. English hadn't counted right, she'd overlooked her own hack and two unbroken two-year-olds.

The yards were approximately thirty miles apart and each shuttle, with loading and unloading, was taking me two hours. By dusk at seven in the evening all but the oddments were safely settled in and Marigold for once looked tired. Her head lad had given best to the flu and gone home to bed and my own muscles were aching. When I suggested finishing the job early the next morning, the lady resignedly agreed. I tentatively kissed her cheek, an intimacy I would normally not have attempted, and to my utter astonishment her eyes filled with tears, instantly repudiated with a shake of her woolly hatted head.

I offered, "It's been a long day."

"A day I've looked forward to . . . and planned . . . for years."

"Then I'm glad it went OK."

She was lonely, I perceived, surprised, the hard outer lady had a gallant way of playing the cards life had dealt her. I knew moreover that I had indeed secured her future business, and was happy I'd had to do the shuttle myself.

Leaving her trudging with reviving voice round the new stables, I drove the nine-van along to the farmyard, pulled up by the pumps and wrote up the logbooks, both the van's and my own. I'd spoken to Isobel on the phone several times during the day, hearing at one point that Jericho Rich had actually turned up in her office checking her records. Cheek, I thought. I'd also learned from Harve that all the planned work had been completed without trouble except that one of Jogger's pair of broodmares had started to foal on the way to Surrey and that Jogger, mechanic, had unwillingly become midwife.

Jogger in his turn had reported the incident to me with shocked indignation because the stud groom at the destination had refused to move the mare from the horse van until the foaling was complete, delaying Jogger's return to Pixhill by a couple of hours. Jogger, it appeared, had never seen a foal born before: he had found it both eye-opening and disgusting.

"Did you know the mare *eats* all that stuff? Fair turned me up."

"Don't think about it," I advised him. "Tell me which vans have sprouted little strangers."

"Eh? Oh . . . Phil's and the one Dave's driving, which is

Pat's van usually. But, see, most of the others had gone out by the time I found those. There may be more."

He sounded cheerful, but then it wasn't his business at stake. By the time I'd completed the logbooks, filled the tanks and moved the nine-van to the corner where we customarily cleaned the fleet, he had still not returned.

Under the strong outdoor lights I hosed down the nine-van and squeegeed the windows, not a big job for once as the weather had been dry all day. In the farmyard, the cleaning water came out like a mist under pressure, driven through a pump with compressed air: more effective and more economical with water than a plain hose.

The interior took me more time, as forty-five horses and a relay of grooms had left their mark despite the intermittent sweepings out, and I was dog-tired myself by the time I'd mopped the floors with disinfectant and fastened all the partitions ready for the morrow.

The front cab itself was a mess, littered with screwed-up sandwich wrappers and awash with ropes, reins and other paraphernalia used and borrowed from the underseat locker.

I opened the locker and replaced all the gear in it. Even inside the locker the grooms had left their meal-remains. I picked out a small paper carrier and replaced it with a couple of refolded horse rugs. Shutting the lid, I noticed again the stain on the seat from the previous night and wondered how to get rid of it, short of re-covering the whole thing. Certainly none of the grooms that had sat on it that day had complained, but then they hadn't known about Kevin Keith Ogden's last ride.

Smiling a shade ruefully I swept the rubbish into the sack I'd provided but the grooms had resolutely ignored and stood it beside the small carrier, which would have gone into the sack also, except that it proved heavier than empty and contained, I found, a thermos flask and a packet of uneaten sandwiches. Yawning, I thought I would get it back to Marigold's grooms in the morning, whether or not I did the last shuttle myself.

Finally I drove the van along to its usual parking space, locked everything, threw the rubbish sack into our own dumpster, carried the thermos flask and bag into the offices and typed my day's records into Isobel's computer. That done, I sat for a while calling to the screen the requirements for the next day, trying to work out if we would have enough drivers and hoping no one else would be ill by the morning.

I phoned Jogger to find out where he was. Ten minutes from the boozer, he said. The boozer, Jogger's natural home, was the pub where he drank with his cronies every night. Ten minutes to the boozer meant maybe twelve to the farm.

"Don't stop on the way," I said.

While I waited for him I ran through the computer notes for the day; everything, that's to say, that had been entered before Isobel and Rose had left at four o'clock.

The only hiccup, a very minor one, seemed to have been that Michael Watermead's fillies had set off an hour and a half late to Newmarket.

"Nigel reported," the screen informed me, "lads from Newmarket didn't show until ten-thirty. Tessa's message yesterday ordered van for nine A.M. Nigel set off with fillies at eleven. Reported arrival Newmarket one-thirty. Reported leaving Newmarket two-thirty."

Nigel had returned uneventfully, Harve had said, and his van stood clean and shipshape in its accustomed place.

The Tessa in question was Michael's daughter, so no

one's head would roll over the mistake; mixups over time were all too common. If that was the worst that had happened, it had been a near-perfect workday.

Isobel's last snippet of information read, "Mr. Rich in person called at the office, checking our records on his transfer. I satisfied him on all points."

Jogger's lights swooped in through the gates and he rolled along to the pumps. I went out to meet him and found him still shaken by the confrontation with the bloody realities of birth. I myself had seen several foals and other animals delivered but never, I idly reflected, an actual human baby. Would I, I wondered, have found it more traumatic? My only child, a daughter, had been born in my absence to a girl who'd persuaded another man he was the father, and married him quickly. I saw them all sometimes, along with their two subsequent children, but I felt few paternal longings and knew I would never seek to prove the truth.

Jogger filled his tanks, moved to the cleaning area and grumbled his way through the mopping out. In the belief that if I interrupted I would be left with an incomplete job, I waited until he'd finished before I asked him the vital question.

"Where exactly are these limpet strangers?"

"You'll never see them in the dark," he said, sniffing.

"Jogger . . ."

"Yeah, well, you can't hardly see them in broad daylight." He wiped his nose on the back of his hand, "unless you want to get under on the slider with a flashlight?"

"No."

"Didn't think so."

"Just tell me about them."

He walked along the row with me, pointing.

"Phil's van. I had it over the pit. There's a tube container stuck on top of the rear fuel tank, in that space above the tank but under the van's floor. It's hidden by the side of the horse van, and you can't see it either from the front or the back of the van if you're looking casually under the chassis. Bloody neat job."

I frowned. "What would it hold?"

"Search me. Half a dozen footballs, maybe. It's empty now, though. It must have had a screw-on cap. The screw-thread's there, but the cap is missing."

Phil's van was a super-six, as were half of the fleet. A super-six carried six horses in comfort, had an extra-spacious cab, a generous general layout, and could accommodate a seventh horse standing crossways at a pinch. I liked driving them better than the longer nine-vans. Half a dozen footballs in a tube on the underside sounded macabre as well as downright improbable.

"Pat's van," Jogger said, pointing, "that's the one Dave drove with the broodmares, remember?" He broke off, recalling his own frightful day. "Don't never ask me to drive no broodmares no more."

"Er, no, Jogger. What about Pat's van?"

Pat's van, smaller, took four horses. Five of the fleet were that size, handy, less thirsty, the runabouts. In the Flat racing season, Pat's van was retained full time by another Pixhill trainer with a phobia about sharing journeys with other trainers' horses. Pat's van went often to France, though not with her driving.

"Under there," Jogger said, "is another tube, not so big. It unscrews at the end and it's empty. The screw-on cap is there, on that one."

"Been there a while?" I asked. "Dirty?"

"Natch."

"I'll take a look in the morning. And Jogger, keep it to yourself, will you? If you spread it around the boozer you'll frighten off whoever stuck the things there, and we'll never have a chance of finding out what's going on."

He could see the point of that. He said he'd be as silent as the wash (wash and shave; grave) and again I wondered if his reticence would outlast the evening's pints.

On Saturday morning early I drove one of the four-vans to Salisbury Plain, collected Marigold's oddment horses and delivered them to her by nine, realizing along the way that I'd forgotten to take with me her grooms' lunch carrier bag. When I mentioned it to her she inquired loudly of her employees about ownership but received no claims.

"Throw it away," she counseled. "I'm sending horses to Doncaster. You can take them, I hope?"

Doncaster races, twelve days ahead, represented the prestigious opening of the Flat season. I assured her I'd be delighted to take anything she wanted.

"In a van on their own," she added. "I don't want them picking up other stables' germs. My horses never share transport."

"Fine," I said.

"Good." She brought forth a smile, more a matter of eyes than of lips: as good a pledge as shaking hands on a contract.

Home again I drank coffee, ate cornflakes, talked to Harve, talked to Jogger ("Didn't say a dicky bird down the boozer") and checked the day's list, again juggling the dearth of drivers and pressing Dave and Jogger again into behind-the-wheel service.

Rather against his will I redrafted Phil into the nine-van and took his super-six myself, picking up jumpers from three different stables and delivering them and their grooms to Sandown racecourse for the afternoon's sport.

Over Sandown's fences I'd ridden more winners than I could remember, its testing course so imprinted in my subconscious that I could probably have ridden it blindfolded and had certainly navigated its intricacies familiarly in countless dreams. Of all courses it evoked in me the strongest nostalgia for the close world I'd lost, the intimate body-to-body blending with a nonhuman powerhouse, the mind-into-mind flowing of courage and intent. One could speak to strangers of race-riding as being a "job like any other" but the slightest introspection gave that the lie. Racing on horses over jumps at thirty or more miles an hour was, to me at least, a spiritual exaltation never achieved or even envisioned in any other way. To each his religion, I supposed. Big horses over big fences had been mine.

Nowadays at Sandown I felt excommunicated; no doubt a blasphemy, but a deep truth nevertheless.

I met Patrick Venables outside the weighing room, as he'd promised.

The head of racing's Security service, a tall thin man with suitably hawklike eyes, had, in his time, one understood, been "something in counterespionage," no details ever supplied. Racecourse wits said he'd been sired by a lie detector out of a leech, in that one couldn't fool him or shake him off.

Like others in his job before him, he ran the comparatively small Security section with brisk efficiency and was largely responsible for the reasonably honest state of racing, sniffing out new scams almost before they were invented.

He greeted me with the usual skin-deep friendliness, never to be mistaken for trust. Looking at his watch he said, "Five minutes, Freddie. Is that enough?"

Condense it, he meant, and, faced with his deadline and obvious lack of time, I began to retreat from asking his advice.

"Well, it doesn't really matter," I said lamely.

My hesitancy, instead of releasing him, seemed to switch on his attention. He told me to follow him into the weighing room and led me through to a small inner office containing a table, two chairs and very little else.

He closed the door. "Sit down," he said, "and fire away."

I told him about the three containers Jogger had so far found under the vans. "I don't know how long they've been there or what they contained. My mechanic says he can't swear he won't find more, as they're pretty well camouflaged." I paused briefly. "Has anyone else come across anything like this?"

He shook his head. "Not that I know of. Have you told the police?"

"No."

"Why not?"

"Curiosity, I suppose. I wanted to find out who's been using me, and what for."

He pondered, studying my face. "You're using *me* as insurance," he said eventually, "in case one of your vans is caught smuggling."

I didn't deny it. "I'd like to catch them myself, though."

"Mm." He pursed his mouth. "I'd have to advise you not to."

I protested, "I can't just do nothing."

"Let me think about it."

"Thank you," I said.

"I suppose"—he frowned—"this hasn't anything to do with the man who died in one of your vans? I heard about that."

63

"I don't really know." I told him about the masked searcher. "I don't know what he was looking for. If it was the dead man's belongings he wouldn't have had any success because the police had them all. But then I wondered if he'd been *leaving* anything. And he had dirt and dust on his clothes, which was why I wondered if he'd been on the ground, and why I asked my mechanic to see if he'd stuck anything on the van underneath."

"And you think he had?"

"No. The container under there had been in place for some time. It was filthy, with layers of grime."

I told him that the van I had driven to Sandown that day had a capacious tube stuck above the fuel tank. "You can't see it at all easily even if you're looking for it, up from underneath," I explained. "Horse vans are all coach-built so that the sides are nearer the ground than the chassis. For aerodynamics and good looks. I expect you know that. Mine are built in Lambourn. They're very good. Anyway, the sides hide and shield the underside mechanisms, same as cars. Bombs can be hidden there."

"I do understand," he assured me. "Are bombs what you fear?"

"I suppose drugs are more likely."

Patrick Venables looked at his watch and stood up. "Have to go," he said. "Come back to the weighing room after the last race."

My nod of agreement was made to his departing back. I wondered what he would make of it; shrug it off or take a look. Sometime during the afternoon he would decide, but in telling him I'd come to my own conclusion, that I really did need and mean to find out what was going on, with or without his help.

I went outside and spent a good deal of the afternoon in

conversation, useful sometimes for business but a far cry from the urgency of race-riding, changing colors, weighing out and in, hurrying, racing, changing colors . . . Oh, well. On the good side I no longer starved to remain artifically thin, no longer broke my bones and hid large bruises, no longer feared losing big races, good owners, my nerve or my job. I was now free in a way I'd never been and reflected that if I still had to please owners and trainers, then to prosper almost everyone had to please *someone*, performers the paying public, presidents and prime ministers, their population.

On afternoons like that at Sandown I'd found I behaved like all my drivers, that is to say I took special note of those particular runners that I'd brought to the course. A winner lifted the spirits of every driver: a horse killed, as occasionally happened, sent them home in depression. The undoubted if illogical feelings of proprietorship had a noticeable effect on how cheerfully, fast and thoroughly the vans got serviced on their return.

As two of the horses I had ferried that day belonged to a trainer I'd ridden for intermittently in the past, it was natural that I'd end up talking to him and his wife.

Benjy Usher and Dot appeared to be quarreling as usual when he shot out an arm and grabbed my sleeve as I passed.

"Freddie," he demanded, "tell this woman which year Fred Archer shot himself. She says 1890. I say that's rubbish."

I glanced at Dot's normal mixed expression of resignation and anxiety. Years of living with an irascible man had carved permanent facial lines that even her infrequent smiles could barely override, yet although they'd been fig-

uratively spitting at each other for as long as I'd known
them, the pair were still grimly together.

They were both unusually good-looking, which only
made it odder. Both were well dressed, in their forties, so-
cially practiced and intelligent. Fifteen years earlier I
wouldn't have given their union five minutes, which just
shows how little an outsider can see of a marriage.

"Well?" Benjy challenged.

"I don't know," I said diplomatically, though I did know
actually that it had been in 1886, when the brilliant champion jockey was twenty-nine, and had won 2,749 races,
traveling everywhere by train.

"You're useless," Benjy said, and Dot looked relieved.

Benjy changed the subject, mercurial as always. "Did my
horses get here all right?"

"Yes, they did indeed."

"My groom tells me you drove them yourself."

I nodded. "Three of my drivers have the flu."

Many trainers came out into their stable yards to see
their runners loaded safely into the transport, but Benjy seldom did. His idea of supervision was to yell out of the window if he saw anything to displease him, which I
understood was often. Benjy's turnover of grooms was
higher than most. Benjy's head traveling groom, who
should have accompanied the runners to Sandown, had
walked out on the previous day.

Benjy asked if I knew of that awkward fact. Yes, I'd
been told, I said.

"Then do me a favor. Saddle my runners and come into
the ring with us."

Most trainers in the circumstances would have saddled
their own runners, but not Benjy. He scarcely liked touching them, I'd observed. I guessed the question about Fred

Archer had been only a pretext; grabbing me on the wing had been the purpose.

I told him I'd be glad to saddle the horses. Not too far from the truth.

"Good," he said, satisfied.

Accordingly I did the work while he and Dot chatted to the first runner's owner, and the same for the second runner later in the afternoon. The first ran respectably without earning medals and the second won his race. As always in the winner's enclosure on such occasions, Benjy's handsome face reddened and sweated as if with orgasmic pleasure. The owners patted their horse. Dot told me seriously I would have made a good head groom.

I smiled.

"Oh dear."

"Well, I would," I said.

There was always something I didn't understand about Dot; some deep reserve in her nature. I knew her no better after fifteen years than I had at the beginning.

Benjy's odd training methods were due, one understood, to his not having to make training pay. Benjy's inherited multimillions, moreover, had been deployed in acquiring good horses overseas which were trained there by other trainers and which won better events in France and Italy than Benjy's horses in England. Benjy, like many owners, preferred the higher prize-money of mainland Europe, but he chose still to live in Pixhill and to train for other people as a hobby and to use my horse vans for transport, a fact guaranteed to earn my approbation.

He and Dot took me for a drink: double gins for them, tonic for me. The one thing I couldn't afford to lose was my driving license.

Benjy said, "I've a colt in Italy that's pulled a tendon. I want him back here to heal and rest. Care to fetch him?"

"Very much so."

"Good. I'll tell you when." He patted my shoulder. "You do a good job with those vans. We can trust you, can't we, Dot?"

Dot nodded.

"Well . . . thanks," I said.

One way and another the afternoon passed quickly and after the last race I waited for Patrick Venables outside the weighing room. He came eventually at a half-trot, still pressed for time.

"Freddie," he said, "you told me yesterday you were short of drivers. Is that still the case?"

"Three have flu, and one's left for good."

"Er, um. Then I suggest I send you a replacement; one who can look into your problem."

I wasn't immediately enthusiastic. "He'd have to know the job," I said dubiously.

"It's a she. And you'll find she does. I've arranged for her to go to Pixhill tomorrow morning. Show her your operation and let her take it from there."

I thanked him unconvincingly. He smiled faintly and told me to give her a try. "Nothing lost if nothing comes of it."

I wasn't so sure, but I'd asked his help and could see no way of backing out. He hurried off with a last piece of information. "I gave her your address."

He'd gone before I thought to ask her name, but it hardly mattered, I supposed. I hoped she would have the decency to arrive before I went to Maudie Watermead's lunch.

Her name was Nina Young. She swept up the drive onto my tarmac at nine A.M., catching me unshaven and reading newspapers in a terrycloth robe, coffee and cornflakes in hand.

I went to the door to answer her ring, not realizing at once who she was.

She'd been driving a scarlet Mercedes and, although not young, she wore slender skin-tight jeans, a white shirt with romantically large sleeves, an embroidered Afghan vest, heavy gold chains and an expensive scent. Her shining dark hair had an expert cut. Her high cheekbones, long neck and calm eyes reminded me of noble ancestor portraits, bone structure three hundred years old. My idea of a working van driver, she was not.

"Patrick Venables said to come early," she said, offering a nail-varnished hand. The voice was Roedean—Beneden—St. Mary's, Calne, the social poise learned in the cradle. From my male chauvinist point of view, the only drawback was her age, nearer mid-forties than my own.

"Come in," I invited, standing back and thinking she was good for the scenery if not for the matter in hand.

"Freddie Croft," she said, as if seeing a cardboard cutout come to life. "The man himself."

"Well, yes," I agreed. "Like some coffee?"

"No, thank you. Do I detect a faint air of exasperation?"

"Not in the least." I led the way into the sitting room, and indicated any chair she chose to sit on.

She chose a deep armchair, crossing the long legs to show fine ankles above buckled leather shoes. From a shoulder bag of equal pedigree, she produced a small folder which she waved in my general direction.

"Driving license with Large Goods Vehicle qualification," she assured me. "The real McCoy."

"He wouldn't have sent you without it. How did you get it?"

"Driving my hunters," she said matter-of-factly. "Also my show horses and eventers. Any questions?"

The sort of horse vans she would have been driving had home-from-home large living quarters in front of the stalls, the nomadic luxury motors for eventing at Badminton and Burleigh. She had to be a familiar figure in that world, widely recognizable to too many people for the present purpose.

"Perhaps I ought to know you?" I suggested.

"I shouldn't think so. I don't go racing."

"Er," I said mildly, "here you'd need to be able to find the racecourses."

"Patrick said you were bound to have a map."

Patrick, I thought, had taken leave of his senses.

She watched my no doubt obvious misgivings with cool amusement.

"My horse vans are basic transport," I said. "No fridges, no cookers, no bathrooms."

"They've Mercedes engines, haven't they?"

I nodded, surprised.

"I'm a good driver."

I believed her. "All right, then," I said.

I reflected that whatever she might lack as an investigator, I definitely did need an extra pair of hands for my wheels. What Harve and Jogger would make of her I dreaded to think.

"Good," she said prosaically and after a brief second's pause asked, "Do you take *Horse and Hound*?"

I fetched that week's as yet unread copy of the magazine from a side table and handed it to her, watching as she flicked through towards the end, to the many pages of classified advertisements. She came to the horse-transport section where about once a month I advertised Croft Raceways, and tapped the pages with a rose pink fingernail.

"Patrick wants to know if you've seen this?"

I took the magazine from her and read where she'd pointed. In an outlined, single-column-width advertisement were the simple words:

TRANSPORT PROBLEMS?

WE CAN HELP.

ANYTHING CONSIDERED.

A fourth line gave a telephone number.

I frowned. "Yes, I've seen that. It's in the transport ads now and then. Rather pointless, I've thought."

"Patrick wants me to check it out."

"No one," I objected, "would advertise a smuggling service. It's impossible."

"Why don't we try?"

I passed her a cordless telephone. "Go ahead."

She pressed the numbers, listened, wrinkled her nose and switched the phone off.

"Answering machine," she reported succinctly. "Leave name and number and they'll get back."

"Man or woman?"

"Man."

We looked at each other. I didn't believe there was anything sinister in the advertisement, but I said, "Perhaps Patrick Venables could use his muscle on *Horse and Hound* and find out where that ad comes from."

She nodded. "He's doing it tomorrow."

Impressed despite my disbelief, I went over to the desk and consulted the chart.

"I've probably got two vans going to Taunton races tomorrow," I told her. "My woman driver Pat's got the flu. You can take her van. It can carry four horses but you're only likely to have three. You can follow my other van to Taunton so that you arrive at the right place at the right time, and for the pickup this end I'll send a man called Dave with you. He knows the stable the horses are going from. After you've collected the horses, drop him back at our base and follow the other box from then on."

"All right."

"It would be better if you didn't report for work in that car out there."

She gave me a glimmering smile. "You'll hardly know me in the morning. And what do I call you? Sir?"

"Freddie will do. And you?"

"Nina."

She stood up, tall and composed, every inch the opposite of what I needed. The trip to Taunton, I thought, would be her first and last, especially when it came to cleaning the van after the return home. She shook my hand—her own was firm and dry—and went unhurriedly out to her car. I followed her to the door and watched the scarlet excitement depart with its expensive distinctive Mercedes purr.

No one, I reflected, had mentioned pay. Rose would want to know what I'd agreed. Not even undercover missions for the Jockey Club could be conducted without ubiquitous paperwork.

Sundays were always comparatively quiet, businesswise, with rarely as many as half the fleet on the road. That particular Sunday, the driver shortage posing no problem, Harve, Jogger and Dave could all take their accustomed day off, along with a bunch of others. Most of the drivers liked Saturday and Sunday work as they were paid more for weekends, but I was lucky in general with all of them as a team, as they hated to see work go to rival firms and would drive on their allotted days off to prevent it. According to the law, their hours and compulsory rest periods were strictly set out: I sometimes had difficulty persuading them that I could be prosecuted if they bent the rules too far.

Like most jobs in racing, driving horse vans was more a way of life than simply a means of earning a living and, as a result, only people who enjoyed it, did it. Stamina was essential, also good humor and adaptability. Brett had been a mistake.

The news of his leaving had spread already through the racing grapevine, and before eleven that morning two applicants had phoned for his job. I turned them both down: one had worked for too many other firms, the other was over sixty, too old already for the intense physical demands and no good as a long-term prospect.

I phoned Harve and told him I'd engaged a temporary woman driver to take Pat's place until she was well again. She would be doing the Taunton run planned for Pat.

"Good," Harve said, unsuspecting.

So far the week ahead looked less busy than the one just completed, not a bad thing in the circumstances. I would be able to go to Cheltenham races in spectator comfort, to watch other lucky slobs win the Gold Cup and smash their collarbones.

Jericho Rich on the telephone bounced me out of unprofitable regrets.

"You got my fillies to Newmarket safe and sound, then," he shouted.

"Yes, Jericho." I held the receiver an inch from my ear.

"I expect you know I checked everything in your office. A good job well done, I'll say that for you."

Good grief, I thought. The heavens would fall.

"I've got a daughter," he said loudly.

"Er, yes, I've met her at the races."

"She's bought a show jumper, some damned fancy name. Can't remember it. It's in France. Send a van for it, will you?"

"Pleasure, Jericho. When and where from?"

"She'll tell you. Give her a buzz. I said I'd pay for the transport if it was you who fetched it, so she's doing you the honor." He laughed, fortissimo but for him almost mellow. "Don't send that driver, though. That one that picked up the hitchhiker."

"He's left," I assured him. "Didn't my girls tell you?"

"Well, yes they did." He read out his daughter's phone number. "Give her a buzz now. No time like the present."

"Thanks, Jericho."

I buzzed the daughter as directed and began on the details of the show jumper: age, sex, color, value, all for the agents who would arrange the paperwork for the horse, and overnight provision for the driver. She sounded straightforward and less fussy than her father, merely asking me to complete the transfer as soon as I could as she needed to practice before the show-jumping season started. She gave me an address and phone number in France and asked if I could arrange for a groom to travel over with the horse.

"I could provide a good man from here," I suggested. "One I trust."

"Yes. Great. Send the bill to my father."

I said I would and, to do him justice, Jericho Rich was a prompt payer. Mostly I billed the trainers for the transport of all their runners, the trainers then billing the individual owners, but Jericho always wanted his bills sent direct to himself. Jericho believed trainers would charge him more than they'd paid, all of a piece with his general mistrust of anyone working for him.

On the whole people accused others of doing what they would do themselves. Dishonesty began at home.

He'd accused me in his time of taking bribes from a bookmaker to lose on one of his hurdlers. I'd told him very politely that I wouldn't ride for him anymore, and a week later, as if nothing had happened, he'd offered me an enormous retainer to ride all his jumpers the next season. It had turned out profitably: I put up with his yelling and he gave me lavish presents when I won. A permanent standoff perhaps described our ongoing relations.

I took a quick look at the time and switched the phone through to Isobel, who took bookings on Sundays when I was busy. Then I got on with such small things as dressing and tidying and going out into the garden to pick flowers. This peaceful activity was the result of strong promptings from my absent sister and brother, who considered that flowers should occasionally be put on our parents' grave. As it was I, the youngest, who had inherited the family home, and as it was I who lived near the cemetery, they felt it only right and proper that it was I who picked the flowers and put them in place. The whole point, for them, was that the flowers should come from the right garden. Bought flowers would not be the same.

There was little but daffodils in the first week of March, though I scavenged also some crocuses and an early hyacinth along with the evergreen sprigs of cupressus, and drove them to the gates of the orderly cemetery on a hillside where we'd buried the parents within two years of each other some time ago.

Actually, I never minded the errand. The grave was high on the hill but the view was worth the walk up there, and as I had no sense of their being around in any way, I tended to leave the flowers as thanks for my own satisfactory childhood, their gift.

The flowers would die, of course. It was delivering them that mattered.

Maudie Watermead's lunch began in spring sunshine in the garden, with her younger children and guests bouncing on a trampoline and their elders playing tennis. Still too chilly for standing around in, the March air drove faint-hearts back through the garden door to the sitting room to enjoy the bright log fire and Maudie's idea of champagne cocktails, which began with angostura bitters on sugar lumps and fizzed to the brim with cold pink bubbles.

Benjy and Dot Usher were playing in long trousers on the hard court, arguing about balls being in or out. We engaged in unathletic mixed doubles, Dot and I being outargued by Benjy and the Watermeads' daughter, Tessa. Benjy and Tessa were enjoying their partnership in a way that had Dot hissing, to my private amusement and our public defeat.

Benjy and Tessa, as victors, took on the Watermeads' son, Ed, and Maudie's sister, Lorna. Dot glowered until I persuaded her into the sitting room, where the numbers had swelled and the chatter level risen to the point where individual voices were lost in conglomerate noise.

Maudie handed me a glass and gave me a smile with the friendly blue eyes that as usual set me thinking powerfully adulterous thoughts. Thoroughly aware of my dilemma, she was forever trying to transfer my feelings to her sister, Lorna, who, while alike in platinum hair, shapely waist and endless legs, simply lacked for me anything but physical attraction. Maudie was fun, Lorna was troubled. Maudie laughed, Lorna earnestly championed praiseworthy causes. Maudie cooked roast potatoes, Lorna worried about her weight. Maudie thought I would be good for Lorna but I had no intention of becoming her therapist: that way threatened boredom and disaster. I thought Lorna would be perfect for Bruce Farway.

The worthy doctor himself was at that moment standing near the fire with Maudie's husband. The bubbles in the Farway glass were colorless. Mineral water, I surmised.

Maudie followed my gaze and answered my unexpressed surprise.

"Michael thought that as it looks as if he intends to stay in Pixhill, we'd better teach the good doctor that we're not all rogues and fools."

I smiled. "He'll have trouble being supercilious with Michael, that's for sure."

"Don't you believe it."

My attention moved on towards the woman now talking to Dot, a younger woman, blonde like Maudie, blue-eyed like Maudie, lighthearted, left-handed, a pianist and thirty-eight.

"Do you know her?" Maudie asked, again following my gaze. "Susan Palmerstone. Her family are all here somewhere."

I nodded. "I used to ride her father's horses."

"Did you? It's easy to forget you were a jockey."

Like many Flat-racing trainers' wives, Maudie seldom went to jump meetings. I'd come to know her only through the transport.

From across the room Susan Palmerstone looked in my direction and finally walked over.

"Hello," she said. "Hugo and the children are here."

"I saw the children on the trampoline."

"Yes."

Maudie, making nothing much of the exchange, wandered over to Dot.

Susan said, "I didn't realize you'd be here. We don't know the Watermeads very well. I would have said we couldn't come."

"Of course not. It doesn't matter."

"No, but ... someone told Hugo he couldn't have a brown-eyed child and he's been fussing about it for weeks."

"Hugo's a green-eyed redhead. He can have anything as a throwback."

"I thought I'd better warn you. He's halfway to obsessed."

"OK."

The tennis players came in from the garden and also Hugo Palmerstone, who'd been watching the children. Through the window I could see my daughter standing on the grass, arms akimbo, disparagingly critical of her straight-haired blond brothers' bouncing. Cinders, my daughter, had brown eyes and dark curly hair like mine and was nine years old.

I would have married Susan. I'd loved her and been devastated when she chose Hugo, but it had been a long time ago. Nothing remained of the emotion. It was difficult, even, to remember how I'd felt. I didn't want the long-buried past casting a shadow over that child's life.

Susan moved from my side the moment Hugo entered the room, but not before he realized we'd been together.

His expression as he made his way directly to me was not promising.

"Come outside," he said curtly, stopping a yard away. "Now."

I could have refused him but I thought, perhaps wrongly, that if I didn't give him the opportunity to say what he clearly intended to say it could fester in his mind and do harm to his family. Accordingly I quietly parked my glass and followed him out onto the lawn.

"I could kill you," he said.

It was a remark to which there seemed to be no answer. When I said nothing he added bitterly, "My bloody aunt told me to open my eyes. My father-in-law's ex-jockey! Take a look at him, she said. Do some sums. Cinders was born seven months after your marriage. Open your eyes."

"Your aunt has done you no service."

He could see, of course, that she hadn't, but his anger was all for me.

"She's *my* daughter," he insisted.

I glanced over towards Cinders, now somersaulting high with exuberance.

"Of course," I said.

"I saw her born. She's mine, and I love her."

I looked regretfully at Hugo's furious green eyes. He and I were almost totally unalike in nature as in looks. A middle-rank City executive, he had an incandescent temper as fiery as his hair, allied to a strong streak of sentimentality. Our lack of affinity with each other had proved, until now, a natural barrier to my getting too close and too fond of my daughter, and I saw clearly, even if he didn't, that allowing myself to be drawn into a fight with him would destroy what should never be touched.

He was clenching and unclenching his fists but with still a degree of control.

I said, "You won the girl I wanted. You've a daughter and two sons. You're lucky. You'd be a fool to light a bonfire. What good would it do?"

"But you ... you." He spluttered with hurt incoherent rage, wanting me dead.

"Hate me if you like," I said, "but don't take it out on your family."

I turned away from him, more than half expecting him to haul me back and hit me, but to his credit he didn't. I thought uneasily, all the same, that if he came across a less direct and physical way of doing me harm, he might take it.

I walked back through the garden door and Maudie, by the window, said, "What was that about?"

"Nothing."

"Susan Palmerstone looks scared."

"Yes, well, I had a disagreement with Hugo, but forget it. Introduce Lorna to Bruce Farway and don't put me next to her at lunch."

"What?" She laughed, then looked thoughtful. "If I do, in return you can detach Tessa from Benjy Usher. I don't like her flirting with him, and Dot is livid."

"Why did you ask them?"

"They live practically next door, dammit. We always have Benjy and Dot."

I did my best for her, but detaching Tessa from Benjy proved impossible. Tessa was a great whisperer and thought nothing of turning her back to prevent people hearing what she was spilling in Benjy's ear. I got the turned-back treatment a couple of times and left Benjy alone to his foolishness.

Bruce Farway was taking an interest in Lorna, the delectably pretty sister full of good works. Susan stood with her arm through Hugo's, talking brightly to Michael about horses. Intrigue and woven threads, typical of racing villages. Change partners and dance.

We ate Maudie's splendid ribs of beef with the crunching roast potatoes and honey-walnut ice cream after. I sat between Maudie and Dot and behaved with propriety.

The younger children chattered about the rabbit run in the garden where the family pets had doubled themselves in number within the past year. "They'll go to the butcher one of these days," Maudie muttered to me darkly. "They get out and eat my dahlias."

"One of the bunnies is *missing*," her younger daughter was insisting.

"How can you possibly tell?" Michael asked. "There are so many of them."

"There were fifteen last week and today there are only fourteen. I counted them."

"Probably the dogs ate one."

"Daddy!"

Lorna talked to Bruce Farway about pensioned-off steeplechasers, one of her current charities, and he listened with interest. Unbelievable.

The talk turned to Jericho Rich and his desertion of Michael's stable.

"Ungrateful beast," Maudie said vehemently. "After all those winners!"

"I *hate* him," Tessa said with enough intensity to earn a sharp glance from her father.

"Why especially?" he asked.

She shrugged, tight mouthed, denying him an answer. Seventeen, full of unspecified resentments, she was one of those children who'd never lacked for anything but couldn't settle for being one of life's favored mortals. She was a head-tosser besides a whisperer and she didn't like me any more than I liked her.

Ed, her brother, sixteen and pretty stupid, said, "Jericho Rich wanted sex with Tessa and she wouldn't, and that's why he took his horses away."

As a conversation stopper it was of Oscar-earning caliber, and in the breath-held aghast silence the front doorbell rang.

Constable Sandy Smith had called. Apologetically he told Michael that he needed Dr. Farway and also Freddie Croft.

"What's happened?" Michael asked.

Sandy told Michael, Bruce Farway and myself privately out in the front entrance hall.

"That mechanic of yours, Freddie. That Jogger. He's just been found along at your farmyard. He's in the inspection pit. And he's dead."

4

Jogger's neck was broken.

We stood looking down at him, the sideways angle of his head to his body impossible in life.

"He must have fallen in," Farway said as if stating the obvious.

From the other side of the pit Harve met my eyes, clearly thinking, as I was, that for Jogger to have fallen accidentally into an inspection pit he would have to have been reeling drunk, and even then I would have bet on his instincts to save him.

As if catching the thought, or at least the first half of it, Sandy Smith sighed. "He had a right skinful last night in the pub. Raving on about aliens under the trucks. Lone rangers, stuff like that. I took his car keys off him and drove him home in the end. I'd've had to arrest him for being drunk in charge, otherwise."

Bruce Farway asked him officiously, "Have you informed his wife of this?"

"Not married," Sandy said.

"No next-of-kin at all," I amplified. "I have next-of-kin listed for all my employees, and Jogger said he hadn't any."

Farway shrugged, climbed down the metal ladder bolted to the inspection pit wall and bent clinically over the crooked body, lightly touching the bent neck. Then, standing upright, nodding, he reported to me almost accusingly, "Yes, this one's dead as well."

Two corpses found on my property in four days, he seemed to imply, were suspiciously excessive.

Michael Watermead, who had deserted the tail end of his lunch party to follow me along to the disaster in the farmyard, asked curiously, "As well as what?"

"The hitchhiker," I said. "Thursday."

"Oh yes. Of course. I was forgetting. On the way back from taking Jericho's two-year-olds." The thought of Jericho brought a scowl to the naturally patrician features, his son Ed's appallingly casual revelation as yet undigested, unprocessed.

Michael, I guessed, had been prompted to be present now in my barn by a mixture of straightforward morbid interest, supportive friendliness and the typical fuzzy overall sense of responsibility in the community which kept much of rural English life within sane parameters. He brought anyway a weight of authority to the proceedings which Harve, Sandy, Farway and myself might have lacked.

"How long has he been dead?" I asked. "I mean . . . hours? Last night?"

Bruce Farway said hesitantly, "He's pretty cold, but I'd say fairly late this morning."

We understood, all of us, that a closer guess was impossible at that point. The pit itself and the air temperature were cold also. The doctor climbed up the ladder and suggested that he and Sandy should again call for the ultimate in removers.

"How about photographs?" I said. "I've a camera in the office."

Everyone solemnly agreed on photographs. I walked through the yard, unlocked the offices, collected my Nikon and returned to the barn. The others were still where I'd left them, standing round the pit looking down at Jogger with unreadable thoughts.

Although there was a certain amount of daylight in the barn from a window looking into the farmyard, we always had to top it up with electricity for work. The overhead lights were all on, but even so I used flash for the pictures, taking several shots from round the rim of the pit and several others from its floor, down beside my poor mechanic.

I didn't touch him, though I bent near to photograph his head. He lay in the angle between wall and floor; rough grease-streaked concrete walls, oil-blackened floor. He seemed to be looking at the wall six inches from his nose, his eyes, like those of so many suddenly dead, still open. The yellow teeth showed in two uneven rows within his mouth. He wore the old army jersey, the dirt-clogged trousers, the old cracked boots. He still smelled, extraordinarily, of oil and dust; of earth, not death.

The pit was five feet deep. Standing upright, my direct line of sight was roughly level with the ankles of Sandy,

Harve and Michael. Bruce Farway was behind me. For a petrifying second a primitive instinct warned me against standing up with my neck sticking out of a hole in the ground and I turned quickly but saw Farway harmlessly writing in a small notebook, and felt foolish.

I hauled myself up the ladder out of the pit and asked Harve how he'd happened to find Jogger at that particular time.

Harve shrugged. "I don't know. I just wandered round the yard, like I often do. The vans working today had all left. I was here earlier checking them out, see, to make sure. Then to waste time, sort of, while I was waiting for lunch to be ready, I walked round again."

I nodded. Harve liked to be on his feet always, and on the move.

"So then I noticed the lights were on in the barn," he said, "and I thought I might save us a bit of electricity so I walked over here thinking that I hadn't seen anyone come over here earlier. No one needed to. I wasn't worried, see, only I just came over for a look around and, like I said, to switch the lights off." He paused. "Don't ask me why I got as far over as the pit. I don't know why. I just did it."

The pit in fact was well over to the far side of the barn, expressly to stop people stepping over its edge unawares. A large rollback door at one end of the barn made it possible to drive a horse van straight in over the pit. The small door nearest the farmyard, which people on foot used, opened onto a general workshop area, with tools kept in a large locked storeroom in one corner.

I asked, "Do you think Jogger was lying here all the time while drivers came in to work and took the vans out?"

Harve was troubled. "I don't know. He could have been. Gives you the shudders, doesn't it?"

"The postmortem will tell us, eh, Bruce?" Michael said, and Bruce, preening slightly at the intimacy of the use of his first name, agreed that speculation could be safely left for that event.

Michael caught the satirical glance I gave in his direction and came very close to a wink. The winning over of the doctor was clearly succeeding.

Farway and Sandy between them produced their mobile phones and summoned the necessary cohorts. Michael asked if he could use the phone in my office. Help yourself, I said, it's open. He sauntered off on his errand and when Harve and I followed, feeling upset and insecure, Michael was saying, "Damned shame for poor old Freddie," into Isobel's phone, the first one he'd come to, and "Oh, accidental, undoubtedly. Must go now. See you."

He rang off, said thanks and goodbye and left smiling with universal benignity, happy in the knowledge that he wouldn't have to feel any personal repercussions from Jogger's death.

"What do you reckon?" Harve asked as we reached our jointly used sanctum and paused for consideration.

"Do you believe he fell in?" I asked.

"Don't want to think of the alternative."

"No," I agreed.

"But if he didn't fall . . ."

He left the words hanging, and so did I.

I said, "Who was in the pub last night with Jogger?"

Harve began answering automatically, "Sandy, of course. Dave was bound to be . . . I wasn't . . ." He broke off, aghast. "Do you mean . . . who was in the pub to hear

him talking about aliens under the vans? You can't mean
... you *can't* ..."

I shook my head, though how could one help wondering?

"We'll wait for the cause-of-death report," I said. "If it's
proved he skidded on a patch of oil and fell and hit his
neck on the edge of the pit ... which is possible ... we'll
decide then what to do."

"But the cash box hiding-place was *empty*," Harve insisted. "No one would kill Jogger just because he'd found
an empty thing like that. They wouldn't. It *can't* be anything like that."

"No," I said.

Harve stared worriedly out at the row of vans.

"When I found him," he said, "I went back home and
phoned your personal line from there, but I got your answering machine saying you'd phone back soon, like it
does when you're only going to be away an hour or two.
But, well, I didn't think it could wait, so I phoned Sandy.
Was that all right?"

"The only thing you could do."

"We didn't know where you were. In the end we tried
Isobel and she said she thought you'd be at the
Watermeads', as Nigel had told her you were going to
lunch there when he phoned to say the daughter had mixed
up the departure time. It seems Tessa told Nigel. So Sandy
said he'd go round and fetch you."

"Mm." News traveled in Pixhill in dizzying spirals.

Harve began showing troubled signs of indecision,
which from our long proximity I identified immediately as
doubt over whether or not he should tell me something I
might not want to hear.

"Spit it out," I said resignedly.

"Oh! Well . . . Nigel said Tessa wanted to go to New-market with him, with the fillies. She climbed into the van and sat ready in the passenger seat."

"I hope he didn't take her."

"No, but he was flummoxed. I mean, he had you on one side threatening the sack to anyone giving lifts, and her on the other side, the trainer's daughter, wanting a ride." He paused. "She's a proper little madam, that girl, and Nigel's a sexy hunk, so my wife says, and . . . don't take me wrong . . . I thought you'd better know."

"I'm grateful," I said with truth. "That's a mess we can do without. I don't want to lose Michael Watermead's work just because his daughter fancies one of our drivers. We'd better not send Nigel there again, though it's damned an-noying, to say the least."

Lewis, of course, was Michael's driver of choice, but very often Watermead horses needed more than one van. Not being able to send Nigel cut down my options.

Harve said with humor, "We could put Pat on the extra Watermead runs, when she's better, and your temporary re-placement could do any before that."

"Good thinking!" I stifled too broad a smile and made a note for Isobel to allocate Nigel chiefly to Marigold En-glish, whose pulses he might race to good effect.

In time a police car crept carefully through the gates, bringing CID investigators, an official doctor and a photog-rapher. Harve and I went out to the barn, where Sandy was showing Jogger to his plainclothes colleagues and Bruce Farway was talking importantly to his police counterpart. The official photographer took bright flash official photo-graphs from the same angles as my own.

A statement from Harve about finding the body was taken down and read out to him in the curiously stilted English such proceedings seemed to incur. Harve signed the result even though the words weren't his own, and Farway, Sandy and I confirmed that the body was as we'd found it, and that nothing had been added or subtracted from the scene.

Sandy's colleagues were impersonal, without humor. All fatal accidents had to be thoroughly investigated, they said, and there would be further questions, no doubt, on the morrow.

The same black hearse that had collected Kevin Keith Ogden, or one very like it, arrived in the farmyard, and presently another finished life left my land under canvas and straps in a metal coffin.

The police, unsmiling, followed. Farway, Sandy and I watched them go, I, at least, with relief.

"All very sad," Farway said with a certain briskness, not caring one way or the other.

"A local character," Sandy said, nodding.

Not much of an epitaph, I thought. I said, "Sandy, when you drove Jogger home last night, was it in your car or his?"

"Last night? My car. That old wreck of a runabout will still be at the pub."

"That old wreck is actually mine," I told him. "I'll collect it later. Do you still have the keys?"

They were in his house, it seemed, for safekeeping. I said I would pick them up shortly and with a sigh of relief he left to salvage the remains of his Sunday off.

Bruce Farway followed, not wasting on me any of the slightly fawning regard he'd lavished on Michael or the police doctor, merely nodding a cool farewell. Harve walked back to his own house for his long-postponed lunch and I wandered round in the barn, staring into the now empty pit and checking that nothing in the tool storeroom was out of place.

The tool storeroom was a spacious twenty feet by ten, windowless. I unlocked the wide door, switched on the light and stood looking at Jogger's domain; at the pair of heavy-duty hydraulic jacks, the vast array of spanners and wrenches, the labeled boxes of spare parts, the rolls of cable, the chains, cans of oil, drums of grease, a set of six new Michelin tires waiting for installation.

The floor was filthy but the tools were clean, often the way with Jogger. As far as I could see, nothing had disturbed the general tidiness he miraculously maintained in the storeroom. The truck in contrast would contain a hopeless-looking jumble from which he would nevertheless pluck just the pliers he needed.

I switched off the light, locked the storeroom, and walked out beside the long workbench in the barn, a sturdy shelf which bore nothing at that moment but a small and a large vise, both bolted on. There were no tools anywhere lying about. Nothing a man could trip over, however drunk.

Morosely I left the barn, turning off the lights but as usual not locking the door to the yard. Enough was enough, I'd always thought. We kept the tools locked away and there was the padlock on the outer gate. Security could become an obsession, and anyway I'd been guarding against thieves, not against smugglers.

Not against murder.

I shied painfully away from that word. I couldn't believe it. Didn't want to believe it.

Murder couldn't happen. Not to Jogger. Not because of an empty cash box and two empty tubes. Not because he'd shot his mouth off down at the boozer.

I had a sense of jumping to overdramatic conclusions. It would be best to wait for the postmortem findings.

I sat in the office thinking of Jogger: not of the manner of his death, but of the man he had been.

A loner, an old soldier, a driver of army trucks whose only active service war zone had been the Northern Irish border. He almost never spoke of it, though his mates in a truck ahead of him had been blown apart by a bomb.

I'd acquired his services as a fixture or fitting along with the farmyard and the horse vans, the transaction apparently to his liking: and I'd counted myself lucky to have him and didn't now know where I would find anyone else as expert, undemanding and committed.

I mourned him also simply, without self-interest. Grieved for him as a man. In his own way he'd been a whole person, not needing what others might think he lacked. No one should impose their own perception of fulfillment on anyone else.

A little later, when the afternoon faded to dark, I walked down to Sandy's house and collected the keys to Jogger's truck. Sandy gave them to me without question: I signed for them merely, as Sandy knew the truck belonged to me. It didn't seem to occur to him that perhaps a couple of keys on the ring were Jogger's own. Continuing on, I walked to the pub that Jogger favored and duly found the truck in the car park there. At first sight there was nothing wrong with it. On second sight, I found that the two rear doors were slightly ajar, and inside, where there should have been the slider and a jumble of tools in a big red crate, there was nothing but rusty dust on the bare metal floor.

I sighed. A whole pubful of people had seen Sandy take

Jogger home, leaving a truckful of easy pickings behind him. I supposed I should be pleased that the truck itself hadn't gone too, and that it still had wheels, tires, gas and an engine.

I drove it the short distance to Jogger's quarters, which I so far knew only externally as a rickety-looking garage with an upper story.

In some distant past, the place had been a chauffeur's lodging, though the house it had served had long gone. Keeping me up to date on developments, for months and months Jogger had conducted a running battle with good souls on the local council who wanted to declare the building unfit for habitation, Jogger maintaining that his home was as it always had been and that it was the council whose ideas had changed. I thought that one could probably defend even a cave on those terms, but Jogger's strong and quasi-logical indignation had to date won him the day.

I laboriously opened one of the old creaking wooden front garage doors, leaving the truck outside and letting enough streetlamp in to show me the empty space inside. The way to Jogger's room, he'd said, lay across the garage and up some narrow stairs by the back wall, and up there I came to a flimsy door that opened easily when I tried the handle. No need for keys. I found a light switch and stepped for the first time into Jogger's private world, feeling both that it was a terrible intrusion and also that he would have wanted someone to care enough to go there, to see it for him one last time and make sure there was no desecration.

Jogger's home was as he'd left it, a mess untouched by whoever had stolen the tools. He'd earned good money for years yet had evidently chosen to live as if poverty breathed down his neck, his sagging armchair covered

with a grubby old tablecloth, the table covered with newspaper, the floor with linoleum. The army might once have
coerced him into spit-and-polish in general, but only in his
work had that training prevailed over what I guessed might
have been the familiar manner of his childhood. This was
the way he felt comfortable, this his old shoes.

There was no kitchen, merely a few mugs and plates on
top of a chest of drawers with tea, sugar, dried milk and
biscuits in packets alongside. The one drawer I opened revealed a tangle of old clothes. The suit and shirt he wore
for driving were draped on a hanger on a hook on the back
of the door.

His bed, a matter of jumbled khaki-colored blankets on
a divan, was by conventional standards unmade. Impossible to tell whether or not he'd slept there during the past
night.

I realized that the place wasn't as cold as the day outside and came across the first sign of luxury, a small con-
vection heater taking the edge off nature. There was also
a color television, three crates of beer, a shining electric
kettle and a telephone. Against one wall leaned a stack of
mildly pornographic magazines, representing one copy a
week for a couple of years, and in a shoe box on a shelf
I came across his birth certificate, his army discharge papers and the passbook of a building society, the total of his
savings raising my eyebrows and showing exactly what
he'd done with his pay packets.

I left his papers where I'd found them and looked into
a sketchy bathroom which was what I by then expected,
hardly spotless but not disgusting, basic with throwaway
razors and a gap-toothed comb.

Walking back through his room I left everything as it
was, including the heater. The whole place still smelled of

him, of oil, earth and dust. While his smell remained, so would he. The worthy council would sweep it all away soon enough.

I locked his door, closed the outer garage door and drove the truck to the farmyard wondering why Jogger had gone to the barn without his keys or his wheels . . . and when . . . and how . . . and *who with*?

In the offices, Jogger's logbook lay on Isobel's desk, ready for her to type the details into the computer. I took the book with me into my own office and sat reading what Jogger had written.

The bare bones of the trip only. No comments. No frills. He'd collected four named steeplechasers from a Pixhill stable and driven them down the M4 to Chepstow races. Time of leaving base, time of pickup, time of arrival, time of departure from racecourse, time of delivery back at stable, time of return to base. Diesel intake recorded in liters. Odometer readings entered. Cleaning completed. Total number of hours worked. Number of those hours spent behind the wheel.

Nothing about aliens or lone rangers.

Depressed, I replaced the logbook on Isobel's desk and thought I couldn't do any more there that was useful. Four of the fleet were still out, not counting the one in France and the one in Ireland, but Harve would see them return. I would hear soon enough if anything went wrong. I yawned, locked up and went home.

Revived by the product of Scotland, I sat in my swiveling armchair and rewound the tape of the answering machine on my private line. I'd transferred the business line to Isobel for receiving and making bookings for the fleet, but personal calls came on a different number. On that Sunday, I'd switched the private answering machine on when I went upstairs to shower, left it on while I picked flowers and took them to the cemetery, left it on of course for the Watermead's lunch, and it had been on ever since. The tape wound busily back.

I pressed the play button and nearly fell out of the chair.

The first voice was Jogger's, hoarse, cockney, unhurried, unafraid.

"I hate this bloody machine," he said. "Where have you gone, Freddie? Someone's half-inched the truck. It's not in the garage here, some tea-leaf's bloody nicked it while I was zizzing. You'd better tell Sandy ... No ... wait ... hang about ..." His voice stopped for a while and then in some embarrassment went on, "Er, um, cancel that, Freddie. I know where it is. It's down the boozer. Forget I said it, OK?"

The line clicked off, but the second call was also from Jogger. "I remembered, like, about the truck. Sandy's got the keys. I'll walk along to the farmyard first for a decko and then I'll get the keys. Anyway, I want to tell you, take a butcher's at them nuns. I found a dead one in the pit last August, and it was crawling and Poland had the same five on a horse last summer and it died. What do you think?"

His voice stopped, leaving me with the problem that I didn't know what he'd been talking about.

Nuns in the pit! Dead, moreover, like himself. Poor old Jogger, poor old exasperating man.

Why couldn't he ever say things straight out? His rhyming slang hadn't seriously mattered before this, but now it was infuriating. Half-inched meant pinched, a tea-leaf was a thief, a butcher's came from butcher's hook, look. All those were common parlance, part of the general language. But what were nuns and crawling and Poland?

What I needed, I decided, was a rhyming dictionary, and in the morning I would buy one.

I'd switched my private-line answering machine on at about eleven o'clock that morning. Jogger had been alive then. To be "pretty cold" in the pit by three in the afternoon, he must have died not long after his phone calls. I sat for a while simply looking at the machine as if in some stupid way it could bring my mechanic back to life. If I'd been able to speak to him myself, maybe he *would* have been still alive. I couldn't hear the phone's chirrup when I was in the shower or through the buzz of my electric razor. Perhaps he'd phoned then, but I hadn't noticed the "message received" light shining. More likely he'd tried when I'd left to pick and take the flowers. I must have missed him by seconds.

With unassuageable regret I ran through a couple of other messages on the tape and I told one or two people about Jogger. The whole village, one way or another, would know of it by bedtime.

By seven-thirty the next morning, after a troubled night's sleep, I was along at the farmyard talking to the two drivers who were taking runners to Southwell. There was an all-weather track up there, just northeast of Nottingham, giving an underfoot surface which had proved popular because it didn't crack, freeze or flood like turf. Its only drawback as far as Pixhill trainers were concerned was its distance of a hundred and fifty miles from home: as far as Croft Raceways was concerned, the distance filled the coffers. It was about the furthest the vans went out and back in one day, entailing early starts and late returns. Anything much further meant overnight stops or two drivers to work in spells.

On that Monday we had six vans going to racecourses,

two taking broodmares, two abroad and four standing idle, which in view of the persistent flu situation was just as well.

I was out in the farmyard when a woman drove through the gates in a small Ford runabout that had been a long time out of the showroom. She stopped outside the offices and emerged from behind the wheel stretching to a tall thin height in jeans, padded jacket and dark hair scrapped back into an untidy ponytail. No makeup, no nail polish, no pretense of youth.

She was, as she'd said she'd be, almost unrecognizable.

I went across. "Nina?" I said.

She smiled briskly. "I'm early, I'm afraid."

"All the better. I'll introduce you to the other drivers . . . but I'd better tell you what's filling their minds."

She listened to the finding of Jogger with a frown and immediately asked, "Have you told Patrick Venables about this?"

"Not yet."

"I'll do it. I'll reach him at home."

I took her into my office and listened to her make the call. "It could well be an accident," she told her boss. "Freddie hopes so. The local police have it in hand. What do you want me to do?"

She listened for a while and said "Yes" a few times, and then handed the receiver to me. "He wants to talk to you."

"Freddie Croft," I said.

"Let me get this right. This dead man is the one who found the empty containers stuck to your horse vans?"

"Yes. My mechanic."

"And besides you and me, who knew he'd found them?"

"Everyone who heard him saying so in a pub in Pixhill on Saturday night and understands rhyming slang." He cursed with feeling and I explained about Jogger's linguistic habits. "The local policeman heard him but it didn't make total sense to him. It *would* have made total sense, though, to anyone who knew the containers were there. Lone rangers and aliens under the vans, Jogger said. By lone rangers he meant strangers. Clear as daylight."

"I agree." Patrick Venables paused. "Who was in the pub?"

"It's a popular place. I'll ask the landlord. I'll go in at lunchtime and tell him I'll stand a pint to everyone who was there on Saturday night, on Jogger's last visit. In memory, sort of."

With humor in his voice he said, "It can't do any harm. Apart from that, I'll put out feelers towards your local police to see what they're thinking. This Jogger's death may be just an unfortunate coincidence."

"I hope so, indeed," I said fervently.

He wanted to speak to Nina again and she said "Yes" a few more times, and "Goodbye, Patrick" at the end.

"He wants me to phone him later," she said. "And on second thoughts, he advises you to be careful in the pub."

I told her about Jogger's last message on the answering machine.

"I'll write it down for you when I go home," I said, "but it's pretty incomprehensible. He used to make up his own rhymes and I've never heard him use these before."

She gazed at me. "You've had more practice than most."

"Mm. I thought of buying a rhyming dictionary, though it's more a matter of guessing. I mean, when he said carpets he meant drugs. Carpets and rugs. You don't have to just find the rhyme, you have to find the word that goes with the rhyme, and the association arose solely in Jogger's own brain."

"And if he hadn't died," she said, nodding, "you could simply have asked him what he meant."

"Yes. He just liked to play games, to challenge me, I suppose, in a quiet sort of way. But don't get me wrong, he thought naturally in that rhyming fashion. It was no sort of effort. It would come out spontaneously. The trouble is that I don't know if what he said yesterday morning was of desperate importance or only a passing comment. I don't know if desperate importance would come out in a rhyme. Passing comments did often."

Harve came into the office at that moment and I introduced Nina as the new temporary driver. Harve tried not to look dubious, knowing I preferred younger drivers because of their relative tirelessness and seeing the present substitute as older even than I.

"We have to give Pat at least two weeks to recover from this sort of flu," I pointed out, having discovered from past experience that too early a return to such a physical job caused further days off in the end. "Nina's very experienced with horses and with driving horse vans and we'll give her good help with directions."

He listened to the firmness in my voice and made the best of it. I asked him to show her the canteen and then how to fill out a temporary log and also to explain to her the refueling and cleaning routines. She followed him meekly out of the office, a shadow of yesterday's woman and not half as interesting.

The day's work began. The two Southwell vans set off to pick up their loads, and the other drivers began arriving, most of them making straight for the tea and the toast in the canteen. Dave creaked along on his rusty bicycle. Nigel came running, keeping fit. All of them already knew about

Jogger, as did Isobel and Rose, who drove to work in small cars, collecting milk and newspapers on the way.

Out in the yard I had a quick private word with Nina before she set off with Dave to collect her horses for Taunton.

I said, "The van you're driving is one with an empty container stuck on the bottom. You'd better know, though I can't think it will be used for anything today."

"Thanks," she said dryly, "I'll keep a lookout."

I watched her start up and drive off. She certainly managed the horse van competently, maneuvering through the gates easily and turning economically into the road. Harve, watching her departure with his head on one side, could find nothing to criticize. He gave me a shrug and raised eyebrows, judgment deferred.

Half an hour later, when she returned, pausing outside the gate, Dave jumped down from the cab and with a grin reported to Harve and me that "The old girl can twiddle a horse van on a penny and the horses are purring all over her. Where did you find her?"

"She applied for Brett's job," I said. "So did four others by phone yesterday. I've two coming for interviews this morning. The word's flown around that we're short of a driver."

"Isn't this Nina bird staying then?" Dave asked, disappointed.

"We'll see how it goes."

The second van bound for Taunton rumbled past Nina, hooting, and she set off after it, following in convoy.

"Could do worse," Harve said generously. "She seems sensible so far."

I told Dave that once the paperwork was fixed he would be going to France to collect Jericho Rich's daughter's new show jumper. Phil would drive, and they would stay overnight. Dave looked pleased, as he liked such excursions, but when he'd ambled off, Harve queried my choice of Phil.

"Do you mean Phil in his super-six? Just for one show jumper?"

I nodded. "He's experienced. It's best he goes. It's a valuable horse and I don't want anything going wrong with any other journey to do with Jericho Rich. Phil will come back without hitchhikers, dead or alive."

Harve winced, smiled and agreed.

Back in the office I urged Isobel to chase the agents for documentation for that trip. We used the services of specialists for overseas paperwork, as they understood the needs, worked fast and seldom made errors.

"Prompt and perfect," she said cheerfully. "Croft Raceways motto."

"Er . . . prompt and passable will do."

I took the day's newspapers along to my own office and flicked through them. There was never much hard racing news on Mondays. Jogger wasn't mentioned. The lead story in one paper was about the equine flu plaguing several racing stables in the north, virtually putting whole yards out of action for months. There was speculation that the virus might spread to Newmarket. Trainers, the writer said, were unwilling to share transport with horses from other stables in case of infection.

Hooray for that. I was all for separate journeys. Just as long, of course, as Pixhill itself stayed free. It was bad enough having *drivers* home sick, but the equine version of flu could hang around much longer, severely depleting the number of runners needing my services.

Equine flu, an infection of the upper respiratory tract, the paper said, had been known in the past as "the cough." There was no cure but time. So what else was new?

I turned to another paper. This one, still on the gloom and doom trail, discussed the previous summer's outbreak of debilitating fever and diarrhea in horses in mainland Europe. No one had satisfactorily identified the cause and trainers feared there might be a recurrence.

Diesel prices might rise again, I read. I hated "might" stories; nonstories. Like "Doctors warn," I put "might" stories at the bottom of my list. Anxiety raisers, all of them. Doctors should warn against "Doctors warn."

It was a "might" sort of morning. Sunny Drifter might not run in the next day's Champion Hurdle. There might be an increase in betting tax in the Budget. Michael Watermead might run the brilliant Irkab Alhawa in a warm-up race before the 2,000 Guineas.

Marigold English, I read open-eyed, reported that she had successfully completed her move to Pixhill. "Owing to Freddie Croft's personal services, the transfer went smoothly in all respects." Bully for the old trout, I thought, and phoned her on the spot to thank her.

"You did a good job," she said, pleased.

By nine-thirty the phone was ringing almost continuously as it always did on Mondays, the trainers making transport plans for the week ahead.

Isobel answered everything, coming along to my door at one point and saying, "There's someone inquiring for Brett's job. He sounds all right. What shall I do?"

"Ask him if he can come for an interview this morning."

She went away and returned to say that he would. Ten minutes later we had another applicant, and then another. We would have a line of them round the farmyard if it went on.

I started the interviews at about ten o'clock. Four men had already arrived and a fifth appeared within an hour. All

103

of them had the necessary licenses, all had experience, all said they'd worked in racing before. The fifth one said he was also a mechanic.

Most drivers were mechanics to some extent. This one gave me a reference from a Mercedes garage in London.

His name was Aziz Nader. Age, twenty-eight. He had curly black hair, olive skin, shining black eyes. Confident and outgoing in manner, he was looking for a job but not offering subservience. He spoke with a Canadian accent but didn't look as if he should.

"Where do you come from?" I said neutrally.

"Lebanon." He paused a second and amplified his answer. "My parents are Lebanese but they went to Canada when the trouble started. I was raised in Quebec mostly and I'm still a Canadian citizen, but we've been here eight years now. I've got a resident's work permit, if that's what's worrying you."

I looked at him thoughtfully. "What language do you speak with your parents?"

"Arabic."

"And . . . um . . . how about French?"

He smiled with white teeth and spoke to me rapidly in that language. The French I knew was racecourse stuff; he was too fast for me.

In the summer I shipped many horses for Arab clients, most of whose employees fumbled along in hopelessly tongue-tied or nonexistent English. A driver who could converse with them, and could also feel at home in France, seemed too good to be true.

"How good are you with horses?" I asked.

He seemed uncertain. "I thought you wanted a driver-mechanic."

No one after all was perfect. "Horse van drivers are better if they can handle horses."

"I'd . . . er . . . learn."

It wasn't as easy as he thought, but it didn't rule him out.

"I've told everyone I'll go with them on a test drive before deciding who gets the job," I said. "You came last, can you wait?"

"All day," he said.

The test drives were important because the cargo had to go steadily on its feet. Two of the applicants were jerky with brakes and gears, one was very slow, the fourth I would have engaged if he'd been the only remaining choice.

I found, as I climbed into the super-six cab beside Aziz, that I already intended to give him the job on the strength of his languages and his mechanical experience, just as long as he was halfway proficient at driving. He proved in fact not dazzling but at least smooth and careful, and my mind was made up long before we returned to the farmyard.

"When can you start?" I asked, as he braked to a halt.

"Tomorrow." He gave me another flashing smile, all eyes and teeth, and said he would work hard.

I thanked the other applicants who were waiting hopefully and got them to give their names to Isobel, in case. They went away disappointed. Isobel and Rose met Aziz with fascination and a visible increase in femininity, and Nigel, it was plain, had found strong competition.

Three months' trial, subject to his references being OK, I suggested, offering appropriate pay and conditions. Rose said she would put him into her computer, asking for his address. He would rent a room in the village, he said, and let her know later. Rose tentatively told him where Brett had stayed: the room might still be available. Aziz thanked her, listened to her directions, and drove off cheerfully, as he'd come, in a very old well-tended small-sized Peugeot.

I wondered how much one could really tell of a person by the car they drove. Sunday's Nina matched her Mercedes; Monday's Nina, her old runabout. Aziz seemed too strong a character for his wheels. I, on the other hand, owned a Jaguar XJS, loved and left over from the jockey days. I took it still to race meetings but moved around Pixhill in a workhorse four-wheel-drive Fourtrak. Everyone, I thought in passing, had a two-car personality, and wondered what Aziz would drive from choice.

To be prudent, I checked his references. The London garage he'd worked for said he knew his job but had left some time ago. The trainer whose private horse van he had driven proved to have gone out of business recently in financial difficulties. Aziz Nader had been a satisfactory employee but everyone on the payroll had lost their jobs.

While I was on the phone two cars arrived together, not, as it transpired, in tandem but both on fact-finding missions. The first disgorged the press in the shape of a spindly young man with a large nose and a spiral notebook, the second, the area bloodhounds in plainclothes, different men from the day before. I went out without enthusiasm to greet them. There were no smiles, no handshakes, merely minimal introductions, badges flapped in my face. No one seemed intent on overfriendliness or engaging my best help trustingly. Both press and police subsequently asked invasive and borderline-rude questions with visible skepticism at my answers.

Apart from Sandy, my experiences with the larger police world had been few but enough to show me one should never say a word to them that one did not have to, on the probability of being adjudged guilty of any old thing before conclusively proved innocent, and very likely after. One should also never, ever, on any account, make jokes. Not even to Sandy. The police, to my mind, had only themselves to blame for the public's prevalent mistrust of them, great chaps though no doubt most of them were. Pouncing, however, came as a natural instinct to them all: they wouldn't have been effective without it. No one that I knew of, particularly if innocent, cared to be prey.

The pressman seemed to see his role as being *Washington Post*-type investigative journalism. The police, to my quiet amusement, saw him as a nuisance who would do no investigating at all if they could help it. I listened to them match verbal swords until the young man retreated discomfited to wait in his car and the force produced notebooks of their own.

"Now, sir," they began, an opener full of menace if ever there was one, "you will hand over the house keys of the man found dead here yesterday, if you please."

I would have given them Jogger's keys willingly. The brusqueness of their demand reinforced my hovering antagonism and ensured I didn't help them as I might have done, as I should have done, no doubt.

Without a word, though, I went back to the office, finding them following me with sharp suspicious eyes as if I were planning to destroy evidence, given half a chance. Isobel and Rose watched the procession with open mouths. I didn't bother with introductions.

The two plainclothesmen drew up beside my desk. I opened a drawer, brought out Jogger's keys and removed his house keys from the ring.

They took the keys without comment and asked what Jogger had been doing in the farmyard on Sunday morning. I replied that all my employees could come and go in the farmyard on any errand they cared to, Sundays included, as it was a workday.

They asked me about Jogger's drinking habits. I said he had never turned up drunk for work. Apart from that, it was his own affair.

If Jogger had been drunk when he fell into the pit, I thought, the postmortem would show it. Speculation was pointless, really.

The elder of the two policemen next asked if anyone had been present with Jogger when he fell. Not that I knew of, I said. Had I, personally, been there? No. Had I been to the farmyard on Saturday night after ten o'clock or on Sunday morning at any time? No.

I asked why they were asking such questions and was told that all accidents had to be investigated, of course. The coroner would want answers at the inquest. In police experience, he chillingly added, people with information could remain silent so as not to become involved. I refrained from asking whose fault he thought that might be.

The interview proceeded for several minutes without fruit to either side, as far as I could see. They watched me keenly while telling me they would be making inquiries from my employees. I nodded neutrally, taking it for granted.

They asked for a list of all drivers who had been working on Saturday or Sunday. I took them along to Isobel's office and asked her for a computer printout of the times everyone had left and returned.

She shook her head disgustedly.

"Look, Freddie," she said, "I'm so sorry, but I can't get a thing out of the computer today. When I've sorted it all out, I'll do the records straightaway." She picked up a pile of logbooks. "The information is all in here, it's just a matter of typing it."

"Sure," I said, easily. "Can you just write down the names, for a start? Using old-fashioned pencil and paper?"

Obligingly she wrote the names from the logbook covers and handed the list to the policemen, who took it stolidly. When they'd gone Isobel made a face after them. "They might have said thanks, even if I did balls up the computer."

"Yes, they might."

The spindly pressman came out of his car like a rabbit from his hole once the police car had driven away and I spent the next ten minutes assuring him that Jogger had been a great mechanic, his loss would be sorely felt, the police had been investigating the accident, we would have to wait the result of their inquiries, and so on and so on, a whole lot of platitudes but the truth as far as it went. He drove away finally in dissatisfaction, but I couldn't help that.

A quick look at my watch showed I'd drifted through much of lunchtime without remembering my intention of organizing the Jogger memorial pints in the pub, so I scooted down there at once to talk to the landlord.

He, comfortably fat with a beer belly of his own, presided over a no-frills house geared to the psychological comfort of those made uneasy by too much luxury. He pleased a clientele of both stable workers and austere local intellects, talking easily with both groups.

"Old Jogger was harmless," he pronounced. "Got pissed regular on Saturdays. Not the first time Sandy's driven him home. Sandy's a good fellow, I'll say that for him. What can I do for you?"

Make a list, I said, of everyone who had been in the pub

with Jogger on his last night and give each of them two or three pints in his memory.

"Very decent of you, Freddie," he said, and began his list there and then, starting off with Sandy Smith and adding Dave and Nigel and two other of my drivers and proceeding to grooms from almost every stable in Pixhill, including a new bunch from Marigold English's yard, individual names unknown. "They'd asked in the village for the best pub," he told me complacently, "and were steered here to me."

"Quite right," I said. "Get their names and we'll make a sort of memorial scroll and frame it and hang it here on your wall for a bit."

The landlord became enthusiastic. "We'll do old Jogger proud," he said. "He'd be tickled pink."

"Um," I said thoughtfully, "I suppose he didn't leave any famous last words?"

" 'Same again!' " the landlord said, smiling broadly. " 'Same again' were his favorite words. He'd been rambling on about aliens under your trucks, I ask you, but by the time he left, 'same again' was about all he could manage. But always the gentleman, that Jogger, never any trouble when he'd had a skinful, never fighting drunk like that Dave."

"Dave?" I asked in astonishment. "Do you mean *my* Dave?"

"Sure. He'll take a swing at anyone, given enough ale on board. He never connects, mind you, he can't see straight by then. I stop serving him then, of course, and tell him to go home. Sandy takes him home too, sometimes, when he's too far gone even to balance on that bike. A good lad, Sandy. Pretty good for a copper."

"Yes," I said, and gave him a cash advance for the memorial pints, promising the rest after the list had been drawn up and everyone served.

"How about it if we get their own signatures, then? Make it more personal. Start tonight, shall I?"

"Great idea," I said, "but put their full names beside the signatures, so everyone will know who was here."

"Will do."

I bought a homemade Cornish pasty from him for a takeaway lunch and left him as he began to seek out a sheet of paper worthy of the roll of honor.

During the afternoon I went through the latest printout of the accounts with Rose and then with Isobel's input drew up my own sort of pencil and paper chart for the week. While Isobel was still in my office I inadvertently kicked the carrier left by Marigold English's grooms, and, picking it up, I asked Isobel to throw it away.

She took it out of the office but in a few minutes came back, undecided.

"There's quite a good thermos flask in that carrier. I thought it was too good to throw away so I took it into the canteen in case one of the drivers would like it. And . . . well . . . would you come and look?"

She seemed puzzled enough for me to follow her along to the canteen to see what was on her mind. She'd taken out the packet of sandwiches and laid them on the draining board of the sink there, and she'd unscrewed the flask and removed the top from the vacuum bottle inside. She'd poured most of the contents away into the sink, and found more in the flask than liquid.

I looked where she pointed, though there was no missing what was worrying her. Lying in the sink were four glass containers, each a small tube three and a half inches long, more than a half inch in diameter, amber in color, with a

111

black stopper fastened on with what looked like waterproof adhesive tape.

"They fell out when I poured," Isobel said. "What are they?"

"I have no idea."

The tubes were covered with the opaque milky liquid that had been in the flask. I picked up the flask and looked into it and, finding some of the liquid still inside, poured it into a canteen mug.

Two more tubes fell into the mug.

The liquid was cold and smelled faintly of milky coffee.

"Don't drink it!" Isobel exclaimed in alarm as I raised the mug to my nose.

"Just smelling it," I said.

"It's coffee, isn't it?"

"I'd think so."

I took a paper plate from the stack always ready to hand and put the four tubes from the sink onto it. Then, onto a canteen tray I put the plate, the mug, the thermos, its screw-on top and the packet of sandwiches, and with the carrier itself under my arm took the whole lot along to my desk in my office, Isobel following.

"Whatever can they be?" she asked for about the fourth time, and all I could say was that I would find out.

With a paper towel I cleared the milky residue off one of the tubes. There were a few numbers etched into the glass, which at first raised expectations, but all they announced was the containers' capacity, 10 cc.

I held the tube up to the light and tipped it up and down. Its contents were liquid and transparent but moved more sluggishly than water.

"Aren't you going to open it?" Isobel asked, agog.

I shook my head. "Not just now." I put the tube back on

the plate and pushed the tray away as if it weren't important. "Let's get back to work and I'll decide about this stuff later."

The tray to one side and with Isobel gradually losing interest in it, we finished my preliminary pencil and paper chart and Isobel went back to her office to bring it up to date in the computer.

She was back in my doorway within five minutes, looking very frustrated, dressed for going home at the end of her shift.

"What's the matter?" I asked.

"The computer is totally on the blink. I can't do a thing with it, nor can Rose. Can you get that man to fix it?"

"OK," I said, stretching a hand to the phone book. "Thanks for everything and see you in the morning."

Before I could find the number, my glance fell on the small glass vials on the tray, and instead of summoning the computer man, I phoned my sister.

5

She was, as usual, hard to find. I left messages for her all over the physics department of Edinburgh University and in the administrative section there and the affiliated research laboratories and in an observatory, and tried the Rector's wife's private line, all numbers left over from former searches. No results.

Waiting until she went home in the evenings was fruitless as she spent all her time in inaccessible meetings and committees, and catching her between waking and departure in the mornings fine-tuned things to a variable five minutes. "Please ask her to phone Freddie": after six attempts I gave up and went back to raising the computer people a dozen or so miles up the road.

From that effort I got the number-unobtainable noise

and also presently a voice assuring me that the line had been disconnected. Trying again produced the same result. Irritated, I phoned my barber, who operated four shops along from the computers, and asked what was going on.

"They vanished overnight one day last week," he told me in carefree tones. "Did a bunk. Just upped and scarpered. Took everything, left the place bare. We're all struggling along here since they put our rents up diabolically and I shouldn't wonder if the shoe shop doesn't go next."

"Dammit," I said.

"Sorry, mate."

I did a bit of yellow-fingers walking and secured a shaky promise from a stranger to "put me on the list." "Can't come tomorrow, sorry, not a chance."

Sighing, I flicked again over the Yellow Pages, as I had them in my hand, and tracked down a rhyming dictionary in one of the bookshops. The last one they had, I was warned, but they would keep it for me.

When I put the receiver down this time, the phone rang immediately. I snatched the receiver up again and said "Lizzie?" hopefully.

"Expecting a lady friend, are you?" Sandy Smith teased heavily. "Sorry, can't oblige."

"My sister."

"Oh, sure."

"How can I help you?"

"Other way round," he said. "I said I'd let you know about your hitchhiker. They did the postmortem and he died of a heart attack. Myocardial infarction. Ticker stopped working. They've scheduled the inquest for Thursday. A half-hour job, evidence of identity, that sort of thing. Bruce Farway's report. That driver of yours might be wanted. That Brett."

"He's left. Won't Dave do?"

"Oh aye, I daresay." Not his responsibility, I gathered.

"Thanks, Sandy," I said sincerely. "How about Jogger?"

"That's a bit different." He sounded cautious suddenly. "There's no report on him so far, like. They're always busy on Mondays."

"Will you let me know when you hear?"

"Can't promise."

"Well, do your best."

He said doubtfully that he would, and I wondered if he'd been subverted by my two plainclothes visitors into casting me as opposition. All the same, he'd kept his word over Kevin Keith Ogden, and maybe our long acquaintanceship would remain a durable bridge.

I sat for a while thinking of everything that had happened over the past five days, until eventually the phone rang again and this time it was indeed my sister.

"Who did you leave unturned?" she demanded. "I've been deluged by a veritable flood of 'Phone Freddie's.' So what's up?"

"First of all, where are you and how are you doing?"

"You surely didn't send all those SOS's just for a fireside chat!"

"Er, no. But if we should get cut off, where are you?"

She read out a number, which I added to the list. "Professor Quipp's lodgings," she said crisply.

I wondered if everyone except me had known where to find her. She'd had several lovers, nearly all bearded, all academics, not always scientists. Professor Quipp sounded the latest. I didn't make the mistake, however, of uttering aloud an unretractable guess.

"I was wondering," I said diffidently, "if you could get something analyzed for me. In the chemistry school, perhaps."

"What sort of thing?"

"Some unknown liquid in a 10 cc tube."

"Are you serious?" She sounded as if she thought me crazy. "What is it? Where did you get it?"

"If I knew what it was I wouldn't need to find out."

"Oh brother . . ." She sounded suddenly more friendly. "Tell me all."

I told her about the carrier found in one of my vans and the six tubes in the thermos.

"Quite a lot of weird things have happened," I said. "I want to know what my horse van was carrying and, apart from you, the only person I could ask would be the local veterinarian or else the Jockey Club. Actually, I'll give the Jockey Club a tube or two to be fair, but I want to know the answer myself, and if I entrust it all to any sort of authority I've lost control of it."

She understood very well about losing control of research results. It had happened to her once, and she'd never stopped resenting it.

"I thought," I went on, "that you'd be sure to know someone with a gas chromatograph or whatever it's called, and could get the job done for me privately."

She said slowly, "Yes, I could do it, but are you sure it's necessary? I don't want to waste a favor I'm owed. What else has happened?"

"Two dead men and some empty containers stuck to the undersides of at least three of my vans."

"What dead men?"

"A hitchhiker and my mechanic. He found the containers."

"What sort of containers?"

"For smuggling, maybe."

She was silent, evaluating. "There's a chance," she said slowly, "that you could be thought guilty of whatever's gone on."

"Yeah. A certainty, given the attitude of the two police-men who came here today."

"And you love the police, of course."

"I'm sure," I said, "that there are any number of civi-lized intelligent cultured policemen doing brilliantly com-passionate jobs all over the place. I just seem to have met those who've had the laugh kicked out of them."

She remembered, as I did, a time in the past when I'd begged the police (not Sandy, and not in Pixhill) to pre-serve a young woman from her violent husband. Domestic affairs weren't their business, I'd been told sniffily, and a week later she'd died from a beating. It had been the sub-sequently shrugged police shoulders which had infuriated me, not any sort of blighted passion, as she'd been barely more than an acquaintance. Official indifference had been literally deadly. Too late that years afterwards a new direc-tive had decreed "domestics" to be worthy of action: in me the damage had been done when I'd been idealistic and twenty.

"How are things in general?" Lizzie asked.

"The business is busy."

"And the love life?"

"On hold."

"And how long since you delivered flowers to the fore-bears?"

"Yesterday, actually."

"Really?" She didn't know whether to be impressed or disbelieving. "I mean . . . truly?"

"Truly. The first time since Christmas, mind you."

"There goes your fatal honesty again. I tell you, it gets you into more trouble . . ." She broke off, pondering. "How do you purpose to get these mysterious tubes up here to me?"

"Post, I suppose. Courier, better."

"Hm." A pause. "What are you doing tomorrow?"

"Going to Cheltenham races. It's Champion Hurdle day."

"Is it? Since you stopped hurling your soul over those fences I've lost touch with racing. What if I fly down? I'm due a couple of days off. We could watch the races on TV, you could tell me all and take me out to dinner and I'll fly back on Wednesday morning. Get my old room ready. What do you say?"

"Will you come to the house or the farm?"

"The house," she said with decision. "It's easier."

"Noon?"

"As near as dammit."

"Lizzie," I said gratefully, "thanks."

Her voice was dry. "You're one tough cookie, brother dear, so less of the sob stuff."

"Wherever did you hear such language?"

"In the cinema."

Smiling, I said a temporary goodbye and put down the receiver. She would come, as she always had, driven by an inbuilt compulsion to hurry to the aid of her brothers. The eldest of the family by a gap of five years, she had mothered first our brother Roger and then six years later myself, a fierce hen with chicks. Had she had children of her own, those instincts might have died naturally on my account, as they had for Roger, who'd achieved a cozy wife and three boys of his own, but as I, like her, had never married—or not so far—I seemed still to be not only brother but surrogate son.

Shortish and thin, her bobbed dark hair lately peppered with gray, she whisked around her own habitat either in black academic gowns or white laboratory overalls, her darting mind engaged with parsecs, quantum leaps and black and white dwarfs. She published papers, she taught intensely, she'd made a name; she was, in or out of bed with the latest beard, as far as I could see, fulfilled.

It was a good six months since I'd taken the train to her Scottish door to spend two days with her. Two days compressed six months' conversation into a span she preferred. Her one-night trip to Pixhill was typical; she would never sit still for a week.

Thinking about her, I sat on at the farmyard until Nina came back, her van empty, the runners safely returned to their stable. She parked by the pumps and filled the tanks and came yawning over to the office to put the day's log through the letter box, as she'd been asked.

I went out to meet her. "How did it go?" I asked.

"Utterly uneventful in any meaningful way. Fascinating in others. Has anything happened here?"

I shook my head. "Not really. The police came again about Jogger. I arranged his memorial at the pub, we should get a good list of names tomorrow. The computer's acting up. And after you've cleaned that horse van I've something to show you."

She glanced in disfavor at the dusty vehicle. "Do you really mean I should clean it?"

"Harve will expect it. Inside and out."

She gave me an old-fashioned sideways look of irony. "I don't think Patrick Venables intended this at all."

"Under cover is under cover," I said mildly. "If I do it

for you, and Harve comes back in the middle, my authority in this place is down the drain with the disinfectant."

To do her justice she complained no more but drove the van to the cleaning area and attacked it with the pressurized water, squeegeeing until the windows shone.

Harve did in fact return while she was busy and took her industry for granted. While he filled his tanks and waited his turn with the water I returned to my office and slightly rearranged the items on the canteen tray, removing four of the puzzling little tubes from sight and stowing them deep in a desk drawer. With time to spare, I picked up the unopened packet of sandwiches and read the label on it: "Beef and Tomato." There was also a price sticker label and a sell-by date, which identified the Friday just past.

Friday was the day I'd done Marigold's shuttle and found the carrier with the thermos. Friday's sandwiches. But I hadn't stopped anywhere for the grooms to buy sandwiches or anything else.

I frowned. "Beef and Tomato." I'd seen a "Beef and Tomato" wrapper, empty, only a day or two ago, but *where* exactly? The answer arrived slowly. In Brett's trash in the nine-van, of course.

Nina came into the office and sprawled in the chair across from mine, the desk between us.

"What do I do tomorrow?" she asked. "I learned a lot about racing today but damn all about smuggling. I think Patrick believed I would instantly spot what's going on, but I could be here a month and see nothing if today's anything to go by."

"No one," I reminded her, "has seen anything going on. Perhaps you're here to see how anything could."

"Which you could see better than me."

121

"No, I don't think so. I'd say nothing much happens when I'm around simply *because* I'm around. I'd like to send you on a trip to France or Italy or Ireland, but there we hit a bit of a snag."

"What snag? I don't mind going. I'd quite like it, in fact."

"I have to send two drivers because of the hours."

"That's OK."

I smiled. "Not really. The wives of the married drivers take exception to me sending their husbands abroad with a woman. My usual woman driver, Pat, consequently never goes abroad, to her disgust. I could of course send you with Nigel, who's not married, but Pat herself won't go with him, he'd seduce a nun."

"Not me, he wouldn't." She was definite, but I wondered.

"We'll see if a trip comes up," I said. "As for tomorrow, we won't be very busy here, we never are in Cheltenham Festival week because there aren't many other meetings held on those three days. We'll be busy again on Friday and it will be hectic again on Saturday, if we're lucky. Can you work Saturday?"

"It looks as if I'd better."

"Mm." I leaned forward, picked up one of the remaining two tubes lying on the paper plate and asked her if she'd seen anything like it before.

"I don't think so. Why?"

"They were being carried in one of my horse vans, hidden inside this thermos flask."

She came to full alertness, all the tired lines shed.

"What are they?"

"I don't know. But it's possible—possible's the strongest I'd put it—that they might be what the masked intruder was looking for in the cab of my nine-van, because that's where they were, in the cab. In a carrier with these uneaten sandwiches in this thermos of undrunk coffee."

She took the tube from me and held it to the light.

"What's inside?"

"I don't know. I thought Patrick Venables might be able to find out."

She lowered the tube and looked at me, smothering excitement and saying, "They're the first concrete piece of evidence that *anything's* going on."

I picked up the packet of sandwiches and showed her the labels.

"Brett, the driver who took the nine-van to Newmarket last Thursday with the two-year-olds . . ."

"And who has left?"

I nodded. "Brett—I think probably Brett because Dave had diarrhea—anyway, one of them bought sandwiches like these on that journey, because there was an empty packet just like this in some trash that came back in the cab. They threw the trash away on Friday morning when they cleaned out the van. Anyway, suppose Brett's sandwiches came from the shop in the South Mimms service station, and suppose . . . well, why not suppose . . . that these sandwiches here came from the same place . . . ?" I paused, but she simply listened, not commenting or disagreeing. I went on. "Dave picked up our hitchhiker at South Mimms. So . . . well . . . what if these sandwiches and this thermos were traveling with Kevin Keith Ogden?"

Given the supposition, her reasoning followed the same path that mine had and came up with the same observations.

"If the tubes belonged to the dead passenger, they can't be relevant to the containers *under* the vans. They might well not have anything to do with you at all. The man didn't know he was going to die. He probably meant to take these tubes with him."

"I was afraid you'd say that."

"All the same, very interesting. And . . ." She stopped pensively.

"Yes?"

She told me her emerging conclusions, and I nodded. "Makes you think, doesn't it?"

"You don't need me, really, do you?" she said.

"I need your eyes."

Harve finished his chores and joined us in the office, asking Nina how she'd fared and whether she had any questions. She thanked him, cutting down, I noticed, on the purity of her blue-blooded vowels, but not to an insulting extent. I wondered how often and how regularly she transformed herself for Patrick Venables.

The phone rang and I answered it, finding Sandy on the line.

"Inquest on Jogger," he said. "It's just come through. Wednesday, ten A.M., Winchester Coroner's Court. All they'll do is open the inquest and adjourn it pending results of inquiries. Normal for accident cases. I asked if they'd need you but they said not yet. They'll want Harve, as he found him, and Bruce Farway, of course. Also the inquest on Kevin Keith Ogden, they want Dave to attend. I'll brief him about where to go, OK?"

"Yes, thanks, Sandy."

I put down the receiver and told Harve he'd be needed briefly on Wednesday. Harve made a face of disinclination and shrugged. The phone rang again at once as if in continuation of the same conversation, but in fact there was a strange nasal voice in my ear, full of self-importance and busy-busy.

"John Tigwood here," he said.

"Oh. Yes?"

"Maudie Watermead told me to get in touch."

"John Tigwood. Friend of Maudie's sister, Lorna?"

He corrected me briskly. "Director of Centaur Care."

"Yes, I know."

"John Tigwood," Harve muttered disapprovingly. "Potty little pipsqueak. Always on the cadge."

"What can I do for you?" I asked the phone temperately.

"Collect some horses for me," Tigwood said.

"Certainly," I agreed with warmth. "Anytime." Business was business, after all. Whatever I thought of John Tigwood personally, I was all for taking his money.

"A retirement farm is closing in Yorkshire," he told me gravely, making it sound portentous. "We've agreed to take the horses and find new homes for them. The Watermeads have agreed to put two in their bottom paddock. Benjy Usher's taking two others. I'm on to Marigold English, even though she's new here. How about yourself? Can I rope you in?"

"Sorry, no," I said firmly. "When do you want them transported?"

"Tomorrow do you?"

"Certainly," I said.

"Good. Lorna herself wants to go with your van, acting as groom."

"All right, fine."

He gave me directions and I told him the fee.

"Oh, look here, I was hoping you'd do it for charity."

"Sorry, no." I was friendly and apologetic as far as it went.

"But it's for Lorna!" he insisted.

"I don't expect Maudie said I would do the job for nothing."

After a pause he said grudgingly, "She did warn me."

"Mm. So do you want me to fetch them, or not?"

A shade huffily he said, "You'll get paid. Though I do think you might be more generous. After all, it's a good cause."

"You could ask someone else to fetch them," I suggested. "You might get someone else to do it for nothing."

His silence suggested that he'd already tried someone else. Several someones, perhaps. It was a long way from Pixhill to the place in Yorkshire from where he wanted me to collect seven geriatric cases, shaky on their old legs, to deliver them to their new homes.

When Tigwood had gone off the line I handed the directions to Harve. Nina, having listened to my side of the exchange, asked what it had been all about.

Harve told her disgustedly, "There's this wacky home for very old horses. This John Tigwood, he boards them out all over the place. He charges the owners of the old horses for looking after them, but he doesn't pay the people who give the horses homes. It's a racket! And then he has the cheek to ask Freddie for free transport, in the name of charity."

I smiled. "It's one of the local good causes. People organize fund-raisers. They twist a lot of arms. I daresay I ought to have offered the transport for nothing but to be honest I don't like being pressured or conned, and as I'll bet the owners of the horses will have to pay Tigwood to get their old pensioners brought down here, I don't see why he shouldn't pay *me*."

"The point is," Harve said, "who's doing the job?"

"Whoever goes, takes Lorna Lipton, Mrs. Watermead's sister, as groom," I told him, looking over the chart. "We'll have to send a nine-van ... The new driver, Aziz what's his name, will be driving Brett's nine-van from now on. He may as well start with the geriatrics."

"What new driver?" Harve said.

"I engaged him this morning, after you'd gone. Best of the five who came for interviews."

I wrote Centaur Care in the chart square for the nine-van, and put "Aziz" at the head of the column.

Centaur Care, the name of Tigwood's outfit, sounded so like *Centre* Care that for years I'd thought that was how it was spelled. A tiny institution of its kind, the Centaur Care office occupied a small one-story economically built *hut*, for want of a grander word, on the edge of a two-acre paddock on the outskirts of Pixhill. Adjoining ramshackle wooden stables, capable of holding six pathetic customers with low expectations, just about passed county regulation inspections, the charitable status of the enterprise shielding it from blasts of ill authoritarian will. John Tigwood's public manner elevated this setup in Pixhill's collective consciousness to major good works: I was sure that many who gave to the noble cause hadn't set eyes on its headquarters.

There were "Centaur Care" collecting boxes scattered throughout Pixhill, round tins with slots into which one was exhorted to pour "long life for old friends." John Tigwood came round regularly to empty the containers and write fulsome receipts. He'd left one tin in our canteen but had fumed to find gifts in it of buttons, crackers and an out-of-date condom. "Be glad it hasn't been *used*," I'd said, which he hadn't seen as funny.

Harve was looking over the whole chart, and shrugging philosophically at the news that the computer wasn't working. Like me, he still preferred a written chart, though he inclined to the blackboard on the wall we'd had until I got rid of it. Too much chalk dust in the air, once we'd installed the computer.

I told Harve that all the tools had been stolen from Jogger's van. He swore briefly but saw no great significance in it. We would need, I said, another slider for inspecting the undersides of the vans and Harve, nodding, suggested I ask Nigel to make one.

"All he needs is a bit of plasterboard and some casters," Harve said. "He's good with his hands, I'll say that for him."

I smothered a smile. "He can do it tomorrow, then," I said. I pondered briefly and came to a decision. "On Wednesday Nigel can go to France to collect the show jumper for Jericho Rich's daughter. Nina, here, will go with him as a second driver."

Harve gave her a startled sideways glance and raised his eyebrows to me comically.

"I did warn her," I said. "She says she's Nigel-proof."

"She doesn't know him!"

"She's experienced with horses," I explained. "Jericho's daughter wants us to send an attendant to travel back with the horse. Nina can double that with driving."

"But you said Dave was to go, with Phil driving his six-van," Harve protested.

"I've changed my mind. Nina's going with Nigel. They can take the four-van Nina was driving today. It will be better, more economical." To her I said, "You'll need overnight things. OK?"

She nodded and, when Harve had gone out to meet the other incoming van, said, "You'll want one of us to sleep in the van, won't you?"

"It has that tube on the underside," I said agreeing.

"Yes. Well, hang out the bait. Let everyone know that that particular van is going to France. Someone might bite."

"Um," I said hesitantly. "No one expects you to do anything dangerous."

She smiled slightly. "Don't be too sure. Patrick can be bloody demanding." She seemed unconcerned. "And I won't exactly be parachuting into occupied France behind German lines."

She was, I saw, exactly the kind of woman who had done just that in World War II and, as if reading my thoughts, she nodded and said, "My mother did it, and survived to have me afterwards."

"That takes a bit of living up to."

"It's in the blood."

"Do you have any children?" I asked.

She wiggled long fingers in the dismissive gesture of unsentimental nanny-assisted mothers. "Three. All grown out of Pony Club age, all flown the nest. Husband long dead. Life suddenly empty, boring, no further point in showing or eventing. So . . . Patrick to the rescue. Need any more?"

"No."

I understood her deeply, and she realized it, moved despite herself to an internal wave of emotion and self-knowledge. She shook her head as if to disown the moment and got to her feet, tall and competent, a horse-woman for whom horses ultimately were not enough.

"If you don't need me tomorrow," she said, "I'll deliver the tubes to Patrick in London and discuss things with him, and be back on Wednesday. What time?"

"You'll need to set off from here at seven. You'll cross from Dover to Calais and reach your French destination at about six. Returning on Thursday, you'll have to go to Jericho Rich's daughter's place, of course, to deliver the horse. You'll be back here late, perhaps ten o'clock."

"Right."

She wrapped the two amber tubes carefully in a handkerchief and stowed them in her purse. Then with a brief nod of farewell she walked out to her car and inconspicuously departed.

Retrieving the four other tubes from the desk drawer, I wrapped each one in a tissue and put them in my jacket pocket. Then I poured the mug's contents back into the thermos, screwed on the inner stopper and the outer cap and restored it with the sandwiches to the carrier for onward transport to my house.

The workday was ending. There were still vans out on the road, though I wouldn't wait for their return. The drivers never expected it and might have taken too much close checking as a lack of trust. There had, however, been phone messages during the day both from the nine-van I'd sent to Ireland with broodmares and from the van in France that was bringing the two two-year-olds over to join Michael Watermead's stable, all the calls to the effect that neither van would be arriving back until two or three in the morning.

For us, that was quite normal. For Michael Watermead, it was bound to be an intolerable inconvenience. I had already arranged with the driver to come straight back to home base and to keep the two young horses in the farmyard's stables until morning, but remembered I'd forgotten to tell Michael himself.

Stifling a yawn, I pressed his numbers and found him at home.

"Two in the morning!" he protested. "You know I don't like it. It disturbs the whole yard, noise and lights when the other horses are asleep. They do need a good sleep, you know."

"If you like we could keep your two-year-olds here in the farmyard stables until morning." I suggested it as if I'd just thought of it. "They'd come to no harm. They're traveling well, my driver says. They're calm and eating."

"You might have organized it better," Michael grumbled, gently reproving, as usual converting any strong feeling into good-mannered restraint.

"There's been a holdup with the ferry in Calais," I explained. "Your horses won't reach Dover until about ten tonight, they say. I'm very sorry, Michael, but it's out of our hands."

"Yes, yes, of course I do see. But blast it, it's bloody irritating. Still, yes, I suppose those two-year-olds won't come to much harm. Bring them over first thing, though. Six-thirty or soon after, when my grooms come to work. Eh?"

"First thing," I confirmed.

"All right then." He paused for a change of subject. "Any ... er ... more news of your mechanic, poor fellow?"

"The police were asking accident-type questions."

"Too bad he fell."

"Rotten."

"Let me know if I can do anything."

"Thanks, Michael."

"Maudie sends her love."

I put the receiver down with a sigh, wishing Maudie meant it, and after a moment's thought got through to the stud farm that was expecting the delivery from Ireland.

"Your four mares with foals," I said soothingly, "are on the ferry right now but they won't get to Fishguard until eleven tonight and if we bring them straight on to you they'll be with you sometime after three. Is that all right with you?"

"Fine. We'll be up all night anyway, with mares foaling."

Jobs done, I stood up tiredly, picked up the carrier, locked the outer office door, leaving the canteen open for the drivers, and went out to shift gears in the Fourtrak, my workhorse buggy. I sometimes felt, climbing behind that practical wheel, as if the Jaguar XJS persona was leaving me altogether; but somewhere below the businessman the jockey still had a pulse, and I now saw that it was essential to keep him alive, not to let him slip away, to be still *willing* for him to risk his neck daily, even if he no longer did.

I drove home, ate, went to bed.

I would unleash the Jaguar more often, I thought.

Soon after six-thirty in the morning I was up, dressed and breakfasted, and driving along in the strengthening daylight to the farmyard to see what was what.

The van from France with Michael Watermead's two-year-olds stood quietly in its accustomed place, its cargo dozing in the stable, its driver nowhere about. There was a folded note from him, however, tucked under the windshield wiper. I opened it and read, "Can someone else take them to Watermeads? I'm bushed, I'm out of hours, and I think I've got flu. Sorry, Freddie." It was signed "Lewis" and dated two-thirty A.M., Tuesday.

Damn the flu, I thought forcefully. Damn all invisible enemies, in fact.

I unlocked the outer office door and went along to my own room to fetch the duplicate keys of Lewis's van, deciding that it was easier to drive it along to Michael's yard myself rather than wait for another driver to be ready. Accordingly I unlocked the horse van, loaded the patient untroubled guests from my stable and took them the scant mile to their destination.

Michael was already out in his yard, looking pointedly at his watch, which stood nearer to seven than the appointed six-thirty.

When I climbed down from the cab his displeasure lessened a little but not altogether. He was, for him, in a comprehensively bad mood.

"Freddie! Where's Lewis?" he said.

"Lewis came back with flu," I said ruefully.

"Dammit!" Michael did some arithmetic. "What about Doncaster? This flu takes so long."

"I'll give you a good driver," I promised.

"It's not the same. Lewis is helpful with saddling and so on. Some of those lazy buggers get to the races and sleep in their cabs until it's time to go home. That Brett was one of those. I couldn't stand him."

Making sympathetic noises, I lowered the ramp for access to the two-year-olds and untied the nearer one to lead him out.

"I thought the bloody French were sending a groom with them," Michael grumbled, his fair head back, his mild voice plaintive.

133

In anyone else, the displeasure level would have come roaring out in full-blown anger. In Jericho Rich, for example, intemperate man.

"Lewis told us yesterday on the phone that the French groom went back home from Calais," I explained. "He apparently thought he would be seasick on the crossing. Lewis assured me he could manage on his own, so we decided not to lose even more time in finding a substitute attendant. Where do you want me to put this fellow?"

The two-year-old was skittering around playfully at the end of his rope. Michael's headman, half running, came to take him into custody and lead him away to his new home.

With the second import safely unloaded, Michael's irritation subsided into his normal bonhomie and he suggested a cup of coffee before I went on my way. We walked together into his house, into the bright warm welcoming kitchen where frequent visitors sat unceremoniously round a long pine table and helped themselves to juices and toast.

Maudie was there in jeans and sweatshirt, blonde hair still tousled from sleep, face bare of makeup. She received my hello kiss absentmindedly and asked for Lewis.

"Flu," Michael said succinctly.

"But he helps the children with the rabbits! Bother and damn. I suppose I'll have to do it myself."

"Do what?" I incautiously asked.

"Clean out the run and the hutches."

"Be careful," Michael teased, "or she'll have *you* mucking out the wretched bunnies. Let the children do it, Maudie. They're quite old enough."

"They'll be dressed for school," she objected, and indeed her two younger children, boy and girl in tidy gray, came bouncing in with gleeful appetites and good-morning hugs for their father. They were followed, to my severe surprise, by my own daughter, Cinders.

She wore the same gray clothes. I gathered from the chatter that she went to the same school and had stayed with the Watermeads overnight. Hugo, I reflected, couldn't have reckoned on my coming to breakfast.

She said "Hi" to me nonchalantly as someone she'd met in passing at lunch two days ago, as someone who knew her parents. Her attention reverted at once to the other children with whom she giggled, at ease.

I tried not to watch her, but I was as conscious of her as if I'd grown new antennae. She sat opposite me, dark-haired, neat and vivacious, secure and loved. Not mine. Never mine. I ate toast and wished things were different.

Maudie's daughter said, "If Lewis has flu, who's doing the rabbits?"

"Why not Ed?" Maudie said, suggesting her elder son.

"Mother! You know he won't. He's a dead loss as a brother. Lewis loves the bunnies. He strokes them, strokes their fur. They hop all over his hands. There's no one as good with them as Lewis. I wish Lewis was my brother."

Michael raised his eyebrows at Maudie, neither of them relishing the promotion of Lewis to son.

"Who's Lewis?" Cinders asked.

"One of Freddie's drivers," the children told her, explaining the fleet of vans, explaining they were mine.

"Oh," she said, lacking much interest.

Michael said he would get one of the grooms to clean the hutches that afternoon and Maudie chivied the three children like a flock of sparrows to finish their breakfast, bundle up in coats and scramble out to the car for her to drive them miles to reach school by eight-thirty.

The kitchen seemed quiet and empty after they'd gone.

I finished my coffee and rose to my feet, thanking Michael for the company.

"Anytime," he said amiably.

My glance fell on one of John Tigwood's ubiquitous round collecting tins standing on the windowsill.

"Oh yes," I said, remembering. "One of my vans is fetching a load of ancient steeplechasers from Yorkshire today. John Tigwood says you're taking two of them in your bottom paddock. What shall I do about them? Do you want the whole lot to come here first? I mean, *which* two do you want?"

Not surprisingly he looked faintly exasperated. "Lorna talked me into it again. Let her and that wretched little man sort them out at that awful little place. But see if you can bring me two here that aren't on the point of expiring. I told Tigwood to take the last two to the knackers to put them out of their misery. It's a lot of sentimental rubbish, keeping those poor tottering wrecks on their feet, but of course I can't say that in front of the children. They don't understand the need for death."

He came out into the stable yard to drive up to the Downs to watch his horses complete their morning exercise, and on an impulse asked if I would like to go with him, as Irkab Alhawa would be up there doing fast work.

I accepted at once, intensely pleased at what I knew to be a compliment and a gift. He drove us in his high-wheelbased Shogun and pulled up at a vantage point near the end of his upland all-weather exercise track. From there we had a clear view of horses galloping uphill towards us three abreast, and a closer look as they swept past us, to pull up a hundred yards further on.

I'd spent innumerable mornings most of my life riding training-gallops. I still did it, given the chance. There

. wasn't going to be any chance I would exercise Watermead horses, though, as steeplechase jockeys of my size, whether retired or not, tended to be too heavy and too strong for young Flat-racers.

"How's Irkab coming along?" I asked tentatively.

"Doing just great."

Michael's voice was full of satisfaction, the anxiety of training a horse fancied to win the Derby hovering well below sweat-level so early in the year. Come June he'd be insomniac.

We watched three or four trios of his string come past us in a prearranged order, and Michael said, "Irkab will be in the next three, on this side nearest to us. You'll see the white blaze down his nose."

"Great."

The three horses came into sight, moving easily, fast shadows on the brown track. Irkab Alhawa, with his awkward Arab name, had been a late developing two-year-old, not revealing the extent of his athletic ability until the Middle Park Stakes in October the previous year. Lewis had driven him to Newmarket that autumn day as merely another Watermead runner and had returned with a revelation that had attracted newsmen to Pixhill like a flock of starlings.

The promise of the Middle Park had been confirmed two weeks later by a scintillating six-length victory in the Dewhurst Stakes, the final top two-year-old event of the season, slaughtering the best that Newmarket could muster on its own turf, with the result that during the peaceful inactive winter Irkab Alhawa had become almost a cult, the odd-sounding syllables part of his mystique. The press had translated the words into English as "Ride the Wind," which had caught the public's imagination, though somewhere I'd heard that that rendering wasn't quite right. Never mind; Irkab Alhawa was good news for Michael, for Pixhill, for Lewis and not least for Freddie Croft.

The brown sensation with the narrow white blaze, recognizable afar off, swept effortlessly up the track towards us in the smooth coordination of muscle and mass that was nature's gift to the lucky few, horses and humans, in whom grace of movement equaled speed.

I felt, as always in the presence of great horses, an odd sort of envy: not to be on their backs, but to be *them*, riding the wind. In rational terms it was nonsense, but after so many years of closeness with the marvelous creatures they were in a way extensions of myself, always hovering in the back of consciousness.

Not everyone had rejoiced with Michael over the emergence of a prodigy in his stable. Human nature being what it was, a certain portion of the racing world would have been happy to hear that ill had befallen the horse. Michael shrugged it off. "There will always be spite and envy. Look how some politicians encourage it! It's not my problem if people grudge and bitch, it's theirs." Michael, easygoing and civilized, couldn't understand the force of unprovoked hate.

Irkab Alhawa galloped past us, majestically strong. Michael turned to me with a glimmering smile and saw he needed to make no comment. For a horse like that, comment was inadequate, banal.

We drove back to the stables. I thanked him. He nodded, and in an odd way, because of that gallop, we'd come closer to a positive friendship, not just friendly business relations.

I took Lewis's super-six back to the farmyard, its daily bustle embracing me, bringing my feet back to earth.

Aziz had reported for work, his vitality and flashing
smile having already produced a sort of glaze in Harve's
less shiny eyes. Harve greeted my arrival with relief and
told me he'd been trying to explain to Aziz, disappointed
with his first assignment, that a job was a job was a job.

"There's a whole lot of no glamour in this business," I
assured Aziz. "Some days you take seven terminal has-
beens. One day, maybe, a Derby winner. Getting the cargo
alive and well to journey's end is all that matters."

"OK."

"And do remember that all horses doze off and dream
while you're driving at a constant speed on a motorway,
but when you leave the motorway and slow down and
come to a roundabout they'll wake up and not know where
they are and judder about trying to stay on their feet. All
horses are like that but these very old ones will be shaky
on their pins to start with, so be extra careful or you'll
come back with all seven threshing around on the floor
and, even if they survive, at the very least we will not get
paid for our efforts."

Aziz listened to this homily at first with a disbelieving
grin and latterly with thoughtful attention. He should,
though, have been nodding throughout.

I said slowly, "You *have* been driving racehorses,
haven't you?"

"Yes," he replied instantly. "Of course. But local, round
Newmarket. And to Yarmouth races. No motorways, really."

Harve frowned but didn't pursue it, and question marks
rose like a prickly hawthorn hedge in my own mind. It
was true there were few if any long motorways in East
Anglia, where Newmarket stable was situated, but it

passed credibility that a Newmarket stable would never have sent runners further afield.

I might have asked Aziz a few searching questions but at that moment Maudie's sister, Lorna, swept through the gates in her expensive crimson Range Rover, the aristocrat of safari cars, built to withstand raw African veldt and the smooth roads of Pixhill.

Lorna, concerned and intense, hopped down from behind the wheel and strode across to give me a peck on the cheek. Blonde, blue-eyed, long-legged, richly divorced and thirty, lovely Lorna looked me firmly in the eye and told me I was a pig to charge for fetching the pensioners.

"Um," I said, "is John Tigwood charging the pensioners' owners?"

"That's entirely different."

"No, that's getting it both ways, or trying to."

"Centaur Care needs the money."

I smiled a usefully bland smile and introduced Aziz as the day's driver. Lorna blinked. Aziz, shaking her hand, gave her a white blinding smile and a flash of dark eyes. Lorna forgot about my meanness and told Aziz animatedly that they were going on a wonderful Errand of Mercy and that it was a Privilege to be involved in Saving Old Friends.

"Yes, I agree," Aziz said.

He gave me the ghost of a sideways grin as if daring me to denounce his hypocrisy. Aziz was a rogue, I thought, but rogues were good for the spirits, up to a point.

John Tigwood chose that moment to give us the benefit of his company, which I could certainly have done without. The potty little pipsqueak, as Harve had called him, emerged from a coffee-colored van emblazoned all over with "Centaur Care for Aged Horses" in titanium-white letters and strode. in our direction with thrusting important steps. He wore gray corduroy trousers, an open-necked shirt and a heavy-knit sweater and was carrying an anorak.

"Good morning, Freddie."

His voice tried hard, but the self-important fruitiness couldn't disguise the lack of substance beneath. Tigwood was essentially an inadequate man inventing a role for himself: not, I supposed, an unusual phenomenon or even one necessarily reprehensible. What else could he do? Slink along, wringing Uriah Heep hands?

I'd always taken the Centaur Care charity to be a long-established facet of the local community. That Tuesday morning I wondered whether Tigwood himself had set it up, and whether he lived off the collecting boxes, and whether, if he did, should Pixhill object? There were always old horses around dozing in sunshine. Such a cause had to be worthy, if compassion meant anything.

"Morning, Lorna," the charity man said.

"John, dear." Lorna pecked his thin cheek somewhere above the sparse beard that straggled round his pointed chin. Even the beard, I thought, trying to stifle my impatience, was inadequate. So in a way was his thin neck with the sharp larynx, neither of which he could help.

"What can I do for you, John?" I asked, welcoming him.

"Thought I'd go with Lorna," he announced. "Seven horses . . . two pairs of hands will be better than one. Is this our driver?"

Lorna gavé a quick glance at Aziz, not sure that she wanted John with her after all, but the potty little pipsqueak had made up his mind, had come dressed for the journey and would stick obstinately to his plan, it was clear.

141

"How nice," Lorna said insincerely.

"You've a long way to go," I told them in general, "you may as well get started."

"Yes, yes," Tigwood said, taking bustling charge. "Come along, driver."

"His name is Aziz," I remarked mildly.

"Oh? Come along then, Aziz."

I watched them climb aboard, two totally incompatible men with the well-intentioned Cause-embracer between them. Aziz looked grimly out of the window in my direction, all relish for the day, small at best, evaporating. I couldn't blame him. I'd have hated to have taken his place.

Under that nine-van, I reflected, as Aziz turned competently out of the gate, was the magnet Jogger had found. I'd taken it on trust that the nails in the insulating block of wood were still holding fast. I hadn't warned Aziz it was there. I hadn't told him to look out for strangers trying to roll under the fuel tank section of the chassis. I couldn't envisage anyone seeking to transport anything in such awkward secrecy between Yorkshire and Pixhill, when all they'd have to do was drive down in a car.

Harve left in Aziz's wake, setting out five minutes after, in time to pick up two runners for the later races at Cheltenham. Another van had already left for the same destination, two had gone to Bristol airport to collect Irish horses flying over for Gold Cup day and three were out with broodmares. Not bad, considering.

I went into the offices where Isobel and Rose were looking in frustration at blank computer screens and asking what they should do with the day.

"Type letters on the old-fashioned typewriter?" I suggested.

"I suppose we'll have to," Rose said, disgusted.

"The man promised he'd come tomorrow," I assured her.

"Not before time."

Tigwood's collecting box stood on Isobel's desk and I picked it up and shook it. The result was a hollow rattle, three or four coins at most.

"Mr. Tigwood came to empty it last week," Isobel said. "There wasn't much in there. He thinks we should try harder."

"Perhaps we should."

I went out to my jalopy and drove to Newbury to leave my film of Jogger with a one-hour developing outfit and to collect the ordered, reserved and ready rhyming dictionary. I hadn't actually seen one of these before and sat in the car park flicking over the pages to pass the hour's wait, finding that the rhymes were listed not in regular alphabetical fashion but all starting with vowels.

"Amely," I read. "Gamely, lamely, namely, tamely.

"Etter / better, debtor, fetter, getter, letter, setter, sweater, wetter . . .

"Oard / board, floored, ford, gourd, hoard, horde, oared, pored, sword, toward, aboard, afford . . ."

Hundreds and thousands of rhymes, available but useless. I realized I needed to have Jogger's cryptic statements under my eyes, not just in my memory. Maybe if I could simultaneously see what he'd said, some spark might fly out of entries like "unch / brunch, bunch, crunch, hunch, lunch, munch, punch, scrunch . . ."

Always remembering, I thought in depression, that in Jogger's cockney accent bike became boike and lady, lidey, and *t*'s and *d*'s could be swallowed and not heard.

Closing the book, I collected the sharp sad pictures of

his death and drove home to ready the house and get my sister's room ready, which meant making the bed and opening the windows to let in whatever March cared to deliver.

I picked more daffodils and put them in a vase, and punctually at noon my sister Lizzie arrived.

She flew in literally, from on high, in a helicopter.

6

Lizzie owned a quarter share of the tiny Robinson 22, her only extravagance and the way she chose to use her inheritance from our parents. To my mind, the helicopter was her equivalent of Roger's cruise ships and my steeplechasing, the elder sister's statement that if boys could have toys, so could girls. She had shown us each in turn as children how to run a complicated train set. She'd taught us how to bat unafraid at cricket, she'd climbed trees like a cat; in her teens she'd led us into jungle woods and scary caves and defended us and lied for us in our wrongdoings. Because of her, we'd grown up understanding many faces of courage.

She cut the engine and, when the rotor had stopped, jumped down from the little glass bubble and walked collectedly to meet me on the tarmac.

"Hi," she said; small, light, wiry, pleased with life.

I hugged her.

"Have you fixed lunch?" she asked.

"No."

"Good. I brought a picnic."

She returned to the helicopter and retrieved a carrier, which we took with us into the house. She never came empty-handed. I never wasted time catering for her except to put champagne on ice. I popped the cork and poured it straight, and she relaxed in a big chair, taking a deep fizzy gulp and looking me over as sisters do.

"How was the flight?" I asked.

"Bumpy over the moors. Some snow still lying about. I dropped down at Carlisle to refuel. Four hours, door to door."

"Three hundred and fifty miles," I said.

"Near enough."

"It's great to see you."

"Mm." She stretched, almost purring. "Tell me all."

I told her a good deal, explaining who everyone was: Sandy Smith, Bruce Farway, the Watermeads, Jericho Rich, Brett, Dave, Kevin Keith Odgen and Jogger. I told her about Nina Young and her metamorphosis.

She inspected the empty cash box standing in all its grime on the newspaper. I showed her the rhyming dictionary and played her the tape of Jogger's last message, but all the mental agility under the graying dark cap of hair couldn't unlock the old soldier's meaning.

"Silly man," Lizzie said. "Did he fall or was he pushed?"

"Pushing someone into a five-foot-deep inspection pit is not a surefire way of killing them."

"An accidental push, then."

"No one has owned up to it."

With some hesitation I offered to show her the photographs of Jogger in the pit.

"I'm not squeamish," she protested. "Hand them over."

She studied them at length. "There's nothing to tell, one way or another."

"No," I agreed, taking the photos back and returning them to their packet.

After a pause she asked, "What about these tubes in the thermos flask?"

I took two of the tubes from my safe, where I'd kept them overnight, and gave them to her. She unwrapped each from its tissue and held them up to the light.

"Ten ccs," she said, reading the small numbers. "In other words, one tablespoonful."

"Only one?" I was surprised. I'd thought the tubes held more.

"Only one," Lizzie confirmed. "A large mouthful."

"Yuk."

"Well, yes, it wouldn't be prudent to drink this." She put the tubes back into the tissues, and into her purse, just like Nina. "I suppose you want the results like, say, yesterday?"

"It would be helpful."

"Day after tomorrow," she promised prosaically. "The best that can be done."

"I'll try for patience."

"Never your best virtue."

She sniffed the contents of the thermos and poured a little into a spare glass, putting her nose down close to the surface.

"Coffee," she said. "And the milk's off."

"It's been in the thermos since Thursday at least."

"Do you want this analyzed as well?"

147

"What do you think?" I asked.

She said, "I'd think the coffee was just there to cushion the tubes."

"Leave it, then," I said.

We drank more champagne and unpacked the picnic, which was the glorious gift of arguably the best restaurant in Scotland, La Potinière at Gullane in East Lothian. "The Browns send you their love," Lizzie said, referring to the owners. "They want to know when you're coming back."

They would want to know six months in advance and even then one might not get a table. Sometimes Lizzie, their close friend, had been down on her knees. This time they'd sent chicken breasts stuffed with a mousseline of cream, hazelnuts and Calvados and a watercress salad with its hazelnut oil dressing packed separately, followed by a light lemon cheesecake that melted to ambrosia on the tongue.

I seldom cared much what I ate. Lizzie deplored it and educated me when she could. I'd have been willing to have graduated at La Potinière.

We companionably watched the first of the Cheltenham races on television, and it was no use looking back, it was three years since I'd finished second in the Champion Hurdle, a bittersweet loss on the day.

"Be glad you're out of the worry of it," Lizzie said, watching me watching the jockeys.

"What worry?"

"The worry of someone else being given your rides."

I smiled. That was, for all jockeys, the worst of worries, and I said, "You're right. It's a relief. Now I only have to worry about other transport firms pinching my customers."

"Which I don't suppose they do, much."

"Not so far, luckily."

The phone rang with a call from Isobel, reporting progress.

"Everything's OK," she said. "That new man, Aziz, has phoned from Yorkshire to say they want him to bring back eight animals, not seven, and the eighth is a half-bald old pony that can hardly walk. What do you want him to do?"

"John Tigwood's there," I said. "If he'll be responsible if the pony dies on the way, we'll ship it. Tell Aziz to get Tigwood to write a note absolving us, and sign and date it, including the time."

"Right."

"How did Aziz sound?"

"Fed up," Isobel said cheerfully. "Can't blame him."

"What's that all about?" Lizzie asked lazily as I put down the receiver, and I explained about the geriatric expedition and gave her a rundown on John Tigwood, profit-making philanthropist.

"A fanatic?"

"He has to be."

We watched the rest of the races, all, that is, that were shown. Isobel phoned again in midprogram at four to report all well; she was going off home. One of the local horses Harve had driven to Cheltenham had won, had I noticed?

"Yes, terrific."

"Good for custom at the pub," she observed, bright girl, reminding me, as it happened, that I hadn't checked that day on Jogger's memorial.

I told Lizzie about the memorial, and the reason for it.

"So you don't think it was an accident!" she said.

"I want it to be."

When the races had finished, we switched off the television and just talked in general, and later Aziz telephoned direct to my house, saying he hoped I didn't mind but the office was shut with my own number on its answering machine.

"No, of course not, I don't mind. Where are you?"

"Chieveley service station; that place north of Newbury. I'm inside, in a phone booth. I wanted to talk to you without them listening."

"What's the matter?"

"It's my first day with you, and I . . ." He stopped, seeking the words. "Do you mind," he said in a rush, "coming to meet this van wherever it is that I'm taking it?"

"Centaur Care."

"Yes. These horses aren't fit to travel. I told Mr. Tigwood but he insisted we bring them. Mrs. Lipton's worried they'll die before we unload them . . ."

"All right," I said decisively. "When you get near Pixhill, call me again on the horse van phone and I'll drive round at once. Don't let the ramps down until I get there. Sit in the cab and write up the log sheet. Do *anything*. Understand?"

"Thanks." One short word; a dictionary of meaning.

"See you," I said.

When I told Lizzie the problem she asked to come with me, and after Aziz had phoned again, round we went.

The scrubby Centaur Care paddock had been overgrazed to the point where dark earth showed between the straggling tufts of grass. The roughly hard-topped parking area had weeds growing through cracks and the small concrete office was streaked with rusty rain marks. Behind it, the stables looked as if a good breeze would flatten them. Lizzie gazed at this magnificent spread speechlessly as we pulled up beside the elderly green paint of the front door.

We'd been there barely a minute before Aziz turned in slowly from the road and brought the nine-van to an exceedingly gentle halt. I walked across to his window as Tigwood and Lorna disembarked from the passenger seats on the other side.

Aziz opened the window and said, "They're all still alive, I hope."

There were sounds of the ramps being unbolted on the far side and I hurried round the front and told both Tigwood and Lorna to stop.

"Don't be silly," Tigwood said. "Of course we must unload them."

"I'd be happier to see them first," I told him reasonably.

"Whatever for?"

"Old horses might like five minutes' rest at this point. There's no mad hurry, is there?"

"It'll soon be dark," he pointed out.

"All the same, John, I'll just rub their noses."

I opened the rear grooms' door without waiting for any further objections and heaved myself up to horse level. Three patient old sets of eyes gazed at me, tiredness showing in the angle of the necks and in the lethargically turning ears.

In the space in front of their heads, where often an attendant traveled, stood an untouched bale of hay and the row of plastic containers, all full.

I jumped down from that compartment and opened the center grooms' door, climbing up again into the space between the middle three stalls and the front three. In the middle three stalls stood another shaky trio, their heads hanging low with fatigue. I wriggled forward through the empty third of the front stalls and inspected the rest of the load, a horse so feeble that it looked as if the partitions themselves were all that were holding him on his feet, and a pathetic pony with acres of hairless skin and its eyes shut.

151

I descended to ground level and told Tigwood and Lorna
that I wanted the veterinarian round to see them before they
were unloaded. I wanted an authoritative opinion, I said,
that my firm had delivered them in as good a condition as
possible.

"It's none of your business," Tigwood said furiously.
"And it's an insult to Centaur Care."

"Look, John," I said placatingly, "if the owners of those
horses care enough about them to give them good homes in
their old age, they'll certainly pay for a veterinarian to make
sure they've come to no harm from the journey. They're nice
old horses but they're very tired and I should think you
should be grateful to have help with their well-being."

"John," Lorna said, "I'm sure Freddie's right. I do think
we should. They were a lot feebler than I expected."

"Did they drink before they set off?" I asked.

Lorna looked at me worriedly. "Do you think they're
thirsty?" she said. "Aziz was driving so dreadfully slowly."

"Hm." Through the open passenger door I asked Aziz to
hand me the phone and without more ado got through to
the local veterinary surgeon, explaining what I wanted.
"Five minutes look-see, that's probably all. But right now,
if you could."

He promised the right now and was as good as his word,
a longtime friend who knew I wouldn't call him out for
nothing. He made the same brief inspection as I had and at
the end gave me a hollow-eyed look, meaning more than he
said.

"Well?" John Tigwood demanded, and listened crossly to
the verdict.

"They're mildly dehydrated and probably hungry. Thin,
too, though they've been adequately looked after in general.

They'll need good hay and water and a lot of rest. I'll stay while you unload, I think."

During the wait for his arrival I'd introduced Lizzie to Tigwood and Lorna. They paid her scant attention, having thoughts only for the horses, and Lizzie herself was content just to watch and listen.

I lowered the rear ramp finally and John Tigwood untied the first of the passengers and led him to the ground, the old legs slipping and unsteady, hooves clattering, eyes frightened. He reached firm footing and stood still, quivering.

"Lorna," I said, "how old are they?"

She produced a list and handed it to me mutely. The names, ages, and owners of the horses were there, some of them so familiar as to raise my interest sharply.

"But I rode two of them!" I exclaimed. "Some of these were great horses."

"Surely you realized that?" Lorna said tartly.

"No, I didn't. Which is which?"

"They have labels on their head-collars."

I went to the horse Tigwood was holding while the veterinarian looked it over and read the name, Peterman. I fondled the old nose and thought of the races we'd won and lost together twelve and more years earlier, days when the shaky frame had been taut and powerful, a proud head-tossing prince, a star in his time. At twenty-one, his age on the list, he was the equivalent of roughly ninety, in human terms.

"He's fine," the veterinarian said. "Just tired."

Tigwood gave me an "I told you so" look of triumph and led my old friend off towards the stables.

"He's the youngest," I remarked, reading the list.

The daylight faded as the unloading progressed and I

switched on all the horse van's lights, inside and out, to give passable illumination. The veterinarian gave a provisional thumbs-up to all the travelers except the last two from the forwardmost stalls, both of which had him shaking his head.

The aged pony was the worst. The poor creature could hardly stand, let alone walk down the ramp.

"Advanced laminitis," the veterinarian said. "Best to put him down."

"Certainly not," Tigwood pronounced indignantly. "He's a much-loved pet. I *promised* a comfortable home, and that's what he'll get. His owner's fifteen. She made me *promise*."

I thought of Michael Watermead's remark about his own children: "They don't understand the need for death." Tigwood understood it all right, but keeping life going at any cost was where both his income and his fanaticism seemed to lie.

"At least let me dress his alopecia," the veterinarian suggested, referring to his hair loss, and Tigwood resentfully said, "Tomorrow, then," and literally pushed the poor little beast until he had to totter down the ramp or fall down altogether.

"It's disgusting," Lizzie said under her breath.

Lorna heard and snapped at her, "It's the people who kill horses just because they're old who are disgusting." She was busy stifling her own doubts, I saw. "Old horses have a right to life. Centaur Care is a wonderful institution."

"Yes," Lizzie said dryly.

Lorna gave her an unfriendly stare which she then transferred to me.

"You don't appreciate John's work," she accused. "And

don't give me all that crap about putting animals out of their misery. You can't be sure they're miserable."

I thought it quite easy to be sure when they were, but I was not going to argue, and besides, I'd known many old horses to live healthily and happily into their middle twenties. My father, the trainer, had looked after his favorite horses until they died in the fields, feeding them oats all winter to keep them well-fleshed and warm. They had all looked better than the thin crowd of today.

I said, "It's nice to see old Peterman again and I'm sure the owners will appreciate your personal attention."

"And John's!"

"And John's," I said.

We all three watched Tigwood lead the pony towards the paddock, the sore hooves flinching at every slow step, the head bobbing low with pain. The fifteen-year-old owner, I thought, was full of love but had no mercy, a cruel combination.

Lorna tossed her fair hair, admitting no criticism. The veterinarian shook his head, Lizzie went on looking disgusted, Aziz shrugged. He'd brought them back alive: his involvement ended there.

Tigwood let the pony loose in the paddock and returned to open his office door. We all trooped in behind him, filling a functional space about fifteen feet square, lit by fluorescent strips and lined with filing cabinets. The brown composition flooring was softened by two large patterned rugs, and framed photographs of old horses in sunlit fields crowded the walls. Tigwood crossed to a pair of metal desks standing side by side, one holding a computer and printer, and the other the normal impedimenta of the pre-computer age. A row of collecting tins stood on one of the filing cabinets and a tea-making machine on another. Bookshelves conspicuously displayed publications on the medical problems and care of aged thoroughbreds. There were three comfortable-looking wool-covered armchairs and some decent blue curtains at the two windows. If any of the horses' owners ever turned up on the doorstep, the setup would give the message that here every penny was devoted to the cause, while at the same time due regard was paid to the luxury level normal to racehorse owners.

Give him his due, I thought, Tigwood had got it right; inside, at any rate.

He demanded, and the veterinarian wrote, a brief statement to the effect that six horses (names attached) had traveled without incident from Yorkshire and had arrived in good condition. One horse (name attached) showed signs of exhaustion and required special care. One pony with laminitis needed veterinarian attention. All had been transported by Croft Raceways and entrusted to Centaur Care.

Satisfied, Tigwood made a photocopy and handed it to me with a smirk, saying, "You've made a lot of fuss about nothing, Freddie. You can pay the veterinarian's bill, I'm not going to."

I shrugged. I'd called for the help and received it, and I didn't mind paying. The statement, in fact, had insulated me from any accusation of negligence Tigwood might think of making once he received my account. I said I was very glad the horses had been all right, but that it was nice to be sure, wasn't it?

With varying emotions we all left the office again, the veterinarian driving off with a wave and Tigwood and Lorna climbing back into the horse van for the run to the farmyard, where they'd both left their cars that morning. Lizzie and I followed the van, Lizzie asking whether it hadn't all been a storm in a teacup.

"Didn't your driver overreact?" she said.

"Maybe. But he's new today. And there can't be much wrong with his driving if he got them all here on their feet."

Lorna and Tigwood left the farmyard separately in individual shades of huff.

Aziz said awkwardly, "Sorry for all that." No white teeth. Shiny eyes downcast.

"Don't be sorry," I reassured him. "You did right."

Lizzie and I left him refilling his fuel tanks and went home, deciding to pause there briefly and go out to eat.

There were three callback messages on the answering machine, two business, and one Sandy Smith.

I called him back first and listened to him tell me that this was out of hours, like, and unofficial.

"Thanks, Sandy."

"Well, they did the postmortem of Jogger yesterday in the morgue of Winchester Hospital. Cause of death, broken neck. He hit the back of his head at the bottom of his skull, the top two vertebrae were dislocated, same as in hanging, but he wasn't hanged, no rope marks. Anyway, the inquest opens tomorrow in Winchester. They'll only want identification, which I'm doing myself as there's no next-of-kin, and Bruce Farway's statement, and the police photos. Then the coroner will adjourn the inquest for three weeks or so for inquiries. Routine for all accidents. You won't be needed."

"Thanks very much indeed, Sandy."

"The Ogden inquest's first thing on Thursday, same place, that's to say the coroner's court, which is a room in the police station in Winchester. The verdict will be natural causes. They won't adjourn that one. Bruce Farway will give his report. Mrs. Ogden's identified her husband. Seems

Ogden had heart trouble on and off but was bad at taking pills. Dave had better attend, though they might not call him. I'll be there too, of course."

"Great, Sandy. Thanks again."

"I drank to Jogger last night in the pub," he said. "There was quite a turnout. Loads of people signing his memorial. You'll get an astronomical bill."

"All in a good cause."

"Poor old Jogger."

"Yes," I said.

Lizzie and I settled for dinner in an old country inn ten miles from Pixhill where the specialty was duck roasted in a honey glaze to a crisp blackened skin with succulence inside. La Potinière it was not, but an old favorite place of Lizzie's, who liked the heavy oak beams, the authentically crooked walls and the low-to-dim lighting.

As Pixhill people often ate there, I was not much surprised to see Benjy and Dot Usher side by side at a booth table across the room from us. Impervious to their surroundings they were in midquarrel as usual, the two faces tight with fury six inches apart.

"Who are they?" Lizzie asked, following my gaze.

"A Pixhill millionaire who plays at training and his inseparable wife."

"Ask a silly question . . ."

"And you get a dead accurate answer."

"Really?"

"I reckon if they ever stop fighting that marriage will collapse from boredom."

I told her about my day with them at Sandown races and about Benjy's odd habit of not touching horses.

"And he's a *trainer?*"

"Of sorts. But he's also a customer, which makes him OK by me."

She studied my face with elder-sister indulgence. "I remember you once saying," she said, "that if you rode races only for people you liked you'd have missed winning the Gold Cup."

"Mm. Same theory. I'll hire out my skills to anyone for the prospect of reward."

"It sounds like prostitution."

"What isn't?"

"Pure research, for one thing. You're an absolute philistine."

"Goliath was a Philistine ... a giant of a man."

"Brought down by a slingshot."

"Sneaky."

Lizzie smiled with pleasure. "I miss you," she said.

"Me too. Tell me about Professor Quipp."

"I *knew* I shouldn't have said that about everyone finding me. You never miss a trick."

"Well, go on."

"He's nice." She sounded fond, not defensive. A good sign, given the characters of some of the past beards. "He's five years younger than I am and he adores skiing. We went to Val d'Isère for a week." Lizzie positively purred. "We raced each other down mountains."

"Um ... What color beard?"

"No beard. You're a beast. No mustache either."

It sounded serious. "What subject?" I asked.

"Actually, organic chemistry."

"Ah."

"Any more ahs and you won't get your tubes analyzed."

"Not another ah shall pass my lips."

We ate the crisp black duck and during our coffee Benjy

159

Usher took his attention off Dot long enough to notice me across the room.

"Freddie!" he shouted uninhibitedly, turning every other diner's head his way. "Come over here, you bugger."

It seemed easiest to go. I stopped at their table and said hello to Dot.

"Come and join us," Benjy commanded. "Bring the bird."

"She's my sister."

"Oh sure, pull the other one."

Benjy had had one drink too many. Dot looked embarrassed. It was for her sake, really, that I went and persuaded Lizzie to cross the carpet.

We accepted coffee from Dot and resisted Benjy's offer of huge glasses of port. When Benjy summoned another for himself, Dot said conversationally, "He's now at impotence. Paralysis next."

"Vicious bitch," Benjy said.

Lizzie's eyes widened.

Dot remarked, "Followed by vomiting, ending in tears of maudlin self-pity. He calls himself a man."

"Pre-menstrual tension," Benjy mocked. "Chronic case."

Lizzie looked at their handsome faces and casually good clothes, at the diamonds on Dot's fingers and at Benjy's gold watch. No comment was possible. None was needed. Their pleasure depended not on money but on spite.

"When are you going to Italy for my colt?" Benjy asked me.

"Monday," I suggested. "It'll take us three days. He could be here by Wednesday evening."

"Which driver? Not that one called Brett. Michael says never Brett."

"He's left. It won't be Brett."

"Send Lewis. Michael swears by *him*, and he's driven my horses a lot. That colt's valuable, you know. And send someone to look after him on the journey. Send that man of yours, that Dave. He can handle him."

"Is he difficult to handle?"

"You know colts," Benjy said expansively. "You send Dave. He'll be all right."

Dot said, "I don't know why you don't stand him at stud in Italy."

"You keep your tongue off what doesn't concern you," her husband replied.

To try to stop their argument, I mentioned that we'd that day brought the load of old horses from Yorkshire and I gathered he was giving a home to two of them.

"Those old wrecks!" Dot exclaimed. "Not *more* of them."

"Do you have some already?" Lizzie asked.

"They died," Dot told her. "I hate it. I don't want any more."

"Don't look at them," Benjy said.

"You put them outside the drawing room window."

"I'll put them *in* the drawing room. That should please you."

"You're utterly childish."

"You're utterly stupid."

Lizzie said sweetly, "It's been terribly nice meeting you," and stood up to leave, and when we were out in the Jaguar asked, "Do they always go on like that?"

"I can testify to fifteen years of it."

"Good grief." She yawned, well-fed and relaxed, sleepy. "Beautiful moon tonight. Terrific for flying."

"But you're not going tonight!"

"No, it's just a habit of mind. I think of the sky in flying terms, you think of the ground as hard or soft for horses."

"I suppose I do."

She sighed pleasurably. "Lovely car, this."

The Jaguar hummed through the night, powerful, intimate, the best wheels I'd owned. The jockeys lately seemed to have stopped buying speed in favor of middlerank family sedans, ultra-reliable but rather dull. My bit of flamboyance, alive in my hands, was no longer politically correct with the new serious lot in the changing room.

Bad luck for them, I thought. Looking back, I seemed to have laughed a lot in those years. And cursed and ached and seethed at injustices. And had a sizzling good time.

The last stretch of the road from dinner to bed went past the farmyard. I slowed automatically to glance at the row of transports gleaming in the moonlight. The gates were open, which meant that one or more vans were still out on the road, and I completed the short distance to the house wondering which one it was.

Lizzie's Robinson 22 shone in the moonlight, standing on the tarmac where the nine-van had stood with Kevin Keith Ogden on board.

"I'll leave about nine in the morning," she said, "and get your analysis started in the afternoon."

"Great." I must have sounded preoccupied. She turned her head to study me.

"What's the matter?" she asked.

"Nothing really. You go in, go to bed. I'll just nip back to the farmyard to lock the gates. There aren't any vans still out, or anyway there shouldn't be. I won't be long."

She yawned. "See you in the morning, then."

"Thanks for coming."

"I've enjoyed it."

We hugged briefly and she went in smiling. I hoped Professor Quipp would love her for a long time, as I'd never known her so at peace.

I drove the Jaguar back to the farmyard and stopped outside the gates. Someone was walking about in the yard, as Harve often did, taking care of things, and I walked towards the half-seen figure, calling "Harve?"

No answer. I walked on, reaching the nearest van, Harve's own, and passing into a patch of shadow.

"Harve," I shouted.

I heard nothing, but something hit me very hard on the back of the head.

I worked out later how long I spent unaware of the world: one hour, forty minutes.

The first sensation of the daze I awoke to was a pain in the head. The second sensation was of being carried. The third was a matter of hearing, with a voice making a nonsensical remark.

"If this doesn't give him flu, nothing will."

I was dreaming, of course.

Of course.

Soon I would wake up.

I felt I was falling. I hated dreams about falling: they were always about falling off buildings, never off horses.

I fell into water. Breathtakingly cold.

I went down into it without struggling. Wholly immersed. Went down deep.

Terrible dream.

Instinct, perhaps, switched me to reality. This was no dream, this was Freddie Croft, in his clothes, drowning.

The first awful compulsion was to take a deep breath,

and it was again subconscious knowledge, no present thought, that stopped me.

I kicked, seeking to go upwards, and felt sucked to one side and clutched by currents, a rag doll in limbo.

I kicked again with growing horror, urgency flooding finally into a response from arms and legs, muscles bunching, working hard, chest hurting, head hammering.

Swim up, for God's sake.

Swim . . . up.

I swam up in crazy panic-driven breaststrokes. Swam as if horizontal, arms sweeping, legs kicking, knowing I was also going sideways, being swept without choice.

Probably I spent barely more than a minute underwater. I breaststroked through the surface into the night and gulped air into my starved lungs with a whooping roar, and the moment I stopped swimming my heavily saturated clothes and water-filled shoes dragged me down again, down like a seesaw, ultimate terror.

The drowning come up twice, and the third time stay down . . . the bad news wisdom. I swam with ebbing strength to the surface against the weight of my clothes and the drag of the water, and its inexorable swirling suction, seeing no light anywhere, only darkness enough for one struggling gasp, and my head went under again, willpower urging me up and the salt sea claiming me for its own.

Salt sea . . . I swallowed it, gagging. Pretty well every vestige of athleticism went into lifting my nose above the surface, and kicking to stay there. In a way I knew it was a losing battle, but I couldn't accept it. If I'd been dropped off a boat, if I were alone far from land, an end would come soon, and it was intolerable. I protested furiously, vainly, against being murdered.

I saw a glitter on the water, a flash of light. The current was taking me into it, out of darkness.

Electric light.

A lamp ... high above the water ... on a *lamp standard*.

I hadn't realized how far I'd lost hope until the knowledge that electric lamp standards didn't grow in midocean hit my brain like a more friendly blow on the skull. Lamp standards equaled land. Land meant life. Life meant swimming to the lamp standard.

Simple.

Not so simple. It was all I could do to stay up. All the same, the current that had floated me from darkness to light continued its benign work, taking me towards the lamp standard, but slowly, casually, indifferent to its flotsam.

Two lamp standards.

They were above me, on top of a wall. I bumped eventually into the wall, no longer able to see the lights on their tall stalks, but knowing they were there. I was in shadow again by the wall but, looking back, I could see little lights everywhere, bright, unmoving, a whole forest of lamp standards.

The wall was smooth and slimy, without handholds. The water carried me along it slowly, sucking me away and slapping me back against it, while I kicked fearfully and with insidiously growing feebleness to stay up to breathe.

I tried shouting for help. The suck and slap and gurgle of the eddies smothered my voice. When I took a deep breath to shout again, the salt water rushed into my mouth and set me choking.

It seemed ridiculous to drown when I could actually

touch land, while the swell lifted me against safety and pulled me away again, while ten feet above me there was a dry place to walk.

I lived by luck. Lived thanks to the designer who'd built a staircase into his wall. One surge of water lifted me into a sort of hollow in the smooth cliff and the retreating ebb all but floated me out again. Almost too late I thrust my arms and hands against slippery concrete, desperate not to be dragged away, waiting . . . waiting . . . for the water to lift me again into the hollow and knowing it was the last chance, the miracle of deliverance if only I had the strength.

I rolled with the water into the hollow and pressed my body onto a sharp step; felt the tug of the receding swell and rolled against it, using the killing weight of shoes, trousers and jacket as anchor. With the next swell of water I rose to the step above and lay there immobile, head and shoulders out of the water, legs and feet still submerged. The next wave achieved for me one more step up so that I was lying on the slope of stairs, feeling hard land embrace me as if in forgiveness, as if saying, "All right, then, not yet."

The stairs were inset, parallel with the wall, the seaward side being always wide open to the water. I crawled up one step more and simply lay there, exhausted, shuddering, frozen and concussed, with almost nil activity going on in the brain box. My feet, still in the water, lifted and fell with liquid rhythm and it wasn't until one wave slapped over my knees and tried to float me out again that I sluggishly realized that the tide had to be rising and that if I didn't climb upwards I would be back where I'd come from with no strength for another fight.

I slithered up two steps. Three steps. At the top, as I looked up, stood a lamp standard.

When some semblance of strength oozed back I continued crawling, pressing myself against the inner wall, cravenly frightened of dropping off the open black edge back into the sea. True nightmares weren't about falling off buildings, I thought, they were about falling off steps built for embarking onto boats.

The endless-seeming climb ended. I slithered onto hard dusty flat dry road-surface, crawled weakly to the lamp standard and lay full length beside it, facedown, one arm hooked round it as if to convince myself that this, at least, was no dream.

I had no idea where I was. I'd been too busy trying to survive to worry about such minor details. My head throbbed. When I tried to work out why, memory got lost in a fog.

There were footsteps approaching, grittily scrunching. For a shattering moment I thought the people who'd thrown me had found me again, but the voice that spoke above me carried a different sort of threat, the heavy resentment of affronted petty authority.

"You can't lie here," he said. "Clear off."

I rolled onto my back and found myself staring straight into the eyes of a large purposeful dog. The dog pulled against a leash held by a burly figure in a navy uniform with a peaked cap and a glinting silver badge. The dog wore a light muzzle which looked inadequate for the job.

"Did you hear what I said? Clear off."

I tried to speak and achieved only an incoherent croak.

Authority looked displeased. The dog, an unfriendly rottweiler, lowered his head to mine hungrily.

Trying again, I said, "I fell in." This time the message reached its target but with moderate results.

"I don't care if you swam the Channel, get up and clear off."

I made an effort to sit up. Got as far as one elbow. The dog warily retreated a step, leaving his options open.

"Where am I?" I said.

"In the Docks, of course."

"Which docks?" I said. "Which port?"

"What?"

"I . . . I don't know where I am."

He was far from reassured by my obvious weakness. With the dog at the ready he said suspiciously, "Southampton, of course."

Southampton Docks. Why Southampton Docks? My bewilderment grew.

"Come on. Get going. No one's allowed on here when the dock's shut. And I can't stand drunks."

"I hit my head," I said.

He opened his mouth as if to say he didn't care if I'd been decapitated, but instead said grudgingly, "Did you fall off a ship?"

"I don't really know."

"You can't lie here, all the same."

I wasn't so sure I could get up and walk and he must, I thought, have seen it, as he suddenly thrust down a reaching hand to be grasped. He pulled me vigorously to my feet and I held on to the lamp standard and felt dizzy.

"You want a doctor," he said accusingly.

"Just give me a minute."

"You can't stay here. It's against orders."

Seen at level height, he was a truculent-looking fiftyish individual with a large nose and small eyes and the thin grim mouth of perpetual wariness. He'd been afraid of me, I saw.

I didn't mind the manner. To be a night watchman in a dock area was to face dangers from knaves and thieves, and a man lying where he shouldn't had to be treated as a hazard until proved to be harmless.

"Do you have a telephone?" I asked.

"In the guardroom, yes."

He didn't say I couldn't use it, which was invitation enough. I let go of the lamp standard and tottered a few shaky steps, lurching sideways off a straight line and trying hard to behave with more sense than I felt.

"Here," he said roughly, grabbing my arm. "You'll fall in again."

"Thanks."

He held my sleeve, not exactly supporting me but certainly a help. With feet that seemed hardly to belong to me I made a slow passage down a long dock and arrived finally at some large buildings.

"This way," he said, tugging my sleeve.

We went through tall iron gates in a high fence and out onto a sidewalk. A car-parking area lay ahead, followed by a low wall, with a public roadway beyond that. No traffic. I tried looking at my watch to see the time and hit a slight snag: no watch.

I peered feebly along the road in both directions while the night watchman fed a key into a lock, and I found I was looking at a recognizable landmark, somewhere I'd been before, an orientating building telling me exactly *where* I was, if still not why.

"Come in," the night watchman invited. "The phone's on the wall. You'll have to pay for it, of course."

"Mm." I nodded my assent, felt for wallet and coins,

and found neither. Nothing in any of my pockets. The night watchman observed the search judiciously.

"Have you been mugged?"

"It looks like it."

"Don't you remember?"

"No." I looked at the telephone. "I can reverse the call collect," I said.

He made an assenting wave. I took the receiver off the wall and realized that if I phoned my own house what I would get would be my answering machine. It was possible to deactivate it from a distance but not on a reverse charge call. Sighing, I got through to the number, listened to my voice saying I was out and to leave a message, and went through the switch-off routine. The night watchman asked crossly what I was doing.

"Getting the operator," I said, redialing.

The operator tried my number and said there was no answer.

"Please keep trying," I said anxiously. "I know someone's there, but she'll be asleep. You need to wake her."

Lizzie's bedroom was next to mine, where the phone would be ringing. I exhorted her silently to wake up, to tire of the ringing to get up and answer it. Come on, Lizzie . . . come on, for God's sake.

Ages seemed to pass before she finally said, "Hello?," thick with sleep. The operator, following my instructions, asked if she would take a call from her brother, Mr. Croft, in Southampton.

When she spoke to me direct she said, astonished, "Roger? Is that you? I thought you were in the Caribbean."

"It's Freddie," I said.

"But you can't be in *Southampton. Roger's* ship goes to Southampton."

170

Explaining was impossible, and besides, the night watchman was listening avidly to every word.

"Lizzie," I said desperately, "come and collect me. I've been robbed of money . . . everything. I've been in the water and I'm freezing and I hit my head, and to be honest I feel rotten. Come in the Fourtrak, it's outside on the tarmac. The key's on a hook beside the back door. Please do come."

"Heavens! Come *where*?"

"Go to the main road to Newbury, but turn south. That's the A34. It goes straight to Southampton. Follow the signs to Southampton and when you get there take the road to the docks and the Isle of Wight ferries. There are signs everywhere. I'm . . . I'm down there by the docks. The Isle of Wight ferry terminal is just along the road. I'll go there . . . and wait for you."

She said, "Are you *shivering*?"

I coughed convulsively. "Bring me some clothes. And some money."

"Freddie . . ." She sounded shocked and unsure.

"I know," I said contritely, "it's the middle of the night. It'll take you three-quarters of an hour, about . . ."

"But what *happened*? I thought you were here in bed, but you didn't answer the phone. How did you get to *Southampton*?"

"I don't know. Look, Lizzie, just come."

She made up her mind. "Isle of Wight ferry. Southampton docks. Forty-five minutes. Five more while I dress. Just hang in there, buddy boy. The cavalry's coming."

"The cinema has a lot to answer for."

"At least your sense of humor's still working."

"It's a close-run thing."

"I'll be there," she said, and put down the phone.

171

I thanked the night watchman and told him my sister would come. He thought I should have telephoned the police.

"I'd rather go home," I said, and realized I simply hadn't thought of asking for police help. That would involve too many questions and I had not enough answers. And also not enough stamina left for sitting on a hard chair in a police station, or for having my bumps read. The source of my troubles lay not in Southampton but back in Pixhill, and if the transit from one to the other was wholly blank, I did vaguely remember driving the Jaguar to the farmyard and calling to Harve.

The troubles lay on my doorstep, in my farmyard, under my trucks, in my business. I wanted to go home, to sort them out.

7

Lizzie, true to form, came to rescue her little brother.

The night watchman let me spend most of the wait in his underheated guardroom, even going so far as to brew me a cup of tea to alleviate my shivers, all under the baleful eyes of his attentive dog. When the hands of the clock on his wall stood at two, he said I'd have to leave as it was time for his rounds, so I thanked him and walked . . . well, shambled . . . along the road to the ferry terminal and sat in shadow on the sidewalk there at one end of the building, my spine against the wall, my arms hugging my knees. I'd known worse conditions, just.

Not far away, on the other side of an openwork metal fence, light glinted on water. I looked at the scene vaguely, then with speculation. I suppose there were many places

173

like that, where in darkness semiconscious people could be slid into the briny with nobody noticing. There were miles of available shoreline in Southampton Docks.

The Fourtrak came, slowed, moved hesitantly into the parking area and stopped. I stood up, pressing against the wall for support, and took a few paces forward into the light. Lizzie saw me and came running from the vehicle, stopping dead a few feet from me, wide-eyed and shocked.

"Freddie!"

"I can't look as bad as all that," I protested.

She didn't tell me how I looked. She came and draped one of my arms over her shoulders and walked with me to the Fourtrak.

"Take off that wet jacket," she commanded. "You'll die of exposure."

Marginally better than drowning, I thought, though I didn't say so.

Once inside the butty little vehicle I struggled out of all the wet things and put on the dry substitutes, including fleece-lined boots and the warmest padded jacket I owned. When Lizzie coped she did nothing by halves.

I got her to drive as near the guardroom as we could manage. The night watchman and his dog were at home again and issued forth suspiciously. When I offered him money for the first telephone call and for his trouble and kindness he at first refused it with indignation, raising one's regard for the salt of the British earth.

"Take it," I urged, "I owe you. Drink to my health."

He took the note dubiously, only half concealing his pleasure.

"You'll get pneumonia anyway, shouldn't wonder," he said.

The way I felt, he might well be right.

Lizzie drove back home the way she'd come, darting glances at me every few seconds. The cold-induced shudders and shakes gradually abated in my body until eventually even my guts felt warmed again, but conversely along with warmth came overwhelming tiredness so that all I wanted was to lie down and sleep.

"But what *happened*?" Lizzie asked.

"I went to the farmyard."

"You said you were going to close the gates," she said, nodding.

"Did I? Well . . . someone hit me on the head."

"Freddie! Who?"

"Don't know. When I woke up I was being dropped into water. Just as well I did wake up, really."

She was predictably horrified. "They meant you to drown!"

"I don't know about that." I'd been puzzled ever since I'd been conscious. "If they wanted me dead, why not finish the job on my head? Why take me all the way to Southampton Docks? If they wanted particularly to drown me, there's a perfectly good pond in Pixhill."

"Don't joke about it."

"May as well," I said. "All I remember about them is someone saying, 'If this doesn't give him flu, nothing will.' "

"But that's nonsensical!"

"Mm."

"How many of them?"

"There had to be two at least. If not, why bother to talk?"

"Are you *sure* that's what they said?"

"Pretty sure."

"What sort of accent? Did you know the voice?"

"No." I answered the second first. "Not an Eton accent. Rough, sort of."

Lizzie said, "You'll have to tell the police."

I was silent, and she glanced at me too lengthily, even for light traffic.

"You'll have to," she said.

"Keep your eyes on the road."

"You're a shit."

"Yep."

She drove, however, with more attention to getting us home safely and I wondered what good it might really do if I bothered to tell the police.

They would take a statement. They might check with the night watchman that I had in fact crawled out of Southampton Water. I could tell them that as I hadn't known until five minutes beforehand that I was going along to the farmyard, there hadn't been any sort of pre-meditated ambush. I'd walked in when I was unexpected and been smartly prevented from finding out who was there and what they were doing.

Taking me to Southampton must equally have been impulsive. Throwing me in alive but apparently unconscious meant they hadn't much cared if I lived or died . . . almost as if they hadn't made up their minds on that point and were leaving it to fate.

Nonsensical, as Lizzie'd said. Anyone, especially the police, would be skeptical. And what would the force do about it? They couldn't and wouldn't guard me day and night against illogical possible attempted murder. If I didn't walk unexpectedly into shadows at night, why should anyone attack me again?

Probably a lot of that creaky reasoning was the result of concussion. More likely it stemmed from the usual aver-

sion to less-than-friendly questioning, where crime was
seen to be the fault of the victim.

I gingerly felt the back of my by then mutedly throbbing
head, wincing at the actual contact. Any blood that had
been there had been washed away. My hair had dried.
There was a lump and a soreness, but no gaping cut and
no dent in my skull. As injuries went, compared with the
assaults of steeplechasing, it was of the "it'll be all right
tomorrow" kind. To have been knocked out racing meant
to be grounded by the doctors for up to three weeks. I
would ground myself for the rest of the night, I thought,
and maybe I wouldn't go to Cheltenham until Thursday.
That should do it.

The Fourtrak hummed us home, the road direct. Southampton Docks was the nearest deep water to Pixhill: the
nearest tidal place where unseen bodies could wash out on
the ebb before dawn.

Stop thinking about it, I told myself. I was alive and dry
and nightmares could wait.

Lizzie turned into the driveway and curled round the
house and we found something absolutely rotten had happened while we'd been away.

My Jaguar XJS, my beautiful car, had been run at full
tilt into Lizzie's Robinson 22. The two sweet machines
were tangled together, locked in deep metallic embrace,
both twisted and crushed, the Jaguar's buckled hood rising
into the helicopter's cab, whose round bubble front had
been smashed into jagged pieces. The landing struts had
buckled so that the aircraft's weight sank into the car's
roof; the rotor blades were tilted at a crazy angle, one of
them snapped off on the ground.

All one could say was that nothing had caught fire or

exploded. In every other way, the two fast engines, our pleasure, our soulmates, were dead.

The house's outside lights were on, raising gleams on the double wreck. It was spectacular, in a macabre sort of way; a shining union.

Lizzie braked the Fourtrak to a jolting halt and sat hand over mouth, disbelievingly stunned. I slowly stepped down from the passenger's seat and walked towards the mess, but there was nothing to be done. It would take a crane and a tow truck to tear that marriage apart.

I walked back towards Lizzie, who was standing on the tarmac saying, "Oh my God, oh my God . . ." and trying not to weep.

I put my arms round her. She sobbed dryly against my chest.

"Why?" She choked on the word. *"Why?"*

I had no answer, just an ache, for her, for me, for the wanton destruction of efficiency.

In Lizzie the grief turned quickly to rage and to hatred and to hunger for revenge.

"I'll *kill* the bastard. I'll kill him. I'll cut his throat."

She walked round the helicopter banging it with her fist.

"I love this bloody machine. I love it. I'll kill the bastard . . ."

I felt much the same. I thought mutely that at least we ourselves were alive, even though in my case only just, and that perhaps, that was enough.

I said, "Lizzie, come away, there's fuel in the tanks."

"I can't smell any." She came to my side, however. "I'm so furious I could *burst*."

"Come inside and have a drink."

She walked jerkily with me to the back door.

The door had a pane of glass broken.

"Oh *no*!" Lizzie said.

I tried the handle. Open.

"I locked it," she said.

"Mm."

It had to be faced. I went into the big room and tried to switch on a light. The switch had been hacked out of the wall. It was only by moonlight that one could see the devastation.

At a guess, it had been done in a frenzy, with an ax. Things weren't just broken, but sliced open. There was light enough to see the slashes in the furniture, the smashed table lamps, the ruin of the television set, the computer monitor sliced in two, the rips in my leather chair, the raw pieces gouged out of my antique desk.

Everything, it seemed, had been attacked. Books and papers lay ripped on the floor. The daffodils I'd picked for Lizzie had been stamped on, the Waterford vase that had held them crushed to slivers.

The framed photographs of my racing days were off the walls and beyond repair. Our mother's rare collection of china birds was history.

It was the birds that seemed to upset Lizzie most. She sat on the floor with tears running into her mouth, holding the pathetic irreplaceable pieces to her lips as if to comfort them. Grieving for our childhood, for our parents, for life gone by.

I went on a wander round the rest of the house but no other rooms had been invaded: only the heart of things, where I lived.

The telephone on my desk would never ring again. The answering machine had been hacked in two. I went out to the phone in the Fourtrak and woke Sandy Smith.

"Sorry," I said.

He came in his car with his uniform pulled on over his pajamas, the navy blue jacket unbuttoned, hairy chest visible. He stood looking in awe at the amalgam of Jaguar and helicopter, and brought a flashlight with him into the house.

The beam shone on Lizzie, the birds, the tears.

"Done you proper," Sandy said to me, and I nodded.

"Morning, miss," he said to Lizzie, the polite greeting bizarre but the intention kind enough.

To me he said, "Do you know who did it?"

"No."

"Vandalism," he said. "Nasty."

I felt the most appalling, heart-bumping apprehension and asked him to drive down with me to the farmyard.

He understood my fear and agreed to go at once. Lizzie stood up, still holding a wing and a bird's head and said she would come with us, we couldn't leave her alone in the house.

We went in Sandy's car, its lights flashing but its siren silent. The farmyard gates still stood open, but to my almost sick relief the horse vans themselves were untouched.

The offices were locked. My keys had long vanished but, seen dimly through windows, the three rooms looked as orderly as usual. The canteen, door open, had been left alone.

I went along to the barn. The tool storeroom was secure. Nothing looked out of place. I went back to Sandy and Lizzie and reported: no damage and no one about.

Sandy stared at me strangely.

"Miss Croft," he said, "tells me someone tried to kill you."

"Lizzie!" I protested.

Lizzie said, "Constable Smith wanted to know where we were when all that . . . that wicked destruction . . . was going on at the house. I had to tell him. I couldn't avoid it."

"I don't know that anyone actually meant to kill me," I said. I told Sandy briefly about waking up in Southampton. "Maybe the reason for taking me there was to give time for attacking my house."

Sandy thought things over, buttoned his tunic absent-mindedly and announced that all things considered he had better report to his headquarters.

"Can't it wait till later this morning?" I said. "I could do with some sleep."

"You've had two dead men on your premises since last Thursday," Sandy pointed out. "And now this. I'll be in trouble, Freddie, if I don't report it at once."

"The two dead men were accidental."

"Your house isn't."

I shrugged and leaned on his car while he telephoned. No, he was saying, no one was dead, no one was injured, the damage was to property. He gave the address of my house and listened to instructions, relaying them to me after. In effect, two plainclothes detectives would come in due course.

"How long is due course?" Lizzie asked.

"There's a major flap on in Winchester," Sandy said. "So . . . whenever they can."

"Why do you say no one was injured?" Lizzie sounded indignant. "Freddie was injured."

Sandy eyed me with long knowledge. "Injured to him means both legs broken and his guts hanging out."

"Men!" Lizzie said.

Sandy said to me, "Do you want me to call out Doc Farway?"

"No, I don't."

He listened to my emphatic reply and smiled at Lizzie. "See?"

"What time is it?" I asked.

Sandy and Lizzie both looked at their watches. "Three thirty-two," Sandy said with precision. "My message to headquarters was timed at three twenty-six."

Still leaning on Sandy's car, I couldn't decide which to guard, my business or my home. The damage already done might not be all. With such wanton pointless behavior as stamping on daffodils, logical prediction could get nowhere. The graffiti mind, the urge to throw stones at windows, looting, destruction for its own sake, they were the natural glee of untamed humanity. It was civilization and social conscience that were artificial.

The side door of Harve's house opened directly into the farmyard. He came hurrying out in jeans, shrugging his arms into an anorak, anxiety plain.

"Freddie! Sandy!" His relief was partial. "One of my kids got up for a pee and woke me to say there was a police car by the horse vans. What's happened?" He looked along the intact row of vehicles and repeated, puzzled, "What's the matter?"

"Some vandals broke into my house," I explained. "We came to see if they'd been here too, but they haven't."

Harve looked more worried, not less.

"I walked round late," he said. "It was all OK."

"What time?" I asked.

"Oh, I'd say about ten."

"Um," I said, "you weren't out here by any chance an hour or so later? You didn't hear anything?"

He shook his head. "When I went in I watched a video

of a football match for a while, and went to bed." He still looked anxious. "Why?"

"I came here at roughly half-past eleven. The gates were open and someone was moving about. I thought it was you."

"No, not that late. I shut the gate at ten. Everyone was back by then, see?"

"Thanks, Harve."

"Who was here at half-past eleven?" he demanded.

"That's rather the point. I don't know. I didn't see anyone close enough to recognize whether I knew them or not."

"But if they didn't do any damage . . ." Harve frowned. "What were they here for?"

It was a question worth answering but I was not at that moment going to put forward the one reason I could think of. It was logical, besides: perhaps too logical for the poltergeist-type irrationality of so much that had happened that night.

Sandy and Lizzie between them told Harve about my bit of seaside bathing, Harve looking increasingly horrified.

"You might have drowned!" he said, exclaiming.

"Mm. But there we are, I didn't." I belatedly asked Harve to keep watch in the farmyard for what was left of the night. "Doze in your own van," I suggested, "and phone me the minute you see anything odd."

With his promise to do that once he'd told his wife and brought a hot drink and a blanket, I went back to my house with Sandy and Lizzie and left them in the kitchen tut-tutting at life over steaming tea. As for me, I went wearily upstairs, decided to shower, lay down instead on top of the duvet for a minute still in fleecy boots and padded jacket, felt the world whirl briefly and fell instantly and comprehensively asleep.

I didn't wake until Lizzie shook me, her voice urgent. "Freddie! Freddie, are you all right?"

"Mm." I struggled from the depths. "What is it?"

"The police are here."

"What?"

Realization and remembrance came back with unwelcome clarity. I groaned. I felt unwell. I inconsequentially thought of Alfred, King of Wessex, who delivered his country from Danish invaders although suffering from half the diseases known to the ninth century. Such fortitude! And he could write and translate Latin as well.

"Freddie, the police want to talk to you."

King Alfred had had hemorrhoids, I'd read once. With all that on his mind, no wonder he'd let the cakes burn.

"Freddie!"

"Tell them I'll be down in five minutes."

When she'd gone I took off the night's clothes, showered, shaved, dressed again in fresh things, combed my hair carefully and, at least on the outside, began to look like F. Croft Esquire, master of a few things he would rather not have surveyed.

The sitting room looked no better in the opal light of dawn, and the soul had gone out of the tangled heap of metal that had been my precious car. I walked from one disaster to the other with the policemen, who weren't the two who had come to Jogger. There were older, wearier, hard worked and unimpressed by my troubles, which they seemed to suggest I had brought on myself. I answered their questions monosyllabically, partly from malaise, chiefly from ignorance.

No, I didn't know who had done the damage.

No, I couldn't guess.

No, I knew of no one who held a business grudge against me.

Had I dismissed a worker? No. One had recently left of his own choice.

Had I had any personal enemies? None that I knew of.

I must have some, they said. Everyone had enemies.

Well, I thought privately, reflecting on Hugo Palmerstone, I had no personal enemy who could be sure my house would be empty at two A.M. on the Wednesday morning of Cheltenham races. Not unless, of course, they'd tapped me on the head ...

Who hated me this much? If I knew, I said, I would certainly tell.

Had anything been stolen?

That question stopped me short. So many things had been smashed that I hadn't thought of theft. My car could have been stolen. My television, my computer, the china birds, the Waterford vase, all had had value. I hadn't, I said lamely, inspected my safe.

They accompanied me indoors again, looking as if they couldn't believe I hadn't checked the safe first.

"There isn't much in there," I said.

"Money?"

"Yes, money."

How much was not much? Less than a thousand, I said.

The safe stood in the corner behind my desk, its fireproof metal casing camouflaged inside a polished wooden cabinet. The unharmed cabinet doors opened easily but the combination lock inside had been chopped about with the same heavy cutting edge as everything else. The lock had withstood the assault, but its mechanism proved to be jammed.

"Nothing's been stolen," I said. "The safe won't open."

The Fax machine on top of the safe's cabinet would send no more messages. The copier on the table alongside had copied its last. A simple blow to each had ended their lives.

My own anger, not blazing, immediate and tearful like Lizzie's, but a slow inner burn of fury, increased sharply at the spiteful splitting of two machines I—and the insurance—could easily replace. The cruelty got to me. Whoever had done all this, whoever had thrown me into the water, had meant me to suffer, had meant me to feel as I felt. I would give no one the extra pleasure, I resolved, of hearing me scream and moan. I would find out who and why, and even the score.

The police asked about my trip to Southampton but I could tell them very little: I'd been dropped into the water, I'd swum, I'd climbed out, I'd phoned my sister to collect me.

No, I hadn't seen who hit me.

No, I hadn't seen a doctor. No need.

In the middle of telling them I didn't remember anything at all of the journey to Southampton, I began to know that at some point or other I had had my eyes open. I'd seen the moonlight. I'd even spoken. I'd said, "Beautiful night for flying." Delirious.

"If this doesn't give him flu, nothing will . . ."

They had known, I thought, that I was at least semiconscious when they tipped me in.

Concussion was unpredictable, as I'd found at other times. Bits of memory could surface long after the impact. One could also appear to be conscious—people would say one had walked and talked—but afterwards one couldn't remember that. Total recall could happen hours, days or weeks after the event, or sometimes remain blank forever.

I could remember the grass hitting my face one time; I could remember the fence I'd fallen at in the second race of the day and I could remember which horse I'd been riding. I still had no memory of driving to the racecourse that morning, or of the first race which, the record books told me, I had won by seven lengths half an hour before the fall.

I had traveled to Southampton in the trunk of an ordinary car. The knowledge drifted in. I didn't know how I knew, but I was sure.

The police had brought a photographer who took a few flash shots and departed, and a fingerprinter who stayed longer but gave his opinion in one succinct word, "Gloves."

Lizzie mooned round her helicopter, stroking it now and then and muttering "Bastards" under her breath. She said she would have to fly back to Edinburgh on the shuttle, as she had a lecture to give that afternoon. She vowed her partners in the helicopter would *strangle* whoever had crunched it.

Find him first, I thought.

The morning seemed disjointed. The police wrote a statement which put what they'd found and what I'd told them into police-force language, and I signed it in the kitchen. Sandy made tea. The other policemen, sipping, said "Ta."

"Ta," I said too. Light-headed, I thought.

One of the policemen said he believed the damage to my property to be a personal vendetta. He suggested I should think about it. He thought I might know who had attacked me. He cautioned me against taking a personal revenge.

"I don't know who did it," I said truthfully. "I would tell you if I did."

He looked as if he didn't believe me. "Think it over, sir," he said.

I stifled a spurt of irritation and thanked him for coming. Lizzie walked into the kitchen saying "Bastards" quite loudly. I wanted to laugh. She took a mug of tea and walked out.

When his colleagues had gone, Sandy said awkwardly, "They're good lads, you know."

"I'm sure."

"They've seen too much," he said. "I've seen too much myself. It's hard to feel sympathy over and over. We end up not feeling it. See what I mean?"

"You're a good lad yourself, Sandy," I said.

He looked gratified and gave me his own commendation in return.

"You're well-liked in Pixhill," he said. "I never heard anyone bad-mouth you. I reckon if you'd had enemies this bad, I'd have heard of it."

"I'd have thought I'd have heard of it, too."

"I reckon this was destruction for its own sake. They enjoyed it."

I sighed. "Yes."

"Three times this last week," he said, "someone's run a supermarket cart straight into the side of a car in the car park in Newbury. Smashed the sides of the cars right in, all crumpled and scratched. Not for any reason except just to do damage. People come back to find it and it's their frustration that's the worst. The supermarket employs a guard, but no one's caught the vandal yet. You can't deal with that sort of vandalism. And if he's caught red-handed one day, all he'll get is probation."

"He's probably a teenager."

Sandy nodded. "They're the worst. But arsonists, remember, are usually a bit older. And it wasn't no teenager, I'd reckon, that got into this house."

"What age, then?"

Sandy pursed his lips. "Twenties. Thirties perhaps. Not much older than forty. After that the driving force weakens. You don't get sixty-year-olds doing this sort of thing. It's fraud that sees *them* in court."

I pondered a few things and said, "You know Jogger's tools were stolen from his van?"

"Aye. I heard."

"He had an ax in the van."

Sandy stared. "I thought it was mechanic's tools."

"There was a slider, and in a big open red plastic crate he had a hydraulic jack, spanners, tire irons, jump leads, pliers, wiring, a grease gun, cleaning rags, all sorts of oddments ... and an ax, like firemen use, that he'd carried ever since a tree fell across one of the vans. Before I owned the business, that was."

Sandy nodded. "I remember. In one of those hurricane-like winds."

"You might keep an eye out for Jogger's stuff, in the village."

"I'll put the word around," he said earnestly.

"Say there would be a reward. Nothing fancy, but worthwhile for good information."

"Yeah, right."

"It'll be Jogger's inquest at any minute," I said.

Sandy looked at his watch in alarm. "I'll have to be going. I've not shaved yet, or dressed."

"I expect you'll phone later."

He promised he would, and drove away. Lizzie yawned into the kitchen and announced that if I needed her she would be upstairs asleep. I would wake her, please, at eleven, and drive her to Heathrow to catch the shuttle. She had just on my bedroom phone told one of her partners of

189

the demise of the Robinson 22. He was speechless, she said. He would inform the insurers when he got his voice back and probably I would be hearing from them, as they were bound to send an inspector. Did I mind leaving my car where it was until after that? No, I supposed I didn't.

She gave me an absentminded kiss on the cheek and advised me to go back to bed.

"I'm going to the farmyard," I said. "Too much to do."

"Then lock the door behind you, there's a dear."

I locked the back door and drove to the farmyard, finding Nina there drinking coffee in the canteen with Nigel. They were discussing the journey to fetch Jericho Rich's daughter's show jumper from France, Nina seeming oblivious to Nigel's dark-lashed eyes and sultry mouth. They had heard from Harve all about the night's alarms and were glad, they said, to find me functioning.

Nina brought her coffee and followed me into the office.

"Are you really all right?" she inquired.

"More or less."

"I've some news for you," she said, and paused, "but . . ."

"Fire away. Is it the little glass tubes?"

"What? No, not those, there hasn't been a report on those yet. No, this is that advertisement in *Horse and Hound*."

I thought back. So much seemed to have crowded in since Sunday. "Oh yes . . . the transport ad. 'Anything considered.' "

"Yes, that's right. Patrick got the magazine to tell him who had inserted it. And it's rather extraordinary . . ."

"Do go on."

"It was a Mr. K. Ogden of Nottingham."

"No!" My eyebrows shot up. "Well, well, that really *is* extraordinary."

"I thought you'd think so. The magazine said they checked him out the first time he ran the ad. They wanted to make sure there was nothing criminal in it. Seems they were satisfied Mr. Ogden was harmlessly offering his services as an adviser or personal courier, rather on the lines of a universal aunt. The phone number in the advertisement is that of his own house. The magazine checked it. They supposed he must be getting work from the ad, as he's kept on paying for the insertions."

"Wow," I said blankly. "He can't have been doing too well, though. He was wanted for bouncing checks and other pathetic bits of fraud. He might have seemed bona-fide to the *Horse and Hound*—and maybe he was once—but I'd guess he'd stopped worrying about the legality of every transaction, as long as he was being paid."

"You can't assume that," she protested primly.

"Stands to reason." I shrugged. "But I'll give him the benefit of the doubt. Maybe he didn't know there were six tubes in the thermos. Just maybe. I wouldn't bet on it."

"Cynic."

"I'd be cynical about anything after last night."

"What do the police think about last night?"

"They didn't say much. They said it was a wise man who knew his own enemies, or words to that effect."

"Oh." She blinked. "And do you?"

"I think Sandy Smith's right. Smashing up my things was out-of-control vandalism, done on the pleasure principle. I think I walked into the farmyard when I wasn't expected, and the rest was embroidery. Infantile glee. Sly childish impulse to hurt."

"Some child, by the sound of things."

191

"An immature adult, then."

"Or a psychotic."

"A better word for it."

She finished her coffee. "I suppose we'd better get on if we're to catch that ferry. Realistically, is anything odd likely to happen on this trip?"

"I don't know. Did I tell you exactly where the container is, under your van?"

"Not exactly, no."

"It's a metal tube fixed fore and aft in a space that runs beneath the floorboards and above the fuel tanks. That space is outside the main longitudinal struts of the chassis, but hidden by the coachwork sides. You can't see the space from the outside or from underneath, but if you know the tube's there, it's easily accessible. You can screw the end of it on and off without trouble, Jogger said."

"I might go under and take a look."

Rather her than me. "Nigel was going to make a new slider for rolling underneath," I said.

"Yes, he made it. He was showing it to Harve."

"If you want to look, use the slider. Tell Harve and Nigel I told you there's a diesel inspection sort of glass bowl screwed on underneath, on the fuel line between the tanks and the engine. You can check by that that the diesel's clean. If it is, the bowl will look clear. Any dirt in the diesel drops into the bowl and one can unscrew it and clean it out. We had a filthy lot of fuel delivered once. The inspection globe was black with muck. Anyway, tell Harve you want to see it."

"I had an inspection arrangement in my own van."

"Sorry, I forgot."

She smiled. "I'll take a look."

She went out and did so. Harve and Nigel thought her

fussy, she said, coming back and brushing off dust. "And you could smuggle anything in that tube," she added. "I'll keep an eye on it." She looked at the telephone. "A quick word with Patrick, do you mind?"

"Go ahead."

She phoned him at home because of the early hour and told him Harve's version of the night's events, checking each statement with me with her eyebrows. I nodded a few times. The gist was right; the omissions had been my own.

"Patrick," she said to me, "wants to know what it was you walked in on."

"When I find out, I'll tell him."

"He says to be careful."

"Mm."

Harve rapped on the window, pointing at his watch.

"Got to go," Nina said. " 'Bye, Patrick. 'Bye, Freddie. I'm on my way."

I was sorry to see her depart. Except for Sandy and Lizzie, she was the only person around that I found I trusted. Suspicion was a nasty, unaccustomed companion.

Nigel drove out of the farmyard. From the cab Nina waved back to me as I watched from the window.

Reckoning that all good horse people by that time would be up and about, I phoned Jericho Rich's daughter and told her that her transport was rolling and she should have her new horse with her by the next evening, soon after eight o'clock, if that would suit her.

"So soon? What service!" she exclaimed. "Did you send that groom—Dave, is it?—that my father suggested?"

"Not Dave, but someone as good."

"Oh, well, great. Thank you."

"A pleasure," I said, meaning it. And that's what it was:

a pleasure to get a neat job done and more than satisfy customers.

Another more-than-satisfied customer at that moment drove into the farmyard in a jeep from which every comfort had been stripped by time and hard usage. Marigold English, again in basic clothes and woolly hat, jumped out of her vehicle almost before it had stopped rolling and looked about her for signs of life.

I went out to meet her.

"Morning, Marigold. How are you settling in?"

"Hello, Freddie. Feel as if I've lived here for centuries." Her smile came and went. Her voice, as always, was geared to the deaf. "I'm on my way up to the Downs but I thought I'd just call in for a brief word. I phoned your house but some female said you were here."

"My sister," I said.

"Oh, yes? Well, look, what do you know about this John Tigwood and some sort of ancient horse retirement scheme? The fellow wants to rope me in. What do I do? Tell me frankly. No one can overhear you. Give!"

I gave it to her as frankly as seemed prudent. "He's a dedicated sort of man who persuades a lot of people round here to give old horses good homes. Michael Watermead's taking two of the new batch we brought to Pixhill yesterday. So is Benjy Usher, unless Dot puts her considerable foot down. There's no harm in it, if you've got room and grass."

"Would you say yes to him, then?"

"It's a regular charity in Pixhill." I thought for a moment and said, "Actually, one of this new lot is a horse I used to ride long ago. A great performer. A great buddy. Could you ask John Tigwood to let you have that particular horse? His name's Peterman. If you'd feed him oats regularly to keep him healthy and warm, I'll pay for them."

"So there's a soft heart inside there!" she teased me.

"Well . . . he won races for me."

"OK, I'll phone this Tigwood and offer the deal. Peterman, did you say?"

I nodded. "Don't mention the oats."

She gave me a slanted glance of friendly amusement. "One of these days your good deeds will find you out."

She sped back to the jeep, revved up the engine and tore another millimeter off the tire treads. Out of where there might once have been a window she yelled as she rolled forward, "My secretary will contact yours about Doncaster."

I shouted thanks which she probably didn't hear above the whine of ancient gears. I thought she would be good for Pixhill and hoped she would prosper.

Various drivers came to work and went into the canteen. Harve's account of my nocturnal experiences had them all coming outdoors again, gaping, carrying coffee mugs and inspecting me as if I were somehow unreal.

One of the drivers was the Watermead family's favorite. Lewis, the whiz with the rabbits, supposedly nursing his woes in bed.

"What happened to the flu?" I asked him.

He sniffed and with a hoarse throat said, "Reckon it's just a cold after all. No temperature, see?" He coughed and sneezed, spraying infections regardless.

"It's better you don't scatter your germs anyway," I said. "We've too many sick drivers as it is. Take another day off."

"Straight up?"

"Come back on Friday, work Saturday too."

"OK," he wheezed nonchalantly. "I'll sit and watch Cheltenham. Thanks."

Phil, obliging, phlegmatic, unobservant, incurious and unimaginatively reliable, said to me, "Is it true your house got trashed?"

" 'Fraid so."

"And *that* Jag?"

"Yeah."

"I'd kill the bugger," he said.

"Just give me the chance."

The others nodded, understanding the feeling. No one, in their collective ethos, no one messed with their belongings without reprisals.

"I suppose," I said, "that none of you came past the farmyard after eleven last night?"

No one had, it seemed.

Lewis said, "Didn't you see who had a go at you?"

"Didn't even hear anyone. Ask around, will you?"

They said they would, dubious and willing.

Many of the drivers looked superficially alike, I thought, surveying the group. All under forty, none of them fat. Mostly dark-haired, all with good eyesight, none very short or over six feet: the physique that went best with the job. In character . . . different matter.

Lewis had joined the force two years ago with ringlets. When the other drivers called him "girlie," he'd grown a slab of mustache and thrown his fists about to silence sarcastic tongues. He'd then produced a blonde bimbo in scarlet stilettos and again thrown his fists about to silence wolf whistles. During the last past summer he'd cut the hair and shaved off the mustache and the bimbo had brought forth a son over which both parents drooled. Lewis couldn't wait, he often said, to play football with his infant. The complete instant father, transformed.

"Don't sneeze on the baby," I told him, and alarmed, he said, "No way."

Dave creaked in through the gates on his rusty bicycle, cheeky and cheery and as irresponsible as ever. His grin and his freckles gave an impression of eternal youth, the Peter Pan syndrome. Dave's wife mothered him along with their two daughters, putting up large-heartedly with his pub-haunting habits and his betting on greyhounds.

Aziz arrived also, dark eyes and white teeth a-flashing. Harve detailed the day's jobs, checking with a list, making sure each driver knew exactly where to go, which horses to collect and when they had to arrive.

I left them all telling Dave and Aziz of my night's adventures, hearing mistakes creeping into the retelling but not bothering to interrupt and put them right.

"Portsmouth Docks," Phil was erroneously saying, with Dave understandingly nodding. Although we never used Southampton for horses we did occasionally ship them by ferry from Portsmouth to Le Havre. The drivers all knew Portsmouth Docks, even though I preferred to send horses by the Dover-Calais route, because the sea crossing was shorter. Many horses suffered from seasickness on long crossings, made all the worse through being unable to vomit. A horse had died once of seasickness in one of my vans, which made me especially aware of the danger.

"Portsmouth Docks." The drivers were all nodding. Portsmouth, just along the coast from Southampton, sounded more familiar. "Bulldozed his Jaguar ..." "Broke all the glass in the house ..."

Down the boozer, as Jogger would have said, they'd have me dropped over the side of the Portsmouth–Le Havre ferry by nightfall, with my car through the window in the sitting room.

Isobel and Rose arrived and complained again about the defunct state of the computer. I thought of the even more defunct state of the terminal in my sitting room and with an effort remembered that this was the day appointed for the man to fix it. Isobel and Rose took the shrouds off the superseded mechanical typewriters and looked pathetically martyred.

I phoned the central agency that kept my credit card numbers and asked them to get busy putting a stop on my accounts, and I got through to the insurance company who said they would send a form. Would they be sending a *man*, I asked, or of course a woman, who would verify the writeoff of the Jaguar and so much else of my property? They said a copy of the police report would be enough.

After that I sat and listened to my head aching while Harve finished getting the day's work organized. Aziz came into the office with his double ration of vitality and asked if there were any personal errands he could run for me. I considered it thoughtful of him, particularly as his manner was casual and, as far as I could see, not self-serving.

"Harve says there isn't a driving job for me today," he said. "He said to ask if you wanted me to do maintenance, as you've lost your mechanic. He said two of the vans need oil changes."

"It would be helpful." I picked up the tool storeroom keys out of the desk and handed them to him. "You'll find all you need in there. Get a check list from Isobel and return it to her when you've filled it in and signed it."

"Right."

"And Aziz . . ." My aching head came up with a therapeutic idea. "Would you mind driving my Fourtrak to Heathrow, to take my sister to catch the shuttle to Edinburgh?"

"Be glad to," he said willingly.

"Eleven o'clock at my house."

"On the dot," he agreed.

With Aziz driving Lewis's van along to the barn for its oil change and with the others thinning out as they left on the day's missions, I drove home to say goodbyes to Lizzie and beg her forgiveness for sending her with Aziz.

"You're more concussed than you want to say," she accused me. "You should be in bed, resting."

"Oh, sure."

She shook her head in older-sisterly disapproval and rubbed her hand down my back in the gesture she'd always used to show affection for two little brothers who'd thought kissing was sissy.

"Look after yourself," she said.

"Mm. You too."

The phone rang: Isobel's agitated voice. "The computer man's here," she said. "He says someone's killed off our machine with a virus."

8

The computer man, perhaps twenty, with long light brown hair through which he ran his fingers in artistic affectation every few seconds, had given up trying to resuscitate our hardware by the time I got back to the office.

"What virus?" I asked, coming to a halt by Isobel's desk and feeling overly beleaguered. We had flu, we had aliens, we had bodies, we had vandals, we had concussion. A virus in the computer could take the camel to its knees.

"All our *records*," Isobel mourned.

"And our *accounts*," chimed Rose.

"It's prudent to make backups," the computer man told them mock-sorrowfully, his young face more honestly full of scorn. "Always make backups, ladies."

"Which virus?" I asked again.

He shrugged, including me in his stupidity rating. "Maybe Michelangelo . . . Michelangelo activates on March 6 and there's still a lot of it about."

"Enlarge," I said.

"Surely you know?"

"If I knew, I've forgotten."

He spelled it out as to an illiterate. "March 6 is Michelangelo's birthday. If you have the virus lying doggo in your computer and you switch on your computer on March 6, the virus activates."

"Mm. Well, March 6 was last Sunday. No one switched on this computer on Sunday."

Isobel's large eyes opened wider. "That's right."

"Michelangelo is a boot-section virus," the expert said, and to our blank-looking expressions long-sufferingly explained. "Just switching the machine on does the trick. Simply switching it on, waiting a minute or two, and switching off. Switching on is called booting-up. All the records on the hard disk are wiped out at once with Michelangelo and you get the message saying 'Fatal disk error.' That's what's happened to your machine. The records are gone. There's no putting them back."

Isobel stared at me, conscience-stricken, appalled and distressed. "You did tell us to make backup floppy disks. I know you did. You kept on telling us. I'm ever so sorry. I'm so *sorry*."

"You should have *insisted*," Rose told me. "I mean you should have *made* us."

"You don't even seem *worried*," Isobel said.

To the computer man I said, "Would the virus activate on backup floppy disks?"

"Pretty likely."

"But we've got hardly any," Isobel wailed.

We did, as it happened, have comprehensive backup disks containing everything the two secretaries had entered up to and including the previous Thursday. I knew they'd found the daily backup procedure a bit of a bore. I'd seen them leave it for days, sometimes. I'd reminded both of them over and over to make copies and was aware they thought I nagged them unnecessarily. The computer seemed everlastingly reliable. In the end I'd taken to making daily backups myself on the terminal in my sitting room, storing the disks in my safe. If you want a thing done properly, as my mother had been accustomed to say, do it yourself.

At that exact moment, though the copies existed, they couldn't be reached owing to the axed state of the safe's combinations.

I could have reassured them all about our records and normally would have done. Suspicion stopped me. Suspicion about I didn't know what. But it was altogether too much of a coincidence for me that the computer should crash at that particular time.

"You're not alone," the computer man said. "Doctors, law firms, all sorts of businesses, have had their records wiped out. One woman lost a whole book she was writing. And it costs *nothing* to make backups."

"Oh dear." Isobel was near tears.

"What exactly *is* a virus?" Rose inquired miserably.

"It's a program that tells the computer to jumble up or wipe out everything stored in it." He warmed to his subject. "There are at least three thousand viruses floating around. There's Jerusalem II that activates every Friday the thirteenth, that's a specially nasty one. It's caused a lot of trouble, has that one."

"But what's the *point*?" I asked.

"Vandalism," he said cheerfully. "Destruction and wrecking for its own sake." He ran his fingers through his hair. "For instance, I could design a sweet little virus that would make all your accounts come out wrong. Nothing spectacular like Michelangelo, not a complete loss of everything, just enough to drive you mad. Just enough to make errors so that you'd be forever checking and adding and nothing would ever come out right." He loved the idea, one could see. "Once you've written a program like that you have to *spread* it. I mean, one computer can catch the virus from another, that's the beauty of it. All you need is a floppy disk with the virus in it. Feed the disk into any computer and transfer the data on the disk into the computer—which is done all the time—and bingo, the computer then has the virus inside it, lying in wait."

"How do you stop it?" I asked.

"There are all sorts of expensive programs nowadays for detecting and neutralizing viruses. And a whole lot of people thinking up ways to invent viruses that can't be got rid of. It's a whole industry. Lovely. I mean, *rotten*."

Viruses, I reflected, meant income to him.

"How do you find out if you have a virus?" I asked.

"The way to do it is to scan the info in any given computer. The disk I use to do that has more than two hundred of the commoner viruses on it. It will tell you if you've been infected by Michelangelo or Jerusalem II. If you'd called me last week, I could have done it."

"Last week we saw no need," I said. "And ... um ... if this Michelangelo thing activates only on March 6, then obviously we didn't have it in our computer *last* year on March 6."

Our expert parted with more information. "Michelangelo was invented sometime after March 6 in 1991 and only works on IBM compatible machines like yours."

"That's no comfort," I said.

"Er . . . no. Still, I can clean up these machines for you and give you a virus-free setup for the future. But you have to be careful what you feed into computers from the outside. Friends can lend you infected disks. And . . . do you have any other terminals?"

"There's one in my house," I said. "But someone's vandalized it."

The expert looked shocked. "You mean, a different virus?"

"No, I don't. I mean an ax."

The physical smashing of a computer pained him, one could see. Internal malignant illnesses were his stock-in-trade. Axes came into malicious damage, he said.

"Computer viruses are malicious damage, it seems to me," I said.

"Yes, but it's a *game*."

"Not if you've lost your life's work," I pointed out.

"If you don't make backups, you're a nutter."

I agreed with him entirely about backups, but I didn't think viruses a game. I thought them as wicked as chemical warfare. I'd heard of a computer virus that had wiped out a whole geological survey with the result that wells for water weren't drilled in time and more than a thousand people in a desert region died. The author of that particular virus had been reported to be delighted with its effectiveness. Too bad about the dead.

I said, "I suppose there's no way of telling whether this virus of ours was introduced into our system on purpose or by accident?"

He stared at me earnestly, hand busy through the hair.

"It would be unfriendly to do it on purpose."

"Yes."

"Most viruses are spread by accident, like AIDS."

"How long can they lie dormant?"

"You could have a virus quite a long time before it was triggered into life." His eyes held all the sad knowledge of his generation. "You have to take precautions."

I told him I wished we'd known him sooner and mentioned the name of the firm we had dealt with in the past.

He laughed. "Half the computers they sold were *awash* with viruses. They used infected diagnostic disks themselves and they used to rewrap vermin-ridden disks that people had returned to them in anger and sell them again to the great unsuspecting public. They vanished overnight because they knew March 6 would mean an army of furious customers suing their pants off. Even though March 6 was Sunday, we've dozens of cases like yours to clean up this week. Not our own customers, but *theirs*."

Isobel looked shocked. "But they were always so nice and helpful, coming out here whenever we needed them."

"And feeding in programs that would *keep* you needing them, I shouldn't wonder," the expert said with only half-disguised admiration.

"If *you* do that to me," I said pleasantly, "your pants will be off for life."

He regarded me thoughtfully. "I wouldn't," he said, and added, as if safeguarding himself from future accusations of which he would be innocent, "Don't forget the commonest reason for losing all files is pilot error. I mean, you can wipe everything off the hard disk just by typing DEL for Delete, followed by a Directory identification."

We looked blank.

He said to Isobel, "Suppose you typed DEL star full stop star, that's all it would take. Just as effective as Michelangelo. You'd lose everything forever."

"No!" She was horrified, predictably.

"Yes," he smiled. "But people who write viruses see no fun in that."

"But why?" Isobel asked, unhappily wailing. "*Why* do people want to write viruses to cause such trouble?"

"To show off," I said.

The expert's eyes widened. He didn't overmuch care for that assessment, I thought. He tended too much to admire the expertise, not despise the self-indulgence.

"Well," he said slowly, "it's true a lot of virus-writers sign their names into the programs. There's one called Eddie, he's invented several."

"Just put us back in business," I interrupted, tiring suddenly of the whole subject. "Keep us clean from now on with regular checks. We'll work out a maintenance agreement."

"Delighted," he said, the hand doing double time through the hair. "You'll be up and running by tomorrow."

I left him preparing to go while writing a list (expensive) of what we would need, and went along to my office to telephone the makers of my safe.

"An *ax*?" they exclaimed, shocked. "Are you sure?"

"I need the safe opened," I confirmed. "What can you do and how soon?"

They gave me the phone number of their nearest agent. The nearest agent would no doubt send a locksmith to look-see. Thank you, I said.

The nearest agent sounded unenthusiastic and doubtfully suggested a visit the following week.

"Tomorrow," I said.

There was a sharp intake of breath. I could imagine the pursed lips, the judicial shaking of the head. Possibly Friday afternoon, they said. Possibly. As a great favor they might manage it.

I put the phone down reflecting that if I myself let that sort of general backpedaling unwillingness creep into responses to requests for my services, I'd be twiddling my thumbs in no time. Not only did I myself drive anywhere anytime if I had no other driver available, but often at five minutes' notice I'd hire an extra horse van from a rival so as not to turn work down. I'd almost never been unable to get wheels out on the road. It was a matter of pride, of course, but the sort of pride that got things done.

Aziz came into the office to collect the keys of the Fourtrak in order to drive Lizzie to Heathrow. I handed them to him and reflexively asked him to drive her carefully.

"Slow down for roundabouts?" he asked, eyes brilliant.

"Oh, God." I felt like laughing for the first time that morning. "Yeah. Get her to the shuttle on time."

When he'd gone I sat for a while thinking of this and that, and then I phoned the computer expert again. He answered at once, reporting contentedly that he was fixing yet another Michelangelo casualty and assuring me he'd be back with us tomorrow morning.

"Fine," I said, "but . . . er . . . could you answer a question?"

"Fire away."

I said, "Can you change the date in the computer? Could you change its internal clock so that March 6 in the computer wouldn't turn up at all? Could you change March 6 to March 7?"

"Sure," he said readily. "It's a well-known way of

avoiding March 6. Switch the clock forward to March 7, then switch it back to the right date a couple of days later. Easy, if you know what you're doing."

"And . . . you could advance or retard March 6 so that it activated on the actual March 5 or on the actual March 7?"

"Yes." A pause. "That would be positive malice. You'd have to know the virus was in there."

"But it would be possible? Possible to change the hours, too?"

"Yes."

"How long would it take you to change the clock?"

"Me personally? Say a minute, maximum."

"And if I did it myself?"

"Well," he said thoughtfully, "if someone wrote down for you exactly what to do, step by step, or if you had an instruction book, you'd have to allow maybe five minutes of privacy, because you'd have to concentrate." He paused again. "Do you seriously think someone changed your clock? Because it's set to the right date and time now, I'll tell you."

"I don't know," I said. "I just asked."

"Anytime," he replied. "So long. See you tomorrow."

I was fighting shadows, I thought. Seeing villains behind every bush. The great probability was that my computer, like so many others, had accidentally crashed. And if it hadn't . . . then somewhere in its records there must be information I needed for unlocking surrounding mysteries. Information that some foe or other must know I possessed.

To destroy the records it was easiest to type DEL star full stop star. Yet to do that one had to be present, and the disk failure would be instantaneous. Changing the computer's clock to activate Michelangelo meant that any future hour could be chosen, like a time bomb going off.

Sandy Smith drove his police car into the farmyard and parked it outside the office window. He came in to join me, taking off his peaked cap and sitting, uninvited but welcome, in the chair across from mine.

"Jogger's inquest," he said, wiping his forehead.

"How did it go?"

He shrugged. "Opened and adjourned, like I said. I identified him. Bruce Farway gave evidence of death. The coroner looked at the photos and he'd read the postmortem report. He adjourned pending further inquiries." Sandy sighed deeply. "I'd better warn you he wasn't happy. I heard it said that Jogger died from crushing and dislocation of the atlas and that there were particles of rust embedded in his skin at the site of the injury."

"Rust!" I repeated, not liking it.

"There must be rust round the edges of your inspection pit," Sandy said.

"I hope to God there is."

We looked at each other blankly, still not wanting to put the obvious surmise into words.

Sandy said, "The postmortem put his time of death at about noon."

"Did it?"

"There will be a lot of inquiries."

I nodded.

"They'll want to know what you were doing at the time," Sandy said. "They're bound to ask."

Picking flowers, putting them on my parents' grave and driving to Maudie Watermead's lunch. Not brilliant, as alibis went.

"Let's go along to the pub for a drink," I suggested.

"I can't." He looked a shade scandalized. "I'm on duty."

"We could drink Coke," I said. "I have to go and settle up for Jogger's memorial."

"Oh." Sandy's face looked relieved. "All right, then."

"Can we go in your car? My Fourtrak's out on an errand."

He was reluctant to take me and uncomfortable in his refusal.

"Don't worry, Sandy," I said, tiredly teasing him. "I won't compromise you. I'll drive Jogger's old van. You don't have to come if you don't want to."

He did want to, however. We drove in convoy to Jogger's boozer and I gave the landlord a heavy check. The landlord was well pleased with the trade and had done his best with the signatures, which filled a sheet of paper the size of a tabloid newspaper and were accompanied by encouraging comments. "Poor old Jogger, jogged his last." "Up the apples and pears to the pearlies. Go for it, Jog."

"Upstairs to the pearly gates," Sandy interpreted, reading with me.

" 'Gone to the great oil change in the sky,' " the landlord said, pointing. "That's mine."

"Most appropriate," I assured him.

Half of Pixhill seemed to have signed their names but unfortunately all over the place, not in the tidy columns I'd envisaged. Most of my drivers were there, including Lewis, who had been in France collecting Michael's two-year-olds on that Saturday night. I commented on it. The landlord agreed that more people had signed the memorial than had been with Jogger on his last evening. "They wanted to pay their respects," he explained.

"And to drink the free beer," Sandy said.

"Well ... old Jogger was a good mate."

"Mm," I agreed. "So which of these people were actually here on Saturday? Sandy, you were here. You'll know."

"I was off duty," he protested.

"Your eyes were still working."

Sandy looked at the crowded names and pointed out a few with a stubby finger.

"Of your drivers, Dave definitely, he pretty well lives here. Also Phil and his missus, and Nigel who was chatting her up to Phil's disgust, and Harve looked in. And Brett, the one who drove that dead man, Ogden, he was there definitely, even though he was supposed to have left Pixhill. He was grousing about you having got shot of him."

His gaze moved over the names.

"Bruce Farway! He's signed it. I didn't see him here."

"The doctor?" The landlord nodded. "He often comes in with those book people who sit in that far corner putting the world to rights. He drinks Aqua Libra." He concentrated on the sheet, reading upside down. "A whole bunch of Watermead's lads were here and some from half the stables in Pixhill. That new lady, Mrs. English, some of her lads came. New faces. Not a bad bunch. And John Tigwood, he's always in and out with those collecting boxes. And Watermead's son and daughter, they were here Saturday, but they haven't been in since so their names aren't down, see?"

I asked, surprised, "Do you mean Tessa and Ed?"

"Aye."

"But they're underage," Sandy said pompously. "They're not eighteen."

The landlord took mild offense. "I'd only serve them

soft drinks. They both like diet Coke." He glanced at me slyly. "She likes that Nigel, too. That driver of yours."

"Does he encourage her?" I asked.

The landlord laughed. "He encourages anything with tits."

"You'll be in trouble serving them without an adult," Sandy said.

"She said Nigel was buying."

"You'll be in trouble," Sandy repeated.

"They didn't stay long," the landlord said defensively. "They'd probably gone before you got here." He sniffed. "I daresay some of those lads aren't eighteen either, if the truth be told."

"You be careful," Sandy warned. "You can lose your license faster than blink."

"How early did Jogger get drunk?" I asked.

"I don't serve drunks," the landlord said virtuously. Sandy snorted.

"How early, then," I rephrased it, "did Jogger start talking about aliens, little green men and lone rangers?"

"He was here from six o'clock until Sandy drove him home," the landlord said.

"What rate of pints per hour?"

"Two at least," Sandy said. "Jogger could knock 'em back with the best."

"He wasn't drunk," the landlord maintained. "Maybe not fit to drive his van, but not drunk."

"Reeling a bit," Sandy said. "He was on about the aliens before I got here at eight or thereabouts. And telling the world, he was, about Poland having five on a horse last summer."

"Why?" the landlord asked me. "What does it matter?"

"Yes," Sandy said, "and what did Jogger mean?"

"Heaven knows."

"Jogger knows in heaven." The landlord was delighted with his own wit. "Hear that? Jogger knows in heaven."

"Very good," Sandy said heavily.

"Did anything else happen?" I asked. "Who stole the tools out of his van?"

The landlord said he hadn't a clue.

"Dave told Jogger to shut up," Sandy said.

"What?"

"Jogger was getting on his nerves. Jogger just laughed so Dave took a swipe at him."

The landlord nodded. "He knocked Jogger's drink over."

"He *hit* Jogger?" I said, astonished. Jogger, because of his fancy footwork, had been instinctively quick on his feet.

"He missed him," Sandy said. "You have to get up early to hit Jogger."

We all listened in silence to what he'd just said.

"Yes, well . . ." Sandy said, stirring. "Time I reported back on duty. Are you staying, Freddie?"

"Nope."

I followed him out, leaving the memorial with the landlord for framing and hanging on the wall.

"That Tessa," Sandy said, putting on his official hat, "she's a wild one. Not high-spirited, I don't mean. I mean, well, borderline delinquent. I'd not be surprised if she ends up in court."

I thought he exaggerated, but I took his estimation seriously. He spent his life with minor offenders: every local bobby did in villages, but he was particularly good at prevention as opposed to retribution. "I don't suppose you could *warn* Michael Watermead, could you?" he asked.

"Difficult."

"Try," he said. "Save Mrs. Watermead's tears."

I was startled by his imagery. "OK," I said.

"Good."

"Sandy ..."

He stopped in midstep. "Yes?"

"If someone killed Jogger ... if he didn't just fall ... well, *catch the bugger.*"

He listened to the commitment in my voice. "And catch the bugger who took you to Southampton? Catch the bugger who smashed your car and your house and your sister's little wings?"

"If it's possible."

"But you don't trust my colleagues. You don't help them."

"If they treated me as an ally, not a suspect, we'd get on better."

"It's just their way."

We looked at each other peacefully, longtime friends up to a point. Alone together, we'd have been allies in any investigation. With his colleagues taking charge, the professional fence rose between us like dragons' teeth. No-man's-land would keep him loyally in the opposing trenches, though surreptitiously he might send me semaphore messages. I'd have to settle for that. So would he.

I drove Jogger's old truck back to the farmyard and parked it again beside the barn. Its two rear doors were still unlocked and inside there was still nothing but some reddish gray dust. I drove my fingers through the dust and looked at them, not in the least happy with what I saw. The reddish particles among the gray were, to the unmagnified eye, suspiciously like rust.

Brushing the dust off my fingers, I went into the barn

and stood looking at the floor there, especially at the edges of the pit. There was grease in plenty, and general dirt. There would certainly be rust embedded in it. Steel and damp weather infallibly shed ferric oxide. Rust would be there.

All the same, in memory I surveyed Jogger's lost tools; the old slider, the sharp ax, the jumbled small wrenches, the loops of wire . . . all those, and the tire iron. An old strong tire iron, as long as one's arm. Ferrous metal, a wide-open invitation to rust.

I walked back to my office and wondered how much of my hovering nausea was due to the blow on my own head or the imagined scrunch of a rusty tire iron into Jogger's.

You'd have to get up early to hit Jogger . . .

He'd died about noon in broad daylight.

It *had* to have been an accident. I didn't want him to have died simply because he'd worked for me. I could deal with attacks on myself. I didn't want to bear the guilt of someone else's death.

Aziz came back from Heathrow, his irrepressible good spirits hovering in a liquid smile even while he commiserated with me over the Jaguar.

"It can't have been easy to get a car to run at that speed into a helicopter. Not on flatland. Not without risking your neck."

"That's no comfort," I pointed out.

"I took a quick decko into the wreck," he said, bright-eyed. "I'd say the accelerator pedal was wedged down with a brick."

"A *brick*?" I haven't any bricks."

"What's a brick doing there, then?"

I shook my head.

"You'd have to be nippy," he said. "You'd have only seconds to get clear once you'd got up enough speed."

"It has automatic gears," I said thoughtfully. "It sets . . . set . . . off slowly, left to itself."

He nodded happily. "Nice little problem."

"How would you solve it, then?"

He had already been thinking about it, as he answered without hesitation, "I'd wind down the driver's window, for a start. I'd have a brick lashed to one end of a stick with the other end through the window. I'd slide into the driver's seat, start the engine, put the gear lever in drive, slide out again at slow speed and shut the door, then through the window I'd push the accelerator down hard with the brick and jump away just before impact." He grinned. "Mind you, it would take nerve. And you'd have to start a good way back from the helicopter to get up enough speed for that amount of damage. You'd have to be running by the end."

"There must be a simpler way," I said. "No one would risk their life like that."

"You're not dealing with common sense," Aziz said. "Your sister showed me the havoc in your sitting room. You've got a gold-plated wrecker on the loose. Can't you hear him? He's shouting at you. 'Look at me, look at what I can do, see how clever I am.' That sort of character *likes* taking risks. It's life's blood. It give him his buzz."

I said flatly, "How do you know?"

The shining eyes flickered. "Observation," he said.

"Observation of who?"

"Oh, this person and that." He flapped a hand vaguely. "No one particular."

I didn't pursue it. He wasn't going to tell me. I was interested all the same, in his assessment. It matched pretty

faithfully what the expert had said about the pattern of
computer virus writers, the look-at-clever-me syndrome.
The overpowering self-regard that could express itself only
in destruction.

"Does one wrecker," I asked slowly, "egg on another?"

His expression was street-smart beyond any other I'd
met. "Ever heard of football yobbos?"

Murderous, I thought.

I thanked Aziz for driving Lizzie.

"Nice lady," he said. "Any old time."

I rubbed a hand over my face, asked Aziz to check with
Harve about jobs for the next day and told Isobel and Rose
I'd be back in the morning.

On the short way home I noticed that my neighbor had
a small pile of bricks beside his gate. The bricks had been
there for weeks, I realized. I'd never paid them any attention.

I stopped the jalopy by the wreck of the Jaguar and
looked through the space that had once been the driver's-
side window. There was indeed a brick—or the remains of
one—jumbled in the squeezed space. The brick had broken into three pieces. Bricks were brittle. Brick dust was
reddish, like rust.

I'm delirious, I thought.

I let myself into the house with the keys Aziz had
brought from Lizzie and switched on the television in my
bedroom to watch the racing at Cheltenham.

I sat in an armchair and then lay on the bed and then
fell inexorably asleep as if brain dead and stayed that way
until long after the last horse had passed the winning post.

Thursday morning, Cheltenham Gold Cup day, once
greeted with raised pulse and thudding hope, found me

that particular week with a creaking stiffness in my limbs
and a craving to curl up and let the world pass by.

Instead, driven by curiosity more than a sense of duty,
I put on shirt and tie and drove to Winchester, pausing for
five minutes on the way with Isobel and Rose. They could
fill in the time before the arrival of the computer-reviver,
I suggested, by making a list of everyone they could think
of who'd set foot in their offices the previous week.

They looked at me blankly. Dozens of people had
crossed their doorstep, it seemed, starting with all the drivers. I would take the drivers for granted, I said. Just list
everyone else, and put a star against those that had been in
on Friday. They were doubtful if they could remember.
Try, I said.

I collected Dave from the canteen and took him with me
to Winchester, though he was reluctant to go and spent the
whole twenty-minute journey in unaccustomed silence.

The inquest on Kevin Keith Ogden proved, as Sandy
had promised, to be a comparatively simple affair. The
coroner, quiet and businesslike, had read the paperwork
before coming to the proceedings and, though thorough,
saw no benefit in wasting time.

He spoke with kindness to a thin, miserable woman in
black, who agreed that yes, she was Lynn Melissa Ogden,
and yes, she had identified the dead man as her husband,
Kevin Keith.

Bruce Farway, consulted, reported that he'd been called
to the house of Frederick Croft on the previous Thursday
evening and had determined Kevin Keith to be deceased.
The coroner, reading aloud from a paper, accepted the
postmortem report that death had resulted from heart failure caused by a string of abstruse medical conditions that

probably no one in the room understood except Farway, who was nodding.

The coroner had received a letter from Kevin Keith's own doctor detailing the patient's history and the pills he had been advised to keep taking. He asked the widow if the pills had been faithfully swallowed. Not always, she said.

"Mr ... er ... Yates?" asked the coroner, looking around for a response.

"Here, sir," Dave answered hoarsely.

"You gave a lift to Mr. Ogden in one of Mr. Croft's horse vans, is that right? Tell us about it."

Dave made it as short as he could, sweating and uncomfortable.

"We couldn't wake him, like, at Chieveley ..."

The coroner asked if Kevin Keith had shown any physical distress before that.

"No, sir. He never said a word. We thought he was asleep, like."

"Mr. Croft?" the coroner said, identifying me easily. "You called Police Constable Smith when you'd seen Mr. Ogden?"

"Yes, sir."

"And Constable Smith, you called Dr. Farway?"

"Yes, sir."

The coroner shuffled the papers together and looked neutrally at those present. "The finding of this court is that Mr. Kevin Ogden died of natural causes." After a pause, when no one moved, he said, "That's all, everyone. Thank you for your attendance. You have each behaved with commendable promptness and common sense in this sad occurrence."

He gave Mrs. Ogden one last sympathetic smile, and

that was that. We trooped out onto the sidewalk and I heard Mrs. Ogden inquiring forlornly about cabs.

"Mrs. Ogden," I said, "can I give you a lift?"

She focused weak-looking gray eyes on my face and indecisively fluttered her hands. "It's only to the railway ..."

"I'll take you ... if you don't mind a Fourtrak?"

She looked as if she'd never heard of a Fourtrak but would have settled for an elephant if all else failed.

I persuaded Sandy to take Dave back to Pixhill and set off with Mrs. Ogden, who was not exactly crying but in a definite state of shock.

"It didn't take long, did it?" she said defeatedly. "It didn't seem much of a thing, did it? I mean, not at the end of someone's life."

"Not a great thing," I agreed. "But you'll have a service of thanksgiving, perhaps."

She didn't look cheered. She said, "Are you Freddie Croft?"

"That's right." I glanced at her, thinking. "When does your train leave?" I asked.

"Not for ages."

"How about some coffee, then?"

She said wanly that it would be nice and settled apathetically into an armchair in the empty front lounge of a mock-Tudor hotel. Coffee took its time coming but was fresh in a Cafetiere pot, with cream and rosebudded china on a silvery tray.

Mrs. Ogden, until then huddled palely into her black shapeless overcoat, began to loosen a little by undoing the buttons. Under the coat, more black. Black shoes, black handbag, black gloves, black scarf. An overstatement.

"A terrible shock for you," I said.

"Yes."

"Your daughter must be a comfort."

"We never had a daughter. He made that up, to get lifts."

"Did he?"

"He had to make things up." She gave me a sudden look of panic, the first crack in the ice. "He lost his job, you see."

"He was . . . a salesman?" I guessed.

"No. He was *in* sales. Under-manager. The firm got taken over. Most of the management were made redundant."

"I'm so sorry."

"He couldn't get another job, you see. Not at fifty-four, with a bad heart."

"Life's unfair."

"He's been unemployed for four years. We've spent the redundancy money and our savings . . . the building society's repossessing the house . . . and . . . and . . . it's all too much."

And he'd bounced checks, I thought, and failed to pay hotel bills, and tried to live on scraps gleaned from a feeble transport scheme, traveling around free by lifts cadged on the basis of a sob story about a nonexistent daughter's wedding.

Lynn Melissa Ogden looked as hammered into the ground as a tent peg. She had graying straight brown hair tied back in the nape of her neck with a narrow black ribbon. No cosmetics. Pinched lines round her mouth. The cords of age in her neck.

I asked sympathetically, "Do you yourself have a job?"

"I used to." The grayness in her skin looked like despair. "I worked in a greengrocer's but Kev . . . well he's

221

gone now, it can't hurt to say it . . . Kev took some money out of their till, and they were pretty good about it, they didn't get the police but they said I'd have to go."

"Yes."

"We were *eating* on that money." She trembled with futile anger. "Feeding ourselves on my wages and the things like rotting fruit and veggies that the shop couldn't sell. How *could* he?"

"He could have sold that ring, perhaps," I suggested. "I saw it on his finger . . . gold and onyx."

"That was a fake," she said dully. "He sold the real one months ago. He missed it so much . . . He cried, you know. So I bought him that one . . . it was rubbish, but he wore it."

I refilled her coffee cup. She drank absently, the cup clattering on the saucer when she put it down.

"Why did your husband want to go to the Chieveley service station?" I asked.

"He had to . . ." She stopped and considered, then said, "I don't suppose it matters anymore. He can't get into any more trouble . . . I told him I couldn't *bear* any more of it, but I did, of course. We'd been married thirty-three years . . . I loved him once but then . . . for a long time . . . I've been *sorry* for him, you see, and I couldn't kick him out, could I? Because where would he go? And he hadn't been home for weeks because the police had been round . . . I don't know why I'm telling you . . ."

"Because you need to tell *someone*."

"Oh, yes. And *appearances*, you see? I can't tell our neighbors and we hardly have any friends left because Kev borrowed money from them . . ."

And never repaid. The words were as stark as if she'd actually said them.

"So why was he going to Chieveley?" I asked again.

"People used to phone the house and ask him to take things for them from one place to another. I said he'd get into trouble doing that. I mean, he could have been carrying bits to make *bombs*, or drugs, or anything. Quite often he took dogs or cats ... he quite liked that. He put an ad in *Horse and Hound* sometimes. People would pay his train fare to take their animals but he'd cash in the tickets and go thumbing. I mean, he hadn't any *pride* left, you see. Everything had come apart."

"Wretched," I said.

"We paid the phone bill," she said. "We always paid the phone bill. And I'd take the messages for him and he would phone me whenever he could use someone's phone for nothing. But we couldn't have gone on much longer ..."

"No."

"It's a blessing for him, really, that he died."

"Mrs. Ogden ..."

"Well, it is. He was *ashamed*, you see, my poor old boy."

I thought of all their awful shared misery and judged that Kevin Keith had been undeservedly lucky to have had Lynn Melissa.

"He wasn't carrying an animal in my horse van, though," I said.

"No." She looked doubtful. "It was something to do with animals, though. It was an answer to the *Horse and Hound* ad. A woman phoned. She wanted Kev to meet someone at Pontefract service station and go to South

Mimms service station and then go in your horse van to Chieveley."

"Ah," I said.

She didn't understand the depth of comprehension in my voice, but looked simply surprised by it.

"Who was he going to meet at Chieveley?" I asked.

"She didn't say. She just said someone would meet him when he got out of the horse van. Someone would meet him and pay him and take what he was carrying, and that would be the end of it."

"And you agreed to that?"

"Well, yes, of course I did. We *lived* on it, you see."

"Who was he meeting at Pontefract?"

"She just said 'someone' would meet him and give him a small carrier bag."

"Did she say what would be in it?"

"Yes, she said a thermos flask but he wasn't to open it."

"Mm. *Would* he have opened it?"

"Oh, no," She was definite. "He'd be afraid of not being paid. And he always said what he didn't know couldn't hurt him."

A recipe for disaster if ever I heard one.

She looked at her watch, thanked me for the coffee and said she'd better get along to the station, if I didn't mind.

"How about the train fare?" I asked.

"Oh . . . they gave me a voucher. The police or the court or someone. They gave me one to come down last Saturday, too, to identify him." She sighed heavily. "Everyone's been kind."

Poor Mrs. Ogden. I drove her to the station and waited with her until her train came, though she said I needn't. I would have liked to give her money to see her through some of her present troubles, but I didn't think she would

take it. I would get her address from Sandy, I thought, and
send her something in remembrance of Kevin Keith, her
poor old boy who seemed to have precipitated me into a
maelstrom.

9

As I was leaving Winchester the car phone rang. Isobel's voice said, "Oh, good, I've been trying to reach you. The police are here about Jogger."

"Which police?"

"Not Sandy Smith. Two others. They want to know when you'll be back."

"Tell them twenty minutes. Did the computer man come?"

"He's here now. Another half-hour, he says."

"Fine."

"Nina Young phoned. She and Nigel have picked up the Jericho Rich show jumper and they're on their way back. No incidents, she said to tell you."

"OK."

I completed the journey and kept the police waiting while I checked with the young computer expert in Isobel's office. Yes, he confirmed, he had brought with him a replacement computer for my house, as requested, and he would come straightaway to fix it up.

After I'd talked to the police, I said.

He looked at his watch and ran his fingers through his hair. "I'm due at Michael Watermead's stables. Same job as this. I'll do him first, then come to you."

"Michael?" I asked, surprised.

He smiled. "Rather apt, I thought, being Michelangelo, but he didn't think it funny."

"No, he wouldn't."

Barely digesting the news, let alone the significance, of the failure of the Watermead hard disk, I went along to where the policemen waited in my own office.

They proved to be the two whose manner had so easily raised my antagonism on their Monday visit. I resolved for Sandy's sake to be cooperative and answered their questions truthfully, politely and briefly. They exuded suspicion and hostility, for which I could see no reason, and they asked most of Monday's questions over again.

They needed, they announced, to take scrapings of the dirt surrounding and inside the inspection pit. Go right ahead, I said. They told me they were in the process of asking my staff what had brought Jogger to the farmyard on the Sunday morning.

Fine.

Had I instructed him to go to the farmyard on that morning?

No, I hadn't.

Did I object to his going there on a Sunday morning?

"No. As I mentioned before, all the staff could go in and out of the farmyard whenever they liked."

Why was that?

"Company policy," I said, and didn't feel like explaining that the drivers' pride in their vehicles led them to make them more personal, which they did chiefly on Sundays. Curtains were hung on Sundays. Seat and mattress covers were fitted. Bits of carpet appeared underfoot. Wives helped with the home-away-from-homes. Metal and furniture polish accompanied pride. Loyalty and contentment were the products of Sundays.

Did Jogger normally go to the farmyard on Sundays?

I said that the horse transport business was always working on Sundays, though usually not as busily as on all other days. Jogger would certainly consider it normal to go to the farmyard on a Sunday.

They asked, as Sandy had predicted, what I had been doing on that Sunday morning. I told them. They wrote it down dubiously. You say you picked daffodils from your garden and put them on your parents' grave? Yes, I did. Was I in the habit of doing that? I took flowers there from time to time, I said. How often? Five or six times a year.

I gathered, both from their general attitude and the limitations of their questions, that there was still in the collective police mind a basic indecision as to how to view Jogger's death; accident or worse.

Rust, I thought, would decide for them.

I went with them and watched them take scrapings from all round the pit. They fed the patches of dirt into small plastic bags, closing and labeling each with its area of provenance. North end of pit floor . . . east, west, south. North interior wall of pit. East, west, south. North rim of pit . . . east, west, south.

They were thorough and fair. One way or another, rust would tell.

They drove away finally, leaving me to my ambivalent feelings and two alarmed secretaries.

Isobel said, scandalized, "They asked us how you and Jogger got along! Why did they ask that? Jogger *fell* into the pit, didn't he?"

"They have to find out."

"But ... but ..."

"Mm," I said, "let's hope he fell."

"All the drivers say he must have. They've been saying so all week."

Trying to convince themselves, I thought.

I drove home, where the computer whiz soon joined me. He stood with his legs apart in the center of my devastated sitting room, the hand combing through the hair nonstop.

"Yes," I said to his stunned silence. "It took a bit of strength and a lot of pleasure."

"Pleasure?" He thought it over. "I guess so."

He put the wreck of the old computer onto one of the few free areas of carpet and installed the new version in its place, attaching it to its phone line to the computer in Isobel's room. Although I would still maintain my pencil charts, it was reassuring to see the screen come alive again with the active link to the office.

"I guarantee that this new disk is clean," the expert said. "And I'm selling you a disk you can use to check that it stays that way." He showed me how to "scan" the disk. "If you find any virus on there, please phone me at once."

"I certainly will." I watched his busy fingers and asked a few questions. "If someone fed the Michelangelo virus into the office computer, would it also infect the computer here?"

"Yes, it would, as soon as you called the office programs onto your screen. And the other way round. If someone fed the virus into here, the office would catch it. It would then spread to all the computers on the same network."

"Like Rose's?"

"Is Rose the other secretary? Yes, sure, into hers in a flash."

"And ... um ... if we make backup floppy disks, would the virus be in those, too?"

He said earnestly, "If you *do* have any backups, let me check them before you use them."

"Yes."

"But your girls said they hadn't made any for ages."

"I know." I paused. "Did Michael Watermead's secretary make backups?"

He hesitated. "Don't know if I should tell you."

"Professional etiquette?"

"Sort of."

"She'll tell Isobel, anyway."

"Then ... er ... yes, she did, and the backup floppy she's been using lately has Michelangelo on it. I'm having to clean up their whole act."

"Will you save their records?"

"Every chance."

He finished the installation and gave me a cheerful pitying look. "You need lessons," he said. "You need to know about write-protect and boot-up floppy disks, for a start. I could teach you, if you like, though you're pretty old."

"How long have you been in computers?" I asked.

"From before I could hold a pen."

The way I could ride, I thought.

"I'll come for lessons," I said.

"Really? Great, then. Really great."

After he'd gone I managed to stay awake to watch all the racing at Cheltenham and had the bittersweet satisfaction of seeing a horse I'd schooled and taught his business win the Gold Cup.

I should have been riding him. I might have been ... Well, it had to be enough to remember the first of his triumphs, a scramble of a two-mile hurdle. Enough to remember his first steeplechase, a high-class novice race that he'd won by outjumping the opposition though nearly giving it away by floundering all over the place in the last hundred yards. I'd ridden him eight times in all into first place past the winning post, and now here he was, nine years old and a star, charging up the Cheltenham hill as straight as a die with all the panache and courage a jockey could hope for.

Goddammit ...

I shook off the sickening self-pitying regrets. I should have got over it by this time, I told myself. A decent period of mourning was reasonable, but three years along the road I should have stopped looking back. I supposed rather uneasily that I wouldn't be free of nostalgia until the last of the horses I'd ridden was heading towards Centaur Care. Not even then, if many like Peterman turned up on my doorstep.

The minute I switched off the set the telephone rang and I listened to Lizzie's voice sounding surprised.

"Hello! I thought I'd get your answering machine. I thought you'd be at Cheltenham."

"I didn't go."

"So it seems. Why not? Is your head all right?"

"Nothing to worry about. I keep wanting to go to sleep."

"Thoroughly natural. Listen to nature."

"Yes, ma'am."

"Thanks for lending me Aziz. What a fascinating young man."

"Is he?"

"Too bright for his job, I'd say."

"Why do you think so? I need bright drivers."

"Most drivers can't discuss the periodic table of elements, let alone in French."

I laughed.

"Just think about it. Anyway," she said, "I've a report on your tubes."

It took me a few seconds to work out which tubes she meant, typical of the sluggish state of my brain.

"Tubes," I said. "Oh, great."

"They each contained 10 ccs of viral transport medium."

"Of *what*?"

"To be precise about the ingredients, the tubes contained bovine albumin, glutamic acid, sucrose and an antibiotic called Gentamicin, all in sterile water at a balanced pH of 7.3."

"Er . . ." I said, reaching for a pencil. "Spell all that slowly."

She laughed and did so.

"But what's it *for*?" I asked.

"For transporting a virus, as I said."

"But *what* virus?" My mind thought irrationally of Michelangelo, which was nonsense. Michelangelo needed a different sort of tube.

"Any virus," Lizzie said. "Viruses are highly mysterious

and barely visible even under an electron microscope. One can usually only see their results. You can also detect the antibodies the invaded organism develops to defend itself."

"But . . ." I paused to organize a few scattering thoughts. "Was there any virus in the tubes?"

"It's impossible to say. It looks likely, considering that the tubes were carefully sealed and were being carried in the dark in a vacuum flask—and incidentally, the vacuum flask would have been necessary to maintain the tubes in a *chilled* environment, say 4°C, not a hot one—but you've had those tubes for days, haven't you?"

"They were being carried in one of my horse vans a week ago today."

"That's what I thought. Well, viruses will only survive outside a living organism for a very short time. Viral transport medium is used for taking virally infected matter from a sufferer to a laboratory for testing, and for infecting another organism for research purposes, but viruses don't live long in the medium or on culture plates."

"How long?"

"It would depend. The conflicting views here in the university say for as little as five hours or for as many as forty-eight. After that, any virus would be inactive."

"But, Lizzie . . ."

"Yes, what?"

"I mean . . . I don't really understand."

"You're hardly alone," she said. "There are about six hundred known viruses, probably there are at least double that number, and they are all unidentifiable by sight. They're particles of DNA or RNA surrounded by a coating of protein. They are cylindrical or polyhedral in shape, but you can't tell what they do by looking at them. They're not like bacteria, where the organisms are recognizable individually by their appearance. Most viruses look the same. They live by invading living tissue and reproducing in animal cells—for animal, read also human. Flu, colds, polio, smallpox, measles, rabies, AIDS, dozens of things. Everyone knows their effects. No one knows how they evolved. Some, like flu, are constantly changing."

In silence I thought about what she'd told me until in the end she said, "Freddie? Are you still there?"

"Yes," I said. "Do you mean," I asked slowly, "that you could take some flu virus from someone and transport it for miles and infect someone else, without the people even meeting?"

"Sure, you *could*. But why would you?"

"Malice?" I suggested.

"Freddie!"

"You could, couldn't you?"

"As far as I gather, you'd have to have a large inoculum in a small amount of medium, the pathogenicity of the virus would have to be high and the receptor would have to be highly susceptible."

"Is that straight Professor Quipp?"

She said tartly, "Since you ask, yes."

"Lizzie," I said apologetically, "it's just that I need it in plain English."

"Oh. Well, in that case, what it means is that you'd have to have a very active virus and as much of it as possible in relation to the amount of medium, and the person receiving it would have to be likely to catch the infection. It wouldn't be any good trying to infect someone with the present strain of flu if they'd been inoculated against it. You couldn't give polio to anyone who'd taken the Salk vaccine, or give smallpox or measles to protected people. There's no proven vaccine yet against AIDS, and AIDS is

234

terrifying because it may be that it changes, like flu, though that's not established so far."

"If it was flu virus in the tubes," I asked, thinking, "would you inject it?"

"No, you wouldn't. Flu is spread through respiratory droplets or saliva. You'd have to squirt the medium up someone's nose. That might do it."

"Or sprinkle in on their cornflakes?"

"Not really reliable. A respiratory virus would have to go into the respiratory tract, not the stomach. From the nose or lungs it could invade the whole system, but it might not have any effect if you injected it into a muscle or straight into the bloodstream." She paused. "You do have gruesome thoughts."

"It's been a gruesome week."

She agreed with the assessment. "Is my dear little helicopter still exactly where I left it?"

"Yes. What do you want me to do with it?"

"My partners suggest putting it on a low-loader and bringing it home."

"Do you think it can be salvaged?" I probably sounded surprised, but there were bits of it, she said, that looked unharmed. The tail rotor, for example, and the main rotor's linkage, the most expensive part of the works. A helicopter could be rebuilt. It would have to stay as it was, though, she said, until after the aircraft crash inspector had been to see it and made a report. Even ground accidents, it seemed, had to go through the mill.

"Talking of viruses," I said, "we've had a doozy in the computer."

"A what?"

"A killer. No vaccine given in time, alas."

"What exactly are you talking about?"

I told her.

"Inconvenient," she said. "Let me know if you need anything else."

"I will. Incidentally, Aziz said you were a nice lady."

"So I should hope."

I laughed with affection and disconnected and from my bedroom window watched a zippy small car drive onto my tarmac and stop with a shocked jolt within first sight of the Jaguar-Robinson embrace.

My visitor, as I was delighted to see as she stood up in the open air to stare at the wreckage, was Maudie Watermead; blonde, slight, forever legs in blue denim.

I opened my window and yelled down to her.

"Hi," she shouted back. "Can I come in?"

"I'll be right down."

I leaped down the stairs and opened the door for her.

I said, kissing her cheek, "I don't suppose you've come to hop into bed?"

"Not a chance."

"Come in for a drink, then."

She took the less dramatic invitation for granted and followed me into the house. The state of the sitting room opened her mouth.

"Wow," she said breathlessly. "All of Pixhill's *heard* about this, but I never . . . I mean . . ."

"The thoroughness," I said dryly, "is impressive."

"Oh, Freddie!" She sounded truly sympathetic and gave me a hug. Too chaste, however. "And your super car . . ." She bent down and picked up one of the chopped photographs, sharp pieces of glass falling in a cascade from an old soaring flight over The Chair fence in the Grand National. "How can you bear it?"

"Without tears," I said.

She gave me a swift sideways glance. "You're as tough as ever."

What was tough, I wondered. Unfeeling? Yet I felt.

"I was talking to the computer boy," Maudie said. "He described all this. He said if anyone had done this to *him*, he'd have taken an ax to him himself."

"Mm. But you have to ax the right person and he didn't sign his name." Something flickered deep in my brain. Something about signing names. Flickered and vanished. "What will you drink?" I asked. "There's champagne in the fridge."

"If you really feel like it," she said doubtfully.

"Why not?"

So we went into the kitchen and sat at the table there and drank from my best glasses, all unshattered inside a kitchen cupboard.

"Michael was furious about our computer. That young genius who's fixed it for us told us we hadn't had the virus lurking inside there for more than a month. Betsy, our secretary, started using new floppy disks as backup disks a month ago. The virus was on those, but it wasn't on the backup disks she'd used earlier. So the wizard says we didn't have the virus then."

I thought about it. "So Betsy hadn't used the old backup disks recently?"

"No. No need. I mean, you only use backups if the computer itself goes haywire, don't you?"

"Yeah."

"The wizard says there are *hundreds* of these wretched viruses about. Michael's on the point of returning to parchment and quill pens."

"Can't blame him."

"Betsy says your Isobel's told her they didn't make backups, even, in your office."

"One lives and learns."

"But what will you *do*?"

"Oh," I said, "start on the parchment and quills, I suppose. I mean, all the records and figures in the computer are still around on paper. Rose kept paper copies of the bills she sent out. We've all the invoices for supplies coming in. The drivers' logbooks still exist."

"Yes, but what a mammoth task."

"Infuriating," I agreed.

"Why aren't you snarling and gnashing your teeth?"

"Doesn't do any good."

She sighed. "You're amazing, Freddie, you really are."

"But I don't get what I want."

She knew what I meant. She almost blushed, then said, "No, you don't," much too firmly, and drank her champagne. "I came to see if I could help you in any way," she went on, and before I could say anything added quickly, "and not in *that* way, don't be a fool."

"Pity."

"Michael said to ask you to lunch on Sunday."

"Tell Michael yes, thank you."

Tell Michael, Sandy had said, that his daughter, Tessa, had criminal potential. I looked at Maudie's high cheekbones, at her fair eyebrows, her delicious mouth; looked at her good sense and generous spirit. How could one warn such a mother or such a father to look out for trouble in their daughter? Maybe a critical aunt could have managed it, but I certainly could not.

I had no right to do it and no inclination, and moreover I wouldn't be believed and would lose a welcome friendship. I might privately suspect that Sandy was on target, but that was what the thought would remain; private. I could, on the other hand, alert Maudie to less nebulous dangers.

I said tentatively, "Have you come across one of my drivers called Nigel?"

The fair eyebrows rose. "We nearly always have Lewis."

"Yes. But ... um ... Nigel's a sexy hunk, my secretaries say, and ... um ..."

"Get on with it," Maudie urged.

"I just thought ... you might not want him seeing too much of Tessa."

"Tessa! Oh God. I thought it was Lewis she was keen on. She's always whispering with Lewis."

"The pub landlord mentioned to me that Nigel was buying Cokes there for Tessa and Ed one evening. I'm sure there's absolutely nothing to worry about, but perhaps you should know."

"Stupid kids!" She seemed basically unworried. "Coca-Cola in a pub!" She laughed. "In my young days it was 'my needle or yours' that had parents hopping."

I refilled her glass. She frowned, not at the champagne, but at a sudden memory, and thoughtfully said, "You sent that Nigel to us last week to take Jericho Rich's damned horses off to Newmarket, didn't you?"

"Yes. Friday. But I won't allocate him to your work anymore."

"Betsy told me ... He came too early, or something, and Tessa climbed into his cab and said she wanted to go with him, but Michael saw her and said she wasn't to go."

That version of what had happened sounded much more likely than the one I'd heard from Isobel, that Nigel had virtuously said he wouldn't take her because of my ban on hitchhikers.

Maudie said, "Michael told me he couldn't imagine why she wanted to go with Jericho's horses when she said she detested the man, but if it was *Nigel* she wanted to go with, it makes more sense. Do you really think we might have a problem there?"

"He's unmarried and has powerful pheromones, I'm told."

"What a way of putting it." She was amused. "I'll keep an eye on things. And thanks."

"I don't like to tell tales."

"Tessa can be a bit of a handful, sometimes." She looked mildly rueful but forgiving. "Seventeen's a rebellious age, I suppose."

"Did you rebel?" I asked.

"No, actually. I don't think so. Did you?"

"I was too busy riding."

"And here you still are, in your father's house." She mocked me gently. "You never even left home."

"Home is wherever I am," I said.

"Wow. How's that for utter security!"

"You wouldn't care to leave Michael, I suppose?"

"And four children? And an integrated life? And I'm older than you, anyway."

The thing that made the game most worth playing, I thought, was the certainty that I wouldn't win it. She finished her drink happily, my desire for her as pleasurable an intoxication as the bubbles. Casual consummation would have spoiled the future and she was too nice to allow it. She put down her glass and stood up, smiling.

"If you need anything, let us know."

"Yes," I said.

"See you on Sunday, then."

I walked out to her car with her and got an affectionate, passionless kiss and a carefree wave as she turned her car and departed. Celibacy, I thought, returning to the house, could go on for too long, and too long, at that point, was a year. The older I grew, the more I saw consequences in advance and the more I cared, like Maudie, about not doing damage for the sake of a passing pleasure. I looked back over the years with horror, sometimes. After I'd lost Susan Palmerstone I'd drifted in and out of several relationships without understanding that I might have awoke much deeper feelings than I felt myself; and I'd dodged a thrown plate or two and *laughed* about it. How dreadfully long it had taken me to stop grazing. All the same . . . I sighed.

I went into the sitting room to see what I could retrieve from the mess, and stood considering the answering machine, which had been split into two pieces with its guts, in the shape of recording tape, unspooling onto the floor.

On the tape, I thought, was Jogger's voice.

I hadn't in the end written down exactly what he'd said, and although I could more or less remember, I wasn't certain of being exact. No amount of rhyming dictionary would help if I got the original words wrong. I rummaged in the kitchen for a Phillips screwdriver and other tools and liberated the hacked pieces of cassette from the answering machine, trying not to tear the tape itself but finding that the ax, in going through one of the spools, had severed a lot of it into very short lengths.

Cursing, I sought and found an old cassette with nothing of note on it, and took that apart and removed all the tape from it. Then I carefully unrolled the whole of the longest section of tape from the answering machine's one undam-

241

aged spool and wound it from its beginning onto one of the newly freed spools. I attached the severed end to the second freed spool and replaced them into their cassette, screwing it shut again.

Then I searched the house for an old seldom-used pocket-sized cassette player which I knew I had somewhere, but naturally when I finally ran it to earth its batteries were dead.

A short pause ensued while I raided another gadget with the same size batteries in working order, but finally, with a sort of prayer, I pressed the play button and held my breath.

"I hate this bloody machine," Jogger's voice said. "Where have you gone, Freddie?"

Loud and clear. Hallelujah.

The whole of his message was there, though slightly distorted by my not having wound the tape evenly enough. When I ran it back and then forward again the distortions had disappeared. I took a sheet of paper and wrote down what he'd said, word for word, indicating his pauses with dots, but I still didn't understand his meaning.

A dead nun in the pit last August.

Most unlikely! Someone would have told me about it even though I'd spent a good deal of August in France (Deauville races) and America (Saratoga, ditto).

What rhymed with nun? Bun, done, fun, run, sun ...

No. What *paired* with nun?

Nun and monk.

Monk ... bunk, chunk, dunk, drunk, funk, hunk, junk, punk, sunk, stunk, chipmunk.

A dead chipmunk? A dead funk? A dead hunk? Hunk of what? Dead junk? Dead punk? A dead *drunk*?

I would give the transcript to Nina, I thought, and let

the collective brains of the Jockey Club Security Service loose on it. I laid the nonsense aside feeling that even if we cracked the code the message could turn out to be irrelevant. Jogger obviously hadn't known he was going to die. He hadn't been leaving me an intensely significant message, fearing it to be his last.

With a shift of focus I switched on the new computer, hoping there wouldn't be a flash and a fizzle and another total collapse of hard disk. Amazingly, however, the wizard had restored me to smooth computer life, everything working as before. I called up Isobel's office machine to see what, if anything, she and Rose had entered and filed since that morning.

They'd been busy, both of them. They'd been quick, conscientious, generous with their time. I'd told both of them to start with that day's entries and go slowly backwards between their other jobs, if they could, but not to go further back in any case than the beginning of the month.

"Leave it on paper for now," I said.

"But the spreadsheets . . ." Rose said.

"Leave the spreadsheets."

"If you say so," she agreed doubtfully.

"It's our own fault we lost everything," Isobel said dolefully.

"Never mind." I still didn't tell them I might produce full backup copies if, first, the safecracker didn't somehow destroy them in getting the safe open, and if, second, the Michelangelo virus hadn't already wiped them out. I also didn't want to incur a repeat attack on myself or my belongings if someone heard the disks existed and knew they could reveal high-risk information. The bruise on my head might be fading, but my car and my sitting room contin-

ually reminded me that melodrama in Pixhill had come
through my gates and might not yet be extinct.

On the screen I read the next day's engagements for the
fleet. Not bad for that week: Steeplechasers to Wolverhampton and Lingfield Park. Broodmares to three studs.
Irish horses to Bristol airport, returning home from Cheltenham.

Advanced plans for Saturday looked good.

I called up the directory of files to see what else Isobel
and Rose had entered and found an unusual one there:
"Visitors."

"Visitors" turned out to be the list I'd asked them for of
everyone they could remember who'd visited the farmyard
office lately.

The dears, I thought, pleased. Helpful beyond duty.

The list read:

All the drivers except Gerry and Pat, who have the
flu. (They'll both be working again next week,
they say.)
Vic and his wife (They both now have the flu.).
Tessa Watermead (looking for Nigel or Lewis).
Jericho Rich (about his horses).
Constable Smith (about the dead man).
Dr. Farway (about the dead man).
Mr. Tigwood (collecting box).
Betsy (Mr. Watermead's secretary).
Brett Gardner (when he left).
Mrs. Williams (cleaner).
Lorna Lipton (looking for FC, but he was driving the
shuttle).
Paul (Isobel's brother, borrowed some money).
Man delivering disinfectant chemicals.

I typed a thank-you message onto the list and made a backup copy of the new work onto a clean unused floppy, though I suspected the office would be ankle-deep in back-ups from now on. I switched off the computer, made some food, drank the rest of the champagne and thought a lot about viruses, both organic and electronic.

Nina telephoned, yawning, at about ten.

"Where are you?" I asked.

"In the cab of the horse van, in the farmyard. We've re-fueled and Nigel's hosing down the outside of the van, thank God. I'm knackered."

"What happened?"

"Nothing, don't worry. The trip went according to plan. We've delivered the show jumper. The owner's father, Jericho Rich, he was there when we unloaded, shouting orders all over the place. What a bloody awkward man. I nearly snapped his head off but thought I'd better not, for your sake. No, nothing much else happened, it's just that this long-distance-driving lark is a job for strong young men; you're right about that."

"How did you get on with Nigel?"

"My God, he's randy. Had his hand on my knee a couple of times and I'm old enough to be his mother. Actually he's not bad fun. No complaints. We chatted a lot. Can I tell you tomorrow?" She yawned again. "He's nearly finished the cleaning. He's got inexhaustible stamina."

"His chief virtue," I agreed.

"See you in the morning. 'Bye."

In the morning I went to the farmyard early, wanting to see some of the drivers before they set off. Harve himself was down for an early start to Wolverhampton, and in such absences of his I very often wandered around in case there were last-minute queries or alterations.

Early starts were normal, as most trainers insisted on their horses arriving at a course at least three hours before they were due to race. In the winter, when racing could start at noon in order to complete the program in the abbreviated daylight, the drivers could be loading at six or seven in the dark and unloading in the dark twelve hours later, according to the length of the journey. By the vernal equinox, we were loading and unloading at dawn and dusk with the long light summer days beckoning, and in the three years I'd had the business I'd seen a regular pattern of energy enhanced by the sun. The workload might be the same in January and June, but not the fatigue level.

Most of the drivers were in the canteen when I arrived on the Friday. The sky outside was gloriously pink and ginger, high, clear and cold. In the canteen the tea looked the color of teak with strength to match, and white plastic teaspoons stood up-right in the sugar bowl.

"Morning, Freddie . . ."

I answered the chorus. "Good morning."

Harve had already set off to Wolverhampton. I checked the other assembled drivers against the list I'd copied from the computer screen and found them all well briefed by Harve and Isobel. I realized I'd left a lot to those two since Tuesday night and had been more affected than I'd acknowledged by the rattling of my brain.

Phil, Dave and Lewis were there, Lewis showing no sign of the flu. Nigel, despite his late return the evening before, exuded undiminished animal strength. Aziz smiled, as ever. A bunch of others looked at their watches, drank their tannin, used the washroom and ambled out on a collective mission to pick up most of the Pixhill horses that were running that afternoon at Lingfield Park.

Dave was down to go with Aziz in the nine-van on a

broodmare mission to Ireland. Both men had arrived in plenty of time, and I asked Dave to come along to my office as I had something to discuss with him. He came in his usual happy-go-lucky way, carrying his tea mug and wearing an amiable unsuspecting expression.

I gestured to him to sit in the chair in front of the desk and closed the door behind us.

"OK, Dave," I said, taking the chair behind the desk and feeling irritation with him, rather than outright anger, "who arranged your diarrhea?"

"What?" He blinked, dismissing the thought crossing his mind. Dismissing the possibility that I knew what he'd done. Dismissing it wrongly, too soon.

"Diarrhea," I reminded him, "needing a stop at South Mimms service station to buy Imodium."

"Oh . . . yes. That. Mm. That's right."

"Who arranged that stop?"

"What? Well, no one. I had the squits, like."

"Let's just face it, Dave," I said a shade wearily, "you did not pick up Kevin Keith Ogden by accident."

"Who?"

"The hitchhiker. And let's stop playing games. You know perfectly well who I mean. You went to his inquest yesterday. You and Brett stopped at South Mimms not because of any mythical squits but to pick up a passenger in order to take him to Chieveley. All of which you did not tell the coroner."

Dave's mouth opened with automatic denials ready and closed on account of what he saw in my face.

"Who arranged it?" I repeated.

He didn't know what to say. I could almost chart the tumbling thoughts; could clearly see the indecision. I waited while he consulted his tea and searched for answers in the brightening sky beyond the window. The little-boy freckles as always lent his expression a natural air of innocence but the half-sly artful assessing look he finally gave me spoke of a more adult guilt.

"There was nothing wrong with it," he said wheedlingly.

"How do you know?"

He tried one of the ingratiating grins to which I was by then immune. "What makes you think it was arranged? Like I said, there was this geezer cadging a lift . . ."

"Stop it, Dave," I said sharply. "If you want to keep your job, you'll tell me the truth."

Shock stopped him. I'd never looked forbidding to him before. "The truth," I urged.

"Honestly, Freddie, I didn't mean no harm." He began to look worried. "What harm could it do?"

"What was the arrangement?"

"Look, it couldn't do no harm to give a man a lift."

"Who paid you?"

"I . . . well . . ."

"Who?" I insisted. "Or you get on your bike now and you don't come back."

"No one," he said desperately. "All right. All right. I was supposed to be paid, but I never was." His disgust looked genuine. "I mean, you weren't supposed to know about him, but then he died . . ." His voice faded, the realization of his admission hitting home. "They said I would find an envelope in the cab of the nine-van first thing Friday, but of course the van was outside your house and there was no envelope in it in the morning, though I looked for it when we were cleaning, like, and I've never heard no more, and it's *not fair*."

"Serves you right," I said unsympathetically. "Who are *they*?"

"What?"

" 'They' who said you would find an envelope in the cab?"

"Well . . ."

"Dave!" I said, exasperated. "Get on with it."

"Yes, but, see, I don't *know*."

I said sarcastically, "You agreed to do something you knew I had over and over again forbidden, and you don't know who you jeopardized your job for?"

"Yes, but . . ."

"No buts," I said. "How did 'they' get in touch with you, and were 'they' a man or a woman?"

"Er . . ."

I would strangle him, I thought.

"All right," he said, "all right." He took an unhappy breath. "It was a she, and she phoned me at home and my wife answered it and she didn't like it being some strange woman, not Isobel, like, but anyway she just said it would be worth my while just to give this man a lift, and you don't turn down windfalls like that. I mean . . . well . . . it's all beer money, isn't it?"

"Did you recognize her voice?"

He shook his head miserably.

"What accent did she have?"

He seemed merely puzzled by the question. "She was English," he said, "not foreign."

"What did she say?"

"Like I said, she said to pick up this man . . ."

"How were you to know him?"

"She said he would be near the diesel pumps and he'd see us pull up and he would speak to me . . . and he did."

"Who thought up the diarrhea?"

"Like, she did. See, she said I had to have some way of getting Brett to stop at South Mimms. So I told Brett if he didn't stop, I'd have to drop my trousers in the cab and he would have to clean it up." He laughed uneasily. "Brett said he would rub my face in it. But anyway, he stopped."

"So Brett wasn't in the scheme?"

Dave looked furious. "Brett's a *shit*."

"Why, exactly?"

Dave's sense of injustice overcame caution. "He said he wouldn't take the man unless he paid us. So I asked this Ogden, but he said he hadn't any money. He *must* have had some, but he said that wasn't in the bargain, I would be getting paid later, and I said Brett wouldn't agree to it without being paid first, and this Ogden got sort of purple, he was so upset, and he found some money after all, but not a lot, and Brett said it wasn't enough and so *I* gave Brett some money and I had to tell him I'd be getting it back, so then he said he'd be wanting some of that if I didn't want him to tell you that I'd fixed up a hitchhiker for money. And not only *that*," Dave's fury increased, "but Brett came to the pub on Saturday evening and made me pay for his beer and he was effing *gloating*, and I told him the pay envelope hadn't turned up but all he said was, 'Too bad, mate, that's your bad luck,' and went on drinking."

"And you took a swipe at Jogger," I said.

"Well, he wouldn't shut up and I was raging about Brett, and Jogger was going *on* and *on* about things stuck on the bottom of the horse vans, on and on about the cash box in your sitting room, that filthy old cash box, on and on about things being carried under the trucks . . ."

"Did you understand what he was talking about?" I asked, surprised.

"Yes, of course."

"About lone rangers?"

"Yeah, of course. Strangers."

"What about nuns and Poland?"

"Eh?"

His face was blank. Nuns and Poland meant nothing.

"Did Jogger," I asked, "know about your private enterprise?"

"What? Do you mean that Ogden? Of course Jogger knew he'd died, like. I didn't tell him the ride had been fixed in advance. I'm not loony, see, he'd have been round to you in five minutes telling of me. Always on your side, was Jogger."

"I thought *you* were, too," I observed.

"Yeah." He looked very faintly ashamed. "Well, like, there's no harm in a bit of beer money on the side."

"There was, this time."

"How was I to know he'd *die*?" Dave asked aggrievedly.

"What was he carrying?" I asked.

"Carrying?" His forehead wrinkled. "A bag. One of them briefcases. And, um, a sort of carrier bag with sandwiches and a flask. I helped him put them all up in the cab."

"What did he do with the sandwiches?"

"Ate them, I suppose. I don't know."

"Did you and Brett buy sandwiches?"

He looked puzzled by the questions but found them easier to answer than earlier ones. "Brett did," he said readily, though sourly. "He went off laughing and bought some with *my* money, the *turd*."

"Brett said you'd picked up hitchhikers on other occasions."

"He's a *shit*."

"Well, did you? And were they arranged in advance?"

"No, they were casual, like. Brett never minded, if he got some of the dosh."

"What about the other drivers? Have they done the same?"

"I'm not snitching on anyone," he said virtuously.

"Meaning that they have?"

"No." He physically squirmed.

I left it. Instead I asked, "How long before you went to Newmarket was the stop at South Mimms arranged?"

"The night before."

"Time?"

"After I got back from Folkestone races."

"That means late."

He nodded. "My wife didn't like it."

"Had the woman tried to reach you before you got back?"

"My wife would have gone on about it if she had."

He seemed to be well under his wife's thumb, and it didn't seem to have occurred to him to ask how the woman on the telephone had known he wouldn't be home until late, and had also known he could be going to Newmarket the next day. She had known, moreover, that he could be bribed to pick up a hitchhiker.

She had known a good deal too much.

Who, for God's sake, had told her?

10

Dave and Aziz set off for Ireland, Dave looking only moderately chastened, apparently confident that I wouldn't actually sack him. He was probably right, as he didn't appear to have broken any laws except my own and could go off to an industrial tribunal muttering about wrongful dismissal if I gave him grounds and he had a mind to. There was nothing new in his irresponsibility. He was still very good and reliable with horses and an adequate driver. I hoped he would think twice in the future about taking money for lifts, but I wouldn't bet he'd never do it. The main change, as far as I could see, was in my own attitude towards him, my indulgent liking having faded towards irritation.

Out in the farmyard Lewis was showing photographs of

his baby to Nina, who had arrived in her working persona and her working car.

"He's a right little raver," Lewis said, looking adoringly at his offspring. "You know what, he likes soccer on the telly, he watches it all the time."

"How old is he?" Nina asked, dutifully admiring.

"Eight months. Look at this one, in the bath, sucking his yellow duck."

"He's lovely," Nina said.

Lewis beamed and said, "Nothing's too good for him. We might send him to Eton, why not?" He tucked the photos away in an envelope. "Better be off to Lingfield, I guess," he said. "Two for Benjy Usher. Last time I went to that yard," he told Nina, "they led out the wrong horse, and not for the first time, either. I'd loaded up and was driving out of the gate when one of the grooms came tearing along yelling and screaming. I ask you! The wrong horse! And there's Mr. Usher yelling out of his upstairs window as if it was my fault, not his head lad's, the stupid git."

Nina listened, fascinated, and asked me, "Is it easy to pick up the wrong horse?"

"We take the horses they give us," I said. "If they're the wrong ones, it's not our fault. As you know, our drivers have work sheets with times, pickup points, destinations, and the names of the horses, but it's not their job to check identities."

"We took two of Mr. Usher's all the way to the wrong races, last year," Lewis said, enjoying it.

I enlarged. "We were taking one from Usher's to Leicester and one to Plumpton, and although Lewis and the other driver each said clearly which van was going to which destination, the Usher head lad mixed them up.

They didn't find out until the first one arrived at the wrong place. There was quite a fracas."

"Frack-ass," Lewis said, grinning. "I'll say."

"Look in a newspaper and check you've got the right names of the Usher runners," I told Lewis, "so we have no more mixups today."

"OK."

He walked off to the canteen where he could be seen consulting the racing programs, then with a wave took himself over to his super-six to set off on his journey.

"When he came here first," I told Nina, "Lewis had ringlets. Now he has the baby instead. He's handy with his fists if you ever need defending. There won't be many people messing with his boy."

"School bullies beware?"

"And their dads."

"They're all very different from each other when you get to know them," Nina said.

"The drivers, do you mean? Yes, they are." She came with me into my office. "Tell me about Nigel."

She settled herself comfortably into the second chair while I perched on the edge of the desk.

"He drove nearly all the way, there and back, regardless of hours, but we wrote up the logbooks as if we'd shared it more evenly."

"Tut."

She smiled. "He said I could look after the horse. He's not too fond of horses, did you know? He said some drivers he talks to at race meetings are downright scared of them."

"So I've heard."

"Nigel thinks you aren't too bad to work for. A bit fussy, like, he said."

"Oh, really?"

"He's proud of his body. He gave me a rundown of the state of his muscles, practically each of them separately. He told me how to develop my pectorals."

I laughed in my throat. "How useful."

"I have a message for you from Patrick Venables."

Abrupt change of subject. "What is it?" I asked.

"Those tubes you gave me for analysis. He says," she frowned indecisively, "he says they held something called viral transport medium."

I made no immediate comment, so she went on. "It's a liquid apparently made up of sterile water, sucrose—it sounds odd but that's what he said—and bovine albumin, which is what keeps the virus going, and glutamic acid, that's an amino acid or something, and an antibiotic called geranium ... er, no ... Gentamicin ... which kills off invading bacteria, but won't act on a virus. The whole stuff's used for transporting a virus from place to place."

"Did they find a virus in it?"

"No. They said a virus wouldn't last very long out of a body. They apparently don't use the word 'live' with viruses, as viruses can't go on working or reproducing, or whatever it is they do, once they're away from a living host cell. It's all a bit complicated, it seems to me. Anyway, Patrick wants to know where the tubes came from."

"From Pontefract service station in Yorkshire. Before that, I don't know."

I told her what I'd learned from Lynn Melissa Ogden, relict of Kevin Keith.

"Poor woman," I said. "They led a wretched existence."

"There are so many awful lives. And you never expect it when you're starting."

I told her about my confrontation with Dave, earlier that morning.

"So you were right!" she exclaimed. "You said he had to have arranged that hitchhiker in advance."

"Mm. But he didn't react when I asked him what Kevin Keith was carrying. I'm sure he didn't know."

"So it couldn't have been him who came in the black balaclava to search the cab."

"I'm certain it wasn't. He wouldn't have needed to disguise himself. He could have come back openly. He was hoping for his pay to be left in the cab, but, not surprisingly, it wasn't. The person who came disguised was *searching*, not leaving an envelope."

"So who was it?"

"Good question." I thought a bit. "There are two minds at work here. Two at least," I said. "One is logical but destructive. The other's as illogical as a poltergeist."

"Two at least? You mean, more than two?"

"I think it was two *men* who dropped me into the Southampton Docks. One was male, certainly. And they carried me easily. But the person who arranged the transport of the virus medium was female."

"Or falsetto?"

"What would be the point? And not easy to do." I paused. "What we *don't* know," I said, "is whether Kevin Keith was supposed to take the virus medium with him when he got off at Chieveley, or whether he was supposed to leave it in the cab so that it would arrive in Pixhill. Arrive here at the farmyard, that is. Also we don't know whether there was in fact any virus in the tubes on the way here, or whether someone in this general area had ordered the medium for future use."

"Oh Jeeze."

257

I fished in a pocket and gave her a folded piece of paper bearing the transcript of Jogger's phone call.

"Get Patrick Venables's cockney friends to unscramble it," I suggested.

"What cockney friends?"

"He's bound to know the London brotherhood."

"Such faith. All right." She read the words aloud. "Take a butcher's at them nuns . . . ye Gods."

"Does it mean anything to you?"

"Poland had the same five on a horse last summer . . . It's all rubbish." She put the paper in her handbag. "No one came near us on the French trip," she said. "No one anywhere showed the slightest interest in the underside of the horse van. Nigel said he didn't like driving Phil's super-six because it has heavier steering than his own. He approves of the one-man-one-box arrangement and he likes driving for some trainers more than others. He would like to drive for the Watermeads more often, but Lewis is jealous if he does. Lewis drives for Benjy Usher too, but Nigel doesn't like Benjy Usher's ways. He says Harve told him he'll be driving for a new trainer, a Mrs. English, and he's heard she's a dragon."

"Mm." I smiled. "She'll get on well with Nigel, all the same. He'll chat her up. She's demanding, but he's tireless. By the end of the summer she won't want anyone else."

"You go in for quite a lot of applied psychology," she observed, "pairing the drivers to the jobs."

"Happier drivers work better. It's obvious. Happier trainers don't employ my rivals."

"So it's all for profit?"

"And . . . um . . . no harm in all-round contentment, is there?"

"I do see," she said, half mocking, "why everyone likes you."

I sighed. "Not everyone, by a long shot." I stood up off the desk, pleased to talk to her but with things to get on with. "You're not on the driving chart today, are you? You could take a day off after the French trip."

"I don't want to. I'll spend the morning here, looking around in general and available if you get a last-minute driving job."

"Fine. Good. Well, Isobel's arrived." We'd both seen her car drive in. "Come and listen while I try to find out who knew that Dave would be going to Newmarket the day he picked up Kevin Keith."

Her eyes widened in comprehension. "Like I said before," she said, "you don't need me here."

"I like you here."

"As a witness, Patrick said. I'm the insurance you apparently wanted. Your vindicator. He said you were that subtle, and I didn't really believe him."

"Devious, he probably meant."

"He approved of the idea, anyway. That's why I'm here."

I thought her almost too frank and wondered what her boss would have said. We went along to Isobel's office, where I said thank you for the visitors' list, and Isobel brought it onto the screen. She gave me a flashing smile of thanks for my message at the end, but shook her head when I asked her if she could remember which actual day each of the people on the list had been to her office.

"Can you remember," I asked neutrally, "which of them were here the day before Brett and Dave picked up the hitchhiker? That would be nine days ago, on the Wednesday."

She shook her head. "I could call up the drivers' list for that day." She turned automatically to the computer and then looked stricken. "Oh . . . that day's wiped out."

"It's all right." I'd pieced together various scraps of the pencil and paper chart that had been on the desk in my sitting room, and had written them down in a list.

"Harve took the first load of Jericho Rich's horses from Michael Watermead to Newmarket," I said. "Was anyone from the Watermead yard here in the office that day? Was Jericho Rich here? Was anyone here from Newmarket? Anyone who could have had a sight of the Thursday schedule? You usually have the schedule on the screen a lot of the time. Who could have seen it?"

She looked bewildered. I'd asked the questions too fast. I went back and asked them again slowly.

"Oh, I see. Well, obviously all the drivers could see who was going where. I mean, they always come in for a look."

"And beside the drivers?"

She shook her head. "It's so long ago. People are in and out of here all the time." She considered. "They didn't need to come here themselves to know who was doing that trip. I told Betsy when she called here that it was down for Brett and she said both Mr. Rich and Mr. Watermead wouldn't be thrilled about it because Brett was such a whiner, and I said . . . well, I said don't tell them, but I expect she did."

I read the list on her screen. "What about Dr. Farway?"

"Oh no, he came the day *after*, when that hitchhiker had died. He came on the Friday."

"And . . . er . . . John Tigwood?"

"He's such a bore with those collecting boxes. Sorry, I shouldn't say that."

"Why not? He is. Which day did he come?"

"That must have been Friday as well. Yes, Sandy Smith was here too. I remember them all talking about the dead man."

"OK. What about Tessa Watermead?"

"She must have come before Friday because that was the day she wanted to go with Nigel to Newmarket and he wouldn't take her." Isobel frowned. "Tessa's often in and out. I think she gets bored. She wants me to teach her how to do this job . . . do you mind if I show her?"

"Not as long as she's not a nuisance to you, or wastes your time."

"She does a bit," Isobel said frankly. "I asked her why she didn't go to a secretarial college and learn properly and she said she'd think about it."

"Well," I said, "how about Mr. Rich?"

"Friday. While you were doing the shuttle."

"Any other day?"

"Um . . . yes, of course, he came in on the Tuesday, fussing about his transfer. I told you, do you remember?"

"Yes, vaguely."

"I told him you'd arranged it for three consecutive days. I went through it all with him."

"Mm. How about Lorna Lipton, Mrs. Watermead's sister?"

"She walks her dog past here. Well, you know that. She . . . or . . drops in to see you, now and then. She came in on that Friday when you were doing the shuttle."

"What about earlier in the week?"

Isobel said doubtfully, "I can't remember which days."

"Um," I said, "do you remember if anyone asked for Dave the day before he went to Newmarket?"

"What?"

I repeated the question. "Did anyone want to speak to him?"

Her forehead wrinkled. "I don't remember anyone asking, but I couldn't *swear*. I mean . . . oh yes! Mr. Rich wanted to know if Dave was going to Newmarket with his first lot of horses but I said no, we were short of drivers because of the flu and he'd have to take some runners to Folkestone. It was Folkestone, wasn't it?" She looked despairingly at the computer, feeling lost without its memory but doing not too badly with her own. "I expect I did tell him Dave would be going with the nine two-year-olds on the Thursday, though."

I thanked her with a stroke down her arm and went on out into the yard, Nina following.

"It's a maze," she said. "How do you keep it all in your head?"

"I can't. I keep losing bits." And I still kept wanting to go to sleep, which didn't help.

The fleet was steadily leaving, the farmyard looking empty with most of its heard of monsters out on the trail. Only three vans remained in separated slots, quiet, clean, gleaming in the sunshine and in their way majestic.

"You're proud of them," Nina exclaimed, watching my face.

"I'd better not be, or something will happen to them. I loved my Jag . . . oh, well, never mind."

Isobel came to the office door and looked relieved to see me still there. She had Benjy Usher's secretary on the phone, she said: could we please send another van immediately as Mr. Usher had forgotten he was running a pair in the second division of the novice hurdle at Lingfield, the last race of the day?

"She says he clean forgot they were declared," Isobel

reported. "Then just now he let out a yell and said they must be sent off at once. She says the blacksmith's there now, putting racing plates on them and swearing blue murder. What shall I tell her? She's waiting to know. Mr. Usher's yelling at her elbow. I can hear him. Lewis has left there with the first two and Mr. Usher says there's no time for him to go back. What do you think?"

"Say we'll send another van at once."

"But . . . will you drive it yourself? Everyone else has gone."

"I'll do it," Nina said.

"Oh, yes. Sorry . . . Yes, of course." Isobel hurried inside and presently came out again to confirm the journey, pleasurably saying, "Mr. Usher's frantically trying to reach his second jockey."

"Find a good map for Nina, will you?" I asked her. "Mark the racecourse." To Nina I said, "I'll lead you to Benjy's stable. Can you manage from there?"

"Sure. Which horse van?"

We looked at the remnants. "Pat's," I said, pointing at a four-van, "the one you drove the first day. There's a lone ranger under it, don't forget, though I can't see that mattering."

"I'll keep a look out anyway." She smiled. "What an incredible trainer, forgetting his runners!"

"Not so incredible, really. Trainers make shattering mistakes, declaring the wrong horse sometimes, even in big races, and forgetting others altogether. Benjy's eccentric, but he's not the only last-minute merchant we deal with. Many trainers change their minds violently, some when the clock's begun striking. Makes life more interesting."

"As long as you're happy."

I checked the map with her, marking the road clearly,

made sure she had the right paperwork and then drove ahead of her to Benjy's yard, not the easiest of places to find.

He was leaning out of his upstairs window when we arrived, issuing a stream of invective and instructions to his luckless grooms and greeting me personally with, "Don't let your driver go without the jockeys' colors."

Nina helped the grooms load the two young upset hurdlers, who were reacting with trembles and rolling eyes to the general scramble. Nina, I saw, had a calming effect as powerful and natural as Dave's, so that in the end the nervous creatures walked docilely up the ramp without needing blindfolds or brute force. Benjy stopped complaining, Nina and the head lad closed the ramp, the jockeys' colors were put on board, a couple of scurrying grooms climbed into the passenger seats to accompany their charges and the circus was ready to roll.

Nina gave me a laugh through the window. "They say there's a new head traveling lad in Lewis's van ahead of us, and he doesn't know these other two horses are coming. He has to declare them, *and* saddle them. What a to-do."

"Phone Isobel and ask her to tell Lewis," I said.

"Yes, boss."

She went on her way in good humor and I found myself regretting her stay would be temporary. Highly competent and good company, Nina Young.

Benjy withdrew and closed his window like one of the characters exiting in *Jeffrey Bernard Is Unwell*. I half expected him to reappear on his doorstep but when he didn't I drifted off in the Fourtrak to go home.

A short way along the road I slowed before passing a man leading a horse, hardly an unusual sight in Pixhill.

The horse was swinging from side to side with his attendant yanking down again and again on the leading rein in a sharp manner guaranteed to produce more skittering, not less. I passed the pair with caution, stopped ahead, and walked back to meet them.

"Can I help you?" I asked.

"No, you can't." He was brusque, if not downright rude. Young, belligerent, surly.

I realized with minor shock that the badly behaved horse was my old friend Peterman, his name plain on his head-collar.

"Would you like me to lead him?" I asked. "I know him."

"No, I wouldn't. It's none of your effing business."

I shrugged, went back to the Fourtrak and sat watching the erratic and potentially dangerous progress along the road. When he passed me, the groom raised two fingers in my direction with a jerk.

A fool, I thought him. I watched him turn right a good way ahead, taking the road towards Marigold English's yard. I followed slowly to the turning, stopping on the main road but watching until horse and man turned off the side road and in through Marigold's gates. At least, I thought, old Peterman had reached his new home safely, and I would check with Marigold to make sure he was all right.

Outside my own house, when I reached it, there seemed to have sprouted a well filled car park. Clustered around the Jaguar and the Robinson 22 were cars in all directions with their drivers in chatting groups. These, on my arrival, attempted to introduce themselves all at once.

"Hey," I protested, "who got here first?"

The simple order of precedence identified the crowd

into various insurances assessors, air-accident inspectors, a transport firm surveying the possibility of shipping the helicopter to Scotland, a salesman hoping I would order a new Jaguar and the man to open the safe.

I took the last one pronto into the house, even though he was apparently the latest on the scene. He looked at the hatchet job, scratched his head, asked if there was anything fragile inside (yes, I said, computer disks) and said he thought it a case for a drill.

"Drill away," I said.

The rest of the men outside had sprouted notebooks and were discussing the mechanics of bricks-on-sticks on accelerators. By no means impossible, they agreed. Very dicey, but possible. The helicopter-shipper asked questions about fuel in the tanks. Not much there, I told him. My sister had said she would have to refuel at Oxford. Full, the tank and auxiliary tank held about 130 liters, she'd said, but she'd flown from Carlisle on that. The shipper began discussing technical ways to disassemble the tri-hinge rotor, and lost me.

The air-accident inspector produced a letter from Lizzie which he asked me to read and confirm. Neither of us had seen the collision, she wrote. I confirmed it.

Insurance assessors, hers and mine, said they'd never seen anything like it, not right outside someone's back door, that was. They'd studied Sandy's report. They asked me to sign various forms. I signed.

The Jaguar salesman told me about the Jaguar XJ220. Made in Bloxham, near Banbury, he said. Only 350 of them built, costing four hundred and eighty thousand pounds each.

"*Each?*" I repeated. "Four hundred and eighty thousand pounds each?"

Did I want to order one?

"No," I said.

"Just as well. They're all sold."

I wondered if it were I who was surreal and whether my concussion was worse than I suspected.

"Actually," the salesman said, "I came to see if your XJS could be salvaged."

"And can it?"

Shaking his head, he looked with regret at the whole-looking white rear end of my pride and joy. "I might find you another one like it. That same year. Advertise for one, secondhand. And they're still in production. I could get you a new one."

I shook my head. "I'll let you know."

I wouldn't seek a twin, I thought. Life had changed. I was changing. I would buy a different car.

The flock of notebooks returned to their vehicles and drove away, leaving only the workmanlike van of the safe-cracker beside the wreck on the tarmac. I went in to check on his progress and found my safe door open but minus its lock mechanism, which lay bent on the floor.

We discussed the possibility of mending the safe but he advised me to take the insurance money and buy a newer and better model which he would be happy to sell me. It would not, he assured me, have a lock that could be assaulted by an ax.

He went out to the van for a pamphlet with illustrations and an order form, and I signed my name again. He shook my hand. He asked me to check that the contents of the old safe were untouched and, when I'd done that, to sign his work sheet. I signed.

When he'd gone, I retrieved the packet of money and the backup floppy disks and went into the kitchen to phone the computer wizard. Sure, he agreed, bring the disks in for a check as soon as I liked; he would be in his workshop all afternoon and would wash Michelangelo out of my hair with his little virus scrubbers. Did all computer wizards talk like that? I wondered.

"Great," I said.

I made coffee and drank it and thought a bit, and after a while telephoned the local Customs and Excise office.

I explained who I was. They knew of me, they said. I explained that as my horse vans went fairly regularly across the Channel, I wanted an up-to-date list of what could and could not be carried in them, in view of the ever-changing European regulations. My drivers were confused, I said.

Ah, they said understandingly. They didn't themselves deal with import and export, but mostly with tax. If I wanted the up-to-the-minute info on international movement of goods I would need to see their Single Market Liaison Officer in the regional office.

"Which regional office?" I asked.

"Southampton," they said.

I almost laughed. They enlarged. The Southampton regional office was actually in Portsmouth. The Single Market Liaison Officer there would answer all my questions and give me the latest copy of the Single Market report. If I wanted to go there in person, they suggested I should arrive well before four o'clock. It was Friday, they explained.

I thanked them and looked at my watch. Plenty of time. I drove to Newbury, shopped for a week's food and ran the wizard to earth in his workshop, which proved to be a smallish room half lined with large brown cardboard boxes bearing words like "Fragile" or "This way up ALWAYS." A busy desk bore piles of papers—letters, invoices, pamphlets—held down by public-house ashtrays used as paperweights. Ceiling-high bookshelves supported instruction manuals and catalogues by the score. Plastic-covered leads snaked everywhere. A table along one wall bore a keyboard, two or three computers, a laser printer and a live color monitor showing a bright row of miniature playing cards apparently halfway through a game of solitaire.

"Black jack on red queen," I said, looking.

"Yeah." He grinned, ran his hand through his hair, and with a mouse moved the cards around on the screen. "It's not coming out," he observed, and switched it all off. "Did you bring your disks?"

I handed them to him in an envelope. "There are four," I said. "A new one for each calendar year since I took over the business."

He nodded. "I'll start with the latest." He fed it into a drive slot in one of the computers on the table and called up onto the monitor the directory of the files stored for the current year.

Muttering under his breath, he pressed a series of keys on the keyboard and in a while the screen was flickering rapidly with letters and numbers as he scanned my disk for deadly strangers.

Lone rangers, I thought. Aliens everywhere.

"There we are," he said, when the flickering steadied to a single message. "Scan complete. No virus found." He grinned at me. "No Michelangelo. You're safe."

"That's ... er ... rather more than extremely interesting," I said.

"How?"

"I used the disk last to back up the work entered on the main office computer a week ago yesterday," I said. "That was March 3rd."

His eyes savored the knowledge.

"On March 3rd, then," he said, "I'd say there was no Michelangelo in your office. Right?"

"Right."

"So you caught it on the Friday or Saturday . . ." He pondered. "Ask your secretaries if they fed anyone else's disks into your machine. Say, for instance, someone lent them a game disk, like the solitaire game, which no one should do, really, it's an infringement of copyright, but say they *did*, well, Michelangelo could have been lurking in the game disk and it would leap across to your machine instantly."

"The monitor in the office is black-and-white," I said.

"Kids would play solitaire in black-and-white," he replied. "Like Nintendo. No problem. Did you have any kids in the office?"

"Isobel's brother, Paul," I said, remembering his name on the list. "He's fifteen. Always cadging money from his sister."

"Ask him, then. I'll bet that's where your trouble lies."

"Thank you very much."

"I may as well scan your other disks, just to be safe." He fed the three others through the scanning process, all with nil results. "There you are, then. At present they're clean. But, like I said, you have to patrol your defenses all the time."

I thanked him and paid him, took my clean disks out to the car and set off on the drive south to Portsmouth, giving Southampton Docks a wide berth.

Customs and Excise were fortunately helpful, extending the impression that talking to the general public made a change from regular bureaucracy. The near-top man I was finally steered to, who introduced himself briefly as "Collins," offered me a seat, a cup of tea and a willing expression. An office around us: desk, green plant, second-generation Scandinavian decor.

"What may your drivers carry and what may they not?" Collins repeated.

"Yes," I said.

"Yes. As you know, it's all different from the old cut-and-dried days."

"Mm."

"We're positively forbidden to make spot checks on anything coming in from the E.C." He paused. "European Community," he said.

"Mm."

"Even drugs." He spread his hands in what looked like a long-standing frustration. "We can act—search—only on specific information. The stuff floods in, I've no doubt, but we can't do anything about it. Customs checks on goods are now allowed only at the point of entry into the Community. Once inside, movement is free."

"I expect it saves a lot of paperwork," I said.

"Tons of it. Hundreds of tons. Sixty million fewer forms." The plus side lightened his scowl. "Saves time too, saves days and months." He searched briefly for a booklet, found it and slid it towards me across the desk. "Most of the present regulations are listed in there. There's very little restriction on alcohol, tobacco and personal goods. One day there'll be none. But of course there'll still be duty and restrictions of goods entering from outside the E.C."

I picked up the booklet and thanked him.

"We spend a good deal of our time juggling with tax," he said. "Different rates, you see, in different E.C. countries."

"I was wondering," I murmured, "what one may still *not*

bring into this country from Europe, and ... er ... what one may not take out."

His eyebrows rose. "Not take *out*?"

"Anything that doesn't have free movement."

He pursed his lips. "Some things need *licenses*," he said. "Are your drivers breaking the law?"

"I came to find out."

His interest sharpened as if he'd suddenly realized I was there from more than normal curiosity.

"Your horse vans come and go through Portsmouth, don't they?"

"Sometimes."

"And they're never searched."

"No."

"And you have the necessary permissions, of course, to move live animals across the Channel."

"All that's done for us by a specialist firm."

He nodded. He thought. "I suppose if your vans carried *other* animals than horses, we'd never know. Your drivers haven't been bringing in cats or dogs, have they?" His voice was censorious and alarmed. "We maintain the quarantine laws, of course. The threat of rabies is always with us."

I said calmingly, "I've never heard of them bringing in cats or dogs, and if they had it would be common knowledge in my village, where news travels faster than lightning."

He relaxed slightly; a fortyish man with receding hair and white careful hands.

"As a matter of fact," he said, "thanks to vaccines, no one has died of rabies contracted in Europe for the past thirty years, but we still don't want the disease here."

"Um," I said, "what do you need a license for?"

"Dozens of things. From your point of view I suppose veterinary medicines would be interesting. You'd need to get a separate license for each movement, a Therapeutic Substance license from the Ministry of Agriculture and Fisheries Veterinary Medicines Directorate. But there would be no check on the substance here on entry through Portsmouth. Enforcement of licensing would be a matter for MAFF itself."

MAFF? Oh, Ministry of Agriculture, Fisheries and Food. Shades of Jogger.

"Well," I said, "what else isn't one supposed to bring in and out?"

"Guns," he said. "There are still exit checks, of course, for firearms in baggage at airports. No import checks here. You could bring in a vanful of guns, and we'd never know. Smuggling in the old sense has vanished within the E.C."

"So it seems."

"There are intellectual property rights," he said. "That's about the infringement of existing patents between member states."

"I don't think my drivers are into intellectual property rights."

He smiled briefly, a quick movement of lips. "I'm afraid I haven't been of much help."

"Indeed you've been most kind," I assured him, rising to go. "Negative results are often as helpful as positive."

I thought, however, as I drove back to Pixhill with the Single Market booklet on the seat beside me, that I was as far as ever from understanding why anyone should need or want to fix hiding places under my lorries. If smuggling was out, what were they *for*?

At home I sat in my poor green leather chair with the stuffing coming out of the ax holes and one by one fed my clean disks and their information into my new computer. Then, feeling rusty and all thumbs and impatient to begin my lessons with the wizard, I looked up my original computer manuals and worked out how to organize all the data now inside the machine into various categories, both chronological and geographic.

I studied in turn each driver's work over the past three years, looking for I knew not what. A pattern? Something worth destroying my records for, if that should happen not to be the work of Isobel's brother. I tended to doubt it was Paul's doing as, first, he was more idle than bright and, second, Isobel would never let him play games in the office.

The patterns I was looking for were definitely there, but told me nothing I didn't know. Each driver went most often to the racecourses favored by the trainers they mostly drove for. Lewis, for instance, drove most regularly each summer to Newbury, Sandown, Goodwood, Epsom, Salisbury and Newmarket, Michael Watermead's preferred prestigious destinations. At other times he went where Benjy Usher sent his jumpers, Lingfield, Fontwell, Chepstow, Cheltenham, Warwick and Worcester. Most of his overseas journeys had been for Michael, all to Italy, Ireland or France.

Although there was horse racing all over Europe, British trainers rarely sent horses anywhere but Italy, Ireland and France. Often British runners traveled by air (and had to be taken to the airports), but Michael much preferred to go all the way by road; all the better for me.

Nigel had made the most overseas journeys, but that was my doing, owing to his long-distance stamina. Harve had made few, both my choice and his. Dave had made dozens as relief driver and horses handler, often with broodmares rather than racers.

All in all, the categories were informative but told me nothing surprising, and after about an hour I switched off, as puzzled as ever.

I phoned Nina, reckoning she would be in her horse van on the way back from Lingfield, and she answered immediately.

"Phone me when you get to Pixhill," I said briefly.

"Will do."

End of conversation.

I phoned Isobel at her home. Nothing unusual had happened during the day's work, she assured me. She'd told Lewis that Nina was following him, and all the Usher horses had run in the right races at Lingfield. Aziz and Dave had arrived in Ireland with their mares. Harve and Phil had each taken a winner to Wolverhampton, great rejoicing. None of the other drivers had hit snags.

"Great," I said. "Um . . . your brother Paul . . ."

"I've *told* him not to bother me at work." She sounded guiltily apologetic.

"Yes, but, um, how is he with computers?"

"Computers?"

I explained the wizard's game-virus theory.

"Oh, no," she said positively. "I'd never let him near your computer and to be honest he wouldn't know *how* to load data in our machine."

"You're sure?"

"A hundred percent."

Another good theory down the drain.

"Did anyone else," I asked, "know enough to get near enough to the computer last Friday to feed any disk into it?"

"I've thought and thought . . ." She stopped. "Why last Friday?"

"Or Saturday," I said. "Our computer wizard thinks we picked up the infection as late as that."

"Oh golly."

"Nothing comes to your mind?"

"No." It was a wail of regret and worry. "I wish I knew."

"Did you leave any of those people on your list of visitors alone in your office?"

"But . . . but . . . oh dear. I can't remember. I might have done. I wouldn't have seen anything wrong in it. I mean, there weren't any *strangers* there, not right in my office, and I can't believe . . ."

"It's all right," I said. "Don't think about it."

"I can't help it."

I put the phone down just as Sandy Smith rolled onto my tarmac. He came towards the back door, taking off his peaked cap and combing his flattened hair with his fingers.

"Come in," I said, meeting him. "Whisky?"

"I'm on duty," he said doubtfully.

"Who's to know?"

He squared it with his conscience and took the scotch with water. We sat in the kitchen, one on each side of the table, and he relaxed as far as unbuttoning his tunic.

"It's about Jogger," he said. He frowned at his glass, his round face troubled. "About rust."

His gloom spread to me fast. "What did they find?" I asked.

"I've heard," he began, and I reflected that this was Sandy's semaphore at its best. "I've . . . er . . . *unofficially* heard that they did find rust all round the pit and on the edges. But the rust was everywhere mixed with oil and grease. And there wasn't any oil or grease in the wound on Jogger's head."

"*Damn,*" I said.

"They're going to treat it as murder. Don't say I told you."

"No. Thanks, Sandy."

"They'll be asking you questions."

"They've asked questions already," I said.

"They'll want to know who had it in for Jogger."

"I want to know that too."

"I knew old Jog for years," Sandy said. "He wasn't one to have enemies."

"I would think," I said neutrally, "that he may have done what I did on Tuesday night, which was to walk into the farmyard unexpectedly. Maybe both of us were hit on the head to prevent us seeing . . . whatever . . . but Jogger *died*, and was put into the pit to make it look like an accident."

Sandy gazed at me thoughtfully.

"What's going on there, in the farmyard?" he asked.

"I don't know. I bloody don't *know*, and it's driving me crazy."

"Did Jogger know?"

"It's possible he found out. That's perhaps why he died, and I didn't want it to be that. I've been sort of praying for it to be proved an accident."

"You've thought all along, though, that it was murder." He scratched his neck absentmindedly. "What did Jogger mean about lone rangers under your lorries? My colleagues will want to know."

"I'll show you," I said. "Come into the sitting room."

We went into the jumbled wreckage and I led him

across to where I'd left the cash box Jogger had prised from under the nine-van a week ago.

I led Sandy to the place, but the cash box wasn't there.

"That's odd," I said. "It was right here on this spot on the newspaper . . ."

"What was?"

I described the cash box: gray metal, ordinary, fresh-smelling inside, empty, unlocked by Jogger, the round mark of where it had been held onto a magnet the only bright section on its filthy grime-laden exterior.

I looked round the room for it and so did Sandy, poking about in the general mess.

No cash box.

"When did you last see it?" Sandy asked.

"Tuesday, I suppose. I showed it to my sister." I frowned. "When this room was done over, I didn't think to look for the cash box."

He supposed, he said, that he could understand that, and asked if anything else was missing.

"I don't think so."

"Jogger said lone rangers. Plural. There must have been more than one."

"Two of the other vans have been trundling about with containers fixed to their undersides: but the containers are empty, same as the cash box was."

Sandy said doubtfully, "Everyone in the pub last Saturday heard him talking about it. I mean, he can't have been killed to stop him telling anyone about them because he'd already done it."

"What's more," I said, "Dave, Harve and Brett, besides Jogger, saw the cash box here in this room, just after Jogger levered it off the nine-van. It was on my desk at that point, in plain sight. I put it down on the floor sometime later."

"You must have an idea what it was for," Sandy said, a policemanlike suspicion creeping into his voice despite the nonadversarial status between us.

"We thought of drugs, if that's what you mean? Harve, Jogger and I discussed that. But drugs don't just appear out of thin air. Someone had to supply them. Harve and I don't believe that any of our drivers deal in drugs. I mean, there would be *signs*, wouldn't there? And money going around. We would *notice*."

"Why didn't you tell me about this last Tuesday?" Still the suspicious tone. "You should have told me, I reckon."

"I wanted to find out for myself what's happening. I still do, but I haven't much chance if there's a murder investigation going on. You'll have to admit that once your colleagues get to looking at the containers under the vans, those containers will never be used again. I wanted to leave them in place, to keep quiet about them and to *wait*. I implored Jogger not to talk about them in the pub, but the beer got the better of him. I'm afraid that he said too much. I'm afraid he blew the whole operation and frightened the fish away. I've been hoping he didn't. But your colleagues will certainly frighten him away forever and I will never find out . . . and that's why I didn't tell you, because you're a policeman first and a friend second, and your conscience wouldn't have let you keep silent."

He said slowly, "You're right about that."

"It's Friday evening," I said. "How long can you sit on what I've told you?"

"Freddie . . ." He was unhappy.

"Till Monday?"

"Oh shit. What do you want to do before then?"

"To get some answers."

"You have to ask the right questions," he said.

He didn't promise even temporary silence and I didn't try to crowd him with a decision. He would do whatever sat comfortably in his own mind.

He buttoned his tunic round his solid waist. He said he'd better be going. On his way out he picked up his peaked cap and put it on, reaching his car as a fully uniformed and thorough policeman, looking uncompromising in his vocation.

I poured the remains of his whisky down the kitchen sink and hoped our friendship wasn't sliding away with it down the drain.

11

I drove along to the farmyard when Nina phoned to say she was back, and found her filling her tanks, yawning as before.

Lewis had finished cleaning his van and was positioning it in its usual place. Harve and Phil weren't back so far from Wolverhampton but except for Aziz's nine-van, which had gone to Ireland, the broodmare force had returned.

Lewis slid his completed log through the office letter box, told me briefly that he'd taken his pair safely back to Mr. Usher and that he'd had to help the Usher head traveling lad saddle all the runners as their grooms were useless and Nina had said she wasn't dressed for it. He thought little of Nina, I gathered, for letting him do so much work. The approval she'd lavished that morning on the photos of his baby had, I thought in amusement, been wasted.

Nina drove along to the cleaning area and set to work with the pressure hose. Looking at her old jeans, the unsmart sweater and the scraped-back hair escaping in wisps, one could see why she'd back away from public gaze, quite apart from the fact that someone in the horse world might have recognized her and asked astonished questions.

Lewis left. I went over to Nina and offered to clean her van for her if she would do a small different job for me. She agreed with relief, saying, "What if Harve comes back?"

"I'll think of something."

"OK. What do I do?"

"Fetch the new slider from the barn and look at all the fuel tanks to see if there are any containers stuck on them."

She was surprised. "I thought Jogger looked and there were only the three."

"Looking back," I said, "he told me of three. I don't know for sure if he'd looked under all the others. I just want to check."

"All right," she agreed. "Don't you want to do it yourself?"

"Not particularly."

She gave me a curious look but made no comment, just fetched the slider from the barn and started methodically along the row. I finished the cleaning, inside and out, and positioned her van where it belonged, joining her afterwards by the office door.

"Well," she said, rubbing dirt off her elbows, "there's one more, and it's under Lewis's van, but it's empty, like the others. Lewis! So we took *two* hidden containers to Lingfield today, but I stayed with the lorries the whole time, to Lewis's disgust, but he could perfectly well manage to help the head traveling lad saddle up on his own, he didn't need me really, but I'm in his bad books." The thought hardly upset her. "No one came near either van, I'd swear it. No one showed the slightest interest in their undersides."

I thought back. "Lewis's van was on its way to France when Jogger found the second and third containers. Lewis went on Friday, and got back at about two on Tuesday morning."

"There you are, then. Jogger didn't know about Lewis's van. He was dead before Lewis got back."

Harve drove into the farmyard, his lights bright in the gathering dusk.

"Do you want me to check Harve's?" Nina asked.

"If you have a chance. And any others we've missed."

"OK." She yawned again. "Am I driving tomorrow?"

"Isobel's got you down again for Lingfield."

"Oh, well . . . at least I know the way, now."

I said penitently, "I don't even know where you live. Do you have a long drive home?"

"Near Stow-on-the-Wold," she said. "It takes me an hour."

"That's a fair commute. Um . . . How about if I give you dinner somewhere on your way home?"

"I'm hardly dressed for going out to dinner."

"A pub, then?"

"Yes, all right. Thank you."

I went over to talk to Harve as he filled his tanks and found him happy to have taken a winner to Wolverhampton, as he'd also backed it. The groom with the horse had told him it was a certainty. "For once, he was right."

When his tanks were full I asked him to come over to the office to look at the next day's schedule. He came as a matter of course while, looking back, I saw Nina taking the opportunity to slide underneath his van for an inspection.

We went through the list, which was healthily busy. He himself was down for Chepstow, one of his favorite runs. "Good," he said. I told him about Benjy Usher overlooking the hurdlers. "How he ever trains a winner I'll never know," he said. "Mind you, he has the luck of the devil. Who else had *three* walkovers last summer? You remember there was that bug going about in Pixhill? All those Classic Trial weight-for-age races, they always cut up to five or six runners every year anyway, and Mr. Usher's always keen to win them. He won the Chester Vase last year against only two opponents. I know, because I drove his winner myself, if you remember?"

I nodded. "He's always tended to enter horses in races that are likely to have very few runners," I agreed. "I won several two- and three-horse races for him myself, mostly three-mile chases."

"He runs the poor buggers on rock-hard going too," Harve went on disapprovingly. "Doesn't seem to care if they finish lame."

"They limp all the way to the bank."

"You can laugh," Harve objected, "but he's still a rotten trainer."

"We have that colt of his to bring back from Italy next week," I reminded him. "Isobel's arranged the paperwork and the ferry for Monday."

"A broken-down colt," Harve said, sniffing.

"Er . . . yes."

"Who's going?"

"Who do you suggest? He asked for Lewis and Dave."

Harve shrugged. "We may as well please him."

"I thought so, yes."

Across the farmyard Nina emerged from her search and shook her head exaggeratedly.

I said to Harve, "You remember that cash box container that Jogger found stuck under the nine-van? Has anything occurred to you about what it could be for?"

"I haven't thought about it," he said frankly. "Jogger found two more, didn't he, and they were all empty? Whatever was in them is history." He sounded as unconcerned as ever. "Poor old Jogger."

As Sandy had told me off the record that the Jogger inquiry was veering to murder, I didn't mention it to Harve. Everyone would find out only too soon. Harve and I went back towards his van and he eyed the backview of Nina, who was disappearing into the barn.

"This job's too much for her," he observed, not unkindly. "She's a good driver by all accounts, but Nigel says she gets tired easily."

"She's temporary," I said. "One more week, if we get no one else down with flu."

The other Wolverhampton van returned. I left Harve to supervise the end of the day and followed Nina's car as she waved to Harve and drove through the gates. She stopped after half a mile to walk back and suggest I follow her to a place to eat that she passed every day, and half an hour later we both pulled into the busy car-park of a restaurant where good cheap food was important and the bar itself secondary.

She had loosed and combed her hair and applied lipstick, so that the Nina I had dinner with looked younger and halfway back to the original. The place was crowded, the tables small and close together. We ate steak, french fries and fried onions with a carafe of house red wine and a chunk of cheddar cheese. "I get fed *up* with healthy eating," Nina said, secure in her slender body. "Did you starve when you were a jockey?"

"Grilled fish and salads," I said, nodding.

"Have some butter." With a smile she passed me a small silver-wrapped packet. "I adore junk food. My daughter despises me."

"Black Forest chocolate cake?" I suggested, handing her the menu.

"I'm not that crazy."

Companionably we drank coffee, neither of us in much hurry to be gone.

I told her the police thought Jogger had been murdered and that perhaps I now only had hours to find solutions before we were swamped by heavy boots.

"You're unfair to the police," she observed.

"I daresay."

"The solutions, I do agree, seem as far away as ever."

"Sandy Smith," I said, "says it's a matter of asking the right questions."

"Which are?"

"Yes, well, there's the rub."

"Think of one." She drank her coffee, smiling.

"All right," I said. "What do you think of Aziz?"

"What?" She was surprised; almost, I would have said, disconcerted.

"He's odd," I remarked. "I don't know how he could have caused any of my troubles, but he turned up in my farmyard the day after Jogger died and I gave him Brett's job because he speaks French and Arabic and had worked in a Mercedes garage. But my sister says he's far too bright for what he's doing and I respect my sister's insight. So why is Aziz working for me?"

She asked how my sister knew Aziz and I explained about the day he fetched the old horses, and that he'd driven Lizzie to Heathrow the next morning.

"That Tuesday night, when I ended up in Southampton Docks, I don't know if Aziz helped to put me there."

"Oh, no," she said, shocked. "I'm sure he didn't."

"Why are you so sure?"

"It's just . . . he's so cheerful."

"One can smile and smile and be a villain."

"Not Aziz," she said.

To be honest, my gut reaction to Aziz was the same as Nina's: he might be a rogue but not a villain. Yet I did have villains about me, and I badly needed to know them.

"Who killed Jogger?" she asked.

I said, "Who would you put your money on?"

"Dave," she said, without hesitation. "He's got a violent streak that he never shows you."

"I've heard about it. But not Dave. No, I've known him too long." I could hear the doubts creeping into my own voice, despite my conviction. "Dave didn't know about the containers under the floorboards."

"One can grin a little-boy grin and be a villain."

Against all probability I laughed, my cares unaccountably lifting.

"The police will find Jogger's killer," Nina said, "and you will have no more trouble and I will go home and that will be that."

"I don't want you to go home."

I said it without thinking, and surprised myself as much

as her. She looked at me thoughtfully, unerringly hearing what I hadn't meant to say.

"That's loneliness speaking," she said slowly.

"I'm happy alone."

"Yes. Like I am."

She finished her coffee and patted her mouth on a napkin with an air of finality.

"Time to go," she said. "Thanks for the dinner."

I paid the bill and we went out to the cars, hers and mine, both our workhorse wheels.

"Good night," she said matter-of-factly. "See you in the morning." She climbed without pause or tension into her seat, adept at unembarrassing partings. "Good night, Freddie."

"Night," I said.

She drove away with a smile, friendly, nothing else. I wasn't sure whether or not to feel relieved.

Sometime during the night I woke suddenly, hearing again in my mind Sandy's insistent voice, "You have to ask the right questions."

I'd thought of a question I should have asked, and hadn't. I'd been slow and dim. I would ask the question first thing in the morning.

First thing in the morning, rousing me from depths of renewed slumber, the telephone bell brought Marigold's loud voice into my wincing ear.

"I'm not too happy about your friend Peterman," she said, coming at once to the point. "I'd like your advice. Can you call round here? Say, at about nine o'clock?"

"Mm," I said, surfacing as sluggishly as any half-drowned swimmer. "Yes, Marigold. Nine o'clock. Fine."

"Are you drunk?" she demanded.

"No, just asleep." In bed, supine, eyes shut.

"But it's seven already," she pointed out severely. "The day's half over."

"I'll be there." I fumbled the receiver towards its bedside cradle.

"Good," her voice said from a distance. "Great."

Sleep was alluring, sleep a temptress, sleep as beckoning as a drug. Only the remembrance of the essential question I hadn't asked got me out of bed and into the bathroom.

Saturday morning. Coffee. Cornflakes.

Still bleary-brained, I padded from the kitchen into the wreck of the sitting room and switched on the computer. There was no crash of hard disk. I called up Isobel's new entries of details of the drivers and found them still basic and abbreviated: names, addresses, dates of birth, next-of-kin, driving license numbers, journeys driven that week, hours spent at the wheel.

Invading her privacy, I typed Nina's name, and read her address, care of Lauderhill Abbey, Stow-on-the-Wold, and her age, forty-four.

Nine years older than myself. Eight and a half, to be accurate. I drank my second cup of coffee very hot and wondered how much that age gap mattered.

I answered four telephone calls in quick succession, receiving, altering, agreeing to trips for that day and typing them into the program for Isobel, who worked in the office most Saturday mornings from eight until noon. At ten to eight she phoned me herself, reporting her arrival, allowing me gratefully to switch the business line to the farmyard.

I drove along there myself to watch the day's journeys begin and to sort out any last-minute hitches, but again

Isobel and Harve seemed to have everything running smoothly.

Nina (forty-four) gave me a small hello smile as she arrived to go to Lingfield, her appearance as determinedly unattractive as ever. Harve, Phil and the crowd were in and out of the canteen, stretching, picking up work sheets, flirting mildly with Isobel. Any Saturday morning. Another race day. Twenty-four hours in a life.

Most of the fleet had gone by eight-thirty. I went into Isobel's office to find her typing the day's adjusted programs into her computer, working mostly from what I'd typed in at home.

"How's things?" I asked vaguely.

"Always frantic." She smiled, happy enough.

"I want to ask you to remember something."

"Fire away." She went on typing, looking at the screen.

"Um," I said, "last August . . ." I paused, waiting for more of her attention.

"What about last August?" she asked vaguely, still typing. "You go away in August."

"Yes, I know. When I was away last August, what did Jogger find in the inspection pit?"

She stopped typing and looked at me in puzzlement.

"What did you say?" she asked.

"What did Jogger find in the pit? Something dead. What did he find dead in the pit?"

"But Jogger . . . *he* was dead in the pit, wasn't he?"

"Last Sunday Jogger was dead in the pit, yes. But last August, apparently he found something else dead there . . . a dead *nun*, he said, but it can't have been a dead nun. So can you remember what he found? Did he tell you? Did he tell anyone?"

"Oh." Her forehead developed lines of thought as she

raised her eyebrows. "I do vaguely remember, but it wasn't anything to worry you about. I mean, it was so silly."

"What did he find?"

"I think it was a rabbit."

"A *rabbit*?"

"Yes. A dead rabbit. He said it was crawling with maggots or something and he threw it in the dumpster. That was all."

"Are you *sure*?" I asked doubtfully.

She nodded. "He didn't know what else to do with it, so he threw it in the dumpster."

"I mean, are you sure it was a rabbit?"

"I think so. I didn't see it. Jogger said it must have hopped in there somehow and once it had fallen into the pit of course it couldn't get out."

"No," I agreed. "Do you remember what day it was?"

She shook her head decisively. "If you can't remember it, it must have been when you were away." She turned automatically to the computer and again the familiar frustration crossed her face. "It might have been in the records we lost, though I don't really think so. I can't remember bothering to enter anything like that."

"Did anyone else see Jogger's rabbit?"

"I simply can't remember." It was clear from her expression that she couldn't see any importance in it either.

"Oh, well. Thanks anyway," I said.

She smiled without guile and turned back to her work.

Nuns, I thought. Rabbits. Nuns and monks, nuns and sisters . . . nuns and *habits*.

Jogger's words. "Take a butcher's at them nuns. There was a dead one in the pit last August—and it was crawling."

The only rabbits that I could think of that he might mean were the rabbits belonging to the Watermead children, but even if one of those rabbits had somehow escaped and got as far as the inspection pit, it would hardly have been crawling with maggots, unless, of course, it had been there dead for days when Jogger found it. It didn't seem to be of any importance ... but to Jogger it had seemed important enough for him to tell me about it—in his own unintelligible way—seven months after the event.

I looked at my watch. Approaching nine o'clock. What was I supposed to be doing at nine o'clock? The sleep-filled assignation with Marigold English swam to the surface.

I told Isobel where I was going and to reach me by mobile phone for a while if she needed me, and drove to Marigold's yard.

She was outside in her woolly hat and came hurrying towards me when I appeared, carrying with her a bowl of horse nuts.

"Don't get out," she commanded. "Drive me to look at Peterman."

Accordingly I followed her directions, which involved bumping down a grassy track to a distant paddock behind her house. The paddock sloped down to a brook and was edged with tall willow trees that would give great shade for old horses when the leaves came out.

Peterman, however, was up near the gate and looked thoroughly miserable. He put his nose down to Marigold's offered horse nuts and then moved his head away as if offended.

"See?" she said. "He won't eat."

"What are the nuts?" I asked.

She mentioned a standard brand much used and well respected. "All horses like them, they never fail."

I looked at Peterman, puzzled. "What's the matter with him, then?"

Marigold hesitated. "I phoned my old veterinarian on Salisbury Plain to ask him, but he said just to give the old chap time to settle in. Then I came down here again yesterday evening, and you know what a nice sunny evening it was? The sun was shining low and yellow on the old horse, and you could see them."

"See what?"

"Ticks."

I stared at her.

"Tick bites," she said. "I think that's what's wrong with him. I phoned John Tigwood not half an hour ago to tell him to do something about it and he said it was rubbish and impossible, and anyway you, Freddie, had got the local veterinarian round on Tuesday when the horses got to Pixhill, and you'd insisted on an examination, and the veterinarian had passed the horses fully fit and had signed a document to that effect which he would show me if I liked, and really, I didn't like his tone much and I nearly told him to fetch the horse back again, but then I'd already asked you to come and look, and knowing that you wanted this old thing well looked after . . . well, I decided to wait until you came and to ask you what you thought." She stopped, running out of breath. "What do you think?"

"Um . . . where were the ticks?"

"On his neck."

I peered at Peterman's neck, but could see only his bay coat, still thick for winter. Come warmer weather he would shed a lot of it, revealing the short cooler coat of summer.

"What were they like?" I asked Marigold.

"Tiny brown things. The same color as his coat. I would never have seen them except for the sun, and because one of them *moved*."

"How many?"

"I don't know . . . maybe seven or eight. I couldn't see them very clearly."

"But, Marigold . . ."

"You think I'm potty? What about the bees?"

"Er . . ."

She said impatiently, "Bees, Freddie. Bees. *Varroa jacobonsi*."

"Start at the beginning," I begged.

"They are *mites*," she said. "They live on bees. They don't kill them, they just suck their blood until the bees can't fly."

"I didn't know bees *had* blood."

She gave me a withering look. "My brother *panics* about *varroa*," she said. "He's a fruit farmer and half his trees don't bear fruit because the bees are too weak to *pollinate*."

"Oh. Yes. I see."

"So he smokes a pipe at them."

"For God's sake . . ."

"Pipe tobacco smoke is about the only thing that knocks out *varroa* mites. If you blow pipe tobacco smoke into a beehive all the mites fall down dead."

"Um," I said. "It's fascinating, but what has it got to do with Peterman?"

"Don't be so *slow*," she commanded. "Ticks carry illnesses, don't they? I can't risk the ticks on Peterman hopping onto my two-year-olds, now can I?"

"No," I said slowly, "you can't."

"So regardless of what John Tigwood says, I'm not going to keep this old horse here. I'm very sorry, Freddie, but you'll have to find him another home."

"Yes," I said. "I will."

"When?"

I thought of her star-studded stable and of my own strong desire to transport them forever to the winners' enclosures.

I said, "I'll walk him down to my house. There's a patch of garden he can stay in temporarily. Then I'll walk back for my car. Would that do?"

She nodded with approval. "You're a good lad, Freddie."

"I'm sorry to have given you this trouble."

"I just hope you understand."

I assured her I did. I drove back along the grassy track to her stable yard, where she lent me a leading-rein for Peterman and then led me by the arm to peer over a half-door at her absolute pride and joy, the three-year-old colt that, if all went well, would be contesting the 2,000 Guineas and the Derby against Michael Watermead's sensation, Irkab Alhawa. In her, as in Michael, the fledgling excitement shimmered in the eyes, the wild hope growing.

"You do see," she reiterated, "about Peterman."

"Of course," I said. I kissed her cheek. She nodded. I could slaughter John Tigwood, I thought, for putting me in such an awkward position, even though, I thought more fairly, it wasn't actually his fault, as I had myself asked Marigold specifically to take Peterman.

Sighing at my folly, I returned to the paddock, put on the leading-rein and led my old friend out of his idyllic pasture and along the road to the very much smaller patch of shaggy lawn in the walled garden behind my house.

"Don't eat the bloody daffodils," I told him.

He looked at me balefully. As I took off the leading-rein

to walk away I noticed he wasn't even interested in the grass.

I collected my Fourtrak form Marigold's yard and went home again. Peterman stood more or less where I'd left him, looking miserable, the daffodils intact. If it hadn't been for the fallacy of endowing animals with human feelings, I'd have said the old horse was depressed. I gave him a bucket of water, but he didn't drink.

Various thoughts had been popping into my mind, almost as if a couple of sleeping cylinders had resumed firing. I sat down at the computer in my battered room and looked up the instruction manuals again for a renewed expedition through the old information on the healthy disks.

In surveying the drivers' journeys I had not, I'd remembered, pulled out Jogger's own. Even when I did, I learned little, as he'd driven very seldom; barely half a dozen times the previous year and nearly all on Bank Holiday Mondays, the days when with all the holiday race meetings country-wide, we were always scraping the barrel for chauffeurs.

I rubbed my nose, thought a bit more, and began to bring to the screen the horse vans themselves, one by one, identifying them by registration number.

The columns on the screen came up looking completely different: the same information as before but illuminated from the side, like Marigold's view of otherwise invisible ticks.

Identified by registration number, each van's history now gave me dates, journeys, purpose of journey, drivers, engine hours logged, odometer readings, maintenance schedules, repairs, licensing, roadworthy certificates, unladen weights, fuel capacity, fuel actually used day by day.

After some taxing cerebration, much consultation with the manuals and a few false starts, I came up next with details of all maintenance work performed by Jogger the previous August. This time I'd sorted the work by chronology, and had provided myself more simply with the date, the horse van registration number and the work done.

Day by summer day I looked back through that one month in Jogger's life, and there I found her, the dead nun.

August 10th. The registration number of the horse van regularly driven by Phil. Oil change over the inspection pit. Tanks of air for the air brakes drained. Air brake compressor checked. All grease nipples filled. At the end, a note entered on the day by Isobel and forgotten: "Jogger says a dead rabbit fell out of the horse van into the pit. Crawling with ticks, he said. Disposed of in dumpster."

I sat looking vaguely into space.

After a while I went back to the beginning and called Phil's records to the screen, to find out where he'd been on August 10th or 9th or 8th.

Phil, my faithful aid told me, had not been driving that particular horse van on any of those days. He'd been driving another van, an older one, which I had, I remembered, subsequently sold.

Back to the drawing board: back to registration numbers, the sideways illumination.

On August 7th the horse van Phil nowadays drove had gone to France with two runners for Benjy Usher. They had run on the 8th at Cagnes-sur-Mer, down on the Mediterranean Sea, and returned to Pixhill on the 9th.

That horse van, on that journey, had been driven by Lewis.

Lewis had actually driven that particular van most of the previous year, as I knew perfectly well once I'd thought about it. I'd transferred Lewis to the sparkling new super-six I'd bought in the autumn to replace the old one; transferred him so that the Usher and Watermead horses should go in my best style to their destinies. Lewis had driven one of Michael's horses to Doncaster in September in the new super-six to win the last Classic race of the year, the St. Leger.

At about ten-fifteen I telephoned Edinburgh.

"Quipp here," a pleasant voice said. English, not a Scot.

"Um . . . Excuse me phoning you," I said, "but do you happen to know where I could find my sister Lizzie?"

After the briefest of pauses he said, "Which are you, Roger or Freddie?"

"Freddie."

"Hold on."

I held, and heard his voice yelling, "Liz, your brother Fred . . ." and then she was, moderately startled, saying, "Is it your head?"

"What? No. Except it's been slow and stupid. Look, um, Lizzie, do you know anyone who knows anything about ticks?"

"Ticks?"

"Yeah. Little biters."

"For God's sake . . ."

She told Professor Quipp what I wanted and he came back on the line.

"What sort of ticks?" he asked.

"That's what I want to find out. The sort that live on horses and . . . er . . . rabbits."

"Do you have any specimens?"

"I've got a horse in the garden which probably has some."

After a silence Lizzie came back. "I've tried to explain to Quipp that you're concussed."

"Far from it, at last."

298

"What horse in the garden?"

"Peterman. One of the geriatrics from last Tuesday. Seriously, Lizzie, ask your professor how I get information about ticks. There are too many multimillion animals in Pixhill for messing about if ticks could make them ill."

"Ye *Gods*."

I listened to three full minutes of silence, then Professor Quipp said, "Are you still there?"

"Yes."

"I've a friend who's a tick expert. He says can you bring him some specimens?"

"Do you mean . . . put the horse in a horse van and drive it to Edinburgh?"

"That's one way, I suppose."

"The horse is terribly old and shaky. Lizzie knows, she saw him. He might not last the journey."

"I'll phone you back," he said.

I waited. My Jaguar and Lizzie's helicopter sat uselessly on the tarmac. Lovely fast transport at a standstill.

Quipp came back quite soon.

"Lizzie says if you say this is urgent, it's urgent."

"It's urgent," I said.

"Right. In that case, fly up here on the shuttle. We'll meet you at Edinburgh Airport. Say . . . one o'clock? Soon after?"

"Er . . ." I began.

"Of course you can't bring the *horse* with you," Quipp said, "just bring some ticks."

"But I can't actually *see* them."

"Quite normal. They're very small. Use soap."

Surreal.

"Wet a bar of soap until it's sticky," he said. "Rub it over the horse. If you find any round brown specks on the soap, you've got ticks."

"But won't they die?"

"My friend says perhaps not, if you don't waste time on the way here, and anyway, it might not matter. Oh, yes, bring a blood sample from the horse."

I opened my mouth to say it would take an hour or more to get the veterinarian, but Lizzie's voice in my ear forestalled me.

"There's a hypodermic needle and a syringe in my bathroom cupboard," she said. "Left over from my wasp allergy days when I lived at home. I saw it the other day. Use that."

"But, Lizzie . . ."

"Get on and do it," she commanded, and Quipp's voice said, "See you on the lunchtime shuttle. Phone if you're going to be later."

"Yes," I said dazed, and heard the disconnecting click at the other end. A far from absentminded don, I reflected. A good match for my sister.

What Peterman himself would think about my sticking needles into him I dreaded to think. I went upstairs to the little pink and gold bathroom off Lizzie's bedroom and found the syringe, as she'd said, in the mirror-fronted cabinet there. The syringe, disposable, instructions "for single use only," was inside an opaque white plastic envelope and looked much too small for anything equine. Still, Lizzie had said to use it, so I took it downstairs along with her cake of soap, moistened to stickiness, and approached the old fellow in the garden.

His apathy seemed complete. I merely held his forelock while I traced the visible vein running along his lower jaw, sticking the fine needle into it gently. His head remained still, as if he'd felt nothing. I found I needed two hands, in my inexperience, to pull back the plunger in order to draw blood into the syringe, and even then he remained unmoving, as if half asleep. The little syringe filled easily with the red stuff. I pulled the needle out again, laid the syringe aside, picked up the bar of soap and wiped it around Peterman's head and down his neck. Despite my doubts and disbelief there were, after three or four passes, a few discernible dark brown pinhead dots on the soft white surface.

Peterman went on paying no attention as I packed my trophies into a nest of scrumpled tissues inside a plastic food container from the kitchen and firmly closed the lid. Automatically I raised a hand to pat the old fellow, to say thanks, and in midgesture stopped dead. What if, I thought, in patting him, I transferred his ticks to myself? What if I'd already done it? Would it matter? I hadn't even thought of wearing protective gloves.

Shrugging, I left my old friend unpatted, washed my hands in the kitchen, and within five minutes I was spinning along the road in the direction of Heathrow Airport.

I phoned Isobel on the way.

"You're going *where*?" she said.

"Edinburgh. Be a dear and keep all the phone lines switched to you until I get back. Bonus, of course."

"OK. How long will you be gone?"

"A day or two. I'll keep phoning you, to stay in touch."

By luck I had a clear run to the airport, parked in the short-stay car park and caught the last seat on the noon shuttle at nothing faster than a flat-out sprint. My only luggage was the kitchen food container and the envelope of money from the safe. My clothes were the jeans and sweatshirt I'd worn to work. Everyone else on the aircraft seemed to be sporting huge scarlet and white scarves and loudly singing bawdy songs. "Swing Low, Sweet Chariot," with the obscenest of gestures. Life grew steadily weirder. I held the container on my lap and slept away the hour in the air.

Lizzie was waiting at the other end beside a man who looked more like a ski instructor than a professor of organic chemistry, the impact of his dark beardless good looks heightened by a rainbow jacket straight off the slopes.

"Quipp," he introduced himself, extending a hand. "I suppose you're Freddie."

As I'd just kissed Lizzie, this seemed a reasonable assumption.

"I told him you'd get here," she said. "He worked out that you couldn't do it in the time. I told him your jockey instincts made you faster across country than a hurricane."

"Hurricanes are slow across country," I said, "actually."

Quipp laughed. "So they are. Forward speed, not much more than twenty-five miles an hour. Right?"

"Right," I said.

"Come on, then." He eyed the kitchen container. "You've brought the goods? We're going straight to the lab. No time to waste."

Quipp drove a Renault with a verve to match his jacket. We pulled up at what looked like a tradesmen's back entrance of a private hospital and entered a light, featureless corridor that led round a corner to a pair of swing doors with "McPherson Foundation" painted in black letters on non-see-through glass.

Quipp pushed familiarly through the doors, Lizzie and I following, and we entered first a vestibule, and then a room windowed solely by skylights.

From pegs in the vestibule, Quipp issued to each of us a white lab overall-coat which buttoned at the neck and needed to be tied round the waist with tapes. Inside the lab itself we met a man similarly dressed who turned from a microscope on our arrival and said to Quipp, "This had better be good, you son of a bitch. I'm supposed to be at the International rugby football match at Murrayfield."

Quipp, unabashed, introduced him to me as Guggenheim, the resident nutter.

Guggenheim, who seemed, like Quipp, to prefer to be identified solely by his last name, was audibly American and visibly about as young as the computer wizard.

"Disregard his youth," Quipp advised. "Remember that Isaac Newton was twenty-four when he discovered the binomial theorem in 1666."

"I'll remember," I said dryly.

"I'm twenty-five," Guggenheim said. "Let's see what you've brought."

He took the plastic container from me and retreated to one of the workbenches that lined two of the walls. With time to look around, it seemed to me that except for the microscope there wasn't a single piece of equipment there that I could identify. Guggenheim moved in this mysterious territory with the certainty of a Rubik round his cube.

He was slight in build with light brown crinkly hair and the well-disciplined eyes of habitual concentration. He transferred one of the brown dots from the soap to a slide and took a quick look at it under the microscope.

"Well, well, well, we have a tick. Now what do you suppose he's carrying?"

"Er," I said, but it appeared that Guggenheim's question was rhetorical.

"If it came from a horse," he said cheerfully, "perhaps we should be looking for *Ehrlichia risticii*. What do you think? Does *Ehrlichia risticii* spring to mind?"

"It does not," I said.

Guggenheim looked up from his microscope in good humor. "Is the horse ill?" he asked.

"The horse is standing still looking depressed, if that doesn't sound fanciful."

"Depression is clinical," he said. "Anything else? Fever?"

"I didn't take his temperature." I thought back to Peterman's behavior that morning. "He wouldn't eat," I said.

Guggenheim looked happy. "Depression, anorexia and fever," he said, "classic symptoms." He looked at Lizzie, Quipp and myself. "Why don't you three go away for a bit? Give me an hour. I might find you some answers. I'm not promising. We've some powerful microscopes here and we're dealing with organisms on the edge of visibility. Anyway . . . an hour."

We retreated as instructed, leaving our lab coats in the vestibule. Quipp drove us to his lodgings, which were masculine and bookish but bore unmistakable signs of Lizzie's occupation, though her expression forbade me to comment. She made coffee. Quipp took his cup with the murmured thanks of familiarity.

"How's my little Robinson?" Lizzie asked me. "Still in the same place?"

"A low-loader's coming on Monday to bring it up here."

"Tell them to be careful!"

"It'll reach you in cotton balls."

"They'll have to disassemble the rotor linkage . . ."

We drank coffee, strong and black.

I telephoned Isobel. All going well, she reported.

"What exactly *is* the McPherson Foundation?" I asked Quipp.

"Scottish philanthropist," Quipp said succinctly. "Also a

tiny university grant. Small public funding. It has state-of-the-art electron microscopes and at present two resident geniuses, one of whom you met. It pushes out the frontiers of knowledge, and people in obscure places cease dying of obscure illnesses." He drank some coffee. "Guggenheim's specialty is the identification of the vectors of *Ehrlichiae*."

"I don't speak that language," I said.

"Ah. Then you won't understand that when I asked him about ticks on horses he was, for him, riveted. It's remotely possible that you've solved a mystery for him. Nothing less would have torn him away from Murrayfield."

"Well ... what are erlic ... whatever you said?"

"*Ehrlichiae?* They are," he said with a touch of mischief, "pleomorphic organisms symbiotic in and transmitted by arthropod vectors. In general, that is."

"*Quipp!*" Lizzie protested.

He relented. "They're parasitic organisms spread by ticks. The best-known make dogs and cattle ill. Guggenheim did some work on *Ehrlichiae* in horses back in America. He'll have to tell you about it himself. All I'm sure of is that he's talking about a new disease that arose only in the mid–nineteen eighties."

"A *new* disease?" I exclaimed.

"Nature's always evolving," Quipp said. "Life never stands still. Diseases come and go. *AIDS* is new. Something even more destructive may be just round the corner."

"How fearful," Lizzie protested, frowning.

"Dear Liz, you know it's possible." He looked at me. "Guggenheim has a theory that the dinosaurs died not of cataclysmic weather upheavals but of tick-borne rickettsial-like pathogens—and those, before you ask, are parasitic microorganisms that cause fevers like typhus. Guggenheim thinks the ticks and their parasites died with their hosts, leaving no trace."

I pondered. "Could you transport these er—pathogens—in viral transport medium? The stuff in those small glass tubes?"

He looked momentarily startled but decisively shook his head. "No, Not possible. *Ehrlichiae* aren't viruses. As far as I know, they won't live at all in any sort of medium or on a culture dish, which makes the research difficult. No. Whatever was in your viral transport medium, it definitely did not come from ticks."

"That doesn't," I said ruefully, "make anything any clearer."

"Lizzie is an astrophysicist," he said, "listening to the cosmic ripple from the beginning of the universe, and Guggenheim looks inward into parasitic elementary bodies detectable only by magnifying them a million times in a beam of electrons instead of light. Outer deeps and inner deeps, with our puny intellects here and now trying to see and understand incredible mysteries." He smiled self-deprecatingly. "The humbling truth is that with all our discoveries we're only on the fringe of knowledge."

"But from the practical point of view," I said, "all we need to know is that arsenic can cure syphilis."

"You're no scientist!" he accused me. "You need Guggenheim lookalikes to *find out* that arsenic can cure syphilis."

The ultimate squelch, I acknowledged. Lizzie patted my shoulder kindly.

"I suppose you didn't know," Quipp said, "that it was Ehrlich himself, after whom *Ehrlichiae* are named, who first showed synthetic arsenic to be active against syphilis?"

"No," I said, astonished. "I've never heard of Ehrlich."

"German scientist. Nobel prizewinner. A founder of immunology, pioneer of chemotherapy. Died, 1915. You'll never forget him."

In 1915, I thought, Pommern won the wartime Derby. The quirks of life were endless.

After an hour Quipp drove us back to the McPherson Foundation to find Guggenheim pale and trembling, apparently from excitement.

"Where did these ticks come from?" he demanded, as soon as we appeared in our white gear. "Did they come from America?"

"I think they came from France."

"When?"

"Last Monday. On a rabbit."

He peered at me, assessing things. "Yes. Yes. They *could* have traveled on a rabbit. They wouldn't live long on soap. But transfer them from a horse to a rabbit by soap ... there's no reason why they couldn't live on a rabbit ... The rabbit wouldn't be receptive to the horse *Ehrlichiae* ... the rabbit could carry the live ticks with impunity."

"And then one could transfer the ticks to a different horse?" I asked.

"It's *possible*. Yes, yes, I can't see why not."

"I can't see *why*," Lizzie said. "*Why* would anyone do that?"

"Research," Guggenheim said with certainty.

Lizzie looked at me doubtfully but didn't pursue it.

"See," he said to me, "equine ehrlichiosis is known in America. I've seen it in Maryland, and Pennsylvania, though it's a very new disease. Not ten years old yet. Rare. When it's caused by *Ehrlichia risticii* it's been called Potomac horse fever. That's because it's been found mostly near big rivers like the Potomac. How did these ticks get to France?"

"France imports racehorses bred in America. So does Britain, come to that."

"Then why the rabbits?"

"Suppose," I said, "that you know where to find the ticks in France but not in England."

"Yes. Yes." His excitement, though internalized, was catching. "You realize that the ticks you've brought me have *no name*? No one has so far identified the vector of *E. risticii*. Do you realize that if . . . *if* these ticks are the vector—a vector is a carrier of a disease—then we're on the verge of a breakthrough in identifying the path of Potomac horse fever?" He stopped, overcome.

"Practically," I said. "Could you answer some questions?"

"Fire away."

"Well . . . what happens to a horse if it gets Potomac horse fever? Does it die?"

"Not usually. Eighty percent live. Mind you, if it's a thoroughbred racehorse, which presumably you're most interested in, it will probably never win another race. What I've seen of the disease, it's very debilitating."

"How, exactly?"

"It's an enteric infection. That's to do with the intestines. Apart from the anorexia and so on, there is usually fierce diarrhea and colic. The horse is much weakened by the fever."

"How long does the fever last?"

"Four or five days."

"So short!"

"The horse develops antibodies, so the *Ehrlichiae* don't affect it anymore. If the vector is a tick, the tick would go right on living. Ticks, I may say, are themselves not much understood. For instance, only the mature ones are brown. Your soap was crowded with nymphets, young ticks, which are almost transparent." He paused very briefly. "Do you mind if I come to see what you've got there, down in Pixhill? Can I see, for example, your rabbit?"

"I'm afraid I deduced the rabbit."

"Oh." He looked disappointed.

"But come," I invited him. "Stay in my house."

"Soon? I mean, I don't want to upset you, but you said your horse was *old*, and it's typically old retired horses out at pasture that get this illness, and the older they are, the more likely to die. Sorry. Sorry."

"Can younger horses be affected?"

"If it's racehorses in a stable that you mean, then yes, they can, but they're *groomed*, aren't they? The grooming might get rid of the tick. Yes, that's a theory. In America it is mostly horses out at pasture that get ill."

"Um," I said, "is there a cure for it?"

"Tetracycline," he said promptly. "I'll bring some for your old boy. It may be in time. It depends."

"And ... er ..." I said, "can humans catch this disease?"

He nodded. "Yes. They can. It's usually not properly diagnosed as there are so many confusing symptoms. It gets mistaken for Rocky Mountain spotted fever, but it's different. It's rare. And tetracycline does the trick there, too."

"How could it be diagnosed?"

"Blood test," he said promptly. "The amount you brought wasn't really enough."

12

I traveled back on the last Edinburgh-to-Heathrow flight of the day again surrounded by shoals of red and white scarves belting out bawdier-than-ever verses. Bass and baritone voices, tuneful, reverberating. The red and white scarves, it was clear, had won the International match at Murrayfield. Beer disappeared at a Jogger-like pace. A naked flame would have exploded the alcohol fumes in the cabin. The flight attendants got their bottoms pinched. The ecstasy level rose, if anything, during the hour in the air.

I sat with my head whirling from different stimuli, hearing in flashbacks the facts that had poured out of Guggenheim.

The man himself was somewhere among the scarves, sitting separately because there hadn't been two seats

available together. He had brought with him minimal overnight necessities, a huge amount of hope and a large bag
of scientific field instruments. Nothing would have
stopped him in his quest for the unnamed vector of *E.
risticii*. He quivered with hunger. He reached out with per-
cipient fingertips, like Handel to Hallelujah, like Newton
to calculus, like Ehrlich, no doubt, to arsenic for syphilis.
Reached out with genius towards recognition.

"It's early in the year for Potomac fever," he had said.
"It's a warm weather thing, usually . . ."

"The ticks came from down south in France," I told
him. "From the Rhône Valley."

"A river! But usually May through October."

"We had a dead rabbit crawling with ticks in August
last year."

"Yes. Yes. August."

"We had a bug going round locally in Pixhill last summer that put a small number of horses out of action for the
season."

He groaned. With pleasure, as far as I could see.

"They had the same sort of unspecified feverish illness
also in places in France," I said. "I read it again in the
newspaper only this week."

"Find the newspaper."

"Yes, OK."

"No one would have tested for equine ehrlichiosis . . .
it's still almost an unknown infection. Rare. Sporadic. Not
an epidemic. Hard to find. This is *wonderful*."

"Not to the horse owners."

"But this is *history* . . ."

It was a hopeless disaster, I thought, if I couldn't clear
everything up quickly. "Freddie Croft's horse vans brought
Potomac horse fever to Britain." I could just see the head-

lines. "Freddie Croft's *drivers* brought fever to Britain."
Perhaps it would be safer not to employ Freddie Croft's
transport? Sorry and all that, Freddie, but I can't take the
risk.

Confidence was fragile. Loyalty was fickle. Rabbits
bringing ticks? No, thanks very much.

Freddie Croft Raceways out of business.

I sweated.

One of the Watermead rabbits had been missing, on the
previous Sunday. There were only fourteen, not fifteen, the
children had said. Maybe Lewis, the trusted rabbit handler,
had taken that one rabbit with him to France. Taken it in
a hidden compartment, out of sight above the fuel tanks.
Last August it had been Lewis who had brought from
France the dead rabbit crawling with ticks ... Jogger's
dead nun.

Ticks. Jogger's voice came distinctly through the roaring rugby songs ... "Poland had the same five" ... A
childhood rhyme presented itself in synchronizing time
with the singing. One, two, buckle my shoe: three, four,
knock at the door: five, six, pick up sticks ... "Poland had
the same five, six" ... six, sticks, ricks, mix, fix ... Poland had the same ... *ticks*.

Poland had the same ticks on a horse last summer, and
it died.

Who was Poland?

Oh, *God*, I thought. Not Poland and Waleska. Not Poland and coal or Poland and Danzig or Poland and corridor
or Poland and solidarity. No ... Poland and *Russia*.

Russia ... *Usher*.

Benjy Usher had the same ticks ...

Dot's voice, "Those old wrecks. They died. I hate it.
They were always outside the drawing room window ..."

A well-pinched flight attendant asked if she could fetch me anything, raising her voice above the joyful surrounding din.

"Treble scotch ... well, no, just one. Got to drive home."

Pictures crowded my inner eye. Benjy Usher, training through his upstairs window. Benjy never touching his horses. Benjy getting me to saddle his runners at Sandown.

Benjy couldn't have known, surely, that his old dying lodgers probably carried *Ehrlichiae* ... Could he? Benjy ... afraid the microscopic organisms would hop onto himself?

But if he'd feared that, why was he proposing to take two more old horses? Did he know that they, too, might carry ticks?

Lewis drove for him often.

The flight attendant brought my drink.

Benjy entered his horses in small-field races and had had the luck of the devil with walkovers.

It had to be coincidental. Benjy was rich.

What if what he hankered for were *winners*, not money? Harve's voice, "Mr. Usher's a rotten trainer ..."

It was nonsense. It had to be.

From somewhere, mingled with the rugby songs, a sentence I'd read once surfaced into consciousness: "It isn't necessary to speculate about the driving force within us, it leaps out and revels itself. Under pressure, it can't be hidden."

What if Benjy Usher's driving force were a hunger for winners, a hunger his own skill wasn't enough to assuage ... ?

No. Impossible. Yet winners gave him orgasmic pleasure.

Lewis often drove for Benjy.

Lewis had cut off his ringlets last summer.

Had Lewis been afraid he would get ticks in his long hair?

He'd transported the tick-infested nun in Jogger's pit.

Jogger.

Benjy hadn't killed Jogger. Benjy had been playing tennis on the Watermeads' court at about the time Jogger had died.

Lewis hadn't killed Jogger. He'd been in France.

Lewis had come back to the farmyard later than intended, at two in the morning on Monday-to-Tuesday night. He'd stabled Michael's two-year-olds in the farmyard and left me a note to say he had flu. I'd driven his super-six on Tuesday morning with the two-year-olds to Michael's yard, and I'd had breakfast and watched Irkab Alhawa gallop. Then the super-six had gone racing for the day with one of the fleet's other drivers.

What if Lewis had in fact taken the missing rabbit to France to pick up its sick-making cargo? What if it had still been there, now tick-infested, in the hidden container, when I'd driven the super-six to Michael's yard? What if it had still been there until the van returned from the races in the evening? What if Lewis, with only a cold after all, had gone late to the yard to retrieve the rabbit ... and what if I had walked in there while this retrieval was in progress?

Did it make sense?

As much sense as anything else.

What had *Jogger* walked in on, then?

What had occurred on Sunday morning in the farmyard

314

that Jogger had seen, and would tell me about, that it wasn't intended that he should see?

What had happened in the farmyard on that Sunday morning?

"Ask the right questions," Sandy had said.

That Sunday morning had been March 6th, the day the office computer had been switched on in order to activate the Michelangelo virus. Jogger wouldn't have understood the computer. It wasn't *what* he'd seen in the farmyard office that mattered, but *who*.

The rugger songs swelled round me.

I had an acute sense of danger.

On the way home from Heathrow I phoned Isobel, apologizing for the lateness of the hour.

Think nothing of it, she said. The day had gone well. Harve had taken two winners to Chepstow. Aziz and Dave had returned all right from Ireland but Aziz had said Dave wasn't in good shape. Dave, Isobel thought, might be developing flu.

"Bugger," I said.

Nina had taken a winner to Lingfield, and so had Nigel. Lewis had driven three of Benjy Usher's jumpers to Chepstow, and had been reminded to bring his overnight things on Monday for going to Italy. Phil had been phlegmatically to Uttoxeter. Michael Watermead and Marigold English had both booked two vans for Tuesday to take horses to Doncaster sales.

"Great," I said thankfully. Marigold had disregarded Peterman's problem: so far, at least.

Jericho Rich had reportedly fallen out already with his new trainer, Isobel said. She thought we might be bringing the whole string back to Pixhill any day soon.

"The man's mad," I remarked.

"I hear you're going to the Watermeads' for lunch again tomorrow," Isobel said. "I'll go on doing the bookings, shall I?"

"Yes, please," I said gratefully. "And who told you?"

"Tessa Watermead. She came by. I taught her a few things. That's all right, isn't it?"

"Yes, sure."

"Good night, then."

"Good night."

Guggenheim, sitting beside me in the Fourtrak, repudiated my suggestion that we stop for something to eat. I'd had no lunch and was hungry. Guggenheim's hunger for truth won the day. Besides, he said, rationalizing it and silencing me, Peterman needed the tetracycline as soon as possible.

For poor old Peterman, however, it was already too late. When Guggenheim and I went out into the dark garden, my game old partner was lying in the shadows on my lawn barely a yard from where I'd left him, his visible eye already dull, the stillness of death unmistakable.

Guggenheim's grief was for his own career; mine for the long-ago races and the speed of a great horse.

Guggenheim had brought not soap for finding ticks but a very small battery-powered hand-held vacuum cleaner. He tried his best all over Peterman, but an inspection of the collected debris from the horse's skin disappointed him abysmally.

He bent over his microscope in my kitchen uttering soft despairing moans.

"Nothing. Nothing. You must have brought all of them on the soap." He sounded almost accusing, as if I'd ruined things on purpose. "But this is typical. The carrier of *E.*

risticii is brutally elusive. Ticks feed on blood. They burrow their heads right through the skin of their host. The *Ehrlichiae* that live in the tick pass from the tick into the blood of the host and combine with certain blood cells. I won't bore you with it, it's incredibly complicated . . . but they're only viable in *living* cells, and this horse has been dead for *hours*."

"Have a drink?" I suggested.

"Alcohol's irrelevant," he said.

"Mm."

I poured for myself however, and after a minute he took the whisky bottle out of my hand and half filled the glass I'd set out for him.

"Anesthetic for lost hopes," he said. "I suppose you're right."

"When I was your age," I said, "I rode the wind. Quite often."

He looked at me over his glass. "You're saying there will be other days? You don't understand."

"I do, you know. I'll try to get you some more of those ticks."

"How?"

"I'll sleep on it."

We found a dinner of sorts in the fridge and cupboard, and he slept in Lizzie's room silently all night.

In the morning I telephoned John Tigwood and told him Peterman was dead.

Tigwood's voice, pompous as ever, full of bogus fruitiness, was also defensive and querulous.

"Marigold English complained to me that the horse was ill and she said he had *ticks*. Rubbish. Utter rubbish, I told her so. Horses don't have ticks, dogs and cattle do. I'm not having her or you going around spreading such malicious rumors."

I saw with clarity that he feared his whole act would fall apart if no one would board his geriatrics. No more collecting tins. No more self-important bustling about. He had as powerful a reason for keeping quiet as I had.

"The horse is at my house," I said. "I'll get the knackers to collect him, if you like."

"Yes," he agreed.

"How are the other old horses?" I asked.

"Perfectly well," he said furiously. "And it's *your* fault Peterman went to Mrs. English. She refused point-blank to take any of the others."

I made soothing noises and put down the receiver.

Looking about sixteen, Guggenheim came mournfully downstairs and stared out of the window at Peterman's carcass as if willing him back to tick-infested life.

"I'd better go back to Edinburgh," he said despondently, "unless any other horses are ill."

"I can find out at lunch. All the gossip and news in Pixhill will be available then, at Michael Watermead's house."

He said if it was all right with me he would stay until after that and then leave: he had ongoing work in the laboratory that he shouldn't be neglecting. Fine, I agreed; and he could come back instantly, of course, if anything significant happened.

He gloomily watched the knackers position their truck by my garden gate and winch the thin old corpse away. What would become of him? Guggenheim asked. Glue factory, I said. He looked as if he'd just as soon not have known.

He couldn't believe, he said, the state of my sitting

room, still in a mess. He couldn't believe the impact that had destroyed the helicopter and the car. The mind that had done it, I told him, was still wandering around somewhere, still in possession of the ax.

"But aren't you . . . well . . . scared?" he asked.

"Careful," I said. "That's why I'm not taking you with me to lunch. I don't want anyone knowing I know a scientist, especially one who's an expert on ticks. I hope you don't mind."

"Of course not." He looked at the ax-slashed room and shivered.

I took him to the farmyard, though, and showed him the horse vans, which impressed him by their size. I explained about the containers under three of them and said I thought the ticks had come into England that way on the rabbits.

"There would have to be air holes in the containers," he said.

"So there would."

"Haven't you looked?"

"No."

He was surprised, but I didn't explain. I took him back to my house and left him there while I went to the Watermeads' lunch.

Maudie greeted me with affection and Michael with warmth. Many of the usual people were there: the Ushers and Bruce Farway included. Tessa indulged in back-turning and whispering into Benjy's ear. The younger children were missing: they'd gone to stay with Susan and Hugh Palmerstone for the weekend. "They get on so well with Cinders," Maudie said. "Such a nice little girl." I realized that I'd hoped Cinders would again be at the Watermeads'. Don't think about her, I told myself. Couldn't help it.

I asked Michael if he'd accepted any of the old horses yet.

"Two of them," he said, nodding. "Skittish old things. Running about in my bottom paddock like two-year-olds."

I asked Dot the same question and got a different answer.

"Benjy says we can put Tigwood off for a few days. Don't know what's got into the old shit, actually doing what I asked."

"What did that old horse die of, last year?"

"Old age. Some sort of fever. What does it matter? I hate having them about the place."

The veterinarian who'd given my geriatric passengers the all clear was there, comparing notes with Bruce Farway.

"How's trade?" I asked them. "How are the sick of Pixhill? Anything interesting?"

"I hear the knackers were at your house this morning," the veterinarian observed.

"News zooms round," I said, resignedly. "One of the old horses died."

"You didn't call me in."

"I didn't know he was that ill, or I would have done."

He nodded. "They're old. They die. Can't be helped, it's nature."

"Is anyone else in trouble? Anyone got last year's bug?"

"No, thank goodness. Just the usual tendons and teeth."

"What was last year's bug?" Farway asked.

The veterinarian said, "Some unspecified infection. Horses got feverish. I gave them various antibiotics, and they recovered." He frowned. "It was worrying, really, because all those horses lost their speed and form after it. But, thank goodness, it wasn't widespread."

"Interesting, though," Farway said.

"You'll be involved in Pixhill's fortunes before you know it," the veterinarian teased him, and Farway looked disconcerted.

Maudie's sister, Lorna, came proprietorially to Farway's side, taking his arm and eyeing me with the disapproval left over from my not having transported the geriatrics without payment. I found her disapprobation much less alarming than her earlier interest in me. Farway gave her a fond look while sharing her opinions of myself.

I drifted away from them, feeling isolated by how much I had discovered and wondering what else I didn't know.

Ed, Tessa's brother, stood alone, looking surly. I talked to him for a bit, trying to cheer him up.

"You remember your show-stopper last week?" I asked him. "About Jericho Rich making a play for Tessa?"

"It was true what I said," he insisted defensively.

"I don't doubt it."

"He was pawing her. I saw him. She slapped his face."

"Really?"

"Don't you believe me? No one believes a word I say." Self-pity swamped him. "Jericho Rich swore at her and told her he would take his horses away and Tessa said if he did she'd get even. Silly little bitch. How could she get even with a man like that? So, anyway, he did take the horses away and what has Tessa done about it? Bloody nothing, of course. And Dad isn't even angry with her, only with me for telling everyone why Jericho Rich left. It isn't *fair*."

"No," I agreed.

"You're not too bad," he said reluctantly.

I sat next to Maudie at lunch but there was little left of the enjoyment I'd found at the table a week ago. Maudie sensed it, trying to dispel my sadness, but I left after the coffee with no great regrets.

There were no feverish horses in Pixhill, I reported to Guggenheim, and drove him in his own depression back to the airport. On the way home I stopped for gas and, after a bit of thought, phoned Nina's Stow-on-the-Wold number.

"Um," I said, "when you come to work tomorrow, bring a parachute."

"What?"

"For landing behind the enemy lines in occupied France."

"Is this the concussion?"

"It is not. You don't have to go if you don't want to."

"I wish you'd explain."

"Can I meet you somewhere? Are you busy?"

"I'm alone . . . and bored."

"Good. I mean, how about the Cotswold Gateway? I could be there before six."

"All right."

Accordingly I changed direction and drove west and north to arrive an hour and a half later at a large impersonal old hotel on the A40 main road, which ran across the top of the Cotswold town of Burford. I parked outside the great old-fashioned charming pile, a landmark passed endless times in my life on the way to Cheltenham races.

She was already there when I arrived, having had by far the shorter journey, and she was the original compelling Nina, not the scrubbed and workaday version.

She was sitting in a chintz armchair beside a glowing log fire in the entrance hall, a tea tray primly before her on a low table.

Post-Cheltenham but before the summer tourist season, the place was almost empty. She rose when I came in, and enjoyed my admiration of her appearance. No jeans, this time: the long slender legs were covered instead by black tights. No sloppy old sweater but a black skirt, black vest, white silk shirt with big sleeves, large gold cuff links and a long neck-chain of enough half sovereigns to fund a ransom. She smelled, not of horses, but subtly of gardenias. The economical bones of her face were revealed and softened by a dusting of powder. Lips, softly red.

"I hardly like to ask you . . ." I said, kissing her cheek as if from long close habit, "looking as you do . . ."

"You sounded serious."

"Mm."

We sat down near enough to each other to talk, though there was no one to overhear.

"First of all," I said, "I found out what's been carried under my lorries, and it is not as simple as drugs." She waited while I paused, her interest sharpening to acute. "I went to see a top Customs man in Portsmouth," I said, "to ask what *couldn't* move freely in and out of Britain under the E.C. regulations. I expect you know the Customs men never search any traffic nowadays unless they have specific information that drugs will be found in a certain vehicle. In practice, it means that anything—guns, cocaine, whatever, coming here from Europe—has untroubled entry. But he got very excited about cats and dogs, and rabies . . . and it seems the quarantine rules apply, and also one needs a license for things like veterinary medicines. Anyway, my vans *have* been carrying extra livestock, though not cats and dogs, I don't think, because they would both make a noise."

"Make a *noise*?"

"Sure. If you carried a cat in one of those containers, someone would hear it complaining."

"But why? You've lost me. Why take livestock in those containers?"

"So that the grooms with the horses wouldn't know about it. If any horse van carried anything in public out of the ordinary, half the village would hear about it in the pub."

"Then who's been carrying secret livestock?"

"One of my drivers."

"Which one?"

"Lewis."

"Oh no, Freddie. He has that baby!"

"One can love one's offspring and be a villain."

"You don't mean it . . ."

"Yeah. And I don't like it."

"Do you mean . . . you can't mean . . . that Lewis had been deliberately trying to bring rabies into England?"

"No, not rabies, thank God. Just a fever that makes horses temporarily ill, but takes the edge off their speed so drastically that they don't win again."

I told her that Jogger's dead nun had been a rabbit.

"Nun—rabbit—*habit*." She sighed. "How did you find out?"

"I asked Isobel what Jogger found dead in the pit, and she told me."

"So simple!"

"Then I looked at the computer files for last August, for the time when I was away, and there it was. August 10th. Jogger reported a dead rabbit fell into the pit from a van he was servicing, and it was on the day after Lewis brought that van back from France."

She frowned. "But the computer files were lost."

I told her about the backups in my safe.

324

"You didn't tell anyone! You didn't tell *me*. Don't you trust me?"

"Mostly," I said.

She wouldn't meet my eyes. I said, "Jogger told Isobel the rabbit had ticks on it and she put a note about that in the computer. The computer also lists each van's journeys individually, and two of those vans that have hidden containers, Pat's van, that you drove, and Phil's van, both of those were driven to France by Lewis last year. This year he's driving my newest super-six, and it too, as you found, has a container under it. Last weekend, the Watermead children missed one of their tame rabbits, that Lewis looks after for them, cleaning their runs and so on, and also last weekend Lewis drove the super-six to France, and this weekend a horse has died in Pixhill of a tick-borne fever."

She listened wide-eyed, her mouth opening. I went over it all again, slowly, telling her about Benjy's training habits, about Lewis's shorn ringlets, about Peterman and finally about Guggenheim.

Once an old horse had come through the fever stage, I said, he could live with ticks on him all summer. A continual source of potential illness for other designated recipients. An *Ehrlichiae* farm, in fact. A quick wipe over an old horse with a wet bar of soap and, within an hour, a wipe of the same soap onto a new host. Tick-transfer completed. Enough of the ticks would survive. The transfer, I said gloomily, might even have been done by Lewis when he drove the unfortunate victims to the races in my vans.

When the weather grew cold, the ticks would die. A new lot had to be brought in by a temporary host for the new year, and then, without much delay, transferred to their natural host, a horse. Peterman hadn't survived it.

Whatever doubts she had at the beginning, they had gone by the end.

"When we first found the containers," I said, "I begged Jogger not to talk about them. But he did, of course, down at the pub on Saturday night. I reckon he'd been thinking a lot about them. Turning them over in his mind, I'd think he remembered the rabbit, which must have seemed to him at the time to appear from nowhere, and perhaps he'd worked out that it might have fallen out of one of those containers, the one under what is now Phil's van, because that container had lost its screw-on end. I don't know if anyone understood Jogger plainly in the pub. They might have done. Anyway, in the morning he left me the message . . . and he told me, Jogger told me . . . about rabbits and ticks and Benjy Usher's horse that died."

She was silent for a while and then asked, "Was it Lewis who wrecked your car and the house?"

"I don't know. I'm sure he was one of the people who dropped me into the water at Southampton. The one who said, 'If that doesn't give him flu, nothing will.' His voice was hoarse because he had a cold, and in my memory, that voice reverberated a bit, as I was half unconscious, but yes, I'm sure that was him. Whether he hates me enough for the rest . . . I don't know."

"That's *awful.*"

"Mm."

"So what next?"

"Tomorrow," I said, "Lewis is driving the super-six to Milan, in Italy, to fetch home one of Benjy Usher's colts, that has a dicky leg. It's a three-day trip, mostly through France."

She grew still. Then she said, "I'll go. Have parachute, will travel."

"I don't want you to *do* anything," I explained. "I don't want you to alarm him. I want him to have every opportunity to pick up another rabbitful of ticks, because if all of last weekend's cargo were on Peterman and have died with him, and if no other horses are ill, then perhaps this is a chance for them to get some replacements. Those ticks are highly perishable, and also hard to find. I'd think they'd need some more. All I want you to do is to note where you go. The route Lewis will take to Italy is down to the Rhône Valley, which is where he went last weekend also. He should be going through the Mont Blanc tunnel from France to Italy but if he takes another route, don't remark on it. If he wants to stop anywhere at all, let him stop. Don't ask questions. Agree to whatever he suggests. Notice nothing. Don't watch him. Yawn, sleep, act dumb."

"He won't want me with him, you know."

"I know he thinks you tire easily. So *tire*. This time, he may be glad of it."

"And don't, I suppose, look under the van?"

"No, don't. If the place is littered with lettuce leaves and rabbit droppings, ignore it."

She smiled.

"Be careful," I begged. "I'd go myself, except that if I did, nothing would happen. All I want to know is *where* Lewis goes."

"All right."

"You don't have to."

"Nor did my mother."

"Lewis might be just as dangerous."

"I promise," she said emphatically, "that I'll be as blind as a bat." She paused. "There's only one thing."

"What?"

"I want to tell Patrick Venables where I'm going."

"Would he stop you?"

"Probably the opposite."

"Don't let him *do* anything," I said anxiously. "Don't let him frighten them off." My instinct was against the Jockey Club knowing too much, too soon, but perhaps also for this possibly risky mission I might need the insurance of Venables's foreknowledge.

"I don't want to be prosecuted," she said, half playfully, "for trying to nobble half of Pixhill's best colts."

"You won't be. I"—I stopped dead, a revelation presenting itself to me with breath-thieving force. "Bloody *hell*!"

"What is it?"

"Um. Nothing. When you get back on Wednesday you'll be met. Don't worry about anything except not frightening Lewis."

We ate dinner in the dining room, discussing the trip to begin with but passing pretty soon to our lives in general. I enjoyed being with her. I was growing unfaithful to Maudie, I thought ironically. I asked Nina how old her eldest child was.

"Twenty-three." She smiled down at her pasta. "Much younger than you."

"Am I that transparent?"

"You're no toy-boy," she said.

"Your children might think so."

"Your sister is older than her professor, isn't she?"

"Yes, she is," I said, mildly surprised. "Who told you?"

"Aziz told me."

"Aziz?"

"Your sister told *him*. He told *me*. We drivers hang together, you know."

"Wipe that demure smile off your face."

The smile, however, deepened. I thought of all the

empty bedrooms upstairs in the hotel. I thought of the year-long celibacy and felt a strong desire to end it. She must have known what was in my mind. She simply waited.

I sighed. "It's not what I'd prefer," I said, "but I'm going home."

She said passively, "All right."

I rubbed my eyes. "When this is over . . ."

"Yes. We'll see."

We went out together, as before, to our separate cars. She had come in her Mercedes.

I kissed her mouth, not her cheek. She drew her head away, her eyes gleaming in the car-park lights. I saw that I didn't displease her. I could so easily . . . so easily . . .

"Freddie . . ." Her voice was soft, noncommittal, leaving it to me.

"I have to . . . I really do have to go," I said almost desperately. "I'm not sending you off to France without sensible preparations. Bring your overnight things in the morning and pick up a travel kit from the office. It will hold money and phone numbers and a precaution or two against thieves. Lewis always takes a similar kit." I stopped. Travel kits were not what I wanted to talk about. I kissed her again and felt resolution draining away.

"Do the kit in the morning," she suggested.

"Oh, God."

"Freddie . . ."

"I'll tell you tomorrow why I have to go."

I kissed her hard, then turned away and went over to the Fourtrak, feeling clumsy and annoyed with myself for going so far and inexplicably retreating. She didn't seem to mind. There were no hurt rejected feelings in the smile she gave me as she shut herself into the red car.

"See you," she said through the opening window, starting the engine.

"Good night."

With a wave she drove away, as self-possessed as ever. I watched her taillights into the distance and strove to quieten my pulse. The basic drives of nature were so bloody powerful after all. And I'd thought I had the turmoil licked, which only showed that dormant volcanos were simply that; fires temporarily asleep.

Eight and a half years. Did they matter I didn't know, and I understood that she didn't know either. She was attracted to me; I had to believe it. She was also, I thought, in an odd way shy, not wanting me to think she had rushed me. She was making me decide whether what I felt was a passing arousal or a longer commitment.

I belted the Fourtrak back to my house, pushing decisions away for the night, and changed into soft black shoes and the darkest of clothes I could find. Then, with my eyes adjusting to night vision, I walked in the shadows along to the farmyard and unlocked the padlock on the gates to let myself in, locking it again behind me.

It was after midnight. The sky was clear and cold, stars blazing. All those distant suns, I thought; as mysterious and inaccessible as *Ehrlichia risticii*.

All the horse vans were home in the roost, subduedly shining in the light of the night bulb over the canteen door. A quiet Sunday evening, peace after bustle. I had not, this time, walked into a mortal situation.

Harve, I imagined, had done his last rounds, and was watching video football. I unlocked the offices and, without switching on the interior lights, went along to my own room, enough glow creeping in through the windows for me to locate the flashlight I kept in the desk there and to check that its batteries were functioning. Then, relocking the office door on my way out, I padded across the farm-yard to Jogger's old truck from whose front seats I could see all my monsters partially, and one or two of them clearly.

The super-six Lewis would drive to Milan was one of those. I settled into the dark interior of Jogger's truck and tried resolutely to stay awake.

I managed it for an hour.

Dozed.

Woke with a jerk. Two o'clock. Sentries could be court-martialed for sleeping on duty. No one could help going to sleep. When the brain wanted to switch off, it did.

I tried reciting old verses. Nursery rhymes. One two, buckle my shoe.

Went to sleep.

Three o'clock. Four. Half the night passed across my shut eyes. Absolutely no good. Waste of time sitting there.

When he came, the padlock clicked and rattled on its chain, and I was fully alert instantly.

I held my breath, not moving.

Lewis's unmistakable short haircut passed in silhouette between me and the outside light. Lewis, carrying a shape-less bag, moved unhesitatingly towards his own lorry, where he lay down on the ground and disappeared from my sight.

He remained out of sight for what seemed a long time, until I began to think he must have left without my notic-ing. But then, there he was, standing up, moving away, re-turning with his bag to the main gate and fastening the padlock with an almost inaudible click.

Gone.

I sat for another half-hour, not entirely from wanting to

be sure he wouldn't come back but from reluctance to face the next bit.

Phobias were irrational and stupid. Phobias were paralyzing, petrifying and all too real. I slowly emerged from the lorry, took the flashlight, tried to think of race-riding ... anything ... and lay down on my back beside Lewis's van in the location of the fuel tanks.

The cold stars up there didn't care that my skin sweated and my courage shrank to the size of a nut.

The horse van would not collapse on me. It obviously would *not*.

For fuck's sake, do it, I told myself. Don't be so fucking *stupid*.

I shifted my shoulders and hips over the ground and wriggled sideways until I was totally under the tons of steel, and of course they did not collapse on me, they hung over me immobile and impassive, a threat unfulfilled. I stopped under the fuel tanks and felt the stupid sweat wet on my face and came near to complete panic when I tried to raise my hand to wipe the sweat away and hit metal instead.

Fuck, I thought. No word was bad enough. I didn't habitually think in that casual expletive universal on the racecourse, but there were times when no other word would do.

I'd *chosen* to lie where I was. Stop bloody trembling, I told myself, and get on with the matter in hand.

Yes, Freddie.

I felt for, and found, the round end of the container above the rear fuel tank. I unscrewed it and laid it on the ground beside me. I switched on the flashlight and raised my head to look into the container.

My hair brushed against the metal. Tons of steel. Shut

up. My hands were slippery with sweat and I could hardly breathe and my heart pounded, and I'd risked death in racing thousands of times over fourteen years and I hadn't cared . . . it had been nothing like this.

Inside the tubular container there lay what seemed to be a long flat narrow plywood tray stretching away into shadow. Standing on the plywood was an oblong plastic kitchen food-box very like the one I'd taken to Scotland, except that this one had no lid.

Gripping the flashlight convulsively, I stuck my arm with the flashlight into the tube for a deeper look.

The kitchen food-box held *water*.

Little stars appeared above the tubular container, showing on the underside of the horse van floor above. The stars were from the light inside the tube. The stars were the result of holes in the tube.

"There would have to be air holes in the container," Guggenheim had said.

There *were* air holes.

I peered straight into the tube, my head hard against the metal above, arms constricted by metal on both sides, nerves shot to pathetic crumbs.

Deep along in the tube something moved. An eye shone brightly. In his metal burrow, the rabbit seemed at ease.

I switched off the flashlight, screwed the end back onto the tube and wriggled out again into the free night air.

I lay on the hard ground, regrouping, heart thudding, ashamed of myself. Nothing, I thought, *nothing* would get me to do anything like that ever again.

In the morning, life in the farmyard looked normal.

Lewis, predictably, was annoyed that I'd allocated Nina to go with him instead of Dave.

"Dave wasn't well on Saturday," I said. "I'm not risking him getting flu away in Italy."

Dave at the moment creaked into view on his bicycle, obligingly flushed and heavy-eyed. Flu wasn't going to stop him, he said.

"Sorry, but it is," I replied. "Go home to bed."

Nina arrived looking the epitome of feminine frailty, yawning artistically and stretching. Lewis regarded her thoughtfully and made no more objections.

He and she both collected their travel kits from Isobel and went over the paperwork requirements with her. When Lewis went into the washroom I had a private moment to murmur in Nina's ear.

"You're taking a nun with you."

Wide-eyed, she said, "How do you know?"

"I saw her arrive.'"

"When?"

"Five this morning. About then."

"So that's why . . ."

Lewis reappeared, saying if they were going to catch the ferry they'd better be off.

"Phone home," I said.

"Sure thing," he agreed easily.

He drove out of the gate without a worry in the world. I hoped to hell that Nina would come back safely.

From the business point of view it was not an overpoweringly busy day, but the plainclothes police swept in with sharp eyes to take over the place before nine, setting up an interview room in my office. Dispossessed, I showed them whatever they wanted, offered them the run of the canteen and sat for a while on a spare chair in Isobel's office, watching her work.

Sandy drove in in his uniform, still confused in his loyalties.

"Tell them about the containers," he blurted. "I haven't."

"Thanks, Sandy."

"Did you find your answers?"

"I asked some questions."

He knew I wasn't being open with him, but he seemed to prefer ignorance. In any case, he joined his colleagues and ran errands for them all day.

The colleagues found out about the containers from the landlord of the pub.

"Lone rangers?" I repeated when they asked me out in the farmyard. "Yes, Jogger came across three containers under the lorries. All empty. We don't know how long they've been there."

The Force wanted to inspect them. Go ahead, I agreed, though Phil wouldn't be back with his own horse van until evening.

Lewis had reached the ferry in good time, Isobel reported, and was now in France. I metaphorically bit my nails.

The police interviewed everyone they could reach and spent time sliding in and out under the vans. Rather them than me. When Phil returned they removed the tube from above the fuel tanks (with my permission) and brought it out to where it could be easily inspected. Four feet long, eight inches in diameter, empty except for dust, small holes punched through it, screw cap missing.

They took it away for examination. I wondered if they would find rabbit hairs in it.

I drove home. The little helicopter had gone. My poor crunched car stood alone and forlorn, awaiting a tow truck on the morrow. I patted it. Silly, really. The end of a big part of my life. Saying goodbye.

I went early to bed and tossed and turned.

In the morning Lewis reported to Isobel that he had cleared the Mont Blanc tunnel and would collect the colt before noon.

The police asked more questions. Half the fleet set off to take merchandise to Doncaster sales, Nigel driving for Marigold. I progressed from metaphorical nail biting to actual.

At noon Lewis reported that Benjy Usher's colt was unmanageable.

I talked to him myself.

"I'm not driving it," he said. "It's a wild animal. It'll damage the van. It'll have to stay here."

"Is Nina around?"

"She's trying to pacify it. No chance."

"Let me talk to her."

She came on the line. "The colt's scared," she agreed. "He keeps trying to lie down and thrash about. Give me an hour."

"If he's really unmanageable, come back without him."

"OK."

"Anything else?" I asked.

"No. Nothing."

I sat watching the clock.

After an hour, Lewis phoned back. "Nina reckons the colt suffers from claustrophobia," he said. "He goes berserk if we try to shut him in a single stall in the horse van, and also if we try to tie him up. She's got him quiet, like, but he's loose in a big stall, like we arrange it for a mare and foal. You know. Room for three, all to himself. And she's opened the windows. The colt's standing with his

336

nose out of one of them at the moment. What do you reckon?"

"It's up to you," I said. "I'll tell Mr. Usher we can't bring his colt out, if you like."

"No." He sounded indecisive but finally said, "OK, I'll give it a try. But if he goes mad again when we start off, I'll scrub it."

"Right."

A claustrophobic horse. We did sometimes come across animals that no amount of persuasion or brute force would get them up a ramp into a horse van. I sympathized with them, especially after the previous night, but I could have done, this time, with a dozy docile passenger giving Lewis no trouble.

I waited. Another hour crawled by.

"They must be on their way," Isobel said, unconcerned.

"I hope so."

Another hour. No news.

"I'm going to Michael Watermead's," I told Isobel. "Call me on the mobile phone if Lewis reports."

She nodded, busy with other things, and I trundled down to Michael's trying to work out how best to tell him something he wouldn't want to hear.

He was surprised to see me in the hour of afternoon doldrums before the grooms arrived to feed and water the horses and prepare them for the night.

"Hello!" he said. "What can I do for you? Come along in."

He took me into a small friendly sitting room, not the big imposing room of Sunday-lunch champagne cocktails. He'd been reading newspapers, which lay scattered over a low table and nearby armchair, and he roughly gathered them together to make a space for me to sit.

"Maudie's out," he said. "I'll make some tea in a minute."

He waved for me to sit down, obviously waiting for me to begin. And *where* to begin ... that was the problem.

"You remember," I said, "the man who died in one of my horse vans?"

"Died? Oh yes, of course. On the way back from taking Jericho's two-year-olds, wretched man."

"Mm." I paused. "Look," I said awkwardly, "I wouldn't bother you with this, but I do want to clear something up."

"Carry on, then." He sounded receptive, not impatient, simply interested.

I told him that Dave had picked the man up not casually but by arrangement. Michael frowned. I explained about the carrier bag with the thermos flask that I'd found in the nine-van the next evening, and I showed him the last two tubes that had been carried in the thermos, that I'd had in my safe.

"What are they?" he asked curiously, holding one up to the light. "What's in them?"

"Viral transport medium," I said. "For transporting a virus from place to place."

"Virus ..." He was shocked. "Did you say *virus*?"

Virus, to all trainers, meant "the virus," the dreaded respiratory infection that made horses cough and run at the nose. The virus could put a stable out of winners for most of a year. The worst news possible, that was "the virus."

Michael handed the tubes back as if they'd stung him.

"They came from Pontefract," I said. "From Yorkshire."

He stared. "They've got the virus up there. Two or three yards have it." He looked worried. "You haven't mixed any of my horses in with horses from up North, have you? Because, if so ..."

"No," I said positively. "Your horses always travel alone, unless you give specific permission otherwise. I'd never ever put your horses in danger of infection in my transport."

He marginally relaxed. "I didn't think you would." He was eyeing the tubes as if they were snakes. "Why are you telling me this?"

"Because I think . . . er . . . if the hitchhiker hadn't died, the virus that was in these tubes might have found its way into the last of Jericho Rich's string—the fillies—on the last day of the transfer to Newmarket."

He stared some more. He thought it over. "But *why*?" he asked. "That's *criminal*."

"Mm."

"Why?" he said again.

"To get even with Jericho Rich."

"Oh no," he said protestingly, standing up sharply, striding away from me, anger rising. "I would *never, never* do a thing like that."

"I know you wouldn't."

He swung round furiously. "Then *who*?"

"Um . . . I think . . . you might ask Tessa."

"Tessa!" His anger increased; at me, not at her. "She wouldn't. What's more she *couldn't*. This is utter rubbish, Freddie, and I'm not listening to any more of it."

I sighed. "All right." I stood up to go. "Sorry, Michael."

I went out of his house and over to my Fourtrak and he followed me indecisively as far as his door.

"Come back," he said.

I retraced a few steps in his direction.

"You can't make accusations like that and simply bugger off," he said. "Do you or don't you want to go on driving my horses?"

"Very badly," I admitted.

"Then this is not the way to go about it."

"I can't let my business be used for carrying viruses from place to place and do nothing to stop it."

"Huh," he said on a low breath. "When you think of it like that ... But Tessa? It's preposterous. She wouldn't know how to do it, for a start."

"I'd like to ask her," I said reasonably. "Is she at home?"

He looked at his watch. "She ought to be here at any minute. She only went shopping."

"I could come back," I said.

He hesitated, then jerked his head towards the inside of the house, bidding me to follow. "You might as well wait," he said.

I followed him through to the sitting room.

"Tessa," he said, not believing it. "You've got it all wrong."

"If I have, I'll grovel."

He gave me a sharp look. "You'll need to."

We waited. Michael tried to read a newspaper and put it down crossly, unable to concentrate.

"Nonsense," he said, meaning what I'd said about Tessa. "Total nonsense."

His daughter returned, looking into the sitting room as she passed, festooned with boutique bags, on her way upstairs. Brown-haired, light-eyed, perpetually sulky-looking, she glanced at me with disfavor.

"Come in, Tessa," her father said. "Shut the door."

"I want to go upstairs." She peered into one of the bags. "I want to try this dress on."

"Come in," he said, sharply for him, and frowning, ungraciously, she did so.

"What is it, then?" she asked.

"All right, Freddie," her father said to me. "Ask her."

"Ask me what?" She was displeased, but not frightened.

"Um . . ." I said, "did you arrange for some tubes containing virus to be brought to Pixhill?"

It took a moment for my deliberately casual tone of voice to reach her understanding. When she realized what I'd asked her, she stopped fidgeting with her shopping and grew still with shock, her face stiffening, mouth open, eyes wary. Even to Michael it was plain that she knew what I was talking about.

"Tessa," he said despairingly.

"Well, what of it?" she said defiantly. "What if I did? It never got here. So what?"

I took the two tubes out of my pocket again and put them on the table. She looked at them vaguely, then worked out what they were. A bad moment for her, I thought.

"There were six tubes," I said. "What were you going to do with them? Pour the contents up the noses of six fillies belonging to Jericho Rich?"

"Dad!" She turned to him, imploring. "Get rid of him."

"I can't," Michael said sadly. "Is that what you intended?"

"I didn't do it." She sounded triumphant more than abashed.

"You didn't do it," I agreed, "because your courier died of heart failure on the journey and failed to deliver the thermos."

"You don't know *anything*," she said. "You're making it up."

"You wanted to get even with Jericho Rich for taking his horses away because he made a pass at you and you

slapped his face. You thought you would make his horses
ill so they couldn't win, serve him right. You saw an advertisement in *Horse and Hound* magazine saying more or
less 'anything transported anywhere,' so you phoned the
number in the ad and arranged for Kevin Keith Ogden—
the man who died—to pick up a thermos at Pontefract service station and bring it down the A1 to the junction with
the M25 at South Mimms. You arranged with my driver,
Dave, to get Ogden picked up there and to bring him to
Chieveley. You phoned Dave late in the evening after he
got back from Folkestone, as you knew it was no good trying to reach him earlier because you knew his schedule.
You're always in and out of Isobel's office and you could
see the day's list. Ogden was supposed to disembark at
Chieveley and hand over the thermos, but as he'd died my
men brought him all the way to my house. I expect you
may have been surprised when Ogden didn't appear at
Chieveley, but it was soon all over the village why not,
and certainly your father knew about it almost at once." I
paused briefly. Neither father nor daughter tried to speak.

"When you found Ogden was dead," I went on, "you
knew the thermos had to be still in the horse van, so you
came looking for it, Tessa, disguised in dark clothes with
a black balaclava over your head, so that if I saw you I
wouldn't know you. I found you in the cab, if you remember, and you ran away."

It was Michael who said, "No."

"You couldn't find the thermos," I told Tessa. "You
tried twice. Then I decided to sleep in the cab, which put
an end to it."

Michael said, "I don't believe it." But he did.

"I'll make a deal with you," I said to Tessa. "I won't

tell Jericho Rich what you intended for his fillies if you'll answer a few questions."

"You can't prove a thing," she said, narrowing her eyes. "And that's blackmail."

"Maybe. In return for my never mentioning this again to anyone, I want a few answers. It's not a~bad bargain."

"How do I know you'll keep it?"

"He will," Michael said.

"Why do you trust him so much?" his daughter demanded.

"I just do."

She didn't like it. She tossed her head. She said tightly, "What do you want to know?"

"Chiefly," I said, "where did the viral transport medium come from?"

"What?"

I repeated the question. She went on looking blank.

"The liquid in those tubes," I said, "is a mixture used for transporting viruses outside a living body."

"I don't understand."

"If you simply collected the nasal discharge of a horse with the virus," I said, "the virus would disappear in a very short time. To bring the infection to Pixhill from Yorkshire by road, the way it came, you'd need to combine the nasal discharge with a mixture that would keep the virus active. That's what's in these tubes, that mixture. Even in these, a virus won't survive more than two days. This mixture here is harmless now. But where did it come from?"

She didn't answer. Michael said, "Where, Tessa?"

"I don't know. I don't know what you're talking about."

"All you know," I suggested, "was that if you held a

horse's head up and poured the mixture down his nostril, he would be infected?"

"Well, probably. *Probably* be infected."

"Who told you?" I asked. "Who got the stuff for you?" Silence.

"Tessa?" Michael said.

"Was it Benjy Usher?" I asked.

"No!" She was truly astonished. "Of course not."

"Not Benjy," Michael agreed, amused. "But who, Tessa?"

"I'm not saying."

"That's unfortunate," I murmured.

A silence lengthened while the head-tosser, the whisperer, thought it over.

"Oh, all *right*," she burst out. "It was Lewis."

Michael was as surprised as I was not. I would have been astounded if she'd said anyone else.

"I don't *know* where he got it from," she said wildly. "All he said was he could get a pal up North to collect some snot from a horse with the virus—that's what he said, snot, not all posh like nasal discharge—and this pal would take it to Pontefract service station if I could get someone to collect it. The pal couldn't get away to bring it down here and I'd no chance of going to Yorkshire without making endless excuses, so yes, I'd seen the ad in the magazine and suggested to Lewis that I could use it and he said get Dave to pick the man up; Dave was down for the trip to Newmarket and he would do anything for money, and the man would get to Chieveley, where I could meet him easily, and how was I to know he was going to *die*? I phoned Lewis and told him what had happened and asked him to find the thermos for me but all he would do was just give me the key to get into the cab with. And if you want to know, you looked pretty stupid when you caught me searching, when you were trying to run in sleeping shorts and gumboots and a raincoat half off. Pretty silly, you looked."

"I expect so," I said equably. "Did you look *under* the horse van as well as in it?"

"Mr. Know-all, aren't you? Yes, I did."

"Er, why?"

"Lewis told me one day you could carry anything under the horse vans if you wanted to."

"Why did he say that?" I asked.

"Why does anyone say anything? He liked saying things to get you going. He said he'd carried soap in a container under one of your vans, but he'd given it up, it didn't work."

"*Soap,*" Michael said, hopelessly lost, "whyever soap?"

"I don't know. How should *I* know? Lewis just says weird things. Just his way."

"So . . . er . . ." I said, "did you find any soap under my horse van?"

"No, of course I didn't. I was looking for a thermos. There was nothing at all under there. It was all filthy dirty."

"When you tried to get Nigel to take you to Newmarket with the fillies," I said, "were you still hoping to find the virus container and infect the horses on the journey?"

"What if I was?"

"It was a different horse van," I said.

"It wasn't . . . well, they all look alike."

"Many do."

She looked shattered.

"Did you pay Dave?" I asked mildly.

"No, I didn't. I mean, I never got the stuff, did I?"

"And you didn't pay Ogden, because he was dead. Did you pay Lewis?"

After a pause she said sullenly, "He wanted it in advance. So, yes."

Michael said, "Tessa," again, almost wailing.

"Well, I did it for you, Dad," she said. "I *hate* Jericho Rich. Taking his horses away because I slapped his face! I did it for *you*."

Michael was overcome, full of too-easy indulgence. I didn't believe her, but perhaps Michael needed to.

13

Isobel was still in the office when I returned to the farmyard although it was by then nearly five. Rose had gone home.

Lewis had phoned, Isobel said. I had just missed him. He and Nina were back through the Mont Blanc tunnel and had stopped for a sandwich and refueling. Nina had been driving. The colt had had its head out of the window all the way but had not gone berserk. Lewis would be driving north through the night, though he would stop somewhere to fill the jerrycans with French water for the colt.

"Right," I said.

French water, pure and sweet from springs, was good for horses. Such a stop would be unremarkable.

"Aziz asked for tomorrow off," Isobel said. "He doesn't want to drive tomorrow. Something to do with his religion."

"His *religion*?"

"That's what he said."

"He's a rogue. Where is he now?"

"On his way back from taking horses to Doncaster sales."

I sighed. Religions were difficult to argue with, but Aziz was still a rogue, if not something worse.

"Anything else?"

"Mr. Usher asked if we'd collected the colt. I told him he'd be in Pixhill by six tomorrow evening, if there were no ferry delays."

"Thanks."

"Fingers crossed," Isobel said.

"Mm."

"You looked awfully worried," she said.

"It's this Jogger business."

She nodded in understanding. The police, she said, had been irritated to find so many drivers away out on the road.

"They don't seem to realize we've a business to run," she said. "They think we should all down tools. I told them we couldn't."

"Thanks again."

"Get some sleep," she said impulsively, young but no fool.

"Mm."

I tried to take her advice. Concussion no longer did the trick. I lay awake thinking of Lewis stopping somewhere to fill the cans with French water. I hoped to hell Nina would keep her head down and her eyes—partially—shut.

On Wednesday morning I saw off the lorries going out again to Doncaster, where the Flat racing season would open the next day. The March meeting of Doncaster sales and races were the start of Croft Raceways' busiest time: we were entering six months of work, work, improvisation and scramble, an atmosphere I usually loved. Juggling the number of vans, the number of drivers, against the prospects of profitability: normally it excited me, but this week so far I could barely concentrate.

"The whole fleet," Isobel said, cheeringly, "will be rolling tomorrow."

I cared only that Lewis would roll home today.

At nine, when the telephone rang for the *n*th time, Isobel answered it, frowning.

"Aziz?" she said. "Just a moment." She put her hand over the receiver. "What's 'hold on' in French?"

"Ne quittez pas," I said.

Isobel repeated *"Ne quittez pas"* into the instrument and rose to her feet. "It's a Frenchman, for Aziz."

"He isn't here today," I said.

She replied over her shoulder as she went through the door, "He's in the canteen."

Aziz came in hurriedly and picked up the receiver from Isobel's desk.

"Oui . . . Aziz. Oui." He listened and spoke rapidly in French, stretching out a hand for a piece of memo paper and a pencil. *"Oui. Oui . . Merci, Monsieur. Merci."* Aziz wrote carefully, thanked his informant profusely and put the phone back in its cradle.

"A message from France," he said unnecessarily. He pushed the memo sheet towards me. "It seems Nina asked the man to phone here. She gave him money for the phone call and an address. This is it."

I took the paper and read the scant words. "Ecurie Bonne Chance, près de Belley."

"Good Luck Stables," Aziz translated. "Near Belley."

He gave me the usual brilliant smile and smartly left the office.

"I thought Aziz had the day off," I said to Isobel.

She shrugged. "He said he didn't want to *drive*. He was here already in the canteen when I arrived for work. Reading and drinking tea. He said, 'Good morning, darlin'."

Isobel faintly blushed.

I looked at the French address and phoned the Jockey Club. Peter Venables must have been sitting there, waiting.

"Nina sent an address via a Frenchman," I told him. "Ecurie Bonne Chance, near Belley. Can you ask your equivalents in France for any information about it?"

"Spell it."

I spelled it. "Aziz took the message in French," I said.

"Good." He sounded decisive. "I'll ask any French colleagues and phone you back."

I sat for a few seconds looking at the telephone after he'd disconnected, and then went and found Aziz in the canteen and invited him into the open air.

"What's your religion?" I asked, out in the farmyard.

"Er ..." He gave me a sideways look with his bright eyes, the smile untroubled.

"Do you work for the Jockey Club?" I asked flatly.

The smile simply broadened.

I turned away from him. Patrick Venables, I thought bitterly, and Nina also, had trusted me so little that they'd sent another undercover man, one I wouldn't know of, to make sure I wasn't myself the villain I purported to be looking for. Aziz had turned up the day after Jogger died. I suppose I shouldn't have minded, but I did.

"Freddie." Aziz took a step and grasped my sleeve. "Listen." The smile had faded. "Patrick wanted Nina to have backup. I suppose we should have told you, but . . ."

"Stick around," I said briefly, and returned to my office.

An hour later, Patrick Venables came on the line.

"First of all, I think I owe you an apology," he said. "But I'm curious. How did you suss out Aziz? He phoned to say you'd rumbled him."

"Little things," I explained. "He's too bright for the job. I'll bet he never drove for a racing stable. The phone caller from France asked for him specifically, which meant Nina had arranged for Aziz to be available. And you, yourself, didn't ask who Aziz was, when I mentioned him."

"Dear God."

"As you say."

"Ecurie Bonne Chance," he said, "is a small stable run by a minor French trainer. The owner of the property is Benjamin Usher."

"Ah."

"The property is south of Belley and is situated near the River Rhône where the river runs from east to west, before turning south at Lyons."

"Very thorough," I commented.

"The French know nothing against the place. They have had some sick horses there, but none have died."

"Thank you very much."

"Nina insisted on going on the journey," he said, "and she was adamant we don't intercept your van on its way back."

"Please don't."

"I hope you know what you're doing."

I hoped so too.

I phoned Guggenheim. "I can't promise," I said, "but

fly down and come to the farmyard today, in a taxi, and bring something to carry a small animal in."

"Rabbit?" he asked hopefully.

"Pray," I said.

The hours crawled.

Lewis phoned Isobel eventually in the afternoon and said they had crossed on the ferry and were leaving Dover.

After another slow hour Isobel and Rose went home and I locked the office and went over to the Fourtrak, starting the engine. The passenger door opened, with Aziz standing there.

"Can I come with you?" he said. Bright eyes. No smile.

I didn't immediately answer.

"You'll be safer if I do. No one, anyway, will hit you on the head when you're not looking."

I made a noncommittal gesture and he swung into the seat beside me.

"You're going to meet Nina, aren't you?" he asked.

"Yes."

"What do you expect will happen?"

I drove out of the yard, turned out of the village and drove uphill to a place where one could look down on Pixhill below.

"Lewis," I said, "should come over the brow of that far hill and drive into Benjy Usher's yard. If he does, I'll drive down there to meet them. If he goes anywhere else we can see that from here too."

"Where do you think he might go?"

"I don't know how much you know."

"Nina said the method was complicated but the simple matter is that someone is bringing sickness to Pixhill's horses."

"Roughly, yes."

"But why?"

"Partly to make a certain category of races easier to win by methodically infecting all the horses of that category that can be got at in Pixhill." I paused. "Halve the runners in the Chester Vase, for instance, and you more or less double your chances of winning. There are seldom more than six or so runners in the Chester Vase, or the Dante Stakes at York. They are nice prestigious races. Winning them puts a trainer in good standing in the profession."

Aziz sat digesting the implications. "A blanket illness?" he said.

"Occurring here and there." I nodded. "It's not like nobbling the favorite for the Derby."

"Irkab Alhawa," he said. "Ride the Air."

"Ride the Wind."

"No," he said, "in Arabic it means 'ride the air.' It's the way jockeys ride, standing in the stirrups, sitting on air, not the saddle."

"Ride the wind's better," I said.

"But you don't think anyone's going to make *that* horse sick?"

After a pause I said, "Lewis didn't kill Jogger, he was in France. I don't think Lewis destroyed my car or took an ax to my house. I'm sure Lewis didn't crash the hard disk in my computer. As I said, that Sunday he was in France."

"He couldn't have done it," Aziz agreed.

"I thought I was up against two forces," I said. "Muscle and money. But there's a third."

"What is it?"

"Malice."

"The worst," Aziz said slowly.

The driving force within you, I thought, leaps out. Under stress, it can't be hidden.

Apply the stress.

"Do you have any *reason* to think anyone would destroy Irkab Alhawa?" Aziz asked, frowning.

"No. I just intend to use the thought as a lever."

"To do what?"

"Wait and see, and guard my back."

Aziz leaned sideways against the passenger door and assessed me quizzically, the irrepressible smile reappearing.

"You're not like you look, are you?" he said.

"How do I look?"

"Physical."

"So do you," I said.

"But then . . . I am."

An odd ally, I thought; and unexpectedly, I was glad he was there.

A Croft Raceways horse van came over the opposite hill. I raised a pair of binoculars and focused, and saw the horse's head sticking out of the window.

"That's them," I said. "Lewis and Nina."

The van turned into the road towards Benjy Usher's stables, almost next door to Michael's. I started the Fourtrak and drove down the hill, reaching Benjy's yard almost before Lewis switched off his engine.

Benjy's head appeared in his upstairs window, poking out rather like his colt's from the van. He issued orders to his grooms below with his customary force, and Lewis and Nina lowered the ramp. I got out of my jalopy and watched them.

My presence there was taken for granted by everyone. Nina noticed Aziz still sitting in the Fourtrak and threw him an inquiring glance, to which he responded with a quick thumbs-up.

The colt clattered wild-eyed down the ramp, led by

Nina, and limped away in the hands of Benjy's head groom. Benjy shouted an inquiry to Lewis about the journey: Lewis went nearer to the window and shouted up, "It all went right." Benjy, relieved, retreated and closed his window.

I said to Nina, "Did you stop anywhere since Dover?"

"No."

"Good. Go with Aziz, now, will you?"

I went over to Aziz and spoke to him through the Fourtrak's window.

"Please take Nina with you and go to the farmyard. There may be a young man wandering about there, carrying a small animal transporter. His name's Guggenheim. Collect him and in about a quarter of an hour take him on with you."

"Where to?"

"To Centaur Care. That place where you took the old horses. I'll drive this van and meet you there."

"Let me come with you," he said.

"No. Look after Nina."

"As if she needed it!"

"Everyone needs their back watched."

I left him, walked over to the van while Lewis was lifting the ramp back into place, and climbed into the driver's seat.

Lewis was surprised, but when I waved him towards the passenger side he climbed in there without demur. He'd worked for me for two years; he was accustomed to doing what I said.

I started the powerful engine and drove carefully out of Benjy's yard, continuing on down the road towards Michael's place. Opposite Michael's gate, where the road temporarily widened and the space allowed it, I pulled the van over to the side, stepped on the footbrake, rolled gently to a stop, applied the handbrake and switched off.

Lewis looked surprised, but not very. The vagaries of bosses, his manner seemed to imply, had to be tolerated.

"How's the rabbit?" I said conversationally.

His expression gave new meaning to the word "flabbergasted." He looked for a moment as if his heart had actually stopped beating. His mouth opened and no sound came out.

Lewis, I thought, with his biker past, his tattooed dragon, his expert fists; Lewis with his bimbo and his ambitions for his baby, Lewis might be a dishonest muscleman out to make money, but he was no actor.

"I'll tell you what you've been doing," I said. "Benjy Usher owns a stable in France where he discovered last year by chance that the horses there were falling ill with an unspecified fever. He learned that there was a possibility that the fever was carried by ticks. So he thought it a good wheeze to bring the illness to England and give it to a few horses here so as to clear his path a bit to winners he might not otherwise have. The problem was how to bring the ticks to England; and first of all you tried to bring them on soap which you carried in a cash box stuck to the bottom of one of my nine-vans that you were driving at the time."

Lewis went on looking dumbfounded, a pulse throbbing now in a swelled vein on his forehead.

"The ticks didn't survive that journey. They don't, as you now know, survive long enough on soap. A different way of travel had to be found. An animal. A hamster, maybe. Or a rabbit. How are we doing?"

Silence.

"You looked after the Watermeads' rabbits. Perfect. You thought they wouldn't miss one or two, but they did. Anyway, last year, driving Pat's four-van, you went to France to

the Ecurie Bonne Chance, that's Benjy Usher's place outside Belley, down near the River Rhône, and you wiped
ticks onto a rabbit. You brought it back here, wiped the
ticks from the rabbit onto two old horses that Benjy Usher
had in a paddock outside his drawing room window, and although one of them died, there you both were with flourish-
ing live ticks on the other, ready to be transferred to any
horse that Benjy decided on, and that *you* could get close
to by driving it to the races."

I wondered what incipient heart failure looked like.

"The ticks are unpredictable," I continued, "and in the
end probably just disappeared, so in August you went again
to France, but this time taking the van Phil drives now,
which you used to drive regularly at that time. But on that
occasion things went wrong. The van was due for maintenance and was driven straight to the barn on your return.
The cap had unscrewed itself from the tube, perhaps from
vibration. Before you could retrieve the rabbit, it fell into
the inspection pit and died, and Jogger threw it away, ticks
and all."

Strangled silence.

"So this year," I said, "you went in the new super-six to
fetch the two-year-olds for Michael Watermead, and you
took a rabbit with you. The ticks came back alive and were
transferred to the old horse, Peterman. But Peterman went
to Marigold English, not Benjy Usher, and Peterman died.
The ticks died soon after him. So now we have the Flat
season about to start and all the Chester Vase and Dante
Stakes contestants this year are strong and healthy still, so
you set off with the rabbit to fetch Benjy Usher's colt from
Milan, and on the way back you stopped at the Ecurie
Bonne Chance, and what will you bet that in the tube con-

tainer above the fuel tanks of this horse van we'll find a rabbit with ticks on?"

Silence.

I asked, "Why didn't you just wipe ticks straight onto Benjy's colt?"

"He wants it to race again when its leg gets healed."

The admission slipped painlessly out. Lewis's voice was hoarse. He didn't even try to protest innocence.

"So now," I said, "we're going to take the rabbit straight to Centaur Care, where the two old horses destined for Benjy's field are waiting. This time you are not going to have to retrieve the rabbit from the tube at eleven o'clock at night, and hit me on the head when I catch you at it."

"I never," he said fiercely. "I never hit you."

"You did drop me into the water, though. And you said 'If this doesn't give him flu, nothing will.'"

Lewis seemed to have gone beyond being astounded and had reached the stage of anxiety to salvage whatever he could.

"I needed the money," he said, "for my kid's education."

One more shock, I thought, and he would really start talking.

I said, "If it came to a choice, which would you prefer, to drive Irkab Alhawa to the Derby and maybe bring him back as the winner in your own van on the television to this village, or to infect him with ticks to stop him even running?"

"He'd never do that!" he said. His horror, indeed, looked genuine.

"He's violent and spiteful," I said, "so why not?"

"No!" He stared at me, belatedly thinking. "Who are you talking about?"

"John Tigwood, of course."

Lewis closed his eyes.

"Benjy's reward is winning," I said. "Yours is money. Tigwood's is the power to spoil other people's achievements. That's a commoner sin than you may think. Knocking people is a major sport."

To win by cheating. Ambition for one's child. Malice and secretly enjoyed destructive power, bolstering an inadequate personality. To each his driving force.

And mine? Ah, mine. Who ever understood his own?

Lewis looked sick.

"Does Benjy Usher pay Tigwood?" I asked.

Lewis said without humor, "He gives him wads of the stuff in one of those collecting tins, right out in public."

After a pause I said, "Tell me what happened the night you chucked me in the water."

He practically moaned, "I'm no squealer."

"You're a witness," I said. "Witnesses get off lighter."

"I didn't do your car."

"You didn't kill Jogger," I pointed out, "because you were in France. But as for my car, you certainly could have done it."

"I didn't. I never. *He* did."

"Well . . . *why*?"

Lewis stared at me, his eyes deep in their sockets.

"See, he was like a wild thing. Going on about you having everything so easy. Why should you have everything, he said, when he had nothing. There you were, he said, with your house and your money and your looks and your business and being a top jockey all that time and everyone *liking* you, and what did he have, people never looked pleased to see *him*, they turned away from him. Whatever he did, he would never be *you*. He absolutely *hated* you. It turned my stomach, like, but I reckoned he might turn on *me* if I contradicted him so I went along with him . . . and he had the ax with him in his car . . ."

"Did he hit me with the ax?" I asked incredulously.

"No. A rusty old tire iron. He had a lot of tools in his car, he said. When he hit you we put you in the trunk of my car, as there was more room and he told me to drive to the docks. He was *laughing*, see!"

"Did you think I was dead?"

"I didn't know, like. But you weren't. You were talking, sort of delirious, when we got there. I never meant to kill you. *Honest*."

"Mm."

"He said we were in it together. He said how would I like him to get me in trouble. How would I like to lose my job and not drive the best horses anymore."

Lewis stopped talking, looking now at a future which meant all those things.

"Bloody *bugger*," he said.

"So you came back from Southampton," I said, taking it for granted, "and collected the ax and chopped up my house and my car and my sister's helicopter."

"*He* did that. He did it. He was shouting and raving and *laughing*. He chopped all the stuff in your room. So bloody *strong*. I'll tell you, he frightened me rigid."

"You watched him?"

"Well . . . yeah."

"And enjoyed it?"

"Never."

But he had, I saw. He might just possibly have been frightened by the vigor of that attack but deep down there had been an awestruck guilty pleasure.

Ruefully, I restarted the engine.

"Like," Lewis said, "how did you know about the journeys?"

"They're in the computer."

"He said he'd wiped out your records on the Sunday with a Michelangelo or something, and not to worry."

"I had copies," I said succinctly.

Tigwood had been in the pub the night everyone heard Jogger say he'd found the secret containers. From spite he must have stolen Jogger's tools. Then if Jogger found Tigwood tampering with my computer on the Sunday . . . I could see Tigwood going to his car for Jogger's own tire iron, walking along to the barn after him and aiming just one lethal blow. Jogger wouldn't have expected it. He knew of no reason to fear.

I released the brakes and started down the road.

"I suppose," I said, "that it was Tigwood with all his medical journals who understood about ticks? And who knew what you needed for bringing the virus from Yorkshire for Tessa Watermead to infect Jericho Rich's horses? You couldn't give the Jericho Rich horses tick fever, because by then you hadn't been over to collect this year's ticks."

He was again speechless. I glanced at him.

I said, "You haven't much chance if you're not willing to be a witness. Tessa told me and her father what you did."

I phoned Sandy Smith's number and, finding him at home, invited him to drive along to Centaur Care. "Bring your handcuffs," I said.

It took Lewis a slow painful mile to make up his mind, but as I turned through the gates of the crumbling headquarters of a disgraced charity, he said, mumbling, "All right. A witness."

The decrepit place was alive with people.

Lorna Lipton's Range Rover stood in the driveway. Lorna was talking to Tigwood and there were children— *children*—running about. Maudie's two youngest children . . . and Cinders.

Aziz was out of the Fourtrak, also Nina, also Guggenheim. They stood indeterminately, not knowing what to expect.

John Tigwood looked bewildered.

I stopped the van and jumped to the ground. Sandy Smith joined the crowd, lights flashing, uniform buttoned, no siren.

"What's going on?" Tigwood asked.

I wasn't sure how he would react. The trail he'd left with his ax on my property urged any defense I could think of. Keeping the children safe was a first priority.

I said to Maudie's young ones, "Take Cinders and wriggle under the van and play being in a pirate's cave there, or something."

They giggled.

"Go on," I said, urging them. "Crawl in there."

They did, all three of them. Lorna, watching, said merely, "Won't they get dirty?"

"They'll clean."

Tigwood said, "Why are you here?"

I answered him. "We brought back your rabbit."

"What?"

"Lewis and I," I said, "have brought back the rabbit— with ticks."

Tigwood strode to the passenger-seat side and yanked open the door.

"Lewis!" he yelled. It came out as a screech, all fruitiness gone.

362

Lewis shrank away from him. "He knows it all," he said desperately. "Freddie knows *everything*."

Tigwood stretched an arm into the cab and pulled Lewis out. Tigwood's weedy-looking appearance was misleading. Everyone could see the stringy power that tweaked the bigger man out onto the ground with a crash. Lewis's shoulders landed first, then his head, then his legs.

Lewis, rolling in pain, took a rough swing at Tigwood. Tigwood kicked him in the face and turned his attention to me.

"You *bastard*," he said, white faced, intent. "I'll kill you."

He meant it. He tried. He rushed me, smashing me by sheer speed against the side of the van.

He hadn't an ax, however, or a tire iron, but only his hands; and they, had we been alone, might have indeed been enough.

Aziz came up behind him and hauled him off. Aziz displayed a timely and useful skill in twisting a man's arm up behind his back until it reached the point of cracking.

Tigwood screamed. Sandy produced his handcuffs portentously and with help from Aziz locked Tigwood's wrists together behind his back.

Sandy said to me out of the side of his mouth, "What's going on?"

"I think you'll find that John Tigwood axed my house."

"*Bastard,*" Tigwood said, his voice a snarl.

I asked Sandy, "I don't suppose you have a search warrant handy?"

He shook his head bemusedly.

"I don't need one," Aziz said. "What am I looking for?"

"An ax. A rusty tire iron. A thing for sliding under trucks. A bunch of tools in a red plastic crate. And perhaps a gray metal cash box with a round bright patch amid the dirt. They might be in his car. If you find them, don't touch them."

His smile shone out, bright, white and happy. "Got you," he said. He left Tigwood to Sandy and bounced away out of sight.

Lorna bleated in bafflement, "John? I don't understand . . ."

"Shut up," he said furiously.

"What've you *done*?" Lorna wailed.

No one told her.

Tigwood stared at me with unnerving naked hatred and in a taut white rage called me a bastard again, among other things, repeating what Lewis had told me. I'd never imagined the overpowering strength of his murderous corrosive loathing, not even with his ax's handiwork all around me. I felt shriveled by it, and weak. Sandy, who had seen so many dreadful things, looked deeply shocked.

Lorna swung round at me with loathing of her own. "What did you do to him?" she accused me.

"Nothing."

She didn't believe me, and never would.

Aziz reappeared from the direction of the ramshackle stables.

"Everything's there," he reported, beaming. "They're in one of the stalls, under a horse rug."

Sandy smiled at me briefly, pushing Tigwood hard against the horse van. "Reckon it's time to call my colleagues."

"Reckon it is," I agreed. "They can take it from here on."

"And the Jockey Club can take on Benjy Usher," said Aziz.

Another car joined the melee. Not the colleagues yet, but Susan and Hugo Palmerstone, with Maudie. Michael had told them that the children were here with Lorna, they said. They'd come to take them home.

Tigwood in handcuffs appalled them. Lorna told them it was my fault. Hugo believed her easily.

"Where *are* the children?" Susan asked. "Where's Cinders?"

"They're safe." I bent down and looked under the horse van. "You can come out now," I said.

Guggenheim touched my arm as I straightened. "Did you . . . I mean . . ." he said. "Is the rabbit there?"

"I think so."

He, at least, looked happy. He was carrying a white plastic small-animal carrier and wearing protective gloves.

Maudie's two children wriggled out on their backs and stood up, brushing off dirt. One of them said to me, in a quiet little voice, "Cinders doesn't like it under there. She's crying."

"Is she?" I went down on my knees and looked underneath. She was lying flat on her stomach, her faced pressed to the ground, her whole body quivering. "Come on out," I said.

She didn't move.

I lay down on the ground on my back and put my head under the side of the horse van. I shuffled backwards on heels, hips and shoulders, until I reached her. I found there were things I could go under tons of steel for without a second thought.

"Come on," I said. "We'll go out together."

She said, shivering, "I'm frightened."

"Mm. But there's nothing to be afraid of," I looked up at the steel of the chassis not far above my face. "Turn onto your back," I said. "Hold my hand and we'll wriggle out together."

"It'll fall on me."

"No . . . it won't." I swallowed. "Turn over, Cinders. It's easier on your back."

"I can't."

"Your mother and father are here."

"There's a man shouting . . ."

"He's stopped now," I said. "Come on, darling, everything's fine. Hold my hand."

I touched her hand with mine and she grabbed it tightly.

"Turn over," I said.

She turned slowly onto her back and looked upwards to the steel struts.

"It's pretty dirty under here," I said prosaically. "Keep your head down or you'll make your hair filthy. Now, our toes are pointing to where your parents are, so just shunt along beside me and we'll be out in no time."

I began to wriggle out, and she wriggled, sobbing, beside me.

It was after all only a few feet. It can't have seemed much to the people outside.

When we were out I knelt beside her, brushing dirt from her clothes and her hair. She clung to me. Her little face, close to mine, was so like the pictures of myself at her age. The tenderness I felt for her was devastating.

Her gaze slid beyond me to where her parents stood. She let go of me and ran to them. Ran to Hugo.

"Daddy!" she said, hugging him.

He put protective arms around her and glared at me with the green eyes.

I said nothing. I stood up: brushed some grit off myself; waited.

Susan put one arm round Hugo's waist and with the other enclosed Cinders; the three of them a family.

Hugo brusquely turned them away with him towards their car, looking fiercely over his shoulder. He shouldn't fear me, I thought. Perhaps in time he wouldn't. I would never upset that child.

I was aware that Guggenheim and Aziz were slithering under the horse van. Guggenheim scrambled out with visions of immortality in his eyes, cuddling the white plastic carrier as if it contained the Holy Grail.

"The rabbit's here," he said joyfully, "and it's got ticks!"

"Great."

Nina came to stand beside me. I put my arm round her shoulders. It felt right there. Eight and a half years didn't matter.

"Are you OK?" she asked.

"Mm."

We watched the Palmerstones' car drive away.

"Freddie . . .?" Nina murmured tentatively, "that little girl . . . when your heads were together, she looked . . . almost . . ."

"Don't say it," I said.

ABOUT THE AUTHOR

Dick Francis is the author of many bestselling mysteries, most recently *Comeback* and *Longshot*, that are set against a racing background. He divides his time between England and Florida.

Race to finish the complete list of
DICK FRANCIS
national bestsellers published by
Fawcett Books.

BANKER
Young investment banker Tim Ekaterin has decided to
join the exciting world of horse racing. When the
multi-million dollar loan he arranges to finance the
purchase of a champion horse is threatened, Tim desperately searches for an answer. Violence and murder
do not deter him.

BLOOD SPORT
When English agent Gene Hawkins agrees to search
for millionare Dave Teller's prized missing stallion, he
doesn't know his retainer will include the attention of
his boss's beautiful teenage daughter—or Teller's seldom sober wife. He also doesn't know that his search
will lead to murder.

BOLT
In Kit Fielding's breakneck world of steeplechase racing, the ultimate catastrophe strikes. Someone is
shooting the horses with a weapon fiendishly called a
"humane killer." Kit must stop the murdering mad-
ness, and everyone in his upper-crust circle becomes
a suspect.

BONECRACK
Neil Griffon has no choice—an uncompromising crime
czar gives him an ultimatum he dare not refuse. The
czar's son must be hired by Griffon's stable to ride in
the Derby. And his son must be trained to win—or
Griffon's life will be lost.

BREAK IN
Kit Fielding, proud heir to tradition and sporting hero to legions of fans, is drawn into a crusade to save his twin sister's marriage from ruinous scandal. His intercession proves more costly than he'd imagined and thrusts him into a deadly contest with a ruthless media czar, a black-hearted robber baron, and a violent adversary—far too close to home for comfort.

COMEBACK
When Peter Darwin, a globe-hopping diplomat, returns to his childhood home, he comes face-to-face with a case of fatal corruption. Darwin soon realizes the answers involve his own past. This discovery makes Darwin wish he'd never come back, because he might never leave again—alive.

THE DANGER
Kidnapping is Andrew Douglas's business. They take them, he finds them. But it isn't so simple when Alessia Cenci, golden-girl jockey, disappears, followed by the young child of a Derby winner and the senior steward of the Jockey Club. Andrew's caseload is suddenly, violently overflowing.

DEAD CERT
As he rode through the thick English fog, jockey Alan York was looking at an all-too-familiar sight: the back of champion rider Bill Davidson astride the great racehorse Admiral. But this was one race York was destined to win. Before Admiral jumped the last fence, Bill Davidson would be dead. Alan knew racing was a dangerous business, but he also knew this had been no accident.

THE EDGE
The Great Transcontinental Mystery Race is a rail junket that offers passengers the chance to race thoroughbreds and to solve mysteries. For Tor Kelsey, undercover agent for the British Jockey Club, this imaginary mayhem is about to become a nightmare of real murder.

ENQUIRY
Jockey Kelly Hughes and trainer Dexter Cranfield are charged with throwing a race for personal profit and are barred from racing. It is a vicious frame-up, and Hughes refuses to take the phony verdict lying down—even though his personal enquiry might have him lying down permanently.

FLYING FINISH
According to just about everybody, Henry Grey had a bad disposition. But Henry knew all he needed was a new job. The air transport of racehorses would change his luck. His luck changed, all right—when he found there was something more than horseflesh in the cargo hold.

FORFEIT
James Tyrone, racing reporter, knew that fellow writer Bert Chekov was a drunk. When Bert died in an "accidental" fall from a window, Tyrone suspected that Bert's death might be related to some columns he'd written touting can't-lose horses that failed to show up on race day. Tyrone vowed to prove that Chekov was murdered, despite the terrifying risk involved.

FOR KICKS
Daniel Roke couldn't leave his Australian stud farm to look into an English horse-doping scandal. Or so he said. But soon he was in England taking over investigative duties vacated by a racing journalist who had died in an "auto accident." Then Daniel learned that men who would give drugs to horses would do much worse to human beings.

HIGH STAKES
Steven Scott is a novice horse owner who is having an incredible string of luck at the races. He uncovers deceit in his own stables and gets rid of the trouble-maker, only to find that he himself is marked for murder.

HOT MONEY
With five ex-wives and nine children, wealthy gold trader Malcolm Pembroke presides over a motley clan in constant conflict with one another. When Malcolm's least likable ex-wife dies violently, he calls on his son, Ian, the family jockey, to protect him from their nearest, if not always dearest, relatives. Ian must delve into the dark Pembroke past that simmers with greed, hate, and vengefulness to uncover what could motivate blood to strike against blood.

IN THE FRAME
Charles Todd is an artist who must figure out a masterpiece of murder and thereby clear his cousin's name. Todd finds himself involved in a dangerous manhunt for a brilliant and elusive killer.

KNOCKDOWN
For a generous commission from a wealthy American woman, ex–prize-winning jockey Jonah Dereham finds himself bidding for a young steeplechaser. Unfortunately, someone doesn't want Jonah purchasing this horse, and would even resort to murder.

LONGSHOT
John Kendall, writer of travel guides, is impulsive, but taking an assignment because he needs money hardly seems a rash act. Off to rural England Kendall goes to interview a successful racehorse trainer. Soon, Kendall realizes that the perils described in his survival manuals pale next to the dangers in rural England. "Impulse will kill you one of these days," his agent had warned. Kendall should have listened, but he didn't—not by a longshot.

NERVE
Rob Finn was a misfit—a struggling jockey in a family of musicians, a man in love with a beautiful woman who wouldn't have him, a rider who—just as it seemed he was breaking into racing's big time—lost his nerve. Or did he? The horses felt too sluggish beneath him, and he knew there had to be a reason. When he found it he could hardly believe it. And when it found him, he could barely breathe.

ODDS AGAINST
Ex-jockey Sid Halley had a wrecked hand, a mean case of depression, and a need for a new career. He joined a detective agency, took a bullet in his side, and was sent out on a case on his own. Then he met Zanna Martin, a woman who could make life worth living again. But it was an even-money bet that he'd be killed before she had the chance.

PROOF
Wine merchant Tony Beach finds himself caught in the midst of a terrifying mystery beginning with sham scotch and counterfeit claret and escalating to hijacking and murder. Tony must draw on every reserve of hidden courage to crack a sophisticated scam and to save many lives—especially his own.

RAT RACE
Matt Shore is flying some racing fans to the track when he is forced to make an emergency landing minutes before the plane blows up. And this is only the beginning, as Matt is caught up in a flurry of secrets, schemes, and sudden violence that puts him on the wrong side of the odds.

REFLEX
Jockey Philip Nore is no ordinary hero. When he suspects that a track photographer's fatal accident was really murder, he sets out to discover the truth and to trap the killer. Slowly, he unravels some nasty secrets of corruption, blackmail, and murder, and unwittingly sets himself up as the killer's next target.

SLAY RIDE
British investigator David Cleveland comes to Norway in search of Robert Sherman, a champion jockey who had disappeared right before the Norwegian National. Cleveland is sure that Sherman's disappearance is tied to a gruesome string of deaths that he discovers are meant to include his own.

SMOKESCREEN
Edward Lincoln, star of the silver screen, journeys to South Africa to rescue his ailing godmother, Nerissa. Nerissa asks Edward to save her racehorses, but Edward discovers a plot for murder and he must give the performance of his life to find a killer.

STRAIGHT
"I inherited my brother's life and it nearly killed me." So says Derek Franklin, an injured steeplechase jockey, who must try to untangle his brother's complex life—filled with women, precious gems, and horses—without losing his own.

TRIAL RUN
It seems the Prince's brother-in-law has his heart set on riding in the Olympics, but a jealous Russian has her heart set on killing him if he does. So Randall Drew leaves his well-bred horses and high-born girlfriend and goes to Moscow. He does not expect the sabotage and murder he finds there, nor the unspeakable terror that follows.

TWICE SHY
Young physicist Jonathan Derry is given some musical tapes by a friend. But the tapes are really an elaborate computerized horse betting system that can make the owner a rich man—or a dead one.

WHIP HAND
No longer able to jockey, Sid Halley has become quite a good private eye, though he is haunted by memories of his past glories. When the wife of one of England's top trainers comes to beg for his help in preventing some foul play at the track, Sid Halley begins to know what being haunted really means.

DICK FRANCIS

To order by phone, call 1-800-733-3000 and use your major credit card. Or use this coupon to order by mail.

__BANKER	21199-1	$5.95
__BLOOD SPORT	21262-9	$5.95
__BOLT	21239-4	$5.95
__BONECRACK	22115-6	$5.99
__BREAK IN	20755-2	$5.95
__COMEBACK	21956-9	$5.99
__THE DANGER	21037-5	$5.95
__DEAD CERT	21263-7	$5.95
__THE EDGE	21719-1	$5.95
__ENQUIRY	21268-8	$5.95
__FLYING FINISH	21265-3	$5.95
__FORFEIT	21272-6	$5.95
__FOR KICKS	21264-5	$5.95
__HIGH STAKES	22114-8	$5.99
__HOT MONEY	21240-8	$5.99
__IN THE FRAME	22116-4	$5.99
__KNOCKDOWN	22113-X	$5.99
__LONGSHOT	21955-0	$5.99
__NERVE	21266-1	$5.95
__ODDS AGAINST	21269-6	$5.95
__PROOF	20754-4	$5.95
__RAT RACE	22112-1	$5.99
__REFLEX	21173-8	$5.95
__SLAY RIDE	21271-8	$5.95
__SMOKESCREEN	22111-3	$5.99
__STRAIGHT	21720-5	$5.95
__TRIAL RUN	21273-4	$5.95
__TWICE SHY	21314-5	$5.95
__WHIP HAND	21274-2	$5.95

Name_____

Address_____

City_____ State_____ Zip____

Please send me the FAWCETT BOOKS I have checked above.

I am enclosing	$____
plus	
Postage & handling*	$____
Sales tax (where applicable)	$____
Total amount enclosed	$____

*Add $2 for the first book and 50¢ for each additional book.

Send check or money order (no cash or CODs) to:
Fawcett Mail Sales, 400 Hahn Road, Westminster, MD 21157.

Prices and numbers subject to change without notice.
Valid in the U.S. only.
All orders subject to availability.   FRANCIS7